RESERVED

BRIDGET L. ROSE

This book is dedicated to everyone who's been broken by love before. I know it seems impossible, but one day, someone or something will come along and remind you that love can be the most wonderful of things. When that time comes, don't run from it. Embrace it.

Trigger Warnings

The **trigger warnings list includes**: working through grief, topics of loss and fear of loss, child abandonment, toxic parent-child relationships, anxiety and anxiety attacks (fully shown on page), panic attacks (also fully shown on page), as well as sexually explicit scenes and vulgar language

Hello, my dear reader,

Thank you so much for reading Reserved. I am so excited to share this book with you! I just wanted to say that this book does not have a third act breakup, but it does leave off on a cliffhanger. There will be a second book for these characters, so there will be a HEA, just not yet.

Also, I want to clarify that this book is a lot about self-discovery. Adrian is discovering what he wants and Nevaeh is figuring out what she wants in life as well with her job and her love life. They're figuring it out, and you'll see them build a strong friendship, but they're far from perfect (except Adrian of course, he's perfect).

I would like to note that you will see Nevaeh's anxiety. Her experience with anxiety is taken directly from my experience with it as well, just like it was with Scarlette in The Inside of a Rainbow. I want to clarify that her experience is not a universal one and that anxiety can appear in many different forms.

If you have anxiety too, I hope you will feel seen through Nevaeh. I know she has made me feel less alone too in my mental health journey, and bringing her character to life was very therapeutic for me.

Also, in case no one has ever told you before and you have anxiety, you're amazing. You're doing your best. I am so proud of you.

All my love,

Bridget

Pitstop Series
Team Names

Spark Racing

THREE MONTHS AGO

I'VE BEEN FEELING VERY anxious today. Not for a specific reason either. It's right at the surface, building in my chest until I feel my hands shaking and my heartbeat quicken. Whenever I manage to slow it down again, stop my hands from moving of their own volition, I spiral into my thoughts again until my anxiety storms back to the surface.

It's a frustrating cycle.

So, I do what I do best in these moments.

Distract myself with something I love doing.

I take a stroll through Hyde Park, admiring the fluffy snow that sits on the twigs of the bald trees. It's dark outside, which is perfect for the type of photos I'm looking to take.

Photography is my creative outlet, it's what I've loved to do in my free time since I was fourteen years old. Mama and Papa have probably gotten me over a dozen cameras in the past seven years while Nova, my sister, always gets me new lenses to try out. I don't remember getting a present for any occasion that didn't have something to do with photography, and I absolutely love it. There is nothing better than finding new tricks and ways to improve a skill I've been honing for seven years.

Quiet hoots pull me out of my thoughts. I turn my camera on when I see an owl sitting in one of the trees, watching its surroundings with big, brown eyes. A smile lifts the corners of my mouth while I snap some pictures of the magnificent creature. Its white feathers almost give it a camouflage look in the snow. Seeing an owl in London is incredibly rare, which is why I can't stop grinning from happiness. I've been going to this park for years and never spotted one before.

Today must be my lucky day.

After taking about a hundred different photos, trying out various settings and playing around with my portrait and wide-angle lens, the owl decides it has had enough and flies away again, spreading its magnificent wings and disappearing into the night. I watch after it for a while, letting the calming feel of nature settle the anxiety inside of me. It's the only thing that helps on days like these. Going outside. Feeling the cold air on my face. Stepping on the crunchy snow. Connecting with my surroundings instead of falling into my own mind.

If I could, I'd stay longer, but my fingers have started going numb from the December cold. I rush back to my car, feeling a bit lighter now than I did before.

My Volkswagen Tiguan is covered in snow by the time I get back to it, but all of my attention drifts to the car a few parking spots over. It's a red Velocità Rossa SUV. I catch my jaw a moment before it drops and take out my camera again. If there is anything I love as much as photographing wildlife, it's cars.

The glow from the lamps around me offers the best lighting as I squat down and stand up again to take pictures of it from better angles. Papa used to take me to car shows when I was a little girl, explaining everything there was to know about them. Whether it was old-timers or modern cars, he knew every little detail. I retained very little of the information, but I like admiring the way they look. The sleekness or rough edges. The muted colors or bright ones. The futuristic or rustic look.

I adore everything about cars.

A few pictures later, I step back a little and then look at them to see if they're good.

"So handsome," I mumble to myself while I admire how the car looks on my little camera screen.

"Thank you," a deep, smooth voice says, startling me. I quickly lower my camera before my heart stutters, and I forget how to breathe. "But if you wanted a picture of me, you didn't have to hide behind my car to take it," the man adds, all confident and flirtatious. I cock an unimpressed eyebrow.

"Excuse me?" He gives me a wolfish grin, looking more handsome than anyone has a right to.

"I saw you squatting and standing on your tiptoes to get a better angle of me while hiding at the same time." I'm about to deny it when he interrupts me. "Listen, I don't mind, I just wanted to let you know you could have asked for one, you didn't have to go through all this trouble," he says, the amused smirk now spreading all over his face. I lift my tongue to the roof of my mouth and shake my head.

"I'm sure you don't hear this very often, but I wasn't taking pictures of you. Your car caught my attention, and, to be honest, I didn't even notice you were behind it," I reply, which makes him raise his eyebrows. His eyes scan my face, a little surprise hiding in them as he searches for signs of deceit.

"I think I need to see some proof," he says softly, flirtatiously, sending shivers down my spine. I try to ignore them, try to ignore the way his cologne, something warm and fresh and delicious, fills my nose. Instead, I let irritation take control.

"Fine," I blurt out, more than willing to prove him wrong.

The gorgeous stranger takes my camera to look through the photos I took of his car. He seems strangely familiar, but I can't place him. He looks rich, from his clothing to the fact that he drives this beautiful car, which probably means he's either a successful business owner or a celebrity. Maybe that's why I feel like I've seen him before. Could he be an actor? I'm not entirely certain. All I know is, I'm in the presence of the most beautiful man I've ever seen.

"These are incredible. You are a very skilled photographer," he says, studying my pictures closely.

"Thank you," I reply, surprised by his compliment.

My eyes focus on his lips, studying the fullness of them, how plump and pink they look from the cold. Unfortunately, the cocky man notices.

"If you want to take a picture of them, you can," he teases, and I roll my eyes in response.

"You're an arrogant man, do you know that?" I ask, crossing my arms in front of my chest. He stares down at my camera again before refocusing his gaze on my face, letting it travel over my features.

"Perhaps, but do you know what you are?" he asks with an easy smile, taking a step back with my camera still in his hands. He lifts it to his eye, pretending like he's taking a picture of me.

"Please, enlighten me. I'm dying to know what you think of me." I hope the sarcasm is laid on just thick enough.

"You are devastatingly beautiful." My cheeks heat in response to his words. There is fire in the way he looks at me now, heating my skin in a way I've never experienced before.

"Can I have my camera back?" I ask and hold out my hand for him to place it there. He seems confused by my rejection as if it has never happened to him in the past.

"Yes, of course," he says, his face falling a little as he gently places my camera in my hands.

His fingers briefly brush over mine, causing another wave of shivers to run over me. I lift my eyes to meet his, trying to see if the spark of electricity was a mutual sensation. By the way, he watches me, I can tell that it was.

"I apologize for taking pictures of your car," I croak out, watching him lick his lips with utter fascination.

"Why did you?" he asks with an inquiring look.

"Because I love cars, and I've never seen a Velocitá Rossa SUV in real life. It's magnificent," I admit, clearly surprising him.

"It's not mine, it's just a rental," he blurts out, and I nod.

He looks a bit unsure now as if I've completely thrown him off by not flirting back. I can't lie. I kind of want to. He's attractive, and once he drops the whole cocky act, he's actually a little... sweet almost.

"It's a hell of a rental," I reply with a small smile, and he takes a casual step to the side so I can admire it.

"If I'd known it would attract a gorgeous woman like you, I'd have bought it instead."

His eyes rake over my face, stopping at my lips before sliding back up to my eyes. The urge to laugh nervously almost threatens to take over, but I swallow it down well enough with a smile that probably reddens my cheeks.

"Okay then. Again, I'm very sorry about photographing your car, Mister," I say because if I start flirting back, I'm not sure I'd leave here anytime soon.

I attempt to walk away, even when his words threaten to stop me.

"You don't know who I am?" he starts, jogging to catch up with me while maintaining a respectful distance.

"Should I?" I open my car door and grab my camera bag to place it inside. He's grinning at me as if he knows something I don't.

"I guess not." He stops for a second, watching me take off my jacket so I can be comfortable while I drive home. "Do you watch Formula One?" he asks a moment later, and I shift my eyes back to his irritatingly beautiful ones. The way his long, black eyelashes shape his eyes so perfectly is something I've never seen before.

It captivates all of my attention.

"I try not to," I admit. There is no way I'm telling this stranger about the complicated relationship I have with the sport, though. "Why?" I don't know why I ask.

"Have you ever heard of Adrian Romana?"

No, it can't be.

My eyes trail over his face once more. Then, I notice the dirty blonde strands coming out from underneath his beanie, notice the Velocità Rossa symbol—a running horse—painted across his chest pocket area, tiny but there.

Oh my God.

It's him.

A fresh wave of nervousness hits me, but I play it off, something I'm very good at thanks to the years of covering up my anxiety so people around me don't notice the change in my behavior.

"No, but I've heard of his sister," I say and get into my car to turn it on.

Part of me wants to leave while another part is more intrigued by him now than I was before. I've spoken to Formula One drivers before, but never one this young, never one that called me beautiful and looked like an angel sent from heaven.

Adrian closes my door for me, and I roll down my window so we can keep talking for a moment longer.

"Valentina Romana is the best driver there is, so that checks out," he informs me with a bright smile. My heart warms at the adoration in his eyes as he speaks about his sister.

I don't know why I don't tell him that I know who he is. There is no reason for me to hide it. But I like surprising this man. It's fascinating to watch his confidence slip into a bit of shyness because I don't recognize him, even if I do now.

"I've got to go," I say, not because I want to end this conversation but because I can tell he's freezing and so am I.

He nods, and I bite my bottom lip when his tongue runs over his again. I get a strange feeling that he doesn't want this conversation to end either. It makes me smile.

"Will you tell me your name?" Adrian asks, his hands moving to his pockets as he steps away from my car. He remains close enough to hear me, but far enough away so I can leave anytime I want.

"I'll make you a deal. If you see me again, I will tell you my name," I suggest, knowing full well we will probably never see each other again, which is for the best. I already have a complicated relationship with a Formula One driver, and an even more complicated relationship with the Grenzenlos team principal, also known as my father.

"Okay," he mumbles before rubbing the back of his neck and giving me the cutest wave goodbye.

I do my best to ignore the weird feeling spreading through my chest, not to replay the strange yet surprisingly interesting conversation I just had with the vice-world champion of the previous Formula One season, but I fail miserably.

CHAPTER 1

Adrian

"It's been three months, Adrian, do you honestly think you'll ever see this woman again?" my sister, Valentina, asks as I grab my suitcase and place it on my bed. Her eyes, twins of mine, watch me carefully, almost like I'm a wild animal she decided to bring into the house.

"I fucking hope so. The woman has been stuck in my head for months, and no matter what I do, she isn't unsticking herself. So, I have to see her again because it's the only thing that'll hopefully get rid of these—" I cut off and shudder.

Feelings.

That's what I meant to say, but whenever I remember what they are, my whole body cringes. I just need to see this mysterious woman one more time to get rid of this ridiculous notion I have that she is the most beautiful woman I've ever seen.

That's all.

Gabriel, my sister's fiancé and my teammate and rival for the second year in a row, grins at me from where he is sitting on the bed with my sister. One of his hands rests possessively on top of hers because he always needs to touch her in some way when they're together. It's absolutely disgusting, and not just because Val is my sister. They're just *so in love*, and I don't get it. I don't get the appeal of tying yourself to someone and risking your happiness over them. Because I've seen it happen. I've seen the way Gabriel fell apart when Valentina and him were broken up. I watched my sister fight the grief of losing the love of her life, or whatever the fuck she calls him.

It's so unappealing to me.

"What the fuck is so amusing?" I ask Gabriel, but he merely shrugs. Chase, our family dog, jumps off the bed to sit at my feet, demanding attention.

"You are. Watching you struggle with the concept of wanting to be in a relationship because of your stubbornness is my favorite entertainment," he replies and I raise my pinky.

It's always been James', my best friend, and my way of saying fuck you without using the middle finger, especially when we were kids. It started because I accidentally broke his pinky when we were karting, and I made fun of the fact that he couldn't move his finger for two weeks when it was in a cast. He flipped me off with it every chance he got, and it kind of stuck.

"I don't *want* to be in a relationship. They are pointless. You open yourself up to your partner, fall in love, and then it ends. I know how the story goes *every single time*," I say, shuddering at the thought of how my mother ran from my father and her children. Abandoning us. Disappearing like we never meant a fucking thing.

"Not everyone is Mom, you know?" Valentina reminds me, but I just shrug it off, unwilling to let my emotions on the subject show.

"Or Gabriel, I guess," I tease, and my teammate shoots daggers at me while I grin at him. "Too soon?"

It's been months of them happily being engaged and living together after Gabriel left to fix the mess he was in, but Valentina still gets up to nudge her elbow into my side, hard. I fling my arm around her shoulders and press a kiss to the top of her head while breathing through the discomfort of her blow.

Serves me right for attacking her man.

"Lash out all you want, but it doesn't change the fact that something is special about this woman, and if you see her again, I suggest you talk to her without the intention of taking her home and getting her out of your system, or whatever you call it," Valentina says, giving me a pointed look.

A smile breaks out across my face at her words.

"Do you expect so little of me when it comes to dealing with my *feelings*?" I challenge, even if the last word makes my skin crawl, and she steps away from me.

My sister rolls her eyes before Gabriel and her respond, "Yes," at the same time.

They grin at each other while I step into my closet to gather my clothes for the trip to London. The second one in three months. We're not flying there for another few days, but Gabriel, Val, and I have to be in Italy for meetings tomorrow. That means I have to get all my shit ready days in advance.

The image of the mysterious woman slips back into my mind as I look through which clothes to take on my trip. I wonder what she might be up to. What cars she's photographing right now, or if she's taking photos of something else. She's an incredible photographer from what I saw last time. The way she played with angles and lighting was mind-blowing. I could have stared at the pictures all day if she wasn't so fucking beautiful, it made my chest constrict as I looked at her. Not to mention, there was something fiery about her too. She blushed perfectly when I complimented her, but my charm didn't make her like me, not like it does with most people. I mean, it helped me win over the grumpiest man in the world of Formula One, Leonard Tick, and he's one of my best friends now. But with her? Nothing. She didn't even know who the hell I was, and that was the most refreshing of all.

Maybe that's why I can't stop thinking about her.

Maybe that's why I'm hoping to run into her again.

Maybe I've just lost all sense of who the fuck I am because I don't get emotionally involved with people I want to have sex with.

"I love you," I hear Gabriel whisper to Val, who giggles a little before telling him she loves him the same.

Something in my chest dislodges as I listen to their conversation, to their declaration of love. I don't want a relationship, I never have, but I can't pretend that the idea of loving someone as much as my sister loves her fiancé isn't a little appealing, after all. Don't get me wrong. It's as appealing as jumping out of a crashing plane with a fifty percent chance of having a parachute, but there is *something* I can't ignore anymore.

I shudder again before going back to packing and ignoring the direction my thoughts have gone for the hundredth time since I came across *her* in England.

CHAPTER 2
Nevaeh

My leg is bouncing up and down. My heart is pounding and palpitating in my chest. My breathing is awfully uneven. I had one of my full-body anxiety attacks before I got ready this morning, so I was hoping it would ease a little now, as it usually does.

I'm not that lucky, unfortunately.

The shaking of my legs spreads to my hands too, and I have to take several deep breaths to slow my heart rate again. It works somewhat, giving me enough space to force my thoughts into a better direction instead of letting them spiral into the dark hole of what-ifs, worst-possible outcomes, and other fears I don't want to identify right now.

After four years of studying sports journalism and interning at various companies the entire time, I finally scored an interview with one of the biggest sports media companies in England: *Griffin Sports.*

Known for their prestigiousness and sharing reliable information, *Griffin Sports* is *the* media company for every type of sport you could think of. It's a dream for every sports journalist to work here. To either have articles published on their website, or video-recorded interviews shared across all platforms. My dream is to write articles and take photographs of the events I'm reporting on. It's a dream I may have not had for long but am just as passionate about as the one I lost a few years ago.

People pass by the waiting area where I've been sitting for the past twenty minutes, not caring about my presence as they go about their day. I wish I was as calm as them. Instead, my hands are sweating while I wait impatiently for anyone to call my name.

Becoming a sports journalist was my Plan B in life. Plan A was to become a professional tennis player. One rotator cuff tear later, and I haven't been able to pick up a racket since. Familiar shivers of suppressed sadness run down my spine, and I shake my head to focus on my future.

Looking back isn't going to help me get this job, and I desperately need it.

"Ms. Fuchs? Mrs. Lu will see you now." I look up to see a tall, well-dressed man in front of me. He's giving me an indifferent smile before walking away, clearly expecting me to follow him. I jump out of my seat and rush after him, simultaneously trying to calm my heart by taking deep breaths.

It doesn't work.

The *Griffin Sports* headquarters is big and open. There is a lot of natural light coming through the hundreds of windows I walk past. There are also a dozen desks with hardworking people behind them. It's not a cubicle-type office situation, but I cringe nevertheless. An office job is not where I saw myself, quite the opposite actually, but if that's all I get for now, I will make it work.

"Right in here," the man says, and I step through two large wooden doors.

Mrs. Amanda Lu, the CEO of this media company, sits in her office chair while looking over what I assume are potential articles to be published. Another woman is in the chair beside her, staring at her screen. When Mrs. Lu sees me, a genuine smile covers her heart-shaped lips. She tugs her black hair behind her ears before getting up to greet me with a handshake. I quickly wipe my right hand on my skirt, which, luckily, she doesn't seem to notice.

"Ms. Fuchs, it is a pleasure to meet you." Mrs. Lu says with a thick Scottish accent and points to the chair she wants me to sit in. I do as I'm directed, glad that my shaking legs don't have to hold me up anymore. The other woman at the desk smiles kindly at me.

"It's a pleasure to meet you as well, Mrs. Lu. I'm a huge fan of your work," I reply and hope that flattery will make her like me more.

From the smile on her face, I can tell it does.

"Thank you, I appreciate you saying that." She points to the woman beside her next. "I'd like to introduce you to my COO, Ms. Cecilia Martin." I shake her hand as well, smiling at the woman with light eyes and blonde-graying hair. There's something familiar about her, like I've seen her before too. It must have been when I was researching the company and Mrs. Lu. "However, we would like to talk about you."

The nervous laugh bubbling up in my chest almost escapes me, but I cover it up by clearing my throat. I need to get my nerves under control if I want to ace this interview.

"Your resumé states that you were born in Germany, but completed your primary education in Australia, your secondary in the U.S., and your post-secondary here in England. Would you say you are both fluent in German and English?" she asks first, and I nod before I answer.

"Yes, I had a private tutor for German in Sydney and Austin. I studied English for as long as I can remember." My facial muscles are starting to cramp from all the smiling. Mrs. Lu leans back in her chair, her eyes fixated on a piece of paper I can only assume has my resumé on it. Ms. Martin smiles reassuringly at me.

"You also speak a little bit of French," she points out, and, once again, I nod. Mrs. Lu does as well, still studying the words on the page. "I can see here that you are applying for a position in the tennis department since you have fifteen years of experience as a tennis player," she states and lowers the paper to look directly at me. Her brown eyes stare at me with an intensity that makes me shift in my seat. I avert my gaze, bringing it to Ms. Martin instead, but she's gone back to her laptop to work.

"That is correct. I sustained an injury, which unfortunately ended my career in tennis, but I'm very passionate about it. I know everything there is to know about the current top players, their statistics, and—" Mrs. Lu cuts me off before I can finish my sentence.

"I have no doubt that you are well-versed in the language of tennis. Unfortunately, we do not have a position open in that department at the moment," she informs me, causing my polite smile to fade as disappointment washes over me. Ms. Martin notices my change in mood and frowns at her business partner.

"Oh, okay. I understand," I mumble, but Mrs. Lu confuses me when she lets out a small chuckle.

"No, I don't think you do yet. Ms. Fuchs, I hope I'm pronouncing that right—" She stops to look at me, and I laugh a little.

My last name has caused lots of confusion over the years. Every English-speaking person pronounces it wrong, and it always sounds like 'fucks' instead of its actual pronunciation, 'f-oo-ks'.

"Please, call me Nevaeh," I suggest because it's easier than my German last name.

"Alright. Nevaeh, you have great recommendations and spent over three years at media companies as an intern and later an assistant. They speak very highly of you in their letters," she says and leans forward. "I do have one position open, which I would like to offer you." Suddenly, my heart beats faster than it ever has before. "How familiar are you with Formula One?" Mrs. Lu asks, curiosity now written all over her features.

"Pfft, too familiar, if you ask me," I say with a laugh before I remember that this is a job interview, and I'm not behaving professionally. "I apologize, I have a hate-love relationship with the sport."

Probably not the best thing to tell someone I hope will be my boss in the future. Mrs. Lu tilts her head to the side, scanning my face while Ms. Martin grins at me.

"What I meant is, I am very familiar. There is not an aspect of the sport I don't know." My father, the team principal of the Grenzenlos team, made sure of that by always talking to me about his work.

"Brilliant. Then how would you like to shadow and assist our head journalist as he travels with his team around the world to interview the drivers?" Mrs. Lu asks and stands up to walk over to a file cabinet.

I would love to instantly agree, to be excited about this job offer, but I don't know how to feel. Formula One is a great sport, and I've enjoyed watching it my entire life, but it's also the reason why Papa and I have barely spent time together. Not to mention, Lincoln Nash, the guy I hate the most in the world, is now racing for my father's team. I already can't avoid him at home, since our families are close friends, which is why I was hoping my job would have nothing to do with him...

Then again, I can't let my emotions cloud my judgment.

This is an incredible job opportunity.

Can I really pass this up?

I'm about to answer when Mrs. Lu says, "I know this is not a job for everyone, but I think you're highly qualified for it."

I'm surprised she thinks this much of me, but I don't question it. My resumé must be better than I thought it was when I applied.

"Your expenses, such as plane tickets and hotel rooms, will be paid for by us. You will be expected to do everything Mr. Fender tells you to, and we expect an article about the performance of the drivers, teams, or FIA decisions every race weekend. Whatever you think is the most exciting, you write about," Ms. Martin explains with a strong French accent.

I'm overwhelmed by all of the information for a moment. When Ms. Martin looks at me, she must read it on my face.

"Oh, I'm sorry, dear, we haven't even received an answer from you yet, and here we are, piling on information on top of information." A breathless laugh escapes my slightly parted lips, and both of the women across from me smile.

"I would be delighted to be a part of the team," I finally manage to croak out, unsure whether or not this is the right decision.

They flash me approving smiles in response.

Mrs. Lu and Ms. Martin go on to tell me about the weeks of introduction and training I will go through before the season starts.

They also give me the task of writing an article about what exactly Formula One is to get a sample of my writing and point out areas of improvement.

That's not nerve-racking at all.

I take the contract Mrs. Lu hands me and force a smile at them both before leaving my boss's office and making my way home.

CHAPTER 3
Nevaeh

WHEN I WALK INTO my family's ridiculously big house, I let out a sigh of fear. I have no idea how my family is going to react to my news. Nova, my sister, might be the only one who will be excited for me.

She's sitting on the couch with her girlfriend, watching a movie I've never seen. I would ask what it's called, but I couldn't care less. There are more important things on my mind.

My eyes shift from the television back to my sister. Nova is tall, has black hair and brown eyes, light skin, and is covered in tattoos. She loves to wear dark clothes while I always wear light ones. Even now, I'm dressed in a light yellow skirt and a white blouse, and Nova is dressed in black yoga pants and her favorite *From Angels to Devils* crop top. She's worn this outfit a hundred times in her twenty-four years of life.

"Hi," I greet both Nova and Aileen once their heads turn my way so Aileen can see me signing the word with my hands, too. They both smile in response.

"Hey, babes! How did the job interview go?" Nova asks and signs, her accent subtler today than usual. Since she was three years older than me when we lived in Australia, the accent stuck with her. Unfortunately for me, I sound more American.

"It went well. I got a job," I reply in English as well since Aileen is here and while I'm signing the words, she also sometimes likes to read my lips to understand what I'm saying. Nova and I usually speak German so we don't lose our mother tongue, but out of respect for Nova's girlfriend, we always converse in our second language when she's here as well as using sign language. My whole family and I learned it four years ago when Nova and Aileen first started dating. We wanted Aileen to feel comfortable with us and the least we could do was learn the only language she could communicate in. While we speak, we always use our hands to sign the words, too.

Nova sits up to give me her full attention.

"That's amazing! Why aren't you happy?" She sees right through me, not even a fake happy expression could have fooled her.

"You know how I applied for—" I'm interrupted by Mama calling out for me. Aileen furrows her brows at me when I don't continue my story. *Mama is calling me*, I sign to my sister's girlfriend before turning my head to see my mother approaching.

"Nevaeh? Are you home? How was the interview?" My short, curvy Mama runs into the living room in her robe.

After placing a kiss on my cheek, she stands back to look at me. We look a lot alike. Everything from the brown hair with naturally blonde highlights to the round lips and brown eyes is the same.

"I got a job," I repeat, and she jumps up and down in excitement.

"I knew you would. Oh, I'm so proud of you," she says and squeezes my arm. Her eyes shift to the couch, and she beams at Nova's girlfriend. *Aileen! I didn't know you were here, sweetheart. How are you?* she signs, moving her hands around with her usual enthusiasm.

They fall into a casual conversation, and I realize no one is going to ask me more about my interview. My sister is too distracted to remember what we were talking about before. I'm about to walk away when Mama grabs my arm.

"By the way, honey, the Nash family is staying for dinner." *Oh, great, just what I needed.* Also, *staying*?

That means they're already here.

"Is that necessary?" I ask, but it makes her chuckle. She knows that I despise Lincoln, but I never told her why, which might be the reason she thinks whatever happened is merely a childish quarrel. "Do you mind if I eat dinner by myself instead?"

Mama frowns at me then.

"We have dinner as a family every night your father is here. You know the rules," she scolds, and I nod without further complaint. "You have to tell us all about your job later," Mama says cheerfully, and I realize there is no way around it unless I want to be disrespectful.

"Sounds great," I lie before disappearing upstairs and into my room.

The light orange walls are starting to get on my nerves, although I only made them that color two years ago. I must have painted my walls five times since moving here, but it's the only thing about my room that I get to change.

Mama picked out the dark brown mahogany furniture and the thick beige curtains covering my two large windows that lead to a balcony. But one more thing that's mine is the artwork. There are paintings of famous tennis players like Serena Williams and Steffi Graf, which I got for inspiration when I was little. I haven't had the heart to take them down because I was clinging to the hope of having a tennis career.

After my interview today, that hope has vanished.

I walk over to the painting of Steffi Graf first and pull it off my wall. Tears shoot into my eyes as reality hits me. My fingers trace her racket while I swallow the tears.

Aggressive knocking on my bedroom door causes my heart to skip a beat.

"Jesus. Come in," I say, trying to catch my breath.

Regret and anger soon replace my startled feelings when I see Lincoln Nash opening my door. An easy smile lingers on his wide and full lips. He's not very tall. His light skin color is complemented by his blue polo shirt, and his hazel eyes look brighter today than usual.

Lincoln has a lean but trained body, perfect for a Formula One driver. His brown hair sits in wide curls on his head, and I almost groan when his hands catch my attention. I've thought about what his long fingers could do more often than I would like to admit, especially because I despise him. But that's all in the past now. Where he belongs.

"Get out," I say before he can speak. He leans against my door frame, smirking wickedly at me.

"Technically, I'm not in your room, butterfly," he replies, and I roll my eyes. He's been calling me butterfly since we were kids, and I hate that the nickname I once thought was sweet has soured over the years.

"What the hell do you want? You know I don't enjoy your company," I inform him with the fakest smile I can muster. Lincoln's eyes leave my face as he traces my door frame with them.

"Don't be ridiculous. Everybody loves my company." I bite down on the inside of my cheek to hide my amused chuckle. I can't let him see that I found that funny. He'd never let it go. "Your mum told me to come and get you. Dinner is ready unless you want to stay up here and pretend you hate me," he says, completely unbothered by his own words.

"I don't pretend, *Linc*, I just hate you." His eyes grow dark from the way I addressed him. There is nothing he hates more than when I call him "Linc." I don't know why he dislikes it, but it's my secret weapon. He usually leaves once I say it, which is why I'm confused when he steps into my room with a soft expression on his face.

"Why are you taking down your art?" he asks, and I cock an eyebrow.

"That's none of your business," I reply before focusing on taking down Roger Federer's painting.

"Seriously, Nevaeh, you love them. Why would you take them down?" Lincoln is right. I do love them more than any other possession I have, but the reminder of what I'll never have is too painful to keep looking at.

"Don't pretend to care," I spit the words, and he lifts one of the frames I've pulled off the wall to inspect it. The thought of ripping it out of his hands occurs to me, but I'd like to think I'm more mature than that when it comes to him.

"I don't pretend, butterfly, I just care," he says, using my words from before to confuse me even further. "Haven't you lost enough from your injury? Don't let it take more from you."

This makes my blood boil.

"You, out of all people, have no right to say that to me. Get the fuck out of my room, Lincoln, and leave me alone."

Anger has overtaken any other emotion I have ever felt toward him as I stand up and hover over the Formula One driver. He raises both of his eyebrows before lowering my artwork and standing up too, making sure to be close enough so I feel his hot breath on my skin. Once upon a time, I'd have shivered from anticipation.

Now, I just want to kick him where it hurts most.

"When will you ever let go of what happened?" he asks, his lips now merely a few centimeters from mine.

"When will you understand that I can't stand being in the same room as you?" I lift my hair into a ponytail while moving toward my closet.

"Please, Nevs, we both know seeing me is the best part of your day. Gets you all hot and riled up," he says and gives me one last smirk before leaving my room without speaking again.

Part of me is tempted to grab one of my pillows, follow him down the stairs, and hit him over the head with it. Another part is too busy mourning the loss of my friend to do anything other than stand in my closet, swallowing down the tears of anger.

How could I ever forgive him for what he said to me that night?

Chapter 4
Nevaeh

Somehow, I managed to convince Mama to let me stay in my room, using the excuse of having to write an article for my new job. She wanted to argue with me, but Papa stepped in, placed a hand on her shoulder, and told me he'd bring me a plate later.

I've been sitting in front of my laptop for an hour now, trying to do as I said I would. Write the article.

'Formula One is an exciting racing sport with ten teams fighting vigorously for the Constructors' Championship. Twenty drivers make up the starting grid, racing to grasp the Drivers' Championship Title, the most desired trophy of the sport.'

I stop writing because this is not even close to good enough. My new bosses are expecting my best work, and, clearly, I'm not at the top of my game at the moment. There is so much I could write about, like Gabriel Biancheri winning the championship last season, or this season being the first in Formula One history to have a woman racing for a team. Valentina Romana is an inspiration, but, instead, I'm supposed to write a boring article about how the sport works.

I shut my laptop and groan.

"Blocked?" Papa asks, forcing my brain back to German. He places a plate of food on my nightstand.

"Yes, a little," I admit while watching him walk over to me and sit down at the foot of my bed. I bite the inside of my cheek, waiting for the right moment to have *that* conversation with him.

"What's going on, Vaeh? Hmm? I can read on your face that something's wrong. Your mom said you got the job. Aren't you happy?" he asks, his blue eyes scanning my face as if he could figure out what's bothering me by reading it.

"I didn't get *the* job, I got *a* job," I explain before lifting my knees to my chest and wrapping my arms around my legs.

"Okay," he says, obviously still unsure what the problem is. "Don't make me pull it out of your nose, sweetheart. Just tell me," he complains before grabbing one of my pillows and gently hitting my arm with it.

A small laugh escapes me, making him aim for my head next.

"Okay, okay, fine," I say and raise my hands in defeat. The smile on my face fades as soon as I think about what to say. "They didn't have a position available in the tennis department, only in..." I trail off because I'm terrified of his reaction.

My father has separated work from family my entire life, and probably his too, and this is unfamiliar territory for both of us.

"Only in Formula One," I add, and his eyes go wide from surprise. "I know you don't like us interfering in your work, but, theoretically, I won't be in your way. I might interview you at some point if my training goes well, but that's all so far in the future, so I wouldn't worry about that. It's just—" I cut off when I see amusement replacing shock on his face.

"May I speak now?" he asks, smiling. I give him a small nod before resting my chin on my knees. "I think that's terrific, Vaeh," Papa says and gets up to walk over to the artwork I took down earlier.

He lifts up the one of Serena Williams before putting it back on the nails. I wait patiently for an explanation for why he did that, but I don't get one.

"After everything you've been through, I'm so proud of how far you've come. I know tennis meant everything to you, and it's not easy recovering from that kind of heartbreak, but you, Nevaeh, you've exceeded all my expectations."

Tears shoot into my eyes, and I'm not sure if it's from his words or from me reliving the memory of my injury. My hand lifts to my right shoulder so I can run my fingers over my scar. It's five centimeters long and one of my biggest insecurities.

The doctors fucked up during my surgery because they promised me I'd barely see it afterward.

"What about keeping work and family separated?" I ask him to change the subject back to the problem of this situation.

"If I could, I would take all of you with me to every race, but you're so busy with your own lives, I would never put more stress on you. But now, it's great. Your mother and I have discussed her coming with me this season a while ago, and Nova and Aileen will love their privacy," he tells me and sits back down on the bed. I let out a relieved sigh, which doesn't go past him. "Why do you always expect the worst from me?" he asks and tilts his head.

This is a good question with a clear answer, but I don't want to hurt his feelings.

"Will you read over my article once it's done? It's supposed to be about F1 and how it works," I explain, and Papa stands up again, but this time, he gives me a kiss on the top of my head and moves toward the door.

"Of course. Show it to me later," he replies and disappears out of my room.

Something I love about him is that he doesn't force a conversation when he senses I'm done talking. Mama is a little different that way. She likes to pry.

I lean back against my headboard and open my laptop again, trying to come up with something that isn't boring. After all, Formula One is all about thrill and excitement. Every race weekend, the teams perform to the best of their abilities to fight for any of the top ten positions, ideally the top three, to get points counting toward the championships. There are free practices, Qualifying, sometimes sprint races, and then, on Sunday, it's race day.

Papa is usually MIA from Friday morning all the way to Sunday after the race. As the team principal of the Grenzenlos team, he has a lot of responsibilities. He doesn't like to get distracted.

Mama throws herself into work to pretend that she's busy too, but I can always tell how much it bothers her when Papa ignores her texts. It's something we've fought over many times, which is why I'm glad Mama decided to join Papa for the season. She's a very successful author of non-fiction novels and is currently writing her seventh one. This one is about our life in Australia. She doesn't have to stay home to write it.

I shake my head to focus on my article again. My writer's block is trying to distract me, but I have to get over it. I have to get this done by Monday, and I don't have time to procrastinate, as much as I want to right now.

My fingers glide over the keyboard for a moment, searching for any starting point. Still stuck, I decide to look up the drivers for this season. Kyle Hughes and Lincoln are racing for Grenzenlos. Jonathan Kent recently retired, opening up the spot that Lincoln filled, not merely thanks to his talent, which he has a ridiculous amount of, but also thanks to his and my father being best friends. George Nash is also an engineer for Klein Racing, Lincoln's former team. Lincoln *is* an incredibly talented driver, but there is no denying any of this.

Getting what you want in Formula One is a lot easier when you have connections.

I focus on Hawke next. James Landon and Grant Irwin are teammates for the first year this season after what happened with his former teammate Eduardo last season.

My research moves on to the Velocità Rossa team. As much as I've tried to avoid a very specific Velocità Rossa Formula One driver since our conversation three months ago and tried not to think about him, I can no longer avoid him, not when my job will bring us together eventually. All I need to do is approach this as logically as possible.

This is work, nothing but work.

Gabriel Biancheri, last year's World Champion, and Adrian Romana are teammates for the second season now, but they've been doing well together. Papa always says that he hopes to find two drivers that make up such a great team for Grenzenlos one day.

I've watched some races in the past year, and I have to agree. They're always respectful of one another, help the other when their team asks them to, and celebrate each other's highs after the race.

No matter how hard I try to think only about that as I do my research, I can't help getting lost looking through photos of Adrian. He's ridiculously attractive: tall, muscular but lean, with dirty-blonde hair, and blue-green eyes. I get stuck on his smile, the one that has been replaying in my mind every night for the last three months right before I fall asleep too.

I shake my head once more to refocus on the task at hand.

Valentina is racing for Alfa Adrenalina alongside Leonard Tick. From what I've read, they're not only teammates for the first year this season, but they're also opening their own driver's academy called 'Kids Like Us' soon.

Maybe I can focus on the drivers and teams for the article. As long as I get something on the page, it will be fine.

Right?

I stare at the blank page again and take a deep breath.

I can do this.

I can impress Mrs. Lu and Ms. Martin and earn my position at *Griffin Sports*.

New life, I'm about to conquer you.

CHAPTER 5
Adrian

Fucking shoot me.

If I have to listen to another rich, middle-aged man tell me about how many houses he owns and how many wives he's had, I might throw myself off the balcony I was on earlier when I tried flirting with a gorgeous brunette. Nothing but gibberish came out of my mouth, the same thing that's been happening for the last three months. Whenever I try to turn on my charm with a woman, I end up making a fool of myself.

Self-sabotage has taken on an entirely new meaning. The worst of all. I, Adrian Romana, don't know how to talk to beautiful women anymore without sounding like I've never spoken to one before.

I would like to figure out why this keeps happening, but I can't do that with Archibald Whatever-His-Fucking-Last-Name-Is filling my ears with garbage.

"I bought Anna a little cottage in Italy," he informs me.

"What a lucky woman," I say, barely keeping the snort at bay. Gabriel nudges me, and I glare down at him. Archibald doesn't catch the sarcasm in my voice and continues to rant about his fifth wife.

Thank fuck, he turns to the two people beside him after another minute to start the story he just told Gabriel and me all over again.

I practically run from him before having to hear it again.

"You know these people sponsor our team, right? They give us money so we can, you know, *race*," Gabriel reminds me as we make our way toward where Valentina is standing with my date for the evening, James Landon.

If I can't find someone to take to these events, I always take my best friend. He doesn't seem to mind either because he accompanies me every time. I'm glad, too. He always makes me laugh after mind-numbingly dull conversations.

"I understand, but do you understand that men like him make me want to punch my head through a wall?" I ask, making Gabriel chuckle beside me.

"Why? You didn't enjoy the story about the day he went skinny dipping in Mykonos?" I scrunch my nose up in disgust.

"Not particularly. I didn't enjoy picturing him naked."

"No one told you to," Gabriel says with a snicker.

"Are you telling me I'm the only one who instantly pictures things people tell me?" I challenge, but when he walks away after giving me a strange look, I panic a little. "Wait, am I?" I rush after Gabriel, too scared another old dude will tell me things I don't want to know.

"Hi, mon tournesol," Gabriel says as he wraps his arms around Val and leans down for a kiss.

"Hi, mon soleil," she replies a second before his lips meet hers.

I step in front of James, bat my eyelashes, and say, "Hi, mon tournesol," mockingly.

He matches my energy immediately, replying, "Hi, mon soleil," before puckering his lips for me. I burst into laughter, clapping him on the shoulder.

"Ah, thanks, mate, I needed that." I wipe the tears of laughter from under my eyes to see my sister and teammate frowning at me. "Oh, relax, we're just teasing," I say and poke Valetina's side, making her giggle before she smacks my hand away and scowls. "God, you're spending too much time with Leonard. You really mastered the angry face." She tries not to smile and fights against it, but it's useless.

She grins before nuzzling into Gabriel's chest. He kisses the top of her head and wraps his arms around her, resting his hands on the small of her back.

The image of the mystery woman slips into my head in an instant, and I suck in a sharp breath to ward off the panic.

"I'm surprised you're still here. Thought you'd have gone home with someone already," James says after a moment of silence. Gabriel and Val have gone off to dance on the dance floor.

"So am I," I mumble, looking around the room. Plenty of women my age here. Many of them even look at me, smile, and blush.

"Trying out celibacy? Spoiler alert: you're not made for it," James says, and I almost burst into laughter at the absurdity of his suggestion.

"I'd rather hit myself in the balls with a baseball bat three times in a row before choosing celibacy," I joke, and James starts laughing, a deep and full sound.

"You're so dramatic." *Yeah, but you all love me for it, don't you?*

"I know." I smile at him, then bring my attention back to the room. "Time to break the dry spell," I say, rolling my shoulders a little to prepare. James chuckles at my antics, sipping his bourbon.

But, at the end of the night, I go home alone, thinking about the mystery woman all over again.

CHAPTER 6
Nevaeh

MR. FENDER WELCOMES ME with a bright smile on Monday morning. I almost feel starstruck standing in front of him. Gillian Fender is one of the most popular reporters in Formula One. The tall, brown-eyed man with black hair and pale skin has interviewed hundreds of drivers in his fifteen years at *Griffin Sports*. Most of the time when I turn on the television during race weekends, I see him, that's how well-known he is.

"Mr. Fender, it's an honor to meet you," I blurt out when he offers me his hand to shake.

"Please, call me Gillian. Now, let's get you started, shall we?"

Gillian walks away without waiting for a response, and I follow him to a small desk outside of an office three times the size of an average bedroom in London.

"That's my office, and this is your desk," he says while pointing at both to make sure I know exactly what he means. I smile to myself, finally excited to start this chapter of my life.

"So, it's like I'm your assistant?" I say when he reads over the things I will be doing. Gillian chuckles at my words.

"Kind of, but you won't have to get me lunch or answer my calls. We will split our food runs, sometimes you will bring it, other times I will, but don't worry too much about it. We will spend a lot of time traveling, and when we're here at the office, you'll mostly focus on writing your articles. You're responsible for your research, editing, etc.," he goes on before introducing me to how the printer works.

I'm expected to print everything he sends me along with highlighting the titles and doing other small tasks Gillian asks of me. I sit down in my comfortable office chair, watching him point out the drawers I can use to store my things. Then he goes on to outline what the training will look like, such as working on my areas of improvement and familiarizing myself with the publishing process on the website as well as meeting deadlines, and more.

"Have you read the article I sent in or do Mrs. Lu and Ms. Martin look over it?" I ask when I find an opening.

Gillian leans against my black, wooden desk while an easy smile lingers on his thin lips. His features are welcoming and so is his personality.

"I must say, I'm very surprised by how well you engage the reader with the text. You made it exciting to read, which is impressive for someone who is starting out as a journalist. I'm quite happy with your work, but there are small areas I'd like to point out for you to work on."

I impressed Gillian Fender with my writing. It feels like my heart is going to bounce out of my chest from happiness.

"By the way, I don't know if Mrs. Lu told you, but this season we are mostly going to focus on the drivers of the Velocità Rossa and Grenzenlos teams," Gillian informs me before excusing himself and taking a call.

Fantastic.

I really cannot escape Lincoln, no matter how hard I try. Whoever is in charge of my fate loves to force him into my life. I roll my eyes before I realize this might not be the worst thing in the world. Focusing on two teams is a lot less work. Not to mention, I'm dying to meet Gabriel Biancheri. He's an incredible driver.

And as much as I try not to be, I'm excited to see Adrian again too. I wonder if he remembers me, if he has even thought about me since we met.

A part of me thinks this is going to be his season since last year Gabriel and Adrian were head-to-head in the Drivers' Championship. Another part of me has a feeling Lincoln will be on top.

I guess I'll have to wait and see.

"Sorry about that," Gillian interrupts my thoughts, and I look up at him. "That was Mrs. Lu. She informed me that Gabriel Biancheri, Adrian Romana, Lincoln Nash, and Kyle Hughes have accepted our invitation to meet the reporters who will interview and write about them. They will be here on Wednesday," he says. I fake an excited smile.

This is possibly the worst thing he could have told me I had to do this week.

By the end of the day, I'm tired and hungry. I haven't eaten all day because my emotions have been all over the place. I walk out of the building and toward the pickup area. Mama offered to drive me since my car is at the shop.

When I don't see her anywhere, I turn on my phone for the first time today. A message from her pops up.

Mama: Hi, honey. I'm sorry, I won't be able to pick you up, but I sent Lincoln instead. He should be there soon.

Nope, I'm not doing this. I hurry over to the taxi stand when his voice stops me dead in my tracks.

"Butterflyyy," he sings, and I let out a groan so loud, I hope he hears it. "Don't be silly and waste your money on a taxi. My car is all warm and cozy," he says.

At the same moment, I shiver from a cool gust of wind. No part of me is in the mood to take a taxi, but I'd also rather walk home than get in his extravagant car. I attempt to walk again when his voice turns soft.

"Nevaeh, let me take you home."

I take a deep breath before turning around and stepping toward him. He's leaning against his Grenzenlos sports car, arms crossed in front of his chest. Whether I'd like to admit it or not, he radiates hotness with that seductive smirk and confident stance.

Instead of talking to him, I simply get into his car and enjoy the warmth. He's chuckling as he sits down next to me. My fingers fumble around in my bag in search of a distraction. I take out my article to study the comments Gillian left for me.

"How was your first day at work?" Lincoln asks after being able to keep quiet for an impressive five seconds.

"Why are you talking to me?" I challenge, and his lips curl into a smile.

"Because you hate small talk. So, how was your day?"

He's right. I absolutely hate small talk, especially with someone I dislike. Lincoln checks both boxes at the moment. I should ignore him, but if I do, I would do exactly what he expects. If I don't, I'll have to converse with him.

Either way, I lose, which is exactly what he wants.

"My day was great. I got a lot of training done, and Kellan, my performance coach, is happy with my progress," Lincoln informs me when I take too long to answer.

"It's good that you're making progress in one area of your life, considering that your maturity level keeps dropping with every interaction between us."

He chuckles at my response, which only pisses me off more. I don't know what it is about him and the need to bother me. After all, Lincoln is the one who fucked up our friendship, not me. I used to care about him before everything went to shit between us.

He was my best friend.

"I'm very proud of you for getting this job, Nevs. I think you're going to do great." His words startle me. They're sincere, and I can read on his frustratingly handsome face that he means them, which is why I *nearly* regret my next words.

"And you think I give a shit if you're proud of me?" His face falls, making pain shoot through my chest. I forget how to breathe, too surprised by the way my heart responds to hurting his feelings.

"You used to care…" He trails off, his hands securely placed on the steering wheel and his eyes fixated on the icy road ahead of us. It hasn't snowed in a few hours, but the roads are not entirely safe to drive on. "I don't know how many times I can apologize until you forgive me," he complains, and all feelings of compassion evaporate off my skin as anger replaces them.

"How about you start by actually apologizing, Linc?" I suggest while he parks the car in front of my house.

His head turns in my direction, showing me that his bottom lip is tucked between his teeth and his full eyebrows are furrowed. *Why the hell is he confused?* I know he's not stupid, he was at the top of his class when he graduated high school.

"What? You don't believe me that you never apologized? Well, look back at every interaction we had since *that* day, you never did." I open his car door and attempt to get out when he grabs my wrist and drags me back inside the car.

"You can't keep running away from me, Nevs. We have to talk this out," he says, and while I agree, he still hasn't said the one thing I need to hear from him.

"We can talk this out when you've grown up and learned that what you did was wrong. Until then, you'll remain a stranger to me." Lincoln lets go of my wrist but his hazel eyes have a different hold on me. Their familiarity makes me want to stay and figure out how to fix this horrible situation between us.

"You'll never forgive me, butterfly, whether I apologize or not. The sooner you stop lying to yourself about that, the sooner you'll realize you have to let go of your hatred to be ready to hear my apology." Lincoln has lost his goddamn mind. It's the only logical explanation I have for the nonsense coming out of his mouth.

"Next time, don't pick me up, jerk," I say before getting out.

I would slam the door if I didn't love his car and wished I could drive the same. That's the benefit of being a Formula One driver for the Grenzenlos team. They give you the newest models to advertise.

I rush inside to lock the door and let my racing heart find its normal rhythm. My anxiety has spiked so high from our conversation, my hands are shaking again. I hate confrontation. It always makes my skin crawl, panic filling me from top to bottom. One would think after all my fights with Lincoln it'd get easier, but it never does.

"Are you okay? Your cheeks are all flushed," Nova says, and I jump.

"I'm fine," I reply while my voice betrays me and cracks.

If there is one person in the world I cannot lie to, it's Nova. My sister wraps her arm around my shoulders and pulls me close.

"Okay, don't tell me, but I would like to hear about your first day while we drink some tea and eat the scones Aileen baked." Nova pulls me into the kitchen and toward her girlfriend, who is busy finishing the goodies she prepared.

My sister wraps her long arms around Aileen's waist, and I settle down on one of the chairs at the kitchen table. Our modern-styled kitchen has too many mahogany cupboards and only the newest appliances. What for, I have no idea. I'm useless in the kitchen, neither a good baker nor a good cook, just like most of my family. But Aileen loves it here. Her flat barely has a stove or space for one. That's why Nova insists on her coming over so much, and none of us mind.

We love Aileen. She always brightens up our days.

Is Gillian Fender as nice in person as he seems on screen? is the first question Aileen asks, and I smile at her.

She knows that I like specific questions a lot more than the ones Lincoln asked. It makes me feel like the person is actually interested in my day rather than forcing a conversation. I know it's a strange pet peeve to have, but I've felt this way for as long as I can remember.

Aileen's and Nova's faces light up when I tell them how kind Gillian is and they are intrigued as I share what will happen on Wednesday. Nova met most of the drivers because she took a year to travel and went around the world with Papa for an entire season two years ago, but I never had the time.

Now, it will be my job to get to know them, and while I'm somewhat excited about the meeting, I'm also very nervous.

Hopefully, everything will go well.

CHAPTER 7
Adrian

She isn't here. I was hoping to run into her at Hyde Park, the same place where we met three months ago, but the mysterious woman isn't here.

And now I feel like I've officially lost it.

What the hell is wrong with me?

Why does it matter if I see her again or not?

I'd never let it lead anywhere and we might not even be compatible. A ten-minute conversation from months ago doesn't mean that I'll like this woman, even as a friend. If this wasn't the first time I've felt this way, I'd have written her off as just another interaction in my life, but *I can't*. I can't get rid of the image of this woman's face, can't get rid of the way my chest warms at the thought of her.

Every little part of me aches to see her again, and it's beyond frustrating.

I shake my head and wrap my scarf tighter around my neck. England is too fucking cold. It gets cold in Monaco during the winter too, but not like this. Not this mushy snow and rain mix that is simultaneously freezing and also soaks my shoes and beanie. I can't believe I'm out here because of someone I met once, just because she didn't know who I was and I could have a normal conversation without being asked a favor or to sign an autograph. Which I love doing for my fans, but sometimes I don't want to be Adrian Romana the Velocità Rossa Formula One driver. I just want to be Adrian. The guy who cleans up his friends' messes more often than not, but who is also a complete mess on the inside.

Fuck, nope, don't go there.

My phone rings in my pocket, dragging me out of my thoughts and back to reality. My sister's name lights up my screen as I make my way back to my car, the Velocitá Rossa SUV I rented three months ago and decided to rent again this time. It definitely wasn't to attract the attention of the mysterious woman should she live around here somewhere. Absolutely not. It's just because I know this car and am comfortable driving it in the winter conditions here.

I'm not a completely lost cause.

"Yeah?" I say as I hit Answer.

"Can you stop being a creep and come back to the hotel so we can go for dinner?" she asks, giggling at her words.

"Creep? I thought you of all people would think it's romantic I went to the same spot I met her the first time, got completely drenched by this fucking rain-snow combination, all just to see her again," I reply, but Val is still giggling, so Gabriel takes the phone from her to speak to me instead.

"It *is* romantic. I'm proud of you, Adrian," he says, and that's exactly when I realize my mistake. If Gabriel, Mr. Cheesiness himself, thinks I did something right, then I'm way out of my league. "But it's also a bit pathetic, so just come back so I can get ma chérie some food," he adds, and now I feel even worse.

"Yikes, brutal honesty. I appreciate it," I lie, and Gabriel chuckles into the phone.

"No, you don't because you always think you know better when it comes to anything relating to yourself," Gabriel says before not so subtly whispering, "Or even the entire world." I snort, a humorless sound that makes him chuckle again.

"Fuck you too, Gabriel." I hang up before giving him the chance to speak again.

With one last look at the entrance of Hyde Park, I drive off, willing away the disappointment in my chest. If it was meant to be, I would have seen her again, but it's not.

So I can finally let go of that stupid conversation and her drop-dead gorgeous face. With those brown eyes surrounded by long, black lashes. Those full, pouty lips. The round face that was so unimpressed by me. The thick, brown-blonde hair that came out from underneath her beanie.

I can let the thought of her go, *right?*

CHAPTER 8
Nevaeh

AFTER STARING AT MY clothes for a very long moment, I realize it's time for backup. Otherwise, I'll stand in front of my closet for another hour and remain uncertain. I know what could look good, and what I should definitely not wear, but I need to look *wow*. Adrian is going to be at this meeting, and I want his jaw to drop when he sees me.

If anyone knows how to dress to get that reaction, it's Aileen. She always wears the most breathtaking outfits.

I walk down the hallway, finding her in Nova's room.

A curious grin spreads across her face when she sees the uncertainty on my face.

How can I help you, darling? she signs, and relief washes over me.

It takes me a minute to explain the situation to her, and she immediately goes for the black dress that hugs my curves in all the right ways. The long sleeves will keep me warm and so will the turtleneck shape of it. It's sophisticated, but my breasts and ass make it less so. It's perfect.

Aileen tells me to spin once before clapping approvingly.

A dropped jaw won't be the only reaction you'll get from him, I can assure you, she signs and winks, making a small laugh fall from my lips.

I don't know if Adrian will even remember me. Three months is a long time, especially for someone like him who meets thousands and thousands of people, but I hope he'll see me and remember me because I haven't been able to forget him.

"Thank you, Aileen," I say and sign before giving her a brief hug and hurrying into the bathroom to put on some makeup.

I draw a thin line of purple eyeliner on my lid, making sure it's not too much for work. I tie up my hair so half of it is in a bun and half is falling freely down my shoulders with a few strands framing my face.

Once I'm happy with my look, I rush downstairs to my car. I'm close to being late, and today is not the day to be. Luckily, there isn't a lot of traffic, and I even arrive before Gillian does. There is a note on my desk from him, asking me to get some more chairs for the drivers and put them in his office. Holly, a woman from marketing, helps me locate them, and I carry two of them to Gillian's office. I pick up the third one when a too-familiar hand moves on top of mine to stop me.

My eyes shift to Lincoln's hazel ones.

"Let me," he offers, but I smack his hand away and bring the chair to the office myself. "You look beautiful," Lincoln says when he joins me in the big room.

His compliment takes me by surprise, but I don't respond.

"Come on, talk to me, butterfly. Don't you want to make a mean comment or throw an insult my way? Isn't that the greatest part of your day?" His words cause a low, involuntary chuckle to leave me.

"I'm at work, Linc. Unlike you, I'm capable of being professional," I reply while cleaning up some of Gillian's paperwork. It allows me to distract myself from the excitement bubbling in my chest.

Adrian is going to be here soon.

"Ah, there is the mean comment. Thank God, I was starting to think you weren't feeling well," he says as he sinks down on one of the chairs I brought.

I roll my eyes and turn around to hide my smile. *Why am I in such a good mood around Lincoln?* Some of the usual anger I feel toward him has somehow lifted, but not enough to make me forgive him, not even remotely close.

"Actually, I'm feeling great, Linc, despite your presence," I say and spin around to see Adrian Romana standing in the door frame.

His eyes widen as soon as they lock onto mine, and I try to hide my smile by pulling part of my bottom lip between my teeth. He looks very handsome in his blue dress shirt and black jeans. His blonde hair sits in waves on his head, and his lips, the bottom one a bit bigger than the upper one, are pinker than the last time I saw them.

Adrian is smiling now as he takes a step toward me.

"It's you," he states, an expression of awe on his face. "Did you know we'd see each other again?" Adrian asks, and I beam up at him.

He remembers me...

"Wait, how do you two know each other?" Lincoln says, trying to interrupt my moment with the gorgeous Monegasque.

"I didn't. I only found out a few days ago," I reply, focusing solely on Adrian, whose attention hasn't drifted from my face once since he came into the room.

I like capturing his gaze because, when he directs it at me, my heart races. Shivers run down my spine when he smirks at me.

"Well, a deal is a deal," he points out and extends his hand for me to shake. "Hi, I'm Adrian," he says, so I slide my hand into his.

Electricity shoots through me from my fingertips all the way down to my toes. Every cell in my body bursts to life as if they've all been dormant until this very second. Until I got to touch Adrian Romana.

For a moment, I forget to answer, making a blush settle on my cheeks.

"Hi, I'm Nevaeh," I blurt out, my words too quick and breathless to come across in the cool, unaffected way I wish they would.

"Nevaeh. That's 'heaven' spelled backward, isn't it?" Not a lot of people pick up on that, and I'm surprised Adrian did this quickly. I smile at him with a nod.

Lincoln stands up, capturing my attention.

"Yes, it is, now back off, Romana," he growls, his fingers curling into fists.

Adrian cocks an unimpressed brow as he studies the irrational man who is trying, and failing, to intimidate him. I can't help but laugh at how ridiculous Lincoln looks, especially next to the taller, older F1 driver.

Both their heads turn in my direction, and I cover my mouth.

"I'm sorry, but what was that?" I ask, making Adrian turn away from Lincoln to hide his own smile. Lincoln shoots daggers my way, but I merely go back to cleaning up Gillian's paperwork to get my heart to stop hammering so hard in my chest.

The moment is interrupted by Gabriel Biancheri and Kyle Hughes entering the room. The World Champion introduces himself politely and so does the second Grenzenlos driver. I offer for them to sit down when my phone starts ringing. Gillian's name flashes on my screen, sending a bad feeling through me.

"Hello?" I step away from all four drivers to get some privacy.

Eyes burn my backside. I try to ignore them, convinced they're either Adrian's or Lincoln's. They could also both be staring at me, but I have other things to worry about right now.

"Nevaeh, I'm going to be a bit late for the meeting. Please start it without me." Anxiety immediately floods my chest. Sensing my distress from his demand, he goes on, "Just introduce yourself, ask them some questions. You'll be fine." Gillian hangs up on me before I'm allowed to respond.

Perfect.

My feet bring me back over to where all four men are sitting. Kyle is reading something on his phone, and Gabriel is texting someone who is making him grin from ear to ear. I bet it's Valentina Romana. They've been dating for a while now, and from what they've said in interviews, they're quite happy.

"Um, I apologize, but Mr. Fender will be a bit late," I start and decide to sit down in the chair next to Gillian's. Lincoln watches me like a hawk while Adrian's gaze shifts between me and the floor.

"No problem. We're not in a rush," Adrian replies to make me feel better, and I let out a small laugh I don't mean.

I'm too nervous.

"Why don't you introduce yourself? I mean, that's what the meeting is for anyway, right?" Adrian suggests and leans forward to ensure I only look at him.

I could kiss him for giving me a place to start, for distracting me from the way my hands are shaking from anxiety.

"Okay, well, my name is Nevaeh Fuchs, I'm German, and I've been at *Griffin Sports* for two days now."

"And you like photography," Adrian adds, causing my heart to flutter. I nod with a small grin. "Well, it's a pleasure, Nevaeh. We never get to meet journalists and reporters beforehand, especially ones who are as beautiful as you," he says, and my breathing hitches.

Heat rushes into my cheeks at his flirtatiousness. I can't help but flash him a smile.

"Seriously, Romana, watch yourself," Lincoln growls, jealousy dripping from his lips. *What the fuck is wrong with him?* At this point, he's just embarrassing himself with this territorial shit.

"You need to calm down, Nash," Adrian warns. "You're acting like a child." I couldn't agree more.

"Ah, I see. You're still pissed because I got the seat at Grenzenlos that you weren't good enough for all those years ago," Lincoln replies.

I didn't know Adrian had been a candidate for a Grenzenlos seat in the past, but it's unsurprising. He's one of the best drivers I've ever had the pleasure of watching. Papa met Adrian's grandfather and father a few years before their passing, and he always told me what great racers they were in their times.

It must be in their genes.

"Says the guy whose daddy is best friends with my father, the team principal of the Grenzenlos team," I blurt out, causing all of their eyes to go wide.

Adrian snickers and leans forward in the chair to run his hands over his face. Gabriel bites down on the inside of his cheek to hide his amusement, and Kyle pulls his thin lips into a straight line. Lincoln, on the other hand, is boiling from anger. If I look closely enough, I'm sure I could see steam coming out of his ears.

"Can I talk to you in private for a moment?" Lincoln says with a husky, rough voice, letting me know he's more upset with me than he's ever been.

"Mr. Fender is counting on me to—" I'm cut off by Gillian hurrying into the room.

"I'm here. I apologize for being late, gentlemen," he says and turns to me. "Nevaeh, you may take a moment to speak with Mr. Nash in private," Gillian adds, and I want to ask him why the hell he's doing this to me, but, of course, he doesn't know my history with the Formula One driver.

Lincoln gets up and waits for me to walk past him before following closely behind.

I decide to lead him into one of the empty conference rooms.

He moves past me while I hold the door open for him. None of the walls are made of glass as they would be in most conference rooms, which means we have complete privacy.

My heart is beating even faster now, and guilt is slowly creeping in as I think about what just happened, but Lincoln's words make me more mad than anything else.

"Do you feel good now?" is the first thing he asks.

I close the door and lean against it, watching the angry man figure out what to do with himself.

"You humiliated me in there," he points out, but I stay quiet. "Why won't you speak to me?" Lincoln runs his fingers through his hair and then leans against the table in the middle of the room.

"Because you're a hypocrite. You were practically pissing on me to mark your goddamn territory, and I didn't react the way you are about my saying something everyone knows," I say, and he narrows his eyes at me.

"It's not the same, and you know it. You just undermined my ability as a racer. You basically called me a nepotism baby," he replies, rolling up the sleeves of his black button-up before running a hand down the length of his face.

"You acted as if I was your fucking property, Lincoln." My voice is so calm, I'm convinced it irritates him.

"You're the fucking hypocrite, Nevs, do you know that?" Lincoln lets out a dry laugh and then a groan of frustration. "You can't forgive me for something stupid I said, but here you are, using your words to hurt me." This makes my heart drop. No matter how much I dislike him right now, I don't want to hurt him.

"You don't care enough about me to be offended by what I say," I defend, and he closes the distance between us until his hot, uneven breath is on my skin.

"You don't think I care?" Linc asks and lowers his mouth so his lips are almost touching mine. "Your opinion matters to me. Your words affect me. Now, tell me, what makes you think I don't care about you because I sure as hell never gave you that idea," he explains as his hands lift to each side of my face and press against the door, caging me between them.

I don't like this at all. There was a time when I adored his proximity, but that time has long passed. Now, I just want to push him away.

"Do I have to remind you how angry I am with you?" I ask, and he grins for the first time since I made that comment in Gillian's office.

"No, but you might have to remind yourself because I can tell how badly you want me."

I place my hand on his chest before pushing him back to create space between us.

"You're out of your mind if you think anything will ever happen between us. *I loathe you*," I spit the last three words and open the door to get back to the other drivers.

CHAPTER 9
Adrian

Nevaeh walks back into the office with a fake smile on her lips, and Lincoln trails in right behind her. Her cheeks are flushed and his breathing is uneven, but I don't think anything happened between them except fighting. He looks way too unhappy, and, from what I've gathered so far, he seems to have feelings for Nevaeh.

If he'd kissed her, he'd look happier.

There is really no need for jealousy to flood me at the thought, but I think that's what the strange, uncomfortable feeling lingering in my chest is. Jealousy. Not jealous of Lincoln, but jealous that he got her attention.

I sure as fuck am not jealous of the possessive asshole next to me.

I could treat Nevaeh a lot better than he could.

Wait, what the fuck?

"Alright, now that we're all here, let's get started," Gillian Fender says, but my eyes keep slipping to where Nevaeh is sitting with a notepad on her lap and a pen between her fingers.

She's chewing on her bottom lip, her hair falling like curtains to frame each side of her face. She's so breathtaking. And I love the way she didn't let Lincoln act like an alpha male asshole around me without putting him in his place. There is so much fire inside of her, so much passion, I can't help but wonder if she loves as strongly as she despises.

"This season, we're planning on focusing all our resources on—"

Gillian keeps talking, but I'm too mesmerized by Nevaeh to listen.

Freckles are dusting the bridge of her nose and cheeks that I didn't notice before. Her eyes are a warm shade of brown—I think it's called honey brown. She's got long legs with thick thighs to die for and wide hips I can't help but imagine digging my hands into to guide her against me. I have a thing for thick women, always have, and Nevaeh is the kind of curvy that I could spend my days worshiping until I've had enough. Because eventually I would get enough of her and move on.

Yes, I would.

Yes, I would.

Yes, I would.

I repeat the same mantra over and over until I'm at least a little convinced the words will stick. Because they need to stick.

I'm not fucking equipped to deal with... *feelings.*

"Mr. Romana, does that sound good to you?" Gillian asks, and I shift my head to bring my gaze to him.

Nevaeh is blushing beside her boss, staring down at her notepad with the sweetest smile. It fades as soon as Lincoln shifts beside me, catching Nevaeh's attention. Her smile turns into the most vicious glare, making me bite back my own grin because *damn.* I like both of the sides she's showing. I like the no-bullshit side and I like the shy-because-I'm-looking-at-her side.

"Yeah, sounds perfect," I reply, having no idea what the fuck I just agreed to with Gillian. Gabriel grins next to me, clearly seeing the way Nevaeh keeps distracting me.

I very subtly kick him as I lift my leg to place my ankle on my knee, waiting for this meeting to finally be over so I can talk to Nevaeh.

Gillian keeps talking, so I do my best to look anywhere but at Nevaeh, but it's like trying to overtake during a race where you only have three tires and the car in front of you runs on magic fuel.

It's impossible.

So, I look. Again and again, until this god-forsaken meeting is finally done. I stand up along with Gabriel, Kyle, and Lincoln. Nevaeh and Gillian stand too, but I don't get the chance to have a moment alone with my mysterious woman before she's out of the door and on her way somewhere. I've never seen a person in such a rush before, but I'm assuming she doesn't want to deal with Lincoln again.

Understandable.

Unfortunately for me, Lincoln takes that as an invitation to approach me instead.

"Stay the hell away from Nevaeh," he says as we make our way outside the building. Gabriel is on the phone with Val, and Kyle could not be bothered less by all of Lincoln's drama.

"Last time I checked, you're not my boss, rookie, so I don't have to do what you tell me to," I reply, casually crossing my arms in front of my chest and looking straight ahead at the elevator doors. A smile tries to fight its way onto my lips, but I manage to bite it back.

"I'm not a fucking rookie, Romana. I was racing last year already." The annoyance in his voice only amuses me more.

"Were you? I didn't notice. Probably because you were always at the back of the grid and I was winning races."

It's a dick thing to say, but I've had enough of this little boy acting like he's the king of the world. He's only three years younger than me, but the twenty-one-year-old is certainly not acting his age either.

"Well, that's about to change, isn't it? Grenzenlos will be stronger than Velocità Rossa this year, and I'll wipe the floor with you in no time." A yawn slips past my lips as he speaks, but once he's done, I place a hand on his shoulder and give it a reassuring squeeze.

"Sure you will," I say, stepping out of the elevator as soon as the words have left me. Gabriel falls in step beside me, grinning as he tells Val what I just said. He does it in French too, making sure Lincoln won't hear my teammate making fun of him.

"Val says you shouldn't provoke Lincoln unless you want his daddy to snitch on you to the FIA." I burst into laughter so loud, Lincoln shoots me a glare while Kyle leads him outside, mumbling something about it not being worth it.

It really isn't worth it, but I can't deny that it isn't at least a little fun to fuck with people who deserve it.

Nevaeh is her own person. If she wants me to stay away, I'll stay away, but not because of the little rookie telling me to. It'll be because she wants me to, and no one else.

CHAPTER 10
Nevaeh

THURSDAY NIGHT IS BOWLING night whenever Papa is home for the holidays. Mama and I are on one team while Papa and Nova are on the other. Since my injury, I've been too scared to do any heavy lifting or extreme exercise with my right arm, which is why Mama and I are at a great disadvantage. I'm too scared to throw properly.

Lucky for us, however, Nova is extremely uncoordinated. Years of bowling have not improved her skill, and I chuckle every single time her bowling ball lands in the gutter. It happens more often than it should, but it doesn't stop her from having the best time.

We're head-to-head in our first game. Papa picks up his sparkling-purple bowling ball and squats low with it to analyze which angle is best. Mama and Nova burst into laughter while I grin and look around the bowling alley.

My eyes drift to the entrance just in time to notice Adrian, Gabriel, and Valentina walk in. My heart stutters at the sight of him, not entirely sure if I'm imagining it or if he's really here. It can't be that he and I somehow keep meeting unless...

Well, I don't really believe in fate, so what the hell is it?

The couple is holding hands and smiling at each other as Adrian arranges for shoes and a lane. If he didn't look so damn attractive in that long black coat and matching beanie, I'd manage to look away before he catches me staring. But he does, so I ogle him until his gaze meets mine, and I awkwardly turn my head as heat rushes into my face.

"Why are you so red?" Nova asks, and I lift my hands to my cheeks. My skin is on fire, which means she's right. I am red in the face.

"It's hot in here," I lie and remove my sweater to sell it.

My sister's eye twitches as she half closes it, a sign that she doesn't believe a single word falling from my lips. Her inquiring gaze would usually make me confess, but, conveniently enough, it's my turn to bowl.

I jump out of my seat and move toward the bowling balls return machine to grab the blue one I'm using.

Knowing Adrian Romana is here, potentially watching my every move, causes my heart rate to pick up speed. He has a strange sort of effect on me. He makes me a different kind of nervous, not the nervous feeling that comes with my anxiety. He makes me nervous in the butterfly sort of way. The one where those little creatures bat their wings rapidly to create a storm inside of my stomach and chest.

I'm about to throw the ball when his smooth voice fills my ears.

"Mr. Fuchs, it's very nice to see you." Polite, hot, sweet, and capable of pronouncing my last name properly.

It's a combination I've never encountered in a man before.

I mess up my throw and stop a second before facepalming myself. Not the best impression to make, but I pretend it doesn't bother me as I take a couple deep breaths to prepare for what's to come.

"How many times do I have to tell you to call me Robert?" my father replies, and I turn around to see them shaking hands.

Valentina does so next and Gabriel follows afterward.

Papa is highly respected in Formula One. He's seen as one of the best team principals the sport has ever had. He got the team to the top with his planning, commitment, and drive. Almost all the drivers want one of the two seats available because Grenzenlos has one of the best cars and a phenomenal team. Gabriel may have won the championship last season, and Velocità Rossa won the Constructors' Championship, but Papa has been working non-stop to prevent that from happening again.

"This is my wife, Emma, and my daughters Nova and Nevaeh," Papa says to the three drivers as I come closer, catching Adrian's and Valentina's eyes.

"I have already met your lovely daughter," Adrian states as he looks at me, causing my body to react in a hundred different ways, all telling me to take a step closer to him. I manage to keep from doing so, but Adrian moves toward me instead. "How are you, Nevaeh?" he asks softly, and I melt from the way he says my name.

"Oh, um, good," I reply, too perplexed to form a proper sentence. Sensing my confusion, he turns to his sister and waves her over to where we're standing.

"Nevaeh, this is Valentina. Val, this is Nevaeh. You're her favorite driver in Formula One," he says, and I have trouble speaking for another moment.

The first female Formula One driver smiles warmly at me, making my heart drop into my pants.

"Valentina, you're an inspiration. I can't believe I'm meeting you," I admit, my hands starting to sweat. The only time I will get this nervous is in the presence of a powerful, influential woman like Valentina.

Adrian came close, but I got nervous for a different reason with him.

"Thank you, you're too sweet. Adrian has told me a lot about you," she says with a smile before he nudges her, and I grin. "I heard you will be traveling with *Griffin Sports* to all of the races. Are you excited?" My eyes drift to Adrian, who is rubbing the back of his neck and smiling at the floor.

He told Valentina more than I thought he would.

"Yes, I am, and you must be too. This is your first season in Formula One as a driver! That's incredible," I point out, and she gives me an enchanting smile that I can't help but return. I see Adrian in all of her features, except Valentina's are softer and Adrian's are more chiseled.

Both of them are gorgeous though.

"Only took over a decade to fight their misogynistic mindsets to get my seat," she replies. Adrian looks at his sister with a proud smile, warming my insides.

"No one deserves it more than you," Adrian adds, and I think I swoon internally, something I have never, *ever* done before.

Gabriel wraps his arms around Valentina's waist and presses a kiss to her cheek. She gasps in surprise but then giggles happily. My eyes shift to the floor because, whether I'd like to admit it or not, I want what they have. I pretend I don't most of the time because the thought of wanting this impossible thing is cruel to do to myself. But I do. I want to fall hopelessly in love with someone who I can love in every way. Not just as a partner, but also as a friend, an inspiration, and a favorite person.

I want the kind of love where you fall and fall and fall, never hitting the ground.

I want the kind of love where your partner is right there beside you, holding your hands as you drift among the clouds.

I want the kind of love that isn't easy but oh so worth it.

Gabriel and Valentina have something most people don't see, but that I can always identify. They have an unbreakable bond. It often gets chaotic, messy, and painful, but they love each other so much, they will find a way back to one another. Even though I don't know if any of this applies to them, I sense that it does. Just like I know it applies to Mama and Papa. Just like I know it applies to Aileen and Nova. They've had messy times in the past too, but they always came back to each other, every single time.

Adrian's fingers slide onto my arm, dragging me out of my thoughts and back to reality with a wonderful spark of electricity. It settles inside of me until a dozen explosions go off, warming me until my cheeks heat with a blush. I look up at him and he stares down at me, a single look enough to draw me to him.

"How are you feeling? You seemed very upset after your conversation with Lincoln yesterday," he says. I can't pinpoint what makes my heart race anymore. It could be his words, but his skin on mine is also a possibility. Maybe it's the way he's looking at me. Or the fact that he's even looking at me at all.

"Oh, don't worry. Lincoln and I have known each other for years. He did something stupid a while back, so now I despise him. We fight all the time, it's normal," I explain without realizing how much I am sharing with this new acquaintance.

Adrian's handsome face turns serious and part of me is tempted to place a comforting hand on his cheek, wanting to ease what troubles him.

I barely stop my eyes from revealing how surprised I am at that desire.

"You despise him while he has feelings for you. That sounds like a very complicated situation," Adrian responds, dropping his hand from my arm and breaking the source of electricity that was rushing through my body.

"I don't think he has feelings for me." Even though I suspect Adrian is right, I can't go around and confirm things like that when Lincoln hasn't admitted to any of this.

The tall driver cocks an eyebrow at me.

"Okay, if you say so. From what I saw yesterday, I think he does, but you know him better than I do." I cross my arms in front of my chest and study his face.

"Why do you care anyway?" One corner of my mouth lifts, but he soon makes it drop again as he steps toward me until his breath is on my skin. Adrian leans down until I'm the only one who will hear his next words.

"I could lie and say it's mere curiosity that has me wondering about you and Lincoln, but I don't want you to think that's the only reason I'm interested in you."

My breath hitches at his admission, unable to stay steady when his words are so heady and wonderful, they twist my stomach in the best way.

No part of me wants him to back away, so when he does, disappointment consumes every inch of me.

He clears his throat and straightens out his shirt.

"I should let you go back to your family. Have a wonderful evening, Nevaeh." Adrian attempts to walk away, but I hold onto his trained arm.

"You can't say something like that and then walk away," I say, and he steps back in front of me with an intrigued sparkle in his eyes. I've surprised him and he seems to enjoy that a lot.

"Then come with me. Let's go for a walk," he suggests and holds out his hand to gesture for me to go first

I don't hesitate before grabbing my jacket to lead him out of the bowling alley.

Mama and Papa are completely wrapped up in their conversation with Gabriel and Valentina so I only tell Nova where I'm going. She gives me a not-so-subtle thumbs up, and I wink at her.

Adrian waits until I'm finished putting on my jacket, and we go outside into the freezing night air.

Snow falls on us, and Adrian turns to me to adjust my scarf and hat.

"Thank you," I mumble, and he grins at me.

"I know you have a fire inside of you that could probably melt all the snow around us, but just to be safe," he says with a smirk. I bite my bottom lip and shake my head, trying my best not to look at his panty-dropping smile. "I really mean it, Nevaeh. You're full of fire and confidence, and, at the same time, shy and sweet. It messes with my head a little. I don't know what to expect from you," he admits, but I walk past him without responding.

I've never received a compliment from someone that gets my heart racing in the way he does. It makes me feel all tingly inside, and I have no idea what I'm supposed to do with this feeling.

"You must know how good you are with your words," I point out, and Adrian runs his tongue over his bottom lip to hide the amusement I can see creeping onto his face.

"You're a beautiful woman with a name that means 'heaven.' It's your influence on me that makes me good with words," he replies before looking me up and down with desire and fascination.

I stop walking to lean my head backward and let out a laugh.

He must do that on purpose.

"What are you trying to do with me?" I eventually ask. Adrian takes a step toward me and fixes his hair, which is now covered in snow.

"The same thing you're doing to me," he admits, but it doesn't clear things up for me.

"And what might that be?" He takes another step closer, but so do I. The fogs of our breaths intertwine and dance in front of us in perfect harmony.

I have no idea what the hell we're doing. This man is a stranger. And a player. Everyone knows Adrian Romana isn't the relationship type of person—I did my research over the past three months.

They call him the heartbreaker of F1.

He likes to sleep with lots of women but never dates any of them. I know he's directed his charm my way because he might be interested in hooking up. It's why I should step away from him, ignore the way he keeps affecting my body when I don't even know him, but I don't.

"Take over your mind with thoughts of me. You've been in my head for the past three months now, Nevaeh, and I don't know how to get you out," he admits, causing shivers to run down my spine. He smells so good, his cologne filling the space between us until he's all I smell. Until he's all I see.

"I'm sorry?" I say with a laugh, but he shakes his head, smiling as he tugs a strand of my hair behind my ear. Another shiver of pleasure travels down my spine.

He's a player.

I try to keep reminding myself of that, try to rationalize why he's gotten so close, but it's difficult to remember when he looks at me like I'm the only woman in the world that he wants to touch.

"I'm not. I quite enjoy looking at your face, which is probably why my brain keeps replaying the image of you." Fuck, he knows exactly what he's doing, but my cheeks flush red anyway.

His gaze trails over my face, studying me, memorizing me.

"Did you really not know who I was when we met?" he asks, taking a step back to give us both space to breathe.

"Not at first, but by the end, I recognized you." He gives me a thoughtful nod, then smiles even brighter.

"But you were unimpressed?" I almost snort at that.

"Highly," I lie, and he steps closer again, lifting his fingers to my face but stopping before he touches me.

"May I?" I nod before he even voices the entire question.

A chuckle escapes him as he places his thumb on my cheek, rubbing the skin there once before moving on to my lips and tracing them.

"How about now?" There is a lightness to his voice, a flirtiness I welcome.

"Hmmm, still not impressed," I lie with a smile, and he chuckles again, leaning down to bring his mouth toward where his thumb is still tracing my lips.

My father's voice breaks the moment before I have a chance to get lost in a kiss with the hottest man in the world.

"Nevaeh, come back inside, please," he says, and I almost jump away from Adrian.

This is for the best. I don't even know this guy, I shouldn't be kissing him.

Adrian steps back, bringing the thumb that was previously on my lips to his where he runs the pad of it along his mouth. My heart stutters at the intimacy of such a small action, but I do my best not to overthink it.

"I've got to go," I say, but my eyes stay focused on his lips.

"Okay. Next time then," he replies while slowly backing away, shoving his hands into his pockets and giving me another one of those panty-dropping smiles.

"Good night, Adrian," I mutter before walking toward my impatient father. He looks unhappy as I move past him and back inside the bowling alley.

"Vaeh, I think we should talk about what just happened," he says, sounding more demanding than anything else.

"Not today, Papa," I say because before we can talk, *I* need to make sense of the situation myself.

"Tomorrow." He's not asking in the slightest, which bothers the hell out of me.

"You know, you're barely home, Papa. I know you haven't really seen me grow up, but I am. I'm twenty-one years old and what happens between a guy and me is my problem unless I come to you for help. You're a great father when you're here, but I need you to stay behind the line you've drawn, not cross it," I reply firmly, standing my ground in front of him for the first time in my life.

"He's three years older than you, which means he's a lot more mature," is the first thing that comes out of his mouth after a few moments of silence. Hurt laces my expression so he quickly adds, "Look at your behavior toward Lincoln. The fighting between the two of you, it's childish. A grown man like Adrian would never want something serious with someone who can't even be polite to a close family friend."

It's my fault that he doesn't know why Lincoln and I aren't on good terms, but he has no right to say this to me. The wound Lincoln opened in my chest has not closed enough for my father to poke it.

"I will show you real maturity now. Instead of pointing out that you have no idea what you're talking about because *you weren't there when I needed you most*, I'm going to walk away. Nothing I'd say to you right now would be *polite*, so I'll stay at Aileen's flat for the night. At least she knows who I am. Maybe you should get to know me better before throwing something so hurtful at my head." I walk over to Nova to grab my purse and let her know where I plan to be.

"Aileen's spending a few days at her parents' house. You can't go to her," she informs me.

A groan of frustration almost slips past my lips, but I manage to press them shut to keep the sound inside.

There is only one place I can think of going to escape my father, but it comes at a high price. If I wasn't so mad at him, I wouldn't even consider it, but I'm furious.

I have no other option.

Well, here goes nothing...

CHAPTER 11
Nevaeh

Every muscle in my body fights against my intention to knock on the Nashes' door. This is a terrible idea, but Elena Nash is one of my favorite people in the world. Whenever I have problems with my parents, she welcomes me with open arms. Knowing she'll hug me until my anger fades gives me the courage to knock.

Lincoln doesn't even live here anymore, so the chance of seeing him is pretty low. Unfortunately for me, it's not low enough.

He opens the door with a confused and surprised expression, his lips parted and his eyes wide. My gaze drops to his bare chest. His defined abs take my breath away in the same way they have since he started working hard to build them. I hate that my body still reacts to him the same way it used to when we were still friends, when we were very close to becoming more.

Instead of lingering, I focus on the gray dirt on his arms, but his words soon distract me.

"Butterfly, what's wrong? Why are you crying?" Lincoln asks, and I lift my fingers to my cheeks to see he's right.

I hadn't even noticed the tears until he pointed them out. What Papa said must bother me more than I thought. I wipe them away when suddenly, Lincoln takes my face in his hands to remove them for me. My body freezes in place, but I don't pull away. I can't concentrate on my anger toward him when I'm so sick and tired of fighting with the people I care about.

It's weighing heavily on my mental health.

"I came to see your mom," I say with a raspy, barely audible voice, but he doesn't pull away. His concern lingers as he catches more of my tears with his thumbs.

The friend he used to be to me, my best friend, is standing in front of me right now, not the man I've grown to hate, and I have no idea how to act anymore.

"She is in a meeting, Nevs, but come in. I will make you tea," he offers, and I hesitate. I haven't forgiven him, not yet, but I also have nowhere to go.

Elena will eventually have some time for me, and, meanwhile, I will drink a cup of tea with the guy I despise a little less at the moment.

"Okay," I mutter and follow him inside where he removes my coat to hang it in the closet.

"Vanilla Rooibos, right?" Lincoln asks as he pulls the teas from one of the many cupboards in his parents' small kitchen. They recently remodeled it to make it more modern and have white be the dominant color. "Nevaeh?" Lincoln's husky voice pulls my attention to him, and I walk over to the high chairs at the kitchen island.

"Yeah, sure," My tired legs help me settle down on one of the chairs while my eyes never leave Lincoln's muscular back, too suspicious of his next move to look away.

"I can feel you digging a hole into my back with your eyes," he states without even looking at me.

"You're really full of yourself to assume that, you know?" I reply with a harsh laugh, and Lincoln spins around to hand me my cup.

"I am full of myself, but I also saw you staring at me in the reflection of the coffee machine," he informs me, and I glance at the machine to see it's made out of mirror glass.

"I don't trust you enough to not watch you closely," I say because I don't want him to assume desire had anything to do with it.

Lincoln frowns at my words.

"Why are your arms covered in dirt?" I ask to change the subject as he places the cup in my hands, his fingers lingering for moments longer than they should. "Why are you still touching me?" I say, and Lincoln moves around the kitchen island to stand in front of me.

"Because I like touching you," he admits but creates a distance between us to keep me comfortable. "I'm dirty because I was in the garage, working on a vase for my mum," he explains with a shy smile.

Lincoln does pottery? Since when?

Those are questions I should probably ask out loud, but I don't want him to think that I am even the slightest bit interested in his life.

"Come with me. I want to show you," he says and holds out his hand for me to take. I slide out of the chair and make my way toward the garage without accepting his offer. He chuckles but doesn't say anything.

The Nashes' house is wonderful. It's big but significantly smaller than my parents'. There are a lot of windows because Elena loves her natural light, and, unlike my house, it feels like a home. It's not overly sophisticated, and the furniture isn't expensive.

George and Elena had very little when they first bought this house thirty years ago, and it shows in everything they have displayed. In the four years I've lived in England, and in the ten years I've visited this house with my family, it has become more of a home than my parents'.

"Feeling nostalgic, butterfly?" Lincoln interrupts my reminiscing.

"You wanted to show me the vase?" I reply instead of admitting the truth.

"Yes," he simply says before opening the garage door and revealing his workstation.

An electric potter's wheel stands in the middle of the parking spot no one is using. A stool sits behind it and a piece of clay rests on top of the machine. It's already been somewhat shaped into a vase, but I don't think it's anywhere near ready. Lincoln grabs my hand to pull me toward his work.

"My mum asked me to make her a bouquet vase. I'm halfway done." His voice is full of excitement. "Come, sit, please," he says when he gets another stool for me.

I hesitantly take the seat, but Lincoln is already on his stool, wetting his hands and the dough to keep working on it. Silence fills the garage, but it's soon broken when the machine starts to hum.

"How long have you been doing pottery?" I ask.

"Um, a few years now. I don't like to share this with anyone else, which is why no one knows, just my family," he explains, his gaze focused on the clay. "And now you," Lincoln adds before using more water on the clay to get it in the proper shape.

A sad feeling spreads through me.

"I wish my anger toward you wouldn't taint every nice moment we have together, past ones and this one," I admit, causing him to stop everything and look at me.

"Nevaeh, listen to me closely now, would you?" he asks, and I nod. "I was young and stupid—" he says, but I stand up and laugh dryly.

"Would you like to be any more cliché? Being young and stupid is no justification!" I yell as the anger I usually feel toward him returns. Lincoln gets up too before grabbing a towel to clean his hands on and walking toward me.

"I told you you're not ready to hear my apology, and it's bullshit that you choose not to see that. Don't blame all of this on me. I want to apologize. Hell, I'd do it so often, you'd be sick of hearing it, but what's the use when you won't listen to me?" he screams back. My heart thumps against my ribcage from anger.

"I am ready, but that start was *bullshit*, and you know it!" His hands are clean now, which is why he slams the towel on the floor and gets even closer to me. I back away until my body touches a wall.

"I'm sorry! Okay? I'm so sorry for what I said. There is no justification, nothing that can make it better, but please, I can't take you hating me anymore!" he yells at me, his hands moving to each side of me on the wall while both our hearts race and our breathing remains uneven. His lips are centimeters from mine and they get closer with each heartbeat. "Stop me," he whispers, but my body fights against doing so.

Without thinking, without letting myself realize I don't really want this anymore, that I haven't wanted him in so long, I kiss him. I kiss him because I used to be in love with him and this was everything I had wanted to happen between us for so long, I lost track of time. I kiss him because he wants me to.

But as soon as my lips press against his, I *know*, I know I don't kiss him because I'm still in love with him. I don't want him anymore, and the heat of the moment won't change that.

So, I push him away from me to get him to give me space.

"No, Lincoln, we can't do this. This isn't right. I've been mad at you for four years. Kissing you after you just apologized is not the right thing to do," I go on and open the garage door to escape his captivating stare.

"Wait, Nevs!" he calls out, but I'm hurrying into the kitchen to grab my stuff and get out of here.

Lincoln's dad, George, watches me the entire time I collect my things, and I politely wish him a good night.

Lincoln waits until we're alone again before he says, "I'm sorry, I didn't mean to make you uncomfortable."

The problem is, he didn't. *I* kissed *him*. I got lost in the moment, and I kissed him. And it was a mistake I don't intend on making again.

"You don't have to leave. I won't bother you again or speak to you, but don't feel like you have to go home if you don't want to," Lincoln says.

"I'm okay, Lincoln, thanks," I assure him and open the front door to step outside.

"Butterfly," he says softly, and I hesitate. My eyes drift to his hazel ones. "I am sorry about everything."

"I know, but it doesn't make what you said simply go away," I reply and walk away, tears filling my eyes at the memory.

CHAPTER 12
Adrian

"LOOK WHO HAS RETURNED," Gabriel announces, making Valentina snicker next to him.

"Look who's still an idiot," I reply, frowning at him.

"Oooh ouch. Must have not gone well," my teammate whispers to my sister loudly enough for me to hear.

"Your face hasn't gone well," I say, but Gabriel gives me an unimpressed look.

"He's resorting to immature rebuttals. It went worse than not well." Valentina studies me for a moment before giving her fiancé an agreeing nod.

"Definitely didn't go the way he was hoping," my sister chimes in.

"Where's Leonard? I thought he was coming to hang out with us tonight," I say to change the subject.

The thought of Nevaeh and I almost kissing but getting interrupted is as exciting as it is disappointing. I've never wanted to taste a woman as badly as her because there must be something I discover about her that'll turn me off. Maybe she's a terrible kisser. Maybe her mouth on mine isn't as intoxicating as I think it will be. Maybe one kiss will be enough for me to move on from this fascination I have with her.

"I'm here. Sorry I'm late, I was laughing at Adrian getting rejected and had to catch my breath," Leonard replies, a slight lift to the corner of his mouth that is basically a full-faced smile for him.

"First of all, I didn't get rejected. Second of all, I didn't know grumpy assholes were capable of laughing," I say, so he wraps his arm around my shoulders before threatening to cut off my air supply by placing his forearm to my throat.

"What was that?" he asks, and I burst into laughter.

"Nothing. Jesus. I know your wife is a trained fighter, but don't listen to her. Violence is *not* the answer." This makes Leonard chuckle a little.

"Don't worry, I'm way too fucking sore from training to kick your arse in anything but bowling," Leonard says and steps to the side to stretch his back.

"You should take it easy, mate. You're at that age where you could easily injure yourself," I tease, and Gabriel chuckles while Valentina bursts into laughter. My heart beams at the sight of their amusement, knowing I put it there.

"Yes, ha, ha, I am old. Guess what, tick tock, arsehole. Time stops for no one," he says and pats my shoulder.

Valentina and Gabriel are crying-laughing at my dropped jaw, and, as much as I try not to, I join them anyway.

Fuck, I love all of them so much, it scares me.

Do I really want to add another name to my already long list of people I care about and am scared to lose? Because of a woman I met three months ago?

No, no I don't.

CHAPTER 13
Nevaeh

WHEN I WALK INTO my parents' house, Papa is sitting on the stairs at the entrance, waiting for me. He must have heard me get out of the taxi. I drop my jacket and purse from the fright of finding him there in complete darkness, making no sound other than his loud judgment and frustration.

"Good God, what are you doing up?" I ask because it's midnight, and, most nights, he goes to sleep at ten.

Papa gives me a disappointed frown, which I see when I turn on the light in the foyer.

"Oh no, stop that. I hate that face. It always appears a moment before you say, 'I can't believe you chose to go to the Nashes instead of your own home.' I've heard it often enough," I complain and take my shoes off so I don't have to keep looking at him.

"Actually, Nevaeh, I was going to tell you to grow up. I'm sick and tired of you disappearing whenever you don't like what I have to say. I am your goddamn father, and you show me no respect! How do you think that makes me feel?" he asks, and anger fills me from bottom to top until it overflows.

"No, you know what, Papa? I'm tired of you treating me like a child when I try to keep things civil between us. I was mad earlier, and, frankly, fucking hurt from what you said. Distance was the one thing that kept me from yelling at you, from telling you that while I'm proud of your career, I'm angry with you for missing every important event in my life. I'm angry because work is always more important. You have no idea who I am, but you pretend like you do to make yourself feel better.

That needs to stop. You need to observe for once in your life. Even when you're here, you're always busy. So, hear me now: get to know your daughter before you try and make her feel like crap about who she is."

I'm not entirely sure where this came from, but it lifts a weight off my chest, shoulders, and heart.

My father runs his hands over his face before pointing at the ground in front of him, telling me to sit. If I hadn't thrown a lot of bad words his way a second ago, I wouldn't do as he wants. However, I did, and guilt forces my feet to bring me to where he's signaling.

Papa waits patiently until I'm sitting before opening his mouth again.

"You're right about everything you said, but you left something out, Vaeh. How can I get to know you when you barely share anything about your life? When you won't tell me what happened between you and Lincoln?"

I stare down at the floor, ready to retell the one story I've never shared with anyone, not even Nova.

"You called me immature for my relationship with Lincoln earlier, and that was a shitty and unfair thing to say," I point out, and Papa leans back on the stairs, his careful gaze on me.

"Tell me what he did."

"Four years ago, when my rotator cuff tear happened, you weren't there. It was just Mama, Lincoln, and me." He nods once to acknowledge my words. "It was the final game of the season, the one where all the sponsors and recruiters attended, remember?"

Papa nods again, his fingers intertwining as he pays close attention to me.

"I was in the lead when it was my turn to serve. I felt the rip as soon as my racket connected with the ball. Then followed excruciating and unbearable pain. My scream rippled from the court through the crowd as I sank onto the floor, holding my shoulder and crying."

Tears fall down my cheeks, and I see pain shoot through his eyes.

"They took me to the hospital where I got the emergency surgery that sealed my fate as the woman who failed to make her dream come true, even though I was a hair's width away from making it."

This one single sentence always makes me feel lost and helpless. I bring my mind back to the facts instead of the feelings.

"Right after I came out of surgery, the doctors warned me that it is highly unlikely I could ever become a professional with my busted shoulder." They also didn't do a good job fixing it, in my opinion, but whatever. "Lincoln came to visit me after my surgery. Do you know what he said to me?"

Papa shakes his head, and I look at the ceiling, searching for courage.

"He said, 'It's a good thing this happened now before you wasted your time in a career you couldn't have gotten far in any way.'"

My heart rips apart a little because saying it out loud for the first time since it happened is more painful than I thought it'd be.

"So, you see, Papa, it's not a childish quarrel. It's a broken heart that got trampled on at its weakest." My father wraps his arms around me and holds me close, letting me weep like a little kid.

"I'm sorry I didn't hear you before, but I do now. What Lincoln said is inexcusable, but, for your sake, you have to let go of your anger, sweetheart. It's breaking you, not him," he says, and I nod.

This isn't news to me, but things feel different now, at least a little. The pieces of my life are falling into place, and I have to get rid of the negativity holding me back. That means forgiving Lincoln for being the biggest idiot on the planet. I hope I find the courage to let go of my anger because I know it's much easier to hold onto it than to let it go.

Papa releases me, and I turn around to see Mama standing in the doorframe, tears in her eyes. Out of the both of them, finding out what happened between Lincoln and me probably hits her the hardest. She's the one who never took me seriously, never took a moment to ask why I hated him, and, now, I can see regret written all over her aged features.

"Nevaeh, I—I have no words. I'm so sorry, honey." She wraps her arms around me and hugs me too tightly.

"Wait, it's hugging time?" I hear Nova call out from upstairs before she storms downstairs and runs against me to join the embrace. Papa does the same, and we end up standing in the middle of the entrance, looking like a family that doesn't have a thousand problems.

In other words, the complete opposite of us.

CHAPTER 14
Adrian

It's been two days. *Two fucking days.* I've been trying to get this infuriating woman out of my head, but the feel of her lips on my finger still makes my skin tingle. It might be why I asked Nevaeh's sister, Nova, for my mysterious woman's number right before she left the bowling alley with her family.

Now, I'm sitting in the hotel room we're staying at with Val and Gabriel at the table, playing a card game. Leonard and his wife, Chiara, are also here with their three-month-old sleeping in the grumpy man's arms. She's surprisingly silent, smiling like she couldn't be happier to be with her father. Chiara is currently frowning at the floor, looking more tired than I've ever seen her before.

"You alright, Chiara?" I ask, bringing a soft smile to my lips.

Her attention drifts to my face as she slowly nods her head. It's not surprising that she's quiet, Chiara likes to keep more to herself, but she looks tired. I know that having a newborn is one of the toughest jobs in the world, but I still want to check in with her to see how she's doing. I love her. Just like I love Leonard, Gabriel, James, Cameron, and James' son Damian. In a quiet sort of way, playing it off more often than not, but always being there for them when they need me. It's very different from how loudly I love my sister.

She's my favorite person in the world, and I'll never pretend otherwise.

"Yeah, Leonora was keeping me up all night, and this one slept through her screaming, which means I stayed awake," she replies as she points at Leonard, her Italian accent strong.

She shoots her husband a vicious scowl, but I grin at the violence in her eyes, a promise to get payback later. Boy, am I glad I'm not Leonard right now. Chiara is a trained fighter, so getting on her bad side is one of the biggest no-nos for me.

"I'm sorry, sweetheart, I really am. Next time, kick me awake," he says with his thick English accent, earning himself the smallest of smiles from his wife, which is the equivalent of the brightest of smiles for Chiara. They're both grumpy as hell, and it's cute when they let a little bit of sunshine onto their faces.

"See, this is why you should have married me. I would *never* do what Leonard did. I'd be awake for you at all times," I say with a wink directed at Chiara. Leonard steps in front of me, his daughter safe in his arms as he glares at me.

"Chiara just had our baby. What more do you need to stop flirting with my wife?" he asks, looking unhappy when we both know I'm only teasing.

I've been flirting with Chiara from the moment I met her when the two of them were still denying their feelings for each other, and I doubt I'm going to stop anytime soon, not unless she tells me to. Or unless I get a girlfriend, and that's not happening.

"She'll wake up one day and realize she can do better than you, also known as me," I reply with a self-assured grin.

"Hey, Adrian?" Chiara asks, and I twist my head to look around Leonard and at her. "Val told me you had a crush on Robert Fuchs' daughter. How's that going?" I can almost feel the color drain from my face.

My eyes shift to where my sister is sitting, but she's already chuckling at her cards with her pinky raised in my direction.

Well, fuck you, too.

"I don't have a crush on anyone," I say through gritted teeth, trying my best not to stare down at my phone again. "Except you," I add.

Leonard places Leonora in Chiara's arms so carefully, I can tell he's scared of hurting his baby. Once his daughter is securely placed in her mother's arms, Leonard stalks toward me with a murderous look in his eyes. I burst out laughing, covering my head with my arms to protect myself.

"Okay, I'm sorry," I blurt out, still laughing. Leonard places a hand on my shoulder and squeezes until it's painful.

"Chiara is *my wife*. Mine. Either get it through your head, or I'll punch it through your stubbornness. Got it?" Leonard asks, a hint of a smile on his face as he stares down at me.

"Empty threats. You love me too much to ever hurt me," I say and grin at him. I should have seen the slap up the back of my head coming. "Grumpy old man," I complain as I rub the back of my head, but when he gives me a brighter smile, I can't help but return it.

"I think you should text her, Adrian. Maybe ask her on a date and give whatever you're feeling a shot. It's okay to feel fascinated beyond the physical level with a woman. You're intrigued by her, and that's a good thing. Give yourself a chance to like her," Valentina chimes in, and Gabriel smiles affectionately at her.

"You all need to get off my case. I'm perfectly happy with my life the way it is, I don't need to turn into *that*," I say and point at Gabriel. "Or *that*," I add, gesturing at Leonard.

"From what you told me you said to her yesterday, you're already halfway there to becoming me," Gabriel teases with a self-satisfied smirk.

"The possessiveness comes later," Chiara says as Leonard strokes his hand over her short hair, playing with the strands as he stares down at her with so much love, I know he'd destroy the entire planet to protect his world: Chiara and Leonora.

This thought stays with me until everyone's left and it's just me in the hotel room. My phone is heavy in my hands, and before I know it, I'm typing out a message I never thought I'd sent and hitting Send before I can overthink what the fuck I'm doing.

Me: Hi, this is Adrian. I hope this isn't weird, but Nova gave me your number in case I wanted it. Okay, that's a lie, I practically begged her for it. You're stuck in my head, and I wanted to tell you that one more time. I would love to take you out on a proper date someday, but I will also understand if you block me. I am very charming, after all, and some people can't handle it.

For the first time in my life, I don't feel confident talking to a woman at all. Usually, I know exactly what I'm doing. Women love me. I love women. What more do I need? Apparently, I need to go on fucking *dates* now.

Yikes.

When she doesn't respond right away, I add:

Me: I'm flying back to Monaco tomorrow morning, but I hope we'll see each other soon. Good night, Nevaeh.

My fingers tap the side of my phone while I wait. Maybe I misinterpreted the way she seemed drawn to me. Fuck, what if I did? What if this was the worst way to go about this? What if I completely freaked her out?

My phone rings before I have a chance to spiral, a smile lighting up my face at the name appearing there.

"Nevaeh," I say with a soft tone as soon as I hit Answer.

"I hope it's okay that I called you," she replies, causing me to sit up and play with the hem of my shirt nervously.

"I wanted to call you too, but I didn't want to be pushy," I admit, and she chuckles into the phone. I return it.

"So, you can't stop thinking about me, huh?" she asks. I hear rustling as if she stood up to start walking around too.

"Why don't we talk about you instead?" I suggest, trying to keep us from lingering on *that* fact. "Tell me something about yourself," I say. There is a bit of silence for a moment until she breaks it again.

"I wish you weren't leaving so soon," she admits, making my heart skip three beats. It's more forward than anything I was expecting her to say.

"If you want me to stay, I will." *What the fuck is wrong with me? Why would I offer that?*

"Don't you have work responsibilities?" Yes, I have a million meetings to attend and workout schedules I have to stay on top of. Daniel, my performance coach, has already been on my ass to stay focused so close to the start of the season.

"I do, but they can wait another day so I can take you out to dinner." I have no power over my words, none at all. They dance from my lips and turn around to flip me off before flowing through the fucking phone.

Somebody shoot me.

"Pick me up at seven tomorrow evening," she instructs with a firm voice, causing a chuckle to slip out of me because dammit, I like it when women are bossy. It turns me on.

"Seven it is. Good night, gorgeous."

I hang up before I can make more stupid decisions, although I doubt there are any left to make with Nevaeh at this point.

Telling her I can't get her out of my head? Mistake.

Thinking about her constantly? Mistake.

Texting her? Mistake.

Almost kissing her? Big mistake.

Asking her to go to dinner with me? Biggest fucking mistake.

And yet, I find myself wondering when I can make the worst mistake of all. Kissing her until I'm sure I'm the only one left in her head, kicking Lincoln right out into the cold where the fucker belongs anyway.

CHAPTER 15
Neveah

WHAT WAS I THINKING, agreeing to go on a date with Adrian after kissing Lincoln a few days ago? That's easy to answer. I wasn't thinking. I let my body and heart make a decision instead of my head for once. Adrian makes me feel like I'm floating on clouds. I don't want Lincoln, that much has become very clear to me, but I would like to see where things with Adrian could go.

It was a very simple decision to make.

He might be a player, but I'm up for a good game.

Gillian hands me sample articles to look through and learn from, pulling me out of my thoughts. He instructs me to highlight lines I find striking, and, just in general, study every word on the page. I'm not quite sure what the point of this is, but I do as I'm told.

"Neveah, how would you feel about taking French lessons? Since Gabriel Biancheri and Adrian Romana are from Monaco and Kyle Hughes is half French, Ms. Martin is asking if you could turn your little knowledge of it into good enough for conversation," Gillian says or asks, I'm not sure which it is.

Panic grips my chest as I think about what the hell to say to that. I can't say no because I've only been here for a week. If I already start telling my boss I can't do something, it'll undermine my ability as a journalist and one of the strengths I listed on my resumé. I said I'm a quick learner, which wasn't a lie, but how am I supposed to learn French to that extent so fast?

"Um, I can look into getting a tutor," I reply, unsure what else to say, but my boss gives me an approving smile.

"Brilliant. We'll cover that expense, of course," he adds, then walks back into his office, leaving me to get back to work while trying to rack my brain over the fact that they want me to become fluent enough in French to understand native speakers of the language.

A nervous laugh bubbles out of me before I can stop it.

I'm so screwed.

My heart starts racing at the mere thought, my anxiety making my legs shake as I try to focus on the article in front of me. My breathing hitches uncomfortably, so I press a hand to my chest and take several deep breaths, trying to slow my heart rate.

Everything will be alright.

I'll figure it out.

They're not going to fire me because I can't become fluent in French within the next few weeks.

Right?

More anxiety sweeps through me, forcing tears to prick my eyes. I grab my phone and rush toward the bathroom, holding off the tears that always come with my anxiety attacks long enough to lock the door and slide down against it.

I curl into myself, my breathing now heavier than before as I hyperventilate. The lack of oxygen causes my hands and legs to tingle before all feeling leaves them. Nausea builds in my chest too, and I only start panicking more when I realize I don't have time to have an anxiety attack. Gillian will check on me soon, and if I'm not at my desk, he might get upset with me.

"Shit, shit, shit, shit, shit," I mumble over and over again, breathless and with a spinning head.

I fumble with my phone until I manage to dial Nova's number.

"Helloooo," she says as soon as she picks up.

"Code blue," I manage to croak out, wheezing noises leaving me as I try to even out my breath.

"Alright, baby sister, let's take deep breaths together, alright? In, hold, and out. Ready?" she asks softly. I nod over and over, more from the shaking than from acknowledging her words. "In," Nova says, and I suck in a breath until she adds, "Hold." I hold it up until she tells me to let it out again. It comes out shaky, but that small achievement, that one somewhat steady breath, gives me the courage to do it again.

I can do this.

Nova and I repeat the same three steps for another minute until my anxiety subsides enough to stop the shaking and regain the feeling in my legs.

These anxiety attacks have become rare for me. I've had anxiety since my injury happened four years ago, so I know where it originated from. I know what causes my attacks often because I went to therapy for three years. Today, it was my fear of failure that triggered it.

Scared of failing at this job.

Scared of not doing this right.

Scared of failing my family by getting fired.

Scared of not being good enough.

"How are you feeling?" Nova asks, her voice still gentle.

We've been through this often enough that she's figured out a way to get through to me, and it isn't by yelling at me.

It isn't by screaming "Breathe! Why don't you breathe?"

It isn't by starting to freak out too.

It isn't by asking me what's wrong with me.

She's gentle but firm enough to get through to me when I want nothing more than to scream and cry and ask whoever is in charge of my life why I had to get anxiety. It's useless and definitely not rational, but these things become obsolete when it comes to anxiety. There are only feelings. They're not always logical, but that doesn't mean that whatever they are isn't just as real.

"Better now, thanks," I reply, taking one last deep breath to gather all the strength I have to stand up.

"You want to tell me what happened?" I check my watch. Five minutes since I came into the bathroom.

"Later. I have to get back to work," I say before telling her I love her and hanging up.

My makeup, luckily, isn't too messed up, and after a few careful swipes under my eyes with a tissue, I get back to my desk on wobbly legs. My head pounds in complaint at the immediate getting back to work without letting it catch up, but I can't waste any time. I have to get this article back to Gillian before lunch. So, I pop a painkiller into my mouth, hoping it'll ease my stupid post-anxiety-attack headache.

"Nevaeh, I need you to look over these and sign at the bottom to make sure you acknowledge all of the rules and guidelines," Gillian says, handing me a pile of paper.

My eyes scan over the words carefully. There is a lot about how to behave and what to say and not to say around the Formula One members. But the thing that has my breath catching once again is the rule at the very bottom.

No member of this team may date a Formula One driver. This is to avoid accusations of extreme bias and complications during interactions.

Fuck. Me.

"Gillian? What would happen to someone who breaks any of these rules?" I ask, my mouth dry.

I'm in deep shit.

Not only did I have a Formula One driver's lips on mine a few days ago, but another one is taking me out tonight. Well, he was supposed to, but now, everything has changed. I can't go out with him.

"Whoever breaks it, gets fired. Easy as that," Gillian states before strolling back into his office and leaving me to panic by myself. *Again*.

The articles in my hand are no longer captivating as my thoughts get consumed by what I have to do later. My career means everything to me, which is why I won't let a man get in the way of it. There is no hesitation in my mind about it.

Nevaeh: Hi. I really want to go out with you, but I just found out that my job forbids it. I'm so sorry you stayed another day for something that isn't allowed to happen.

I sent this message during my lunch break, and, so far, I haven't gotten an answer. If I were him, I'd be pissed, but something tells me that's not who he is. He strikes me as an easy-going and fun person, someone who doesn't get angry often. At least, I hope so. If he's upset with me because I blew him off, it's going to make this season very difficult.

At the end of the day, I'm miserable. My head is still pounding. My anxiety is a living and breathing thing at the surface of my chest. Not to mention, Lincoln has also texted me a couple of times, asking if everything's alright, but I'm not in the mood to talk to him. He deserves an explanation, but I have none to give him. All I want is to fall into bed, take a nap, and then do some self-care for my mental health.

This job doesn't make me happy, at least not yet, and it's placing doubts in my mind. I shouldn't have taken this job... should I have? I need to speak to someone about this, but Nova and Aileen are busy tonight, and Mama and Papa will tell me to get over it, that it'll get better eventually. They might use a euphemism, but the words will mean the same, and they won't help.

I walk out of the building, half-expecting Lincoln to wait for me. Instead, I notice a red Velocitá Rossa SUV in the pick-up area. It's pitch-black outside, but the lights from the buildings allow me to see Adrian leaning against it with a bag of Haribo gummy bears in his hand. How he knows that those are my favorites, I have no clue.

But I'm going to find out.

His smile is contagious as he pushes himself off his car to take a step toward me.

"Before you ask, yes, I got your message. Yes, I am here to pick you up anyway. No, it won't be a date, but yes, I bribed your sister to drive your car home and tell me what your favorite sweets are," he explains, his green-blue-brown eyes darker in this light and studying my expression to identify how I feel about all of this.

I put my hands behind my back and intertwine my fingers, teasing him by staying quiet. Adrian lets out a nervous laugh, running a hand through his hair as he waits for my response.

"Aren't you supposed to bring flowers?" I ask with a teasing tone as he hands me the gummy bears.

"If this were a date, I would have brought you both," he says before stepping to the side and opening the driver's door for me. "I brought my car for you to drive," Adrian says, causing my jaw to drop and my eyes to widen.

"Are you out of your mind? This car is worth more than my life, I *cannot* drive it," I reply and take a step back.

"You don't have to, Nevaeh, I merely thought you'd want to, considering you adore it," Adrian offers with a smile, and, for the first time since I met him three months ago, he lets a faint Monegasque accent slip through his usual American one.

It's extremely attractive.

"I like the way you say my name," I admit, and Adrian's face turns mischievous.

"You can't tell me things like that. It makes me want to kiss you." His words have a strange way of making my heart race, skip beats, or thump unevenly against my ribcage. Maybe all three of those things combined.

There is no doubt in my mind that if I ever let this man kiss me, it would undo me in ways I'd never be able to put myself together again. So, I simply clear my throat and step toward the car. The grin returns to his face while he closes my door and makes his way to the passenger's side.

Snowflakes sit in his perfectly curly hair, and I get lost in how gorgeous he is for a second too long. All chiseled facial features and yet he has the softest of smiles. He catches me, and I swiftly bring my gaze to the steering wheel to pretend I wasn't ogling him. It's obviously hopeless, but pretending makes me feel less embarrassed.

"Where are we going?" I ask, and Adrian leans his head against the headrest to study me.

"I don't care about the where, as long as—" I have to cut him off then.

"Please don't say 'as long as I'm with you,'" I say with a laugh. He joins me, shaking his head as the sweetest laugh escapes him

"I was going to say 'as long as we get food,'" he clarifies.

I cover my face with my hands and let out a breath of embarrassment. Adrian's fingers wrap around my wrists to pull my hands off my face.

"You don't have to be embarrassed. If this were a date, I would have taken a page out of Gabriel Biancheri's best-cheesy-lines book and said it."

And I wouldn't have minded it one bit. Yet, here we are, in this shitty situation.

The electricity his skin on mine creates disappears as soon as he removes his fingers.

"Well, this is my day off from everything work-related, so, if you're down, I'm in the mood for a burger and fries."

A smile spreads across my face before it's ripped off again by the memories of what it was like to train professionally for a sport. The strict meal plan. The long workout hours. The constant aching somewhere in my body that I grew to love because it always made me feel stronger afterward.

My face falls at the memory of the tear ripping my dreams apart.

"What did I say?" Adrian asks, concern crossing his face.

"Nothing, sorry. I was just thinking about when I was training to be a professional tennis player, but a rotator cuff injury ruined my career. What you said reminded me of those times," I try to explain, and his lips part in a way that tells me he would never want to feel that pain.

His hand reaches out to touch mine, and I watch as his thumb caresses my skin. More tingles of electricity spark.

Something inside of me compels me to remove my jacket and pull down the top of my dress to show him my scar.

His eyes go wide before the tips of his fingers brush over the long and bumpy mark.

"It's ugly," I say before a nervous laugh escapes me. Adrian shakes his head and brings his eyes to mine.

"It's your battle scar, a part of you and your journey. It's a reminder of your strength and determination to make it through the pain of losing your dream. There is nothing ugly about it, Nevaeh, not a thing."

His words are sincere and full of emotion, and I can't help but shiver a little as his thumb trails over my scar so gently, it almost makes me sigh.

"Let's go get something to eat," I say to break the tension. Adrian clears his throat and chuckles, removing his hand from me and looking straight out of the window.

"You think it will satisfy our hunger for each other?" The Monegasque rubs his hands over his thighs, shooting me a flirty smirk as he brings back the casualness and lightness I've grown to expect whenever we spend a moment together.

"Nope, but there is nothing we can do about it, so food it is," I reply and let the engine roar to life.

A thrill washes through me, and I wiggle in the seat.

"This is fucking awesome!"

Adrian laughs whole-heartedly before telling me to go as slowly as I need to be comfortable and get used to the car. Fortunately for him, my father has let me drive cars like this since I was sixteen, and I'm a better driver than most people.

It would be even better if Adrian's eyes stayed on the road instead of me the entire ride.

CHAPTER 16
Nevaeh

EVERYTHING INSIDE OF ME feels light as Adrian and I jump from one conversation topic to the next. We talk to each other like we've been friends for ages, with no awkward or uncomfortable silences because one of us continues to find new questions to ask or a comment to make that the other laughs about.

It's amazing.

My cheeks burn from all the smiling, and my heart is perfectly settled in my chest as we talk, something it hardly ever does. I never feel settled enough around new people for my anxiety to leave me alone, but right now, I do.

There is something special about Adrian, the way he consumes the entire space around us until he's all I see and feel.

"How could you have been on Iron Man's side? Captain America was *trying to save his best friend*," I argue, and Adrian snorts at my comment.

"Yeah, but he should have told Tony what Bucky did! Honestly, woman, how did you watch the reveal scene without feeling the same anger Iron Man did?" he asks, but I shake my head repeatedly. "Tell me you at least cried when he died during Endgame," Adrian adds with a shocked laugh.

"Well..." I trail off, making the Monegasque gasp dramatically. "Did you?"

"Of course. I was bawling my eyes out," Adrian replies and I burst into laughter, earning myself the sweetest smile from him.

"Alright, maybe we should switch topics. Next thing I know, you're going to tell me you hate Doctor Strange, and I don't play when it comes to my favorite superhero," I say, but Adrian's face lights up at my words.

"You've got nothing to worry about there. He's my favorite, too," Adrian says with a chuckle, picking up a fry and popping it into his mouth. He chews while I take a bite out of my burger, smiling happily to myself.

"What made you pick up a racket all those years ago?" he asks, for the first time tonight making a sense of sadness creep into my chest, but the curiosity in his gaze brings back how passionate I was after the first time I tried playing tennis.

"My dad enrolled me in a tennis camp for an entire summer when I was six years old. My coach was amazing. She was so patient and kind, encouraging me the entire time. I got a lot of balls over the net, more than anyone else I was playing with at the time, and it motivated me to get better and better. I like being an overachiever," I admit with a soft laugh. Adrian watches me the entire time I speak, his undivided attention on me.

"I can tell, you know, considering you are probably one of the youngest employees at *Griffin Sports*. That's a hell of an achievement," he says, running a hand over his other arm.

My attention drifts to the way his muscles flex at the motion, and I don't miss the way a cocky smirk curls the left corner of his mouth when he catches me admiring him. A blush creeps onto my cheeks, but I don't look away just because he caught me. I let my gaze trail over his muscular chest, over his trained, veiny forearms.

"What made you decide to follow in your grandfather's and father's footsteps and become a Formula One driver?" I ask, grabbing a few fries and taking a bite out of all of them at once.

Adrian's expression turns thoughtful as he looks at the fireplace next to us where we're sitting on the ground at my house.

"I wanted to be just like my dad when I was growing up. I watched him win races, chase the high of the sport, and be happier than ever when he stepped out of his F1 car. That feeling, that happiness, I wanted it, too," he admits, but the shame is evident in his eyes.

"I feel like there's a but," I say, so Adrian smiles a little in response.

"But, as I got older, I realized I wanted to be nothing like him. He wasn't a good father. After our mother left, he got even worse. He couldn't look at Val and me without seeing her in our faces, so most days, he just dropped us off at our grandparents' house. That's where I learned what Formula One was truly about. My grandfather, one of the best drivers in the history of this sport, taught me everything there was to know about F1. Discipline, sacrifice, dedication. You name it, he taught me the meaning of it."

His gaze shifts back to me, emotion sparkling in his eyes.

"But I didn't want to be anything like my grandfather either. I loved him, but I never aspired to be like him because I always wanted to be like Val." He shrugs with a shy smile. "She was everything I always wanted to be, so I have no idea how, to this day, she thinks I raised her more than she did me," Adrian admits with a small laugh, picking up his water and taking a big sip.

"If Valentina Romana was my sister, I'd want to be just like her, too, so I get it," I reply, chuckling a little when he grins at me. "You two are really close," I point out, and Adrian plays with the wrapping paper his burger was in half an hour ago.

"Val's all I have left in the world. My grandparents and dad passed away."

"I'm so sorry, Adrian," I say softly and reach out to take his hand.

It surprises me that he meets me halfway. If it was Lincoln, he wouldn't have let me touch him while he's vulnerable. I'm convinced most wouldn't, but Adrian isn't most.

His fingers intertwine with mine as he clearly forces a smile.

"It's okay. I loved my grandfather a lot, but Val and he had a special bond. He trained me, but I always felt like his focus was more on her than me. It didn't matter to him if I took my training as seriously as Val. My grandmother and I, on the other hand, were really close. I spent most of my time in her kitchen where we spoke about everything and nothing," Adrian says with an upset frown on his face. "Sorry, I never talk about this, I don't know why I'm oversharing," he adds, but I squeeze his hand to reassure him.

"Don't apologize. I enjoy talking to you, happy and sad alike, and you are *not* oversharing," I promise, and his thumb starts tracing an infinity shape along the back of my hand. "You can tell me more, if you want," I offer, and he sucks in a sharp breath.

"There isn't a lot more to tell. As I said, my father prioritized his job over Val and me. One night, he crashed his car into the middle of our living room. I told Val to stay upstairs while I ran to check his pulse and call an ambulance at the same time. It was useless. He was long gone when they arrived." My heart drops. I wasn't expecting him to be this honest with me. "What's with the surprised expression?" he asks and places his index finger under my chin to tilt my head toward him.

"You're being vulnerable with me, and I didn't think you would be," I explain and close my eyes when his thumb runs over my bottom lip. "I hate my job," I whisper, and Adrian lets out a low, short laugh.

"Because you want to kiss me or for other reasons, too?" he asks, his finger still tracing my lips. Tingles spread from my face all the way down to my toes.

"Both." Adrian drops his hand, and I almost whimper from the loss of contact.

"What are the other reasons?" My eyes drift to the flames of the fire next to us while I enjoy the warmth it brings.

"I never wanted to be a journalist for Formula One. I'm very grateful I got a job, but tennis is my department, not F1, and I know I'm supposed to be happy, but no matter how hard I try, I'm not."

I pause as the realization sinks in, swallowing past the lump building in my throat to keep talking instead of lingering on the existential crisis that's trying to make me fall apart.

"My boss also keeps giving me random tasks without explaining the purpose, and every time I ask, he says it's just important. Part of me is convinced I'm doing his busy work, but it's not my place to say anything, so I don't. Plus, now they want me to become fluent in French, and I have to go find a tutor," I rant and pick up my glass to take a sip of my water. Adrian watches me for a second before responding.

"I'm sorry you don't like your job, Nevaeh. I wish I could help you."

There's a sad look on his face now, but I guide us back to a different conversation to see his smile again.

Time passes as Adrian and I fall back into lighter topics. My stomach cramps from laughing at Adrian's story of standing in front of an automatic door for five minutes and waiting for it to open without realizing he needed to press a button first. I laugh so hard at how upset he is over his stupidity, tears flow out of my eyes.

When I can't stop, he throws a few cold fries at me.

"Okay, alright, yes, I was an idiot," Adrian says, and I finally manage to turn my laughter into amused chuckles.

"At least you were a pretty idiot, so that's something," I offer, and he bursts into laughter, covering his face with his hands.

It takes him a few moments to collect himself again before his gaze drifts back to me and he shakes his head.

Adrian leans back and tilts his head to look at the ceiling.

"Aghh, what are you doing to me, Nevaeh?" he asks, the frustration in his voice clear as day.

"I don't know, but you should move on from whatever it is. Nothing can happen between us." Adrian's gaze focuses on me again, and I forget to remind myself to breathe.

"Tell me how to move on, and I will."

None of this makes sense to me. How did I manage to completely capture the attention of this unbelievably attractive Formula One driver? And why does it give me an ego boost like nothing has ever before?

"Usually, I would suggest we get it out of our systems and just have sex," I blurt out before I can keep my mouth shut. Adrian lets out a loud groan and falls backward onto the carpeted floor.

"Nevaeh!" he complains and covers his face with his arms. "If your job wasn't so important to you, we would be doing exactly that. Unfortunately, my sister raised me right, and I would never get between a woman and her career."

The doorbell rings before I have a chance to respond, to tell him that I adore Valentina for being such an amazing influence and tell him how sweet I find it that he loves his sister so much.

"Are you expecting someone?" Adrian asks, but I shake my head.

"No, not a single person," I say as I walk toward the front door and open it.

Fuck, this is not good.

CHAPTER 17
Nevaeh

LINCOLN SMILES BRIGHTLY AT me, holding a bouquet of flowers in a vase he clearly made for me.

"Before you say anything, butterfly, I don't expect you to have forgiven me or anything of the sort, but you've made me realize it's time I put more effort into my apology. So, here I am—" Lincoln's eyes drift behind me, anger replacing the happy mood he was in before. "—clearly interrupting you while you're on a date." He lets out a sarcastic laugh. "And with Adrian fucking Romana, out of all people."

Lincoln shoves the vase into my hands while watching, without a doubt, Adrian walking up behind me. My left hand burns from the impact, so I look down to spot a little cut. Blood fills the wound, but I don't have time to focus on it when Lincoln grabs my full attention again.

"Feel free to throw the vase and flowers in the garbage," he says through gritted teeth and moves to the side just enough to face Adrian, whose hand moves onto my shoulder.

I give him a confused look, unsure why he's touching me, but one glance at his face tells me everything I need to know. He's trying to protect me. Adrian doesn't trust Lincoln. I look down at my hand, which is barely bleeding, but only the Monegasque notices it. He takes my hand to study the cut, his thumb running over the skin below it.

Lincoln is too busy glaring at him to care.

"I think you should calm down, Nash," Adrian says softly, slowly guiding me behind him. "You made Nevaeh bleed. Wrong fucking move."

This is the first time I've ever heard someone speak with so much authority. Lincoln's eyes go wide, but Adrian gets in the Grenzenlos driver's face.

"I suggest you leave."

I don't think Adrian is a violent person, yet, at this moment, I'm convinced he'd kick Lincoln's ass if he had to.

"You know, Romana, she might be on a date with you, but I was the one who had his tongue down her throat only a few days ago," Lincoln says with disgust on his face before turning to me. "I'm sorry I hurt you, butterfly, it wasn't my intention. Send him home so I can take care of the cut." I know he wants me to, I can read it on his face, but his words have me boiling from anger. His behavior is disgusting, and I want nothing to do with him.

"Get the fuck off my property. I don't ever want to see you again."

I step in front of Adrian to hand Lincoln the vase, a lot gentler than he shoved it at me and then slam the door in his face.

"Jesus," I mumble and run my right hand through my hair, my left one still burning.

Adrian takes my hand to inspect the cut again. It's not deep, and hardly bleeding, but he looks at it like Lincoln personally offended him and his entire bloodline.

"Where is your first-aid kit?" I look up at him, his eyes meeting my gaze. Whatever he spots in my face makes him even unhappier.

Adrian's focus shifts back to the wound, but I pull my hand away to walk into the kitchen. The longer we stand there, the more I'll get overwhelmed by the way he looks at me.

He follows but stays quiet.

"I'm sorry about Lincoln. I didn't know he would show up here and make such a big scene," I say and reach for the kit, which is, thanks to Papa, on the top shelf.

I hear Adrian snicker as he moves toward me and reaches for it. For a split second, his shirt lifts enough to show off his V-line, making my mouth water involuntarily.

"Don't be sorry. Lincoln is the one who needs to properly apologize to you."

Adrian opens the kit and pulls out an alcohol wipe to clean my cut. He does so silently, gently, as if he's scared to hurt me more than Lincoln did. When I suck in a sharp breath from the burning the wipe leaves behind, Adrian blows on the wound to ease the ache.

"So, you kissed him," he points out after a while of silence. I scan his beautiful face for jealousy, but there doesn't seem to be any. He's merely curious.

"Yeah. It was before I found out my job forbids it and we agreed to go on a date."

Adrian nods as he finishes up taking care of my hand.

"It meant nothing," I whisper, causing a smile to break out across his face.

He moves toward me until my back touches the counter. His hands move to each side of me, imprisoning me with his body. My heart hums happily at the proximity of him, at the way his cologne fills my nose.

"Maybe it did, maybe it didn't, but if you ever let me kiss you, whatever it was will turn to dust and that boy will be history in your mind," Adrian says, his mouth yet again too close to mine to be bearable.

I lick my lips as I watch him get closer and closer with every shallow breath of mine.

"I think I should go, *mon paradis*." I furrow my brows.

"What did you just say?" I ask because I'm sure those last two words were French, and I only understood *mon* as *my*. He mumbled the other word too much for me to hear it.

Adrian smiles as he leans away from me.

"Let me tutor you in French, and I will tell you someday," he offers, making my heart stutter for a moment.

"You would do that for me?" I ask, and he raises his fingers to play with a strand of my hair before tugging it behind my ear. Goosebumps appear on my body wherever his fingers graze my skin, my stomach tumbling at the softness of his touch.

"Absolutely." He leans down to press the swiftest of kisses to my cheek, adding, "Text me," and leaving my house again.

I stay in the kitchen for a moment, unsure what to do with myself.

Mama and Papa will be home soon, so I make sure everything is cleaned up and head upstairs into my bedroom. I barely feel the cut in my hand because my mind is stuck on the way Adrian's lips felt on my skin.

Then, I think about him offering to tutor me and everything else that comes with my job. Things will change once the season starts, and I hope that means I'll enjoy it more. Because if I don't, I don't know what I'll do.

If this isn't my passion, what is?

The same question repeats itself over and over again as I sit down on my bed and lose myself in my photo editing.

A lot of people don't realize that a photographer's job isn't just taking pictures. There's a lot of refining them afterward too. Playing with the sharpness or saturation, editing out little things like a random person's shoe at the bottom of the image, or adjusting the sizing to fit whatever I'll use the picture for.

These ones I'm working on today are for Nova's birthday next month. I'm making her a photo album of all of her favorite pictures I've ever taken. I'm planning to make it look more like a scrapbook than a photo album because Nova loves those, but I need to get the pictures ready and printed first.

All of my worries leave me as I use my creative outlet in the way it was meant to be used: as an escape from everything unpleasant in my life.

Chapter 18
Adrian

"Come on, Adrian, fucking push through," Daniel, my performance coach, barks at me, and I grit my teeth as I curl my arms one more time.

The weights seem heavier today, but I know the only heavy thing is the knowledge of the season starting soon. My mind feels like I put a plate of fifty kilos on it. All of the pressure of performing well this season, to finally get that World Championship title I was so close to grasping last year, is fucking exhausting. I want to win this year, I *need* to win, but Gabriel is the reigning champion, and I'm a little worried about Grenzenlos taking back their spot at the top. Last year, they didn't do as well. Hawke came closer to beating our asses than Grenzenlos did, which I know Robert Fuchs is working on with his team to make sure it never happens again.

To simplify, I am scared shitless I won't be good enough to win this season.

Add Nevaeh confusing me and my feelings on top of all of that, and I've never been more of a mess than I am right now.

This is why I never, ever wanted to romantically like someone. It's *exhausting*.

"What's on your mind?" Daniel asks, forcing my attention back to him instead of lingering on the overwhelming panic in my chest.

"I wanna win. Not just the race. Not just the Constructors' Championship. I want to *win*," I explain, taking the towel he hands me and wiping the sweat off my forehead.

"Oh, do you? I thought you were just competing for shits and giggles," Daniel replies, so I flip him off and drop backward to let my back lie flat against the bench.

"Thank you for taking me seriously," I say, but Daniel merely snorts.

"You don't even take yourself seriously most days. Do you really expect me to?" That gets a genuine laugh out of me.

Silence fills the little gym we're in until he smacks my left knee to get me to sit up.

"Listen, you are ready for that title, Adrian. You've worked harder than ever before during the winter break, and it's been paying off. I see how determined you are, and you will get your win. If the car doesn't fail you and you don't make rookie mistakes, I don't see why you don't have the same shot as Gabriel at winning." Daniel hands me my water bottle, gesturing for me to take a sip as I process his words.

He's right.

Our car has excelled in all of the tests so far. Unless Grenzenlos somehow found a way to become two-tenths of a second per lap faster than us, which is what we averaged in almost every race last season over them, then Gabriel is the only thing in my way to becoming a World Champion and following in the Romanas' footsteps. I have to hurry the fuck up too because once Valentina is in a top championship competing car, my chances to win will significantly reduce. That woman is *fast* and skilled and aggressive in her driving, which is a good thing because she isn't disrespectful about it either. She sticks to the rules while she kicks ass, and that is the most dangerous of combinations.

"You have an obscene amount of faith in me. Could I have some of it?" I joke, but the dumbass rubs under his armpits and smears his hands over my hair and face as if that would transfer the confidence onto me. "You're fucking disgusting," I say as I smack his hands away and burst into laughter, grabbing my towel to wipe it away again.

"Great, if you have the energy to insult me, you have the energy for another set. Pick up the weights. Let's go," he instructs, and I curse him out under my breath as I do what I'm told.

Daniel kicks my ass for another hour or so before he lets me go home to rest and reset. The first race of the season is only a little over a week away. I've been training and preparing, but it feels like I'm not ready yet. It feels like there are a million things I should be doing, and none of them include constantly thinking about Nevaeh's laugh or the way her eyes sparkle with mischief before she starts flirting with me. I definitely shouldn't be thinking about the way her attention dropped to my lips when I had her caged between my arms at her kitchen counter. I shouldn't be thinking about this woman at all, but how could I not?

I'm seriously asking you.

How can I get her out of my goddamn head?

This is all so new to me, I don't know how to behave anymore. Do I call her? Do I text her? When do I do either of those things? Whenever I think about her? Well, no, probably not. That would be a little too often at this point.

Using my spare key, I make my way into my grandfather's house, the same place Valentina and Gabriel are living in at the moment. I moved out after Val asked my teammate to move in with her because I wanted to give the two of them their space. It was also because I couldn't stop seeing my grandparents everywhere. I'm usually pretty good at keeping my grief at bay, ignoring it, and fixating on everything else. I have found that if I am busy with something else, my brain doesn't have time to remind me of everything I've lost, of *everyone* I've lost. It works well most of the time, even better now that the constant reminders that Grandfather's households aren't around me, but that doesn't stop me from visiting Val as much as I can.

I miss her now that we're not living together for the first time in our lives.

Chase, the little puppy Valentina found at the side of the road, jumps at me as soon as I walk into the door. I greet him because I miss him now that I've moved out. He's always so excited to see me, too. He follows me as I step into the house before disappearing into the kitchen, probably to look for food.

"What the hell? Adrian, I love you, but you have your own place. Gabriel and I have only been engaged for four months. Do you know what that means?" my sister asks as I place my gym bag neatly in the closet, along with my shoes.

"What does it—" I cut off at the sight of her before smacking a hand over my eyes and saying, "No, Val, why? Why?"

"Because Gabriel texted me to put on this exact outfit so he can put me on the dining table and—"

"If you finish that sentence, I'm going to hurl," I warn, pointing a finger in the direction of where I think she's standing.

"I'm over here, dumbass," she says, but there is no way I'm opening my eyes to look at my sister barely covered by a tiny set of lingerie and a small towel, which she probably grabbed to cover herself when I walked inside.

"Naked dinners are incredibly unsanitary," I point out, grabbing my bag again and throwing one of my clean shirts at her head. I find a pair of extra shorts too, slowly side-stepping toward her to place it in her hand.

"Why are you here?" Val asks, slapping away the hand that's covering my eyes so I look at her.

She's drowning in my clothes now, which is a relief. I love my sister, but we both have boundaries set in place. One of them is that I don't want to see what kind of lingerie she wears for my teammate and biggest rival. A shiver of unease runs through me, along with the desire to deck Gabriel in the face for whatever he does to my little sister. I tried to protect her as best as I could when we were growing up while respecting her boundaries even back then. Should have known the biggest threat would be the pretty boy of Formula One.

I still find it funny that everyone thinks of Gabriel that way.

Naturally, I'm the heartbreaker of F1.

"I miss you," I admit, wrapping her in a hug even though she's standing in front of me scowling and with her fists on her hips.

"You saw me three days ago. We had dinner together while we figured out which car you were going to buy," she says against my chest, and I chuckle before stepping back and placing my hands on her shoulders.

"Well, I have attachment issues. I thought we all already knew that," I reply, knowing full well it's not just with Val, too. I spend all of my time with the people I love.

The days I'm not with Val, I spend with James, but he's really busy with his kid when we're not in our F1 season. Damian, his son, was adopted by Gabriel's aunts a few months ago, but they're more than happy to share custody with James when he's in Monaco. It's a good thing I love spending time with the little guy, too.

"Yeah, come on. I made your favorite. Homemade pizza," she says, so I place a wet kiss on the top of her head. Val's so short compared to me, but I also know she could knock me on my ass if she wanted to.

"And that is why I love you," I say with a grin before stepping toward the kitchen.

Unfortunately, I'm not fast enough and when the door opens again, I hear Gabriel's words loud and fucking clear.

"Get on the table, chérie. I'm starving and I've been thinking about your beautiful, thick thighs wrapping around my head all day."

I cringe once before spinning around to glare at Gabriel. He spots me a moment after frowning at Val's outfit, his eyes going wide for a fraction of a second. My sister's fiancé lets out a nervous laugh, rubbing the back of his neck with his hand.

"Well, there's no recovering from that. Should I dig my own grave or do you want to do the honors?" Gabriel asks, and I flash him a mean smile as I take a step toward him.

"I'll dig yours and you can dig mine because there is no way in hell I'll ever get rid of that visual."

"You're both acting like children. Adrian, you know Gabriel and I have sex, don't pretend we don't. Gabriel, next time, check the room before you start dirty talking. There, problem solved." My sister leaves no room for arguing as she strides into the kitchen to check on the pizza.

"I think our plan is still better," Gabriel points out, earning himself an agreeing nod from me.

"Absolutely. We can start digging after Val goes to sleep."

Gabriel smiles as he claps me on the shoulder.

CHAPTER 19
Nevaeh

The first race of the season is in Bahrain.

Gillian and I arrived a couple of hours ago, along with a few other people like the camerawoman, Fallon, and Gillian's makeup artist, Liz. Luckily, the rooms are small enough so everyone got their own. It allows my anxiety to take a breather instead of overthinking what it would mean to sleep in the same room as three other people I hardly know. They all seem kind and welcoming, but it doesn't mean that my overthinking simply shuts off.

My anxiety is an expert at coming up with every worst possible scenario only to terrify me with it. It makes life ridiculously difficult more times than not. Every decision I make is a battle in my mind, tearing me in two different directions: yes and no. Do it and don't do it. Stay and run. It's exhausting, I won't lie, but eventually, I win those fights with my head, too. All it takes is patience, resilience, and determination. I don't have all or any of these things every single day, but I try my best, and that's good enough for me.

I'm sitting on the bed, a towel wrapped around my body when I see a message light up my phone. This is the first time I've traveled anywhere without Nova or Mama, and they've been texting non-stop to check on me. They're both worried about this huge step that I took, especially because I am terrified of flying, and being on my own isn't my favorite thing either, but I'm so proud of myself for the way I've handled things so far.

For people without anxiety, it wouldn't seem like a big feat to get on a plane and not have an anxiety attack and completely break down, but for me? For me, it's a huge step. It's pure, liquid motivation, too, making me feel like I can do this.

Gillian gave me a couple of articles to edit before tomorrow. He likes the way I edit them, so he's been giving me more and more over the past few weeks I've been at *Griffin Sports*. I hate the work. It's tedious and not at all what I thought I was signing up for when I took this job. I thought I'd be doing what Mrs. Lu and Ms. Martin said I'd do: write my own articles, but Gillian treats me more like an assistant. If I hadn't been an assistant for three years during my internships at university, I probably wouldn't mind as much. Neither would I mind if it wasn't for my bosses telling me how different this job would be.

My screen lights up with another message, this one from a very handsome F1 driver I've been doing my best to keep out of my head. It was working, somewhat, but it doesn't help when he texts me and reminds me how sweet he is.

Adrian: Welcome to Bahrain. I hope we can spend some time together, maybe I can even give you a French lesson.

I let out a laugh before typing.

Nevaeh: You should focus on the race, not on teaching me French. But thank you for the offer.

Adrian: Why can't I do both? You can pay me with those gorgeous smiles of yours.

Nevaeh: Smiles? Plural?

Adrian: Yes, the happy one where you show teeth and the shy one where you don't. Either is an acceptable payment.

That damn Adrian.

I smile to myself. We may not be able to be anything but friends, but that's alright with me.

No one gets hurt this way.

Nevaeh: Time and place?

I should let him concentrate on the weekend, but the selfish part inside of me wants to take advantage of his offer and see him.

Adrian: Wednesday, 20:00. My hotel? Or yours, wherever you're more comfortable. I will arrange for dinner.

Why? I've been asking myself that question a lot since I met Adrian. Why is he such a gentleman? Why is he so infatuated with me? Why did he come into my life at the worst time, when everything doesn't make sense? The list goes on, but these are some of the top ones I can't stop from swirling around in my head.

After giving the pillow on my bed a good, frustrated scream, I tell him I will go to his hotel. It's most likely a lot nicer than my little room. I also feel better about meeting him on Wednesday since Thursdays are for fan meet-and-greets, track walks, and other responsibilities that don't include driving the car yet. Today is only Monday, which means I'll have two days to overthink and try not to change my mind.

I want to be friends with him.

I like the way he makes me feel, heard and understood instead of filled with pain, hurt, and regret.

My phone rings as an incoming call makes it vibrate on my thigh. It says *Unknown* as the caller ID, but I hit Answer anyway.

"Hello?" I ask, curiosity now spreading all the way into my fingertips, making them tingle.

"Hi, Nevaeh, this is Valentina Romana. I'm sorry if this is weird, but I got your number from my brother. I'm heading to the Bahrain National Museum and was wondering if you'd like to join me. Gabriel and Adrian don't want to go. I don't know if you're busy, or even want to. You can of course say no. Oh man, I'm rambling, I'm sorry," Valentina says and lets out a laugh, which makes me smile.

I can't remember the last time I went on a friend-date with someone, apart from Adrian's and mine almost two weeks ago. The only real friend I had growing up was Lincoln and the other people I was "friends" with, well, it didn't work out.

"I would love to go with you, and, no, I'm not busy. I have the day off to do a bit of sightseeing, actually," I reply while getting up and walking toward my suitcase to take out my blue floor-length skirt and a matching white long-sleeve.

"Great! I will meet you at your hotel in an hour," she says, so I give her the address.

We hang up, and I get ready for my friend-date with one of the women I admire the most in the world. I never, ever thought I might become friends with Valentina Romana, the queen of Formula One.

I think I want to be friends with her even more than I want to be friends with her brother, but that's probably because I'd very much like to be different kinds of friends with Adrian.

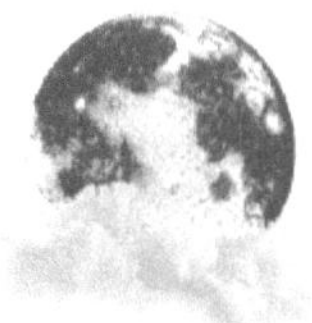

Valentina is standing in the lobby of my hotel wearing jeans that are slightly ripped at the thighs but not revealing any skin, red sneakers, and a matching blouse, and a perfect smile on her lips, which are identical to Adrian's. Her outfit is simple, but she pulls it off. Her dirty-blonde hair sits in perfect curls on her head, framing her face and falling effortlessly down her back. She's trained but curvy, shorter than me by about ten centimeters, and absolutely breathtaking.

She reminds me so much of Adrian, I can't keep the smile off my face.

When she catches me walking toward her, Val's face lights up. My heart flutters because I can't remember the last time anyone was so genuinely excited to see me. I smile back at her and go to hug her.

"It's really nice to see you again," I say first, stepping back to look into her eyes, the same as Adrian's. There is a zero percent chance I won't see him in every single feature of hers, but, for now, I don't mind it.

If anything, I like it more than I should.

"The feeling is mutual. Are you ready to go?" she asks, angling her arm so I can hook mine through hers.

Happiness consumes me, causing the smile on my face to remain the entire cab ride to the museum. We share casual stories about ourselves, but I've never been one for small talk, and I won't pretend to be now. One specific question pushes to the top of my mind, and I ask it before I can stop myself.

"You probably get this a lot, but how did you stay so strong when fighting to drive in Formula One? The misogynists built barriers, and yet, you kept pushing. How? If you don't mind my asking." I add the last sentence because I realize this is a lot more personal than I meant for it to be.

If I'm being honest with myself, I envy her for accomplishing what was impossible for me. Achieving your dream. Getting everything you worked so hard for. Living the life you envisioned for yourself.

Valentina turns to me with a small grin, assuring me I didn't overstep any boundaries.

"Adrian, actually. He gave me strength, and, every time I wanted to give up, he pushed me to believe in myself. All the failed attempts and opportunities didn't matter to him. With his help and connections, we tried over and over again, fought for my place in a driver's academy. Eventually, the Velocità Rossa academy took me in, I got to prove myself, and now, I race for Alfa Adrenalina."

Alfa Adrenalina belongs to Velocità Rossa. It makes sense that she got a seat with them after impressing every single person at the driver's academy. I don't have to ask them to know if it's true. Valentina was called upon as a reserve driver twice last year, racing once for Gabriel and once for Adrian. The second one didn't end so well, and I cringe at the reminder, but the first time did. She kicked ass. As soon as the first race was done, I read everything there was to read about her. Getting accepted into an F3 team, a subcategory of Formula One. Getting kicked out of the team for no apparent reason. Doing test drives and setting amazing lap times but getting rejected. Getting a spot at the Velocità Rossa Driver Academy.

The way Adrian supported her also makes me like him more, and that's a big problem.

"Then again, I'm just amazing, so maybe that's why," Val adds and laughs.

"I know you mean it as a joke, but I've read a lot about your journey into F1, and I think you are incredible. You're a role model to every girl in the world who gets told they can't make it because of their gender. It's incredible, admirable, and one of the reasons why you're my favorite driver," I inform her and watch as tears fill her eyes, making them sparkle.

I'm about to apologize when she speaks.

"Shit, I'm crying on our first friend-date. So not cool," she says, but we both chuckle in response.

Her fingers glide underneath her eyes as she wipes the effect of my words away.

"I'm sorry, I didn't mean to upset you." Valentina shakes her head, making her curls dance with each left-to-right movement.

"You didn't, you just made me a very happy and proud woman. Thank you," she replies and grabs my hand to give it a quick squeeze. "But don't say kind things like that again unless you want me bawling my eyes out," Valentina warns, so I offer her a warm smile.

"Okay, promise."

Soon after, Valentina and I make our way through the Bahrain National Museum, studying the nine different halls and taking in all of the history hiding inside the artwork displayed.

We discuss it like we're both art experts, but we're really just pointing out things we love and grinning when the other person attempts to say something very sophisticated about the piece but neither one of us quite manages the proper language for it. We're having a good time trying though, and the artifacts truly are breathtaking. They're complex and unique, each one more mesmerizing than the last.

Val and I both stare at the artifacts hung in one hall for a long time.

"You know, Gabriel is an artist too, but he mostly just draws me. Every different position and facial expression of mine he has to capture. I think we could fill an entire room with all of the sketches and paintings he's made of me over the winter break alone," she says, a smile lighting up her features as she shares something so incredibly sweet about the man she loves.

"I love that," I reply, and she takes my hand to lead me toward the next painting of animals drinking water. "Do you draw too?" I ask, trying to get to know her a little better.

"No, I'm very uncreative, but I did start a driver academy with Leonard Tick, so that's my creative outlet. Well, in a way," she says, placing a hand on the necklace around her chest. The charm is a Formula One car with the number seven carved into it. Gabriel's number.

"'Kids Like Us.' I've read so much about it, even though the academy hasn't even opened yet. It's remarkable," I say while turning my head to watch a blush settle on her cheeks.

"Thank you." She grins and bumps her hip against mine in a friendly manner. "How about you? Adrian told me you're an incredible photographer," she says, making it my turn for heat to fill my cheeks.

"Yeah, photography is my creative outlet. I love taking photos of nature and cars. Those two are my favorite subjects, but I've done a few photoshoots with people, too, and the pictures turned out great. So, in other words, yes, I like photography," I say, rambling in the same way she was earlier.

I've never spoken to anyone who isn't my family about my passion for photography, so I'm a bit unpracticed.

"Will you show me some of your work?" she asks once we've seen every part of the museum we could visit.

"You want to see my pictures?"

Disbelief fills my voice, something she clearly detects because she gives my arm a reassuring squeeze and lets an excited grin light up her eyes.

"Absolutely!"

Valentina hooks her arm through mine as we walk back to the taxi pick-up and drop-off area, the setting afternoon sun pleasantly warm.

"Give me until tomorrow. I've gotta choose the best ones," I say with a small laugh that she returns.

"I can't wait."

Chapter 20
Nevaeh

Mama and Papa text me to let me know they've landed and will spend some time with George, Lincoln's dad. Valentina invites me to have dinner at her hotel, so we tell the taxi driver where to go. She's staying at the *Four Seasons* along with her fiancé and brother.

We talk the whole way back to the hotel, too, not a silent moment between us because something I say reminds her of something else, or vice versa. It's strangely similar to how it felt when Adrian and I had dinner together, and I soak up every single minute of this carefree moment.

Although she assured me Adrian and Gabriel wouldn't be in her room, there they are, playing a card game with two other drivers. I recognize Cameron Kion and Leonard Tick as soon as I lay my eyes on them.

In the Formula One world, Cameron and Leonard are two of the men I respect the most. In all the interviews, Cameron always finds ways to cheer up the upset drivers if they didn't get their desired results, and he loves to entertain the reporters with his comedic performances. Not to mention, the Australian single-handedly opened up the small minds of people in the sport, specifically the old white men, by having the courage to come out as gay. In Formula One, that was unheard of until Cameron.

Leonard has my respect for being one of the best drivers the world has ever seen while supporting charities, artists, and organizations that do good in the world. He does all of this while also constantly dealing with the racism and ignorance of others. From what Valentina told me, he is one hell of a mentor, too, and I've seen every single one of the projects he is a part of to make this world a better place. He's remarkable, truly someone to look up to not only in this sport, but as a man in general.

My eyes drift from the man I respect to the man I already like far more than I should. His gaze shifts to me before his eyes light up and his back straightens out. Adrian places the cards on the table and gets up to move toward me, a wolfish grin on his full lips.

Gabriel stands up, too, and makes his way to Val before wrapping his arms around her and placing a kiss on her lips. I look away to give them some privacy when I get pulled into a hug as well.

Since Adrian is a lot taller than me but decided to put his arms under mine, he almost lifts me off the ground. My arms fling around him out of reflex, but I don't know why I slide my hands onto the back of his neck.

It feels right but so incredibly intimate.

"Nevaeh," he says softly like he always does when using my name, and I smile.

We've texted a lot over the past two weeks since we had dinner, talking until we both fell asleep. Every time our conversations were about to come to an end, he'd send a random picture from his camera roll or tell me to send one so we could discuss it. It was sweet and let us get to know each other in a way I've never gotten to know someone.

"What are you doing here?" Adrian asks and steps back to look into my eyes. A mischievous smirk spreads over his lips as he adds, "Missed me so much you had to see me earlier?" I let out a laugh and pat his left pec. He's so muscular and *hard*.

"As a matter of fact, I was told you wouldn't be here," I inform him, causing the smile on his face to grow.

"Can't handle seeing me without having a forty-eight-hour notice?" I roll my eyes and shake my head.

"I thought the forty-eight hours' notice was for you to figure out how to be around me without mentally undressing me," I flirt and my gaze drops to his crotch teasingly. Any other guy I've known would have, and has, followed my gaze at a comment like this, not Adrian. He smiles with pure confidence as his attention shifts from my eyes to my lips and then back up.

"I know how to behave myself, Nevaeh. Do you?" he challenges with a low, husky voice, his Monegasque accent slipping through for a brief moment.

My heart flutters at the way his scent fills my nose and his smile makes my stomach tumble.

Clearly, I can't behave myself, otherwise, I wouldn't be flirting with him every time we speak.

"Alright, love, do you want to go out for dinner or stay in?" Val asks me, looking around her fiancé, who's still holding onto her.

"Let's go out," I say because as much as I enjoy Adrian's company, I can't spend too much time with him or I'm afraid I'll start liking him in a way a person doesn't like their friend.

Chapter 21
Adrian

Every Thursday before the start of the season, I ask my team to let me near the car after almost everyone's gone to get a second alone with it. There are still a few mechanics around me, of course, I'm not allowed to be entirely alone with my car, but that's fine by me.

I don't speak.

I don't say a single word aloud as I squat down in front of my car with a single hand resting on its nose.

"You will be a World Champion, son. You will take that title and make it yours, just like I made it mine. You have the heart of a racer, the lungs, the bones, the willpower. You will be one of the greatest in the history of Formula One. I believe in you. You just have to believe in yourself."

My grandfather's words echo in my ears as I study the red color of my car, the eight painted across the nose. My number. The one I chose because I've always liked the way the eight didn't have an end. It's infinite.

Infinite like time.

Infinite like grief and pain.

Infinite like love is supposed to be.

Gabriel chose the number seven because of all the people he lost. Valentina chose the number nine because it chose her first. Leonard chose three for reasons he wouldn't share with me. James chose the number nineteen because he was nineteen when he started racing in Formula One. Cameron chose thirty-four because his little sister liked the number.

But I chose my number because I was hoping it would give me infinite strength. Because I thought if I put it on my car, no one would ever take my seat away. Because I never want to leave Formula One.

Help me get us that championship, I think to my car, pressing my forehead against the cool material of the nose.

This is an incredibly intimate moment, and I'm grateful to find all the mechanics turning away to give me a second. I've done this ritual without anyone, not even Val, knowing since I was a kid. It was for good luck, to feel a deeper connection to my car by treating it like my equal. And it is. All the racing skills and talent in the world won't get me the win if my car doesn't work with me.

I run my fingers over my number one last time before straightening out my back, thanking my mechanics and the rest of the crew working this late, and leaving again.

I want to win.

I want that title.

And I'm going to get it.

No matter what it takes.

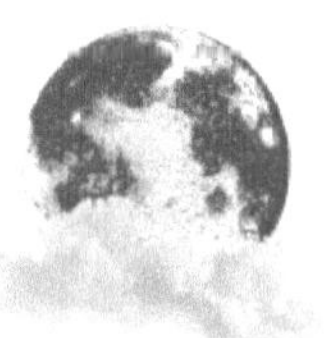

Nevaeh texted me Tuesday night, saying she wanted to reschedule our French tutoring lesson because she was upset about something that happened and didn't feel like she'd be good company. I loved her honesty, wished I could show her that I could cheer her up, and hated the fact that I had no idea what upset her.

She was distant as she stood with Gillian, watching him interview Gabriel, Kyle, Lincoln, and me without saying a single word. Her eyes were locked on her notepad as she scribbled something down.

She looked tired. Beautiful, more so than anyone has a right to, but tired.

I tried talking to her after Gillian was done with his interview, but my PR manager, Fatima, ushered me away to my next one. Being a Formula One driver means I have responsibilities and can't go about doing whatever I want. It's unfortunate because I wanted to ask Nevaeh what I could do to make her smile.

"Hey, big guy, could you get that dreamy look out of your eyes and get in the car?" Chloe, my race engineer, asks with a scowl on her face.

We met five years ago when I was still on a lower-ranking team. I was racing in Brazil, her home race, and she was training to be a race engineer for a different driver. Jonathan Kent never knew I convinced her to work for me instead, but the asshole deserved my sneaky and underhandedness. He was a fucking dick to Leonard.

Chloe is an absolute grump and a hard-ass, but she got us Vice World Champion last year. She's the reason why my races go smoothly. She is the brains behind my successful race strategies.

"I'm waiting for Daniel to get me my gloves," I explain with an easy smile, but she continues to stare me down until I get a little nervous.

She's frightening, but I adore her for it. Nobody from my team fucks with her, which means no one fucks with me, either.

"Sorry, I'm here. My boyfriend's mother was just sent to the hospital for food poisoning," Daniel says as soon as he approaches me with everything I'll need for the Grand Prix today.

I warmed up without him too because he was on the phone with Quinton, his boyfriend, but now I get why. I had food poisoning last year during one of the last race weekends of the season, and it was not fun. It was even worse because Val got into the worst crash Formula One has seen since Gabriel's godfather, Maxime, crashed and passed away from his injuries.

F1 is fun and exhilarating and a thrill until it's not.

Until it's dark and terrifying and life-threatening.

Almost losing my sister last year broke something inside of me I haven't been able to mend yet, which is probably why I'm a little clingy when it comes to her these days. I mean, I've always been a little clingier when it comes to her because she's my favorite person, but watching that crash from the hospital bed, feeling powerless and useless? It's been stuck with me ever since it happened. Whenever I look at my sister, when I see those scars on her skin left behind, the feeling resurfaces.

"Adrian?" Chloe's voice fills my ears, but I don't move. I can't. I've spiraled into the darkest of memories and I kind of need a hug right now.

"Adrian, what's going on? You're usually more level-headed than this," Daniel says, and I manage to lift my head to look at him.

All I have to do is drive the car to the first place position on the grid. Then, I can get out again while the world of Formula One counts down to the first race of the season. Then, I can go see my sister.

Yesterday was Qualifying. It consists of three sessions. Q1, Q2, and Q3. Each time one of the first two sessions ends, five of the drivers get knocked out of Qualifying. In Q1, we position ourselves anywhere from position sixteen to twenty. In Q2, anywhere from eleven to fifteen. Q3 is where it gets most exciting. The top teams compete for the pole position, which means whoever manages to snatch that position will start first the following day for the race. The rest of the ten drivers will position themselves anywhere from two to ten. All of this is to determine the starting grid for the race. Today's starting grid is me, Gabriel, fucking Lincoln, Kyle, James, Grant, Val, Leonard, Cameron, and then the rest of the drivers.

Yeah, I got the first pole position of the season.

I'm *that* good.

"Just drive the car to its place, and then we can figure out how to get your head back inside your body," Daniel says with a light-hearted smile, which I somehow manage to return.

That's who I'm supposed to be, after all. The fun guy. The one who makes everyone smile and laugh, feel good about themselves. I'm not supposed to tear them down. There are only very few people I allow myself to be vulnerable with. Val, James, Gabriel, and my newest addition, Nevaeh.

I shudder a little at the thought, as I remember the night at her home when I told her things I hadn't ever shared with someone I was as attracted to as I am to her. It's easier when feelings aren't involved. Everything's easier when you ignore the most vulnerable part of yourself: your heart.

Since when did I stop seeking the easy route?

You can't live without your brain. Once that's gone, you're done. But you can live without your heart beating inside of your chest for a few minutes before it kills your brain. In those few seconds, there is nothing but agony. Deep pain that floods your entire system. That's not the way I want to die.

I'd rather have the quick death of getting shot in the head, thanks.

"Alright, let's go," I say and take my gloves and helmet from Daniel.

Once I've zipped up my racing suit, slipped my fingers inside my gloves, and placed my helmet on my head, I make my way into my car. My seat is cold and hard, forcing reality back inside my head instead of lingering on the past or fearing the future because of Nevaeh.

I drive the car to my spot on the grid, getting out just in time to see my team approaching me. Daniel is by my side again, waiting for me to hand him my things and get ready to listen to the Bahrain national anthem.

It's part of every race weekend for all of the drivers to stand with the person performing the anthem to show our respect for the country hosting the race. It also gives me time to find my sister and my soon-to-be brother standing off to the side, talking about something I can't hear.

Val is looking at Gabriel with so much concentration, I realize he's telling her everything she needs to remember about this track. Not the things my sister already knows, but probably how the drivers on our grid treat each other during this race.

My heart stutters at the thought of her racing today. At the thought that something else could happen to her. I wonder if that's how she always felt when she was watching me race from my box.

"Don't talk her ear off, Gabriel. She'll need it to listen to Scarlette instruct her during the race," I tease, and my sister grins while my teammate scowls at me.

"She needs to know these things," he points out, and I notice the tension in his shoulders. The way every muscle in his body is flexing to hold off that gut-wrenching fear of Val getting into another accident.

He's as terrified as I am.

"Did you also tell her how fucking aggressive Lincoln is? I didn't get into it with him often last season because he was at the back of the grid a lot, but the three times we raced, he didn't hold back. He pushed me off the track every chance he got," James chimes in as he approaches our little group.

He smiles down at Val and places a hand on my shoulder, squeezing it comfortingly. No doubt he can see how tense I am the same way I see it in Gabriel.

"Yeah, I told her," Gabriel replies, giving James, the man he despises a little less but still fucking hates after all this time, a curt nod.

"I also already studied him and Grant by watching last year's races from their views. They are the two new drivers of the top teams, so I prepared myself, along with studying every other driver on this grid," Val defends and places her fists on her hips. She tied her racing suit around her waist in the same way Gabriel and James have, and when I look down at my body, I realize I didn't.

No wonder I'm sweating my balls off.

"Just be careful. From what I've learned about Grant as a person, he pretends to be nice, but he hates that a woman is racing," James adds, his English accent thick as he stares directly into Val's eyes.

He's been in love with her for as long as he can remember. Everybody knows it. It's the reason he made several dumb decisions in the past, but I think he's gotten a much better handle on his feelings since his son was born.

"Alright, so kick Grant's ass. Got it," Val replies with a little mischievous grin, and I shoot her a proud look. If she doesn't, I fucking will. I'll fight anyone who thinks my sister, or any other woman, doesn't belong in Formula One.

"Uh oh, Val has got her murderous face on. Everybody, take cover," Cameron says as he approaches us, too, a brooding Leonard next to him.

"Better watch out, Kion. If you get in my way, I won't hesitate to remove you," my sister teases, so Cameron flings his arm around her shoulder and presses his lips to her cheek to blow air against it. It makes a farting noise so loud, everyone around us turns their head to furrow their brows at them.

"Alright, Cameron, hands off my wife so she can get ready for her race," Gabriel says, completely ignoring the fact that Val isn't his wife yet. He snatches her away from his best friend to pick her up and carry her over to where we're going to stand to listen to the national anthem, Val giggling the whole way.

"You good?" James asks as we walk together, following the two disgustingly in love people.

"Scared shitless. You?" I reply, and he flashes me an amused smile, his blue eyes practically sparkling in the burning afternoon sun.

"Nah, mate, I'm ready for this season. It's going to be a good one," James says and nudges me with his shoulder.

I look at him one last time before shifting my gaze forward to see Nevaeh standing off to the side with her team. Gillian is interviewing Kyle. Lincoln is standing with them, too, making the hairs on the back of my neck stand up in irritation. He looks guilty as his eyes linger on Nevaeh, but she's paying him no attention. She's focused on her work. The only indicators that something is wrong are the bags under her eyes.

Frustration digs its nails into my back, scratching down the length of it until it burns. I want this man as far away from Nevaeh as humanly possible. I want him to apologize to her for all the pain he's caused her and then fuck off so far, he'll be on the other side of the galaxy. Something about him just rubs me the wrong way, and I refuse to acknowledge that that *something* might just be my very complicated attraction toward a certain curvy goddess of a woman with honey-brown eyes and hair that somehow always looks flawless.

"Focus," James says and nudges me again.

Somehow, I manage to do as I'm told, respectfully listening to the anthem before moving back toward my F1 car. Valentina, Gabriel, and I exchange our family saying before we go our separate ways.

"Breathe, race, and win, as long as it doesn't cost you a limb."

Grandpa used to say this to us every single time before a race. It was his way of reminding us that we should do whatever it takes to win, as long as we're safe and we stick to the rules.

Daniel is by my side, going through my last few pre-race rituals with me. Once I'm in the car, Chloe checks in with me. She tells me about the track conditions such as the temperature of the track and level of humidity before reminding me that tire degradation is going to be a pain in the ass today. Okay, she doesn't use those exact words because she's a professional, but it's the same thing.

"Don't do anything stupid on the opening lap. No risky moves. Gabriel is too fast and smart. He'll overtake you," Chloe reminds me, and I let out a small laugh.

"I'm not a child, you know?" She snorts in response.

"That's debatable." I can't help but shake my hand and laugh again.

Then, it's time for tunnel vision. To shut everything out until racing is the only thing left in my mind. I'm very good at that usually. At least, I was before a certain brunette with blonde highlights in her hair showed up and now I'm thinking about her. Thinking about winning so I can impress her. Thinking about hugging her after the race. Okay, fine, I'm also thinking about kissing her, but that's not going to happen while her job forbids it

"Adrian," Chloe barks. She must have said my name a few times already if her tone is this harsh.

"Sorry," I say, watching the lights turn on above all of us to signal the start of the formation lap.

All twenty drivers take one lap around the circuit to charge the car batteries, warm up the tires, and take in the track conditions. Easy enough. The hard part comes when the lights go on one by one until all five bulbs are filled with bright LED lights.

Then, we wait, all of us getting tested on our reaction times. Once all five lights turn off at the same time, we'll start the race. The better you react, the better you get away.

So, no pressure.

My gaze slips to my mirror, watching Gabriel line up in the second-place spot to the right of me and slightly further back.

No matter how often I race, my heart will never not thump harder and harder the closer we get to the start.

A wave of nerves hits me right in the stomach, but I shove it away.

Gabriel is not overtaking me and neither is the rookie in the Grenzenlos behind me. Yes, I'm still aware he isn't a rookie, but this is only his second year racing and his first with Grenzenlos. He's a rookie to me, and I'm not going to let a fucking *rookie* beat me, especially not a nepotism baby who got his seat through his daddy being friends with Robert Fuchs.

I smell burning rubber from the tires as we all wait, wait, wait, wait, wait...*go!*

My foot slams on the gas pedal as my fingers press the matching buttons. My beautiful Velocità Rossa shoots forward faster than Gabriel's, but only slightly.

He's right up my ass as we head into the first corner, and I bite down on my bottom lip to keep from cursing. All of my muscles tense up as the g-force hits me hard, causing adrenaline to course through my body.

Gabriel shoots next to me when we reach the second corner, but I'm ready for the fight.

I manage to keep him behind me for the entire duration of the first lap. By the time the second one comes around, I've managed to create a gap big enough so that he doesn't get the speed advantage of the drag reduction system, most commonly called DRS. That means, if he's less than a second behind me, he can use it, letting that flap in his rear wing open to get the speed advantage. When he's more than a second behind me, he can't.

Right now, he's more than a second behind me.

According to Chloe, he's slowed down for now to prevent tire degradation. I don't know what the rest of the race will bring, but I'm fucking excited to find out.

And even more excited to win.

Chapter 22
Nevaeh

THERE'S ABSOLUTELY NO WAY to describe Adrian's driving other than mesmerizing. He has me glued to the screens while Gillian talks to his camerawoman Fallon about the interviews they'll be doing later.

I try to focus on them, pay attention and learn, but then Valentina overtakes Grant Irwin with so much elegance and finesse, I let out an excited 'hell yeah!' which earns me a cock of Gillian's brow.

He doesn't say anything, merely looks me up and down disapprovingly once before going back to his discussion with Fallon.

My attention slips back to the screen in front of me to watch Lincoln overtake Gabriel with one of the dirtiest moves I've ever seen. Dirty, but not exactly against the rules. He sped forward enough that his front tire was ahead of Gabriel's front wing, then took most of the track space and pushed Gabriel so far off, he couldn't recover quickly enough to get second place back.

"I was in front!" Lincoln defends after his team tells him the FIA will be investigating this incident.

"We're handling it," his race engineer, Alberto, says.

Then, there's nothing but silence from Lincoln, so I check the gap between Adrian and Linc to see if my former best friend is catching up to the man in first place. He isn't. Adrian keeps up a good pace and the gap of five seconds remains steady right until the first pitstop of the season.

Adrian goes first, and his team performs an effortless stop of two-point-three seconds. Lincoln slips into first place, Gabriel into second, James into third, and Val into fourth. Adrian takes fifth place, barely a second behind Val.

All of the people ahead of him will have to stop soon, too, but that doesn't stop Adrian from overtaking his sister anyway.

I hold my breath as they fight it out, Valentina not making things easy for her brother. No doubt, Adrian is grinning under his helmet as he finally makes it past her a lap later. He has the faster car, for now, and he knows it.

Lincoln is creating a bigger and bigger gap as Adrian fights his way back to the top.

"Nevaeh, can you come over here," Gillian says, his tone harsher than the lightness I've grown used to over the past few weeks. "Go grab us all some coffee," my boss goes on, and I furrow my brows a little.

"Okay." His soft features are hardened into a frown as he tells me exactly what to get all of them and to do it straight away.

"Now, Nevaeh," he adds when I take too long to grab my purse.

There's nothing kind about the way he speaks to me, none of his *you're not my assistant, you don't have to get me food* shit. I don't mind getting us all a coffee, not even a little, but I mind when people speak to me the way Gillian just did.

All weekend, I've been running around, going from one place to another without even an hour for lunch. Gillian only gave me five minutes to inhale a granola bar. But if I've done something wrong, I'd appreciate it if he'd speak to me instead of passive-aggressively barking orders at me.

"Yes, Mr. Fender," I say through gritted teeth, sparing the television one more look to watch Adrian slip back into first place after everyone else pitted too.

If I were a lesser person, I might put salt instead of sugar in my boss's coffee, but when people go low, you have to go higher than you've ever gone before. Which is why I place his coffee in front of him with the biggest smile and the sweetest 'Here you go' that I can muster. It confuses him, but he doesn't comment on it. Instead, he starts telling me more and more things I have to do.

By the time he's finished talking and turns back around to Fallon, the race is nearing the end. I almost curse at how much I've missed before stopping myself and staring at the wall for a minute because *what the hell?* When did I become interested in this sport?

I've always enjoyed watching Formula One, but I didn't seek it out every weekend. Not the way I watched tennis every single day when Wimbledon was on or any of the other Grand Slams.

But now?

Now, I'm irritated because I couldn't watch Adrian, Valentina, Gabriel, James, and Lincoln fight it out for the top five places.

"Come on," I mumble to myself when Valentina slips into James' slipstream and the flap of her DRS opens. There are only three laps left, and she's trying to overtake James, who's struggling in fourth with old tires. He's had them on for too long, which caused a lot of degradation that's slowing him down now. His tire strategy for this race was far from ideal.

She slips beside him, almost overtaking him when James breaks later than her and manages to stay ahead.

My lungs burn, reminding me to take a breath instead of holding it.

Adrian is shown a second later, and I barely keep from complaining that they switched the view during such an intense battle when I watch him go so wide, a cloud of gravel floats into the air from his tires.

That mistake closes the time gap he was building between himself and Gabriel to a little over a second.

Shit, that's not good.

Lincoln is right behind them, too, his car looking like a bullet shot out of a gun, all sleek and dangerous. I'm a big fan of the dark gray they went with this year, something new the Grenzenlos team was trying out. I didn't think I'd like it when Papa first told me about it, but they made it work.

Nothing compares to the deep red Velocità Rossa has chosen though. I like the papaya color from Spark too, and the combination of red and blue Hawke went with. Alfa Adrenalina chose a mix of red, black, and white that I'm also a big fan of.

Focusing on the colors helps me ease the building anxiety in my chest. It distracts from the fact that Lincoln is inching closer to Gabriel, and Gabriel is inching closer toward Adrian and my brain is just swimming in dread at this point.

When the last lap comes around, I debate whether turning around and not watching is the better option. It's only the first race of the season, so in the grand scheme of things, it's not that important, but it *feels* important. It feels like each of these drivers is out there proving themselves and setting the mood for the rest of the reason.

Val has already out-driven everyone in the mid-field and lower teams, her car is currently in fourth place. A wave of pride hits me in the chest for her, but it's replaced by worry the moment Lincoln attempts to overtake Gabriel.

One lap has never felt so long in my entire life. Lincoln is relentless. He fights for Gabriel's place, using DRS to get enough speed advantage to overtake him in the main straight and finish the race in second place.

I can't help the excitement bubbling inside my chest at the sight of Adrian crossing the finish line first, Lincoln following closely behind him.

Celebrations break out everywhere, but Gillian demands my attention, telling me to get a grip on myself—yeah, fuck him—and barks at all of us to get out there and ready for the round of interviews.

We will be interviewing Lincoln, Kyle, Gabriel, and Adrian only, just as we have done the rest of the weekend, too.

I asked Gillian a few days ago why *Griffin Sports* decided to do this, and he said, "There are so many sports media companies out there, we needed something to set us apart. The rest of them can take the midfield teams and perhaps a few questions for the top two teams, but it's us who get the exclusive interviews with Velocità Rossa and Grenzenlos now. It's us that the majority of the fans will watch."

I didn't agree with him then, but I didn't say as much aloud. It's not my company, therefore it's not my decision, but there must be another way to get *Griffin Sports* exclusive content from the drivers to get the fans' attention.

It takes a while for our drivers to make it to the area where the post-race interviews are held. It's shaped into a circle with all of the reporters behind the barriers and the drivers and their PR managers on the other side.

Gillian left me standing here by myself because he doesn't think they're going to be here any time soon, taking care of a problem that arose, but Mr. Romana has a way of surprising everyone, including myself.

Adrian is the first of the top three to be here, all of the reporters surrounding us calling out to get his attention.

There's a bright smile on his full, pink lips and his hair is perfectly wet and curly. He must have just taken a shower to get rid of the champagne they spray on each other during the celebrations.

His eyes catch mine from across the interview pit, and somehow, I don't know how but his smile gets even bigger.

I can't help but return it.

Adrian's PR manager tries to get his attention, but he makes his way toward me without glancing her way. He appears hypnotized by me. Nothing else seems to matter until he's in front of me. He asks his PR manager, Fatima, to give him a second before turning back to me and clearing his throat. His smile reappears as he holds out his hand, waiting for me to shake it.

"Congratulations on your win, Mr. Romana. The car really came alive on this track," I say, and he tilts his head at me.

"Just the car?" he challenges, smirking until a blush settles on my cheeks.

"The car *and* you," I correct. Adrian places his hands against the barrier keeping us apart and nods in approval.

"There you go, *mon ange*, that's better," he praises, turning my cheeks an even darker red.

"What an impressive race," I say to steer the conversation away from making me blush, and he beams down at me, taking pride in my words.

"Impressing you was my number one goal, so I'm glad I can check it off my list," he replies.

"I said the race was impressive, not you," I remind him with a teasing grin, but he's so high on his victory, he merely shrugs.

"I won the race, so it's the same thing," the cocky man replies, taking a step toward me but not too close, always honoring the space I asked for in public.

"So, are you saying you won just so you could impress me?" I ask, crossing my arms in front of my chest.

My cheeks hurt, I'm smiling so hard, and I haven't smiled this much in days.

I tried to stay away from him, to keep my feelings from growing because I can't have feelings for him. I canceled our friendly French tutoring appointment to avoid growing closer, but it's useless. Adrian draws me to him, and there is no escaping the pull he has on me.

"I'm saying, knowing you were watching made me want to show you that I'm the best there is. I wanted you to look at those screens and see that I'm the kind of racer you can be glad to cheer for. I didn't fight dirty, not unlike some other drivers," he says and pauses to shake his head at whatever he's thinking about. "And I wanted you to be proud."

"I *am* proud, Adrian," I say, my voice cracking from all of the emotions his honesty and vulnerability brought out in me.

"Thank God because that race was fucking exhausting. My ass cheeks haven't hurt this much since Abu Dhabi three years ago," he says and attempts to rub them, but when Fatima clears her throat, he seems to remember we're surrounded by enough reporters to turn his joke into something it's not. He turns back to me with that smile of his still on his lips.

"So, Monsieur Romana, tell me, what was the fundamental reason the race went so well for you today?" I ask to switch the subject. With my notebook ready, I look up to watch his gaze gluing itself to my mouth before slowly trailing up my face.

"I am," he says with a wink, ever the smug man. I almost roll my eyes before remembering where I am. "Alright, where's your boss? I would have thought he'd be the first one here to grill me about my race," he says, so I turn around to look for Gillian.

"I have no idea where he is. He was supposed to be here five minutes ago," I reply, spinning back around to face the Monegasque. My hair flies all over the place, making him chuckle as he reaches for me to help me smooth it back down. He stops himself as he thinks better of it, so I tuck it behind my ears and clear my throat.

I'm about to speak again when my boss interrupts me.

"Pardon our tardiness, Mr. Romana. We had a small problem with our camera," Gillian says as he rushes toward us. "But we're here now and ready whenever you are."

Adrian furrows his brows at me, clearly confused, but then puts on a fake smile as he turns to my boss to give his interview.

Fatima holds a telephone next to Adrian, recording the conversation while I take notes. Lincoln is the next of our four drivers to walk up to us, waiting with a scowl on his face behind Adrian. I thought he'd be happy about second place, but he looks as unhappy as if he'd just taken last place.

When he catches me looking at him, his features soften a little, but he makes no attempt to speak to me, and I'm glad he doesn't.

As far as I'm concerned, my relationship with Lincoln is irreparable. After our last conversation, I don't ever want to speak to him again. He hasn't apologized for his behavior, and no matter how much it pains me to lose my best friend, I lost him a long time ago.

There is no pointing holding onto something that slipped through my fingers years ago.

Chapter 23
Nevaeh

It's been over two months since the first race weekend. Four more have passed since, and Gillian seems to despise me more and more with every race. I feel like a burden to him, a little amateur journalist he doesn't want to train or explain anything to. All he does is boss me around, making it infinitely more difficult for me to do as Ms. Martin asked me to: write an article about something captivating I see each weekend. She hasn't published any of my work yet, but I don't blame her.

I have so little time and energy by the end of the day because of Gillian, my writing has suffered immensely.

I tried speaking to Papa about my situation at work, but he told me to have a little faith that things will eventually get better, so that's what I'm doing.

Valentina also told me to give it a bit more time, but she added that if they didn't start treating me better, she'd kick all of their asses without hesitation. It made me laugh so hard, I snorted repeatedly.

Adrian and I speak almost every other day.

The Monegasque got third place in the second race of the season, won the third race, and got second place in the fourth and fifth races. Lincoln has steadily come in second or third. Gabriel Biancheri won the second and fourth races. Valentina has been switching between getting fourth, fifth, and sixth place for the past five races. I know I'm supposed to focus on Velocità Rossa and Grenzenlos, but every single time I watch Valentina race, I wish I could focus only on her.

To tell the entire world to watch her, too.

□We're at the sixth race of the season. Gillian, Fallon, Liz, and I arrived in São Paulo three days ago.

Gillian has been giving me tasks to run from one motorhome to the other, not once letting me sit down to even have a drink of water. He also asked me to prepare for the interviews and come up with a list of questions that kept me up until three last night.

Then, he almost beat down my door at six in the morning to get me out of bed and ready for the day, with no time for breakfast.

□In other words, I'm exhausted. My anxiety has been making me shake all day, and I've done all I could to keep it from taking over and overwhelming me, but it gets very difficult to not fall into an anxiety attack when I'm tired.

My mind doesn't have enough energy to battle itself in this condition. That's why my breathing is uneven. Why my heart is racing. Why panic has its hands wrapped around my throat and squeezes it.

□I'm going through the paperwork Gillian gave me, hyperventilating and slowly breaking down.

□I'm about to call my sister when Gillian storms into the room and says, "Nevaeh, I need you to go to Velocità Rossa and ask for a new interview schedule right now. You've got two minutes, then we gotta head to the Grenzenlos motorhome to interview your dad."

□He disappears before I get a chance to ask for a break, to allow myself to fall apart a little so I can put myself back together. Fighting off the attack is a lot worse than letting it consume me.

The Velocità Rossa motorhome is on the opposite end from the conference room I was working in before. I'm rushing to get there, but the exhaustion of running is making breathing even more difficult.

The path in front of me seems to elongate with every step I take.

Sweat drips down my forehead. It's hotter than usual today, making my hyperventilating even worse. I can't breathe.

My skin burns.

My eyes unfocus until I'm stumbling over my own two feet.

My entire body is trembling and nausea bubbles up in my throat.

I look for anyone who can help me when Adrian appears in my line of sight, blurry but unmistakably him. His eyes find mine, and he lowers the notebook he was holding to wave at me. I try to wave back, but everything spins. No oxygen is getting into my lungs.

I can't breathe.

I can't think.

My anxiety attack is taking over, and I'm too exhausted to keep that thought from making everything worse.

I see someone sprinting toward me, but I'm shaking and crying and still can't breathe.

Then, my legs give out and everything goes black...

CHAPTER 24
Adrian

I BARELY CATCH HER as she drops to the ground, *barely* make it to her in time.

My heart sank at the sight of her. Eyes unfocused, chest moving up and down rapidly, panic all over that beautiful face of hers. She was hyperventilating and according to Scarlette, my sister's race engineer, probably having an anxiety attack. Scarlette has anxiety, too, so she told me that sometimes when her anxiety gets really bad, she also faints.

It's the only thing keeping me from freaking out more than I already am.

I called for a paramedic, who checked Nevaeh's pulse and heart rate, waiting for her to regain consciousness with me. He pressed a cool and wet towel into my hand, telling me to place it on her forehead while we waited.

I do as I'm told, squatting beside the couch Nevaeh's on with one of my arms draped around her middle, my hand drawing an eight-figure on the exposed skin on her hip as more worry fills my chest when she still doesn't wake up.

Finally, her eyes flutter open, those pools of honey-brown finding me.

"*Mon paradis*," I say, but she doesn't seem to understand what I'm saying just yet. She blinks several more times, licking her dry lips once.

The paramedic comes up to her, asking me to step out of the way so he can ask her a few questions.

"How are you feeling?" he asks, checking her pulse once more since she's awake now.

"If you tell me what happened, I'll be fine," she responds with half a smile. She lifts her hand a little to run it over her face, but when she notices it shaking, she adds, "Never mind." Nevaeh balls her hand into a fist with a curse.

"Do you mind telling us? All I saw was you fainting, and I barely caught your head before it hit the ground," I say, catching her attention.

"I had an anxiety attack," she explains, confirming Scarlette's suspicion.

"When's the last time you've eaten anything?" the paramedic asks.

"Yesterday noon. Gillian didn't give me a break today," she admits, but only in a whisper to make sure the paramedic and I are the only ones who can hear her.

And, suddenly, I'm feeling very murderous.

"Did you drink anything today?" he goes on, but she shakes her head. "Alright, Ms. Fuchs, you are dehydrated and probably have very low blood sugar. I'm going to need you to eat and drink something unless you'd prefer to come to the hospital," the paramedic says. She shakes her head again.

"I'll drink more," she replies, and it seems to satisfy the paramedic enough to leave us.

"Nevaeh," I start, but she sits up and lets out a small groan.

"I have to go," she says, but I close the distance between us to place a hand on her shoulder and keep her sitting.

"I'm getting you something to eat and some water. Call your boss, tell him what happened. He should have made sure you got a break for lunch, and the fact that he didn't is unacceptable. Tell him to get his ass here before I get him fired for violating labor laws," I say, making her lips part in surprise.

Nevaeh hasn't seen this side of me yet. The side where I'm ready to tear down everyone who hurt the people I care about.

Yes, you caught me.

I like Nevaeh.

And now that she's wiggled her way into my stone-cold heart, I'm not letting her go again. Above everything, my attraction for her and complicated feelings, she's my friend. I've grown inexplicably fond of Nevaeh over the past five weeks.

Hell, over the last five months. She's just so... *wonderful.* There is no other word my mind comes up with except wonderful. In every way. She's funny, sweet, kind, yet passionate, doesn't shy away from speaking her mind, and has a fire so bright, I really want to play with it. Yes, even if it means I'll get burned. I don't care.

What's a little pain when the pleasure of her company has me addicted to the way I feel when I'm with her?

"It'll be alright, Adrian. I need to get back to work," she says once I return with some water, electrolytes, and an energy bar as well as a bagel.

"Nevaeh, I don't boss women around. It's not who I am, so I'm very sorry about this," I start and lower my face until we're mere centimeters apart. Unable to control myself and needing some contact, I grab her chin between my thumb and index finger and tilt it up so she's looking directly at me. "Sit, eat, and let me take care of you until you feel better. That's not up for debate. Okay?" Her eyes drop to my lips, studying my mouth as I speak before she brings her gaze back to my eyes.

"Okay," she mumbles.

I release her and hand her the water, waiting for her to drain half the bottle before handing her the electrolytes. The softest, sweetest laugh escapes her lips before she takes a few small sips of that, too.

"Can I ask you a personal question?" I start, squatting down next to the couch again while I watch her dig into the bagel.

Nevaeh nods several times as if she's thinking about my question and somehow knows what I'm about to ask.

"You want to know how long I've had anxiety, don't you?" She lowers her bagel to look down at me.

"No. I want to know if your employer and boss know that you have it and that treating you this way can trigger an anxiety attack strong enough to knock you out," I clarify, which seems to surprise her a little.

"No, they don't know," she admits, looking away from my face as she takes a deep breath. "Do you know how people look at you when they find out you have a mental illness like anxiety, depression, ADHD, or any of the other ones? They look at you like you're not a human being. They view you as incapable, less than. I'm a woman trying to make it in a male-dominated field. If they find out I have anxiety? *Pfft*, they'd send me packing the first chance they got."

She pauses to shift her eyes back to my face, a sad smile playing on her lips.

"I'm not ashamed to have anxiety, but I will not give anyone who I don't trust the knowledge of it so they can use it as a weapon against me. It's happened in the past, and I won't let it happen again," she explains, taking another bite of her bagel. As soon as she lowers it, I grab one of her hands and place it in both of mine.

"I won't tell anyone. You have my word," I promise, squeezing her hand where it rests in both of mine.

"I trust you, Adrian." My heart practically expands in my chest at those words. Trust is a big thing for me, and knowing Nevaeh trusts me? Well, let's just say I'm one lucky man.

"When you're ready, will you tell me more about it?" I ask, and she flashes me a genuine smile.

"I'd love to." *She'd love to.*

I smile at that.

Then wonder when the fuck I turned into such a sap.

"Nevaeh, where is the schedule I asked for?" Gillian's voice appears from behind me, and I stand up to walk over to him. Nevaeh rushes to my side, stepping in front of me to talk to her boss first.

"I'm really sorry. I felt a bit dizzy and lost track of time," she lies.

The frown Gillian directs at her in response has me grinding my molars. His eyes shift to me as he forces a smile, clearly realizing he can't yell at Nevaeh while I'm here.

"Don't let it happen again. We have things to do," he states, and Nevaeh nods, ever the polite woman.

"Of course, I apologize." Something protective, and perhaps a little possessive, has me readjusting until my back is almost touching her chest. I offer her boss my hand, and he shakes it, but I squeeze much harder than is necessary.

He winces but doesn't retract his hand.

"Mr. Fender, I'm glad you're here, I have a question for you," I say, letting go of his hand to cross my arms in front of my chest. "Are you interested in an exclusive article about the everyday life of a Velocità Rossa Formula One driver during a race weekend?" Nevaeh twists her head to look at me, surprise widening her eyes.

"That would be incredible. I can have my team—" I interrupt him.

"I don't want your whole team. I want Nevaeh," I say.

Gillian stumbles a step backward, furrowing his brows at me. I have no idea what the fuck I'm doing, but can you blame me? I want Nevaeh safe and sound by my side for the rest of the fucking season. I'll take one weekend if that's all I can get.

"I was thinking that Nevaeh could accompany me this weekend and write the article herself. If you're interested," I offer, watching Nevaeh press her lips together to keep from saying anything while she digests my offer, too.

A journalist following a driver around during a race weekend is unheard of, and I'm pretty sure my team would never agree to this. But I'll make them agree. I'll make them take this deal. If it breaks the rules, I don't give a flying fuck. Nevaeh is not finishing this weekend under Gillian's leadership. I'll sign a contract, she can sign a contract, whatever it takes for her to do this, to get an exclusive like no one ever has before.

"I would—" Nevaeh starts, but Gillian shoots her a warning glare that probably makes her feel stupid for saying anything in the first place.

Fucking dickface.

My head tilts as I force the smile on my face to stay put, even if I want to smash his face against the wall for how he's treating Nevaeh.

"You want Nevaeh to shadow you so she can write an exclusive article? You do understand she has only started on her journalism path, right?"

"If Nevaeh would like to, yes. I think she has great potential and seeing her running around, doing errands like collecting schedules for you seems like a waste of her talents. I read your article on Serena Williams while you were interning for their rival, *Specter Sports*, and I would love for you to write one like that about me, just in more detail," I say, only addressing her with the last sentence.

"I—" Gillian cuts her off again before she can get a second word in.

"We will discuss it and get back to you." I choose to ignore him, waiting for Nevaeh to respond instead.

"I would love to, but you should check with your team first, and I will check with mine."

She doesn't want to undermine Gillian's authority, no matter how much he deserves it right now. It's not who she is, unfortunately. Plus, she told me *Specter Sports* didn't rehire her because they had no position open.

Between you and me, I'd have fired every single person to have Nevaeh on my team.

"Mr. Fender," I say, my focus now drifting back to her boss. "Take this deal. Don't waste Ms. Fuchs' time." I straighten out my Velocità Rossa team shirt and fake another smile. "Oh, and if I ever, no matter which race, watch her faint again because you forget to give her a break, I will make sure your time as a Formula One reporter will be over. I have great respect for you and your years here, but that was unacceptable, and I have taken note of how you treat your employees. Best if that stays between us, wouldn't you agree?" Nevaeh nudges my side, but I don't even flinch. I stand in front of Gillian, immovable as a rock.

"You fainted?" Gillian asks, his whole demeanor changing abruptly.

His hand moves onto her shoulder, and he squeezes a little, probably to comfort her. But it twists everything inside of me until I'm nauseous and angry.

"Why didn't you tell me you weren't feeling well?" *Because you're a disgusting, slimy man who hides behind a nice mask to make people like you, that's why.*

"You didn't give me a chance to," she replies.

"Nevaeh will write that article. You will accompany him starting tomorrow. For today, you're free to go back to the hotel," he says before finally walking away, leaving me alone with the beautiful woman beside me.

"You shouldn't have gotten involved in my business," she points out, crossing her arms in front of her chest and scowling at me. My tongue swipes over my bottom lip as I lower my head and close the distance between us.

"Your health and happiness are my business, Nevaeh," I say, and the frown on her lips fades as her cheeks turn pink. The urge to reach out and run my fingers over her freckles, count them so I know how many dust the bridge of her nose and cheeks, is overwhelming. "Plus, this was to make sure he doesn't disobey labor laws again. Really getting involved in your business would have been me 'convincing' him to drop the no-dating-the-drivers rule," I go on, watching her bite down on the inside of her cheek.

"You can do that?" The corners of my mouth curl into a smile before I can stop them.

She's watching my mouth again. Always watching my lips like she can't wait for me to kiss her. And I want to kiss her. I want to so fucking badly that I can't think of anything better I could do right now. I want to press her up against that wall behind her and explore her mouth until her knees buckle. Until I have to hold her up by pressing my body against hers and she's whimpering into my mouth how good I feel.

"Do you want me to?" I ask.

Her brown-blonde hair flies a little as she moves her head to the side to laugh, and I get lost in the thought of running my fingers through it, wrapping it around my fist, and tugging on it.

Fuck. Me.

"I think it's best if we focus on the weekend for now." She's overwhelmed. I can see it in her eyes, so I don't push. I'd never push her when she's already all over the place because of her boss. Add Lincoln and her anxiety on top, and anyone would crack under that mountain of pressure.

But not Nevaeh.

No, she's a fucking warrior.

Not to mention, I don't know if I could actually make that rule go away, but I'd at least try. I'm not sure I'd give up either if she told me that's what she wanted, and that terrifies me above all.

"Whatever you want, *mon ange*," I say, lifting my arms in the air to stretch and show off my body a little.

Her eyes trail down my chest, lingering on my exposed skin before she forces them away again. The way her cheeks turn red once more has me fucking giddy. I love turning this woman on.

"I want you to eat more and go to the hotel and rest. I'll see you tomorrow," I say, ripping a chuckle from her. I look around the empty room for a moment before leaning down to press a soft kiss to her cheek.

"See you tomorrow, Adrian," she replies as I step away, a shy smile on her lips.

The things I'd do to kiss that smile.

CHAPTER 25
Nevaeh

MY PARENTS WERE TEXTING me non-stop yesterday, worried after they found out what happened, but I felt great. After eating, drinking, and getting some sleep, I was rejuvenated and ready for my day with Adrian. Yesterday were the free practice sessions of the race weekend where the teams tried out new things to get the best performance out of the car on this specific track.

Whenever Adrian wasn't in the car or with his strategists, he was with me, answering whatever questions I asked him. He even allowed me to snap some pictures, which I plan on including in my article. I haven't asked Gillian, Mrs. Lu, or Ms. Martin for permission, but I'm going to as soon as we get back to England.

Journalism and photography go hand in hand, after all.

I'm sure they won't have a problem with it. At least that's what I keep telling myself while I take candid photos of anything and everything that catches my eye.

Velocità Rossa made me sign a contract promising that should I catch any information I'm not supposed to this weekend, I'll keep it to myself or they'll sue me. A non-disclosure agreement. However, Adrian has been very careful not to let me get too close to what his team is doing and keep the focus entirely on him and everything he does during the weekend.

Today is the sixth Qualifying of the year. I don't find it nearly as exciting as the race, but it determines the starting positions of the drivers for the Grand Prix.

Valentina appears on the screen in front of me, beaming up at her performance coach, Isabella, and looking happier than ever before. This is where she belongs. Formula One is her place in the world.

I envy her.

It must be the best feeling on the entire planet to feel like you belong.

"I'm talking to a wall," Adrian's familiar voice says loud enough to fill my ears. The noise in his garage is almost unbearable.

I look at him to see he's dressed in his red racing suit, which hangs at his hips, revealing the red fireproof shirt the Velocità Rossa drivers wear underneath their suits.

"I'm sorry. I was lost in your sister's smile," I reply honestly, and he cocks a brow, handing me a to-go cup. I smell whatever is in it, and the scent of hot chocolate fills my nose. I told this man yesterday that I can't have coffee because of my anxiety, so he brought me this instead.

"I'm sorry to tell you this, but Val's happily taken, Nevaeh. However, she and I do look a lot alike..." He trails off, making me laugh.

"You do look a lot alike, but Val's got curves to die for," I say, tilting my head to the side and causing his jaw to drop. He places his hand on his stomach to imitate getting stabbed.

"Are you telling me my ass doesn't do it for you?" he says while sticking out his ass and making me bend over from laughter. I have no doubt his butt is impressively trained, but his racing suit does nothing for him. "Okay, okay, my ego can only take so much laughter," he reminds me and pats my back to get me to stand upright again. "Just because you have a perfect ass and body."

Adrian pouts, twisting his head to take a peek at his, while my mind lingers on the fact that he likes my body. I do have a nice ass. It's all the squats and running I did when I played tennis.

"Stop looking, it's fine," I assure him, too amused not to smile.

He frowns at me, and I pull out my notebook to focus on what's important: work.

"Alright, first pre-quali question," I start, and Adrian straightens out his back, taking a sip of his water and giving me his 'I'm ready smirk.' He's shown it to me ten times in the last thirty hours, and I seem to like it more every single time I see it. "What is your routine?" I ask, and Adrian goes into detail about every little step, including what he eats, the warm-ups he does, and the responsibilities he has.

I jot down notes, listening closely even though it's quite loud.

"You know what, this is all incredibly boring. Write this in your article instead," he says and leans against the wall we're standing by, crossing his arms in front of his chest. When his gaze fixates on my face and one corner of his mouth lifts, my cheeks burn.

God, why is he so hot?

"For good luck, my performance coach and I have this ritual where we jump rope to see who can go the longest. If he wins, it means I'll have a shitty race. If I win, it means I'll have a great one. We do the same for Qualifying, too." I smile at the visual while swinging my pen around on the page, the ink staining the paper.

"So, he won a lot last season, right?" I tease, making Adrian touch the roof of his mouth with his tongue.

"Nevaeh. Sweet, beautiful Nevaeh, that's the second time in five minutes you've made fun of me. Careful when you do that, *mon ange*, because I have a weak spot for women who tease me," he drawls, only making my cheeks go redder. He takes a step toward me and smiles. "You can also keep going, but don't bring me to my knees if I'm not allowed to taste you the second I hit the ground," he says, and I swallow so hard, it feels like a toad is lodged in my throat.

An unbearable ache appears between my legs, but Adrian leaves me standing by myself when his strategists call him.

He's a player. This is what he does, but he's so damn good at it, sometimes it's hard to remember.

I catch my breath before watching him zip up his suit and place his balaclava over his head. He winks at me one last time before he slides his helmet on, adjusting until it sits right. His body disappears into the car so swiftly, I blink and he's gone.

Qualifying starts, Q1 and Q2 going by painfully slowly. Those two are my least favorite parts about Qualifying since the teams with the drivers I care about the most—Valentina, Cameron, Gabriel, Lincoln, James Landon, Leonard Tick, and

Adrian—usually make it to Q3. Val is the only rookie, but she does incredibly well, just like the first five Qualifyings this season.

I'm so happy for her, I jump up and down a little.

Her team isn't nearly as fast as the top three, Hawke, Grenzenlos, and Velocità Rossa, but she does well with what she's been given. That woman is without a doubt a future Formula One champion, and I've never been prouder to know someone than I am right this second.

Q3 starts, and my nerves get the best of me, making my heart race a little. The first eight minutes are torture. The positions mean little until all the drivers race down the track for the last time this session. Adrian is fastest in the first sector of the track, but Lincoln is fastest in the second. This is absolutely nerve-racking. I cover my eyes and stare at the ground, too nervous about who'll take pole position.

Every single driver crosses the line in the span of another minute, and I wait impatiently for the results.

Adrian and Lincoln are one and two respectively, Gabriel was struggling and ended up in fifth while James Landon is third and Kyle Hughes is fourth. Val is in sixth, and Grant Irwin is ninth. The drivers of the Spark team, Cameron Kion and Michael Lin, are seventh and eighth. Leonard Tick came in tenth.

For some reason, excitement pumps through my bloodstream.

Adrian is first.

I rush outside with the rest of Adrian's team, my camera in hand and ready to snap a few photos for my article. This is not the type of journalism I hoped I'd be doing when I first started studying it, but it's pretty damn close.

After all the drivers get interviewed, Adrian signs the trophy the pole sitter of a race weekend receives, presses his lips to it, and raises it to his chest to take pictures. I hold my camera high, looking through the eyepiece before taking a dozen photos.

When he sees me, he winks and turns his body so I can get a better shot. His bottom lip moves between his teeth, but his attention is ripped from me to another reporter a second later.

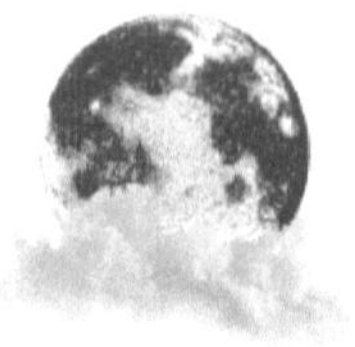

Adrian tells me to meet him outside of the Velocità Rossa motorhome, so I make my way there, sweat running down the back of my neck. The weather here in São Paulo is humid and hot today, something I'm not used to anymore since moving to England, but I love it. I love sweating with every step, as strange as it sounds . I simply love the warmth, even if it's a little overwhelming.

"Nevaeh," I hear Adrian say right as I was about to walk past a gap between the two buildings. His voice comes from the alley, so I smile as I make my way over to where he's standing with Daniel, Gabriel, and Gabriel's performance coach.

"What's going on?" I ask, a little breathless when I take in his bare chest.

My body catches fire at the sight of every hard ridge. At the sight of his light skin having taken on a bit of a tan since coming to Brazil and spending a lot of time in the sun. At the sight of his cocky smile because he knows he's turning me on simply by standing there without a shirt, but I can't help the way my eyes trace every muscle lining his chest. The blonde hair dusting it, and the darker hair trailing from his belly button into his swim shorts.

I've never been more grateful for swim trunks because they pull me out of my ogling trance and back to reality.

"Gabriel and I were just about to take an ice bath to cool off after Qualifying," Adrian explains, watching my mouth as I lick my suddenly dry lips. Fascination makes his eyes sparkle, causing heat to creep up my neck and settle on my cheeks.

"Is that something I'm supposed to write in the article?" I ask, a bit unsure why else I'd be here. Adrian's smirk lingers as he takes a step toward me, while Gabriel turns to Daniel and his performance coach to start up a conversation.

"If you'd like to, sure, but the reason I called you here is so you could admire me the way everyone else does when they see the videos of my ice baths. My fans love them," he says, and I almost snort because, good God, this man.

"I'm not a fan, so I think I'm not the right audience," I tease, but he merely tilts his head down to smile at me. We both know I'm kidding. I am a fan. I've been a fan since the first race, but I will *not* give him the satisfaction of saying so out loud. His ego is big enough, and we still need some room to breathe out here.

"Whether or not you're a fan, I do like seeing you blush at my half-naked body," he says with a wink before spinning around and joining the other three men again.

"Cocky ass," another familiar voice says, and I turn to see Valentina approaching, her sunglasses on her nose and her Alfa Adrenalina team shirt across her body. She's wearing black shorts and sneakers from her biggest sponsor, *Spin*.

Adrian's biggest sponsor is *Trill*, a clothing brand with a parrot as the logo. I've noticed it a few times now when he wore his black cargo pants because the logo is always printed on the left, front pocket.

"What are you doing here?" I ask, and she slips a hand onto my arm to give it a gentle squeeze. Her eyes are glued to her fiancé as he grins at her and cocks a suggestive brow.

"I love it when Gabriel does ice baths," she says and leaves me standing by myself to go admire her future husband as he submerges himself in the ice water, cursing and breathing through groans. She smiles at him but keeps her distance as the social media person films Gabriel.

"Let's go, Adrian," Daniel says, and the gorgeous Monegasque places his left foot in the tub of water and ice, taking several deep breaths before almost throwing himself inside.

"Ah, fuck," he breathes out, the sound a combination of pain and shock, but the little moan that leaves him after has my cheeks heating.

"What is this good for?" I ask Val, and she turns to me to give me her full attention.

"It helps get their body temperatures down quickly. I already did mine," she replies with a smile before turning back to Gabriel.

Now that the social media person is gone, she walks toward him and cups his cheek in her hands. He closes his eyes and puckers his lips to get a kiss from her, my eyes drifting back to Adrian to see the longing in his gaze. The way he's studying my mouth as if he wants nothing more than for me to walk over there and kiss him.

I break eye contact to scribble down some information and try not to smile at the fact that he wants to kiss me.

Gillian, Liz, Fallon, and I are at dinner while I'm being told a hundred things I need to take care of when we return to London. My boss wants me to proofread his articles, type up a report of the entire weekend based on the voice notes he apparently takes, and do countless other tasks.

The entire time he speaks, I feel his anger slicing through me, ruining my mood. He wants to yell at me, I can sense it by the way his eyes narrow slightly every time they drift to me.

Gillian taps his finger twice on the table, and, suddenly, Fallon and Liz excuse themselves to go to the washroom.

That can't be good.

"I don't know what I've done to make you so angry, but I'm truly sorry. I thought taking Adrian's deal would be beneficial for *Griffin Sports*. I apologize if it was the wrong decision."

The voice in my head screams for me to take it back. I didn't mean a single word, but this job is all I have at the moment, and I'm terrified of losing it. I can't fail. I have to be good enough to make it on my own.

"You're a smart girl, Nevaeh. Can't you figure out why I'm angry?" he asks, twisting the coaster of his glass between his fingers.

I've been sitting on a theory since I figured out he's upset with me, but I don't want to be a smartass, which is exactly how I'll look if I answer.

"Spit it out. I know you know." I stop myself from rolling my eyes.

"I fainted, which made you look like an ass in front of a Formula One driver, who has more than just a little power over your job. You let me take that deal because he put you on the spot, and you didn't want to look like a bigger jerk than you'd already seemed at that moment," I explain, wishing I'd never agreed to go to dinner.

Gillian leans back in his chair and smiles.

"I should fire you right now," he spits, causing the hairs on the back of my neck to stand up out of fear. "Unfortunately, Mrs. Lu and Ms. Martin think you're valuable to the company. So, I will suggest this: enjoy this weekend. The next race weekend, you will do what I say and when I tell you to without a single complaint. Got it?"

My hands curl into fists under the table. I need to find another job. There has to be something, anything other than working with someone who hates me for no apparent reason. If my bosses think I'm valuable, I should work for them directly, not Gillian.

"Yes, sir," I reply through gritted teeth.

I excuse myself as well, but unlike Liz and Fallon, I make my way to my hotel room. Today has been a rollercoaster, and I can't take any more of it.

CHAPTER 26
Nevaeh

RACE DAY IS MY favorite day of the weekend. The teams sprint back and forth, gathering all the equipment they need. I do my best to capture candid moments of the hardworking crews, amazed by how much they do and how little credit they get for it. Mechanics working on the car, strategists discussing their plans, and more I don't even know about.

I see Papa running around and snap a few pictures to show him afterward. I think he'll find it funny to see himself sweating through his dress shirt while worrying about the smallest of details.

Right before Adrian left, he appeared in front of me with his headphones half on, half off. Taylor Swift's voice blasted through the earpieces, so loud even I could hear it. I cocked a brow and grinned so hard, my cheeks hurt.

"What? I'm a Swiftie. I have to listen to her music before every race or it won't be a good one. It's my superstition." He winked at me once before placing his headphones on properly and jogging in Daniel's direction.

I smiled the whole time I wrote it down in my notes for the article.

The cars have lined up at the starting grid, and the teams get ready as the clock counts down.

Ten minutes to go until the start of the sixth race of this season.

At the start of the race, all the cars are close together, fighting to push as far ahead as possible. Crashes often happen through avoidable mistakes, miscalculations from the drivers about the amount of space they have, and a million more reasons. It's why I hate the start. It makes me unbelievably nervous.

"Hi, honey," I hear Mama say, grabbing my attention.

I finish the last word of the thought I was jotting down before it has a chance to leave my brain and turn to smile at her. She pushes my hair off my shoulder to let it rain down my back. Concern flickers in her eyes and causes her upper lip to twitch.

"What are you doing?" she eventually asks, making my breathing hitch. Out of all the questions she could have asked, this one confuses me the most.

"With my life or at this very second?" I reply, a smile skipping onto my face. Mama frowns and rubs her temples with the tips of her index fingers.

She hates it when I'm like this.

"Nevaeh, be serious. Your boss spoke to me about your behavior at dinner yesterday. Since when do you walk away from confrontation?" Anger and frustration settle in my chest, weighing heavy on my lungs and restricting my breathing.

Why would Gillian go to speak to my mother?

"Mama, I love you, and I appreciate your concern, but this is my business, and I need you to see it as such."

I know very well this is not an easy thing for her. Being nosy and all up in her children's businesses is her love language, but, for once, she needs to stay out of it. I'm even surprised I've been able to hide what's going on between Adrian and me for this long. She usually sniffs these things out in minutes.

"Okay, but, remember, be glad you got this job. It took you forever to find one," she replies and squeezes my arm before walking away, most likely to get back to Papa.

Something about her words rubs me the wrong way.

Then, as they slowly sink in, I realize she doesn't think I'd get another job, just the encouragement I needed to stay in this shitty one. Fantastic. My eyes dart back to the screens as I force myself to concentrate on the race.

I should take notes in case Mrs. Lu wants me to write an article about the race as well. At this point, I'm not sure what I'm supposed to do.

My main task is to have a constant eye on Adrian, I think.

Finally, the crews clear the track so the drivers can take their formation lap to warm up the tires and charge their batteries. They then reposition themselves on track at the starting light, waiting for the lights to go out. Adrian and Lincoln will go head-to-head, and I can't watch, but I have to, even though it makes my stomach twist into the worst knot.

As soon as the lights go off, every single driver charges forward, inches away from one another. Adrian keeps his first place for now, and Lincoln fights James Landon for the second position. Val stays in sixth as her brother takes off, creating a small distance between himself and the other nineteen drivers. Lincoln eventually moves out of James' reach, keeping his second place.

Once everything settles, I'm able to breathe again.

"Nerve-racking, huh?" A man with brown hair and a matching beard approaches me, and I smile when I realize it's Daniel, Adrian's performance coach. His Irish accent is strong, but I've been around enough people with all types of accents to understand them considerably well in casual conversations.

"Yes." I let out a small laugh neither one of us can hear since it's too loud in the Velocità Rossa garage, but, hopefully, my smile shows it.

"Adrian wasn't kidding," Daniel says as he leans back against the wall, and I pinch my eyebrows together.

"Kidding about what?" He piqued my curiosity. The trainer crosses his arms in front of his chest, looking past me at the screens.

"I think his exact words were 'Her smile matches her name.'" My heart sinks into my stomach as a warm feeling spreads through me. I trap my bottom lip between my teeth while I hide the grin Daniel's words have caused.

That damn Adrian.

As my eyes shift back to the screens, I watch Adrian enter the pitlane to get his tires changed. He loses two places, which is normal and nothing to worry about yet, while Lincoln takes the lead for now.

The race is long.

I sit down after a while of standing on my feet so I can bounce my leg up and down. There are two laps left when Lincoln gets into Adrian's DRS. I cover my mouth and hold my breath as I watch Adrian defend the first place he worked hard to maintain.

Then, Gabriel is right behind Lincoln, pressuring him to stop attacking his teammate and focus on defending his second place. Lincoln gives in, too busy trying to remain where he is when he takes the third-to-last corner too wide by accident, allowing Gabriel to overtake.

A gasp leaves me while I jump to my feet and get closer to the screens. Both of the Velocità Rossa drivers cross the line, scoring a one-two finish for their team. Lincoln comes in third, James in fourth, Kyle Hughes in fifth, and Valentina snatches sixth for herself.

Celebrations take up the next two hours. The drivers get interviewed, then move onto the podium. The Italian and Monegasque anthems fill my ears, one after the other. It's tradition to play the winner's home anthem and the team's before the drivers are handed their trophies and celebrate with champagne.

I watch with the biggest smile and my camera fixated on Adrian as he shakes the champagne bottle, then slams it onto the podium so the liquid sprays everywhere. He directs the bottle at Gabriel, who sprays his teammate in return.

The Velocità Rossa team cheers and celebrates their winner, so Adrian turns toward them after, his champagne raining down on us. He sticks out his tongue, victory painting his cheeks a wonderful pink.

Unsurprisingly, joy looks fantastic on this man.

The story of his father comes back into my mind, causing a sad smile to spread over my lips.

The Velocità Rossa paddock screams out of pure joy because their team has started the season on six separate highs. Then, the top three drivers get back to their garages, changing and getting ready for the post-race conference and interviews with the reporters. Gillian and his team will be there, but he told me not to bother coming. I make my way back inside as well, searching for Adrian to congratulate him.

Instead of Adrian, a very sweaty, very happy Valentina appears in front of me. She shakes her hair from side to side, droplets of sweat and probably water flying everywhere.

"Gross," I say with a laugh, and she giggles. "Shouldn't you be showering to go to interviews?" I ask, wiping a drop off my arm by rubbing it against her racing suit.

"Yes, I should, but I wanted to ask if you'd like to come to the afterparty with me, Gabriel, Leonard, Cameron, James, Scarlette, Chiara, and Adrian," she says, using a towel to wipe the sweat off her forehead.

"I appreciate the invitation but—" I cut off, not quite sure why I'm declining her offer. I love spending time with Val and Adrian, but my anxiety is going to make this evening unbearable.

Exposing myself to new situations triggers my anxiety.

This is a new situation, and my anxiety is already triggered by the mere thought of me going.

What would Nova tell me to do in this situation?

Exposure therapy, Nevi. You gotta go out there and expose yourself to something that frightens you. It'll get easier that way because once you see you can *do these things, it'll feel less like you could never do them.*

"No but, actually. I'd love to come. Where should I meet you?" I ask, ignoring the wave of panic going through my chest.

Valentina takes my arm, giving it a gentle squeeze.

"You'll be with me the whole time, love. I won't leave you alone for a second unless you want me to," she assures me, and if she weren't so sweaty from the two-hour race, I'd give her a hug.

"Thank you."

After she writes down the address of her hotel into my phone, she skips out of the room and straight toward where Gabriel is waiting for her. He gives me a swift nod and a small smile before he beams at Val and wraps her up in his arms.

CHAPTER 27
Nevaeh

"Nevaeh Emilia Fuchs," Valentina says after opening her hotel room door, looking like the most beautiful woman I've ever seen in the world.

She's wearing a red dress that appears to be made out of pure glitter, red heels so high, just looking at them throws me in danger of breaking an ankle, and her necklace with a Formula One car-shaped charm. Her makeup is bright and bold, and I think I could look at this woman for hours and find more beautiful things about her.

"How did you find out my middle name?" I ask as she takes a step toward me and places a kiss on each of my cheeks, the typical *bise*.

"Adrian told me," she says, waving me into her room. "You look beautiful," Val adds, smiling at me.

"Thank you. So do you," I reply, running a hand down the dark orange dress I threw on.

It's tight in all the right places, and loose in all the others, simultaneously highlighting my curves and hiding parts of my body I'm not entirely confident with. I've chosen flats instead of heels, and more simple makeup. But looking at Val, who is shimmering with her dress and the eyeshadow she put on, I wish I'd gone a similar route as her.

"You know, orange is Adrian's favorite color," she says, winking at me as she walks toward her purse and slips it over her shoulder.

"Is it?" I ask, pretending not to know that when it was one of the reasons I chose this dress in the first place. Valentina looks right through me, humming a little after the words have left my mouth.

"Come on, *petite menteuse*, Gabriel, Adrian, and the rest of them are meeting us at the afterparty club," she says, guiding her long, blonde curls over her shoulder and holding out her hand for me to take.

When we arrive at the club, Val and I have to show ID to the bouncers to make sure only members of the Formula One world may enter. This is an exclusive event, after all. I'm sure I wouldn't even be allowed in there, being a reporter and all, if it weren't for Valentina. She takes my hand again as we walk inside, keeping me close to her and reassuring me in the same breath.

I've never had a friend like Valentina Romana.

That thought is followed by another.

There is no one like Valentina Romana.

Just like there is only one Adrian Romana in this world, and he's currently leaning against a high table, smiling at something James Landon is saying. The Monegasque is dressed in a simple black button-down with several of the top buttons left undone to expose his trained chest. His fingers are decorated in several black rings, and a simple black necklace hangs from his neck. The dark blue jeans he's wearing do his round ass a lot more justice than his racing suit, and good God, it is a glorious sight.

All of him is a glorious sight.

Adrian might call me *mon ange*, but he's the one that looks like an angel.

"Need a napkin?" Val teases, lifting her index finger to the corner of my mouth as if she wants to wipe away my drool.

"No, I need a drink," I mumble, walking directly to the bar and ignoring the way my body has caught on fire.

"Don't worry, *bella*, Adrian has that effect on a lot of people," a short woman with bright green eyes, light skin, and short brown hair says. Her Italian accent is thick, and a scowl rests on her lips. "I'm Chiara," she introduces herself, extending a hand. I shake it with a smile.

"Nevaeh. It's nice to meet you," I reply, although her comment about Adrian has me more confused than anything else.

"Pleasure's all mine," she says right as another woman walks up to us with an empty glass and a bright smile on her lips.

"I need another of these passion fruit cocktails. They're so good," the woman says, and Chiara takes the glass from her, shooting the bartender a death glare until his eyes widen and he hurries to make the other woman another drink.

"You must be Nevaeh. I'm Scarlette. Val has told me so much about you!" she says, genuine excitement wafting off her. I look from one woman to the other and almost grin at the polar opposites. Scarlette is pure sunshine. Chiara is a thunderstorm.

Chiara hands Scarlette her refreshed drink, staring at the alcohol longingly. Scarlette catches that look, too.

"Just have one drink. One drink isn't going to mess with your milk," she tells Chiara, but she shoots her a frown in response.

"It's safest for my baby if I don't drink anything, so I won't. Not while I'm breastfeeding," the Italian woman says, lifting a hand to place it on her left boob absentmindedly as a sad expression slips across her face.

"Is breastfeeding as weird as I've always imagined it to be?" I blurt out without really thinking. I half expect Chiara to give me a strange look and walk away, but she gives me several nods and a look that says, 'You have no idea.'

"It's wonderful and so weird, and when your nipples are sucked raw, it's not fun at all," Chiara replies right as Leonard Tick approaches and wraps his arms around her from behind. He whispers something into her ear that makes her blush and bite down on her bottom lip to fight a smile.

"Do you mind talking about taking care of your wife's nipples when I'm not in earshot?" Scarlette asks with furrowed brows and Leonard mumbles a quick apology before whisking Chiara away, making her giggle in his arms.

"I didn't know Leonard was married," I say, Valentina coming up beside me with pink cheeks and her lipstick a bit smudged. Okay, I'm officially a little jealous.

I want a hot Formula One driver to sweep me off my feet, please.

My eyes drift to where Adrian is standing without my permission, but he's already staring at me. His lips are parted ever so slightly before he licks them. My heart races as his gaze trails down my body appreciatively, drinking me in like he's never seen a prettier sight. And I like the way his usual confidence has slipped away a little because when he notices I've caught him staring, a shy smile stretches his lips. I cock a brow at him, and he lets out a laugh I can't hear, shaking his head like he can't believe I just did that. Then, his eyes return to me, fire and lust in them as he takes me in again.

I look away before he has a chance to catch the blush settling on my cheeks.

"Leonard doesn't like talking about Chiara and their daughter in public because the press likes to drag his name through the dirt for no other reason than who he is and where he came from," Valentina explains, turning to the bartender to ask for an iced tea.

"Well, all of those journalists should not have the power and influence they do. Reporters who spread hate about good people, people who have worked their asses off to achieve good in the world, don't deserve to have a platform to speak on," I say, so passionate about the subject, I'm gesturing a lot more than I usually do. Val looks at me with her mouth agape and Scarlette nods in agreement.

"Nevaeh, I don't say this to people often, but I fucking adore you," Val says with a smile. "If the four of us band together, I think we could kick everyone's ass for speaking badly about people who don't deserve it," she goes on. "We could call ourselves *The Revengers*," she says and giggles at her joke.

"What, like in *Thor: Ragnarok*?" I ask with a laugh, and she grabs my arm, pure delight filling her features.

"You got that reference?" I nod, smiling at her excitement. "You're a dangerous woman, Nevaeh. I might grow attached," she says, trying to keep her tone light, but I feel the heaviness of her words deep in my gut.

Valentina doesn't easily let people in, so I wonder why she'd give me a chance. Why I'm the lucky chosen one.

"Come on, let's dance," Scarlette says when a popular song I've heard a million times on the radio starts filling the club.

Val and Scarlette pull me toward the dance floor, both of them dancing a second later. I'm a bit clumsier at first, not as confident as the other two women, but they make me feel so comfortable, I'm swinging my hips before I know it.

We're at a normal type of club. Lights dimmed, neon lights flashing around us with the beat of the music, and alcohol in the air. The difference between this club and others I've been to is that the floors aren't sticky, men aren't trying to grope me or slap my ass every chance they get, and it's not nearly as crowded.

The respectful distance others keep is probably also due to the dozen security personnel I have already spotted around us.

Time passes in a blissful breeze. I'm dancing, having a few drinks, and laughing more than I have in a while. Carefree doesn't begin to cover how I'm feeling, but I'm enjoying myself immensely.

Val outdances me in those heels of hers. She moves like she was born to dance, something Gabriel clearly agrees with because he makes it all of thirty seconds after we started dancing before he joins us, one of his hands on her hip and the other holding a bottle of water he keeps handing her. My friend revels in his touch, his attention, but doesn't hesitate to shoo him away when she wants to dance with me for a song. He welcomes her back every single time she presses up against him again, kissing her cheek, temple, the crown of her head, or her neck.

It's incredibly sweet.

A warm, solid body appears behind me, close enough so the heat radiates off him, but far away enough to give me space. His scent fills my nose, and I almost hum happily.

"I wanna put my hands on you, Nevaeh. Nod if you're okay with that," Adrian whispers after he leans down to bring his lips to my ear. His breath is hot and sweet on my skin, sending a wave of shivers down my spine.

I nod before my brain can catch up, but when I look around, I see we're crowded enough to keep people from noticing us. This is a Formula One event, which means people aren't as starstruck by the F1 drivers and watching their every move.

His hands slip onto my hips, spinning me around so I'm facing him. My arms lift to wrap around his neck of their own volition, but I don't stop them. My head is floating from joy, and having Adrian Romana in front of me, sliding his hands onto my back and resting them right above my ass, has my body vibrating with need and contentment.

I want him.

Wanted him since I first laid eyes on him, and I hate that I have to keep putting distance between us. What I hate even more is that I *know*, even if I didn't put it between us, Adrian would. He doesn't date, and I won't change that.

Right now, I can't bring myself to care.

Chapter 28
Adrian

Nevaeh's soft body is pressed against mine, her heated skin all over me in that dress that almost brought me to my fucking knees earlier.

Never in my entire life has a woman in a dress made me want to rip all my barriers down. Until Nevaeh stepped into this club in that orange dress, her curves getting hugged by the fabric in ways that made me jealous of the piece of clothing for getting to touch her like that.

Jealous of a piece of fucking clothing.

First of all, I don't get jealous. *Ever.*

Second of all, how do you even get jealous of *clothing?*

I'm being ridiculous. Nevaeh is just a woman, and no matter how much I like dropping to my knees for them and making them scream my name in pleasure, she's *just a woman*. I will get over this fascination.

You all agree with me on this, right?

"You know, when a woman is showing off her best moves to impress you, it's impolite to let your mind drift somewhere else," she says with a little laugh, and I bring my gaze down to hers.

A smile tugs at the corner of my mouth when I spot the smirk on her face.

"Trust me, my thoughts may have drifted, *mon ange*, but you were still the center of my attention," I admit, spinning her around once before bringing her back to my chest.

She grinds against me without hesitation, following the rhythm of the music with grace. Her arms fly backward so her fingers can run through my curls. My hands slip over her stomach and down her thick thighs, making her quiver in my arms.

My cock hardens in an instant.

And the beautiful tease in my hands doesn't seem to have a clue what she's doing to me.

A small voice in the back of my mind reminds me we shouldn't be doing this, shouldn't be touching so openly, but all of the fucks I could have given were ground to dust when she started grinding her ass against my cock.

"Careful, Nevaeh, my self-control is slipping away," I mumble into her ear. Her upper body starts shaking with a laugh, and she steps away from me before I have a chance to truly enjoy it.

She spins around and takes one more step away.

"We wouldn't want that, would we?" she replies with a smile before moving toward Scarlette and Valentina and leaving me to subtly readjust myself.

"Tripping all over yourself already?" my best friend asks as he approaches me, a beer in his hand.

We move to the side of the dance floor and out of the way.

"I'm not tripping all over myself." James' eyes drop to my crotch before he lifts them again to smile at me. "I'm horny. There's a difference," I say, realizing with horror that it's been almost five months since I fucked anyone.

Five.

Fucking.

Months.

I raise my palm to my forehead to check if I have a fever because the only reason it would be this long since I've had sex is if I'm sick with the longest flu in the history of mankind.

"How long has it been? A few hours?" James teases, and I let out a small laugh that soon turns into a humorless sound while I question my entire fucking existence.

"Yeah, a few hours." It's a bold lie, one he sees through as he steps in front of me to scan my face.

"Oh my God, how long has it really been?" he asks, sipping his beer as he waits for my answer.

I pull my lips into a thin line, avoiding his inquiring gaze until he slaps my chest.

"Tell me," he insists. I shake my head.

"A week."

"Liar. There's genuine panic in your eyes. It's been longer." I hate that smug look on his face.

"Fine, it's been two weeks. Now, can you leave me alone?" James places his bottle on the table beside us, laughing.

"Just tell me the truth. You're a horrible liar."

"No." I grind my teeth.

"Just say it," he says and laughs again.

"No."

"I'm just going to keep asking. Might as well—" I cut him off.

"Five months!" His jaw drops dramatically at my admission.

"You haven't fucked anyone in five months?" he asks like we weren't just talking about it. I give him a strained nod. "Shit, are you feeling alright?" James says next, raising the back of his hand to my forehead.

I smack it away before he can touch me.

"I'm fine, just off my game apparently," I reply, my eyes drifting to where *mon ange* is dancing with my sister.

"Something happened five months ago... remind me again what it was. That event that had you talking about a very specific woman and wanting to see her again," he says with a smug smirk, tapping his chin like he's thinking really hard about it.

Jerk.

"I met Nevaeh. Okay?" I say, taking a step toward him. I'm only slightly taller than him, but he's wider than me, which is irritating when I'm trying to look intimidating. "I met Nevaeh, laid my eyes on her one fucking time, and now the only woman I want to touch is her. I don't want to look at other women, and I sure as fuck don't want them to touch me, not when my skin only buzzes from excitement from Nevaeh's touch. There. Are you happy now?" I ask, breathing heavily after my rant.

I feel like sitting down. This admission doesn't just catch my best friend off-guard. It has more panic washing through me.

I don't want other women to touch me.

I don't want to touch other women.

I haven't had sex with anyone since I met Nevaeh.

I'm definitely going to be sick.

My head is spinning, trying to process all of this information even though it goes against my nature. I don't get into relationships. I don't date. I especially don't pursue women who are off-limits because it's way too complicated.

Why the hell does none of this apply to Nevaeh?

James pokes me in the forehead, forcing me back into the moment.

"What the hell was that for?" I ask, rubbing the sore spot.

"Just making sure you're real," he replies and picks up his beer again, taking a sip before he stares down at his phone. A picture of his son and him lights up the screen, and I watch his eyes soften.

"Adrian Romana?" *Oh no.*

"Melanie Whitehall," I reply, forcing a smile. The short woman with black hair and clear blue eyes steps in front of me,

"How are you?" she asks, placing a kiss on each of my cheeks. I meet her halfway, hating the fact that my body fights me even more than it usually does.

Melanie is a very nice woman. Smart as hell, too. The problem is, we slept together two years ago, and then her father decided to invest in my team. This means, as much as I would like to avoid her to prevent complications, I see her *a lot* during race weekends. And I don't think she's entirely over me yet.

And no, I know what you're thinking. This isn't me being my typical 'everyone wants me' version. This is just because she keeps making advances.

"I'm good. How are you?" I say, my eyes drifting to where Nevaeh, Val, and Scarlette have moved to, off the dance floor and closer to where I'm standing. Gabriel is with them, and Leonard and Chiara have rejoined them as well. I want to be over *there*. I want to drape an arm around Nevaeh and hug her against my side so she can wrap her arms around me. I don't want to talk to Melanie.

"I've missed you, handsome. Any chance you'll let me buy you a drink?" she asks, running a hand down my chest.

Alarm bells go off in my head. A humorless laugh escapes me because I've never not enjoyed flirting with a woman I am or was attracted to.

This is new territory.

"No, but thank you for offering," I reply. I reach for her wrist to gently remove her hand at the same moment someone clears their throat from behind Melanie.

My eyes drift to Nevaeh's forced smile, sending more panic through me.

Fuck, shit!

"Nevaeh—" I start, but she cuts me off.

"I'm going to head back to my hotel. Congratulations again on the win," she says. I step around Melanie to get to the woman I want to be around as much as I can.

My hands reach for her, but she makes her way to the exit before I have a chance to tell her that I really didn't want Melanie to touch me. That I only want her. There is no way she heard how I turned down Melanie's offer. It's too loud in here, so all she saw was another woman touching me and me smiling politely. Goddammit. I have to tell her she's the only person allowed to put her hands on me. Something I can't fucking do because it's not fair of me to tell her all of these things when we can't be together. In any capacity. Because of her job and my lack of faith in relationships.

"Nevaeh, please," I beg as I chase after her. I sprint in front of her, almost making her run into me.

"Thank you for this weekend and for tonight. I'm happy for you. You drove amazing, and I can't wait to write this article. I'll send it to you once I'm finished so you can approve it," she adds, so I raise an eyebrow in response.

"Don't be nice to me, not when you want to kick me." My words bring a real smile to her face.

"I don't want to kick you, Adrian. You deserve to celebrate, so go, celebrate with her. It looks like she desperately wants you to," she says.

I take a step toward her, making her pull her lips into a thin line.

"Better not make her wait," Nevaeh adds and steps around me, leaving me to sputter nonsense after her, all of my reasons for why I'm not going to go celebrate with Melanie, but she saw what she wanted to see, and I don't think there's a way to convince her to stay without saying all of the things I'm not supposed to.

Kiss me.

Celebrate with me.

Stay with me.

Let's fuck away all of our frustration.

So, instead, I lean down to press the swiftest kiss on her cheek.

"Call me."

I stare after her as she leaves without making any promises of calling me. My eyes drift back to Melanie, and I hate that I resent her a little for making Nevaeh think something that isn't true.

All I can hope is that Nevaeh doesn't care who I do or do not sleep with, but I have a feeling she does, and that I just really fucked things up by saying nothing.

CHAPTER 29
Nevaeh

MY HANDS ARE SWEATING as Mrs. Lu's secretary opens the door to my boss's office, the usual frown on his face as he does so. I've barely slept since I got back home yesterday, which is why a yawn slips past my lips before I can stop it. It doesn't go past Mrs. Lu, nor does it go past Ms. Martin, who raises an amused brow.

"I heard you went out with the drivers. Overdid it?" she jokes, and I wish that was the reason for me being sleep-deprived.

"No, I was working on my article for this weekend," I lie to hide what the hell I was actually doing. Thinking about Adrian and the woman I saw him with. Picturing them together all sweaty and naked. Wondering for the millionth time why Adrian Romana has to be the one to stay in my head when he shouldn't even be there in the first place.

"Come, sit. I understand from your email that you'd like to talk about the events of the race weekend," Mrs. Lu says, and I obey, crossing my legs but leaning toward her before speaking.

"Yes, I hope that's alright." Mrs. Lu sits back in her chair and extends her hand, gesturing for me to go ahead while Ms. Martin keeps working on whatever it is that a COO does.

The smile on Mrs. Lu's face makes me feel better about what I have to do.

"I really appreciate the job you have given me, and Gillian is a great boss, but I don't think I'm a good addition to his team," I start, hating myself for having to look like the ass here.

"Yes, Gillian has informed me about something similar. Lucky for you, I have eyes and ears everywhere. You will no longer be working for him, I won't have it. You gave your all last weekend and ended up unwell because of poor leadership."

My boss stands up, patting down her pencil skirt as she takes a few strides to get to her printer. Her fingers grab hold of a document which she hands me as she leans against her desk beside me. My eyes scan the paper, realizing this is the article I wrote on the plane yesterday and sent to her.

"You won't be working for Gillian anymore. As a matter of fact, you won't be working for anyone," she says, and I feel my heart drop into my stomach.

This is it, this is where I get fired.

My anxiety makes a cold sweat break out across my skin. It doesn't like failure. It usually makes my life more miserable if there is a possibility I could fail at something, whether it's tests, interviews, or anything of the kind. Right now, it's reminding me why it always shows itself during these situations.

To punish me for not being the best version of myself.

"Well, no one except Ms Martin and me, of course." Relief knocks the breath out of me.

"I'm not sure I understand," I reply, but Mrs. Lu's warm smile calms my racing heart once more.

"I sent this article to all ten teams in Formula One yesterday. So far, most of them have responded with a request for you to write an article like this about their drivers. They are even paying more to have you take candid photos like you did with Adrian and the Velocità Rossa team," she says.

Ms. Martin leans forward to chime in.

"This article is brilliant, Nevaeh. The emotion that spills from the pages with every word is phenomenal. So, we would like to offer you a deal," she starts and tucks her graying hair behind her ear.

Mrs. Lu nods, clearly agreeing with her business partner.

"There are eighteen races left as well as nineteen drivers. Only sixteen have asked for articles like this, so we have a bit of wiggle room. Each race weekend, you will accompany a driver whenever they have time for you, which will most likely be less than with Mr. Romana because he took more time for you than he was supposed to," Ms. Martin explains, and a smile creeps onto my face.

I loved writing that article about Adrian, and he sent me a text, assuring me he adored reading it. Getting to write more of them instead of working for Gillian, and taking more pictures, it all sounds like a dream.

"What about Mr. Fender? He's expecting me to do whatever he wants without a single complaint next weekend," I respond, my anger for my former boss coming to the top.

"I realize how uncomfortable it might be for the two of you to see each other daily now, but that's where the last part of the deal comes in." Mrs. Lu walks back around her desk to sink into her chair beside Ms. Martin's and hands me a new contract. "*Griffin Sports* has a location in Monaco, and I'd like to offer you a position there. Moving costs would be covered, however, your living arrangements would come half out of your pockets, half out of ours."

Monaco? Are they serious?

My question is answered when I skim over the contract. My bosses are dead serious. *But I can't just leave everything behind and move to Monaco!* My family is here, but that reason shouldn't interfere with my decision. I need to make it based on all the other factors like money, living costs, and what I want.

If I'll be able to see my new friends more, too, well, then that's a bonus.

"I know this is all very overwhelming, which is why I want you to take today to look this offer over and come back to me with an answer tomorrow." Mrs. Lu smiles.

I have a hundred more questions, but Mrs. Lu stands up, cutting me off before I can even decide on one to ask.

"Now, Ms. Martin and I have a meeting, and you have a big decision to make," she states while stepping out of the room, leaving me speechless and overwhelmed.

There is only one thing to do in a situation like this.

Mama, Papa, Nova, and Aileen sit at the dining room table, watching me closely as I take a deep breath. I hand Papa a copy of the contract since he's the best at understanding them and let out a shaky laugh. Nova rests her arm around Aileen's waist while both of them exchange a worried look. I've never asked them to come together all at once to discuss something, and the unfamiliarity of this situation clearly has them suspicious.

"Okay, you can all stop looking at me like I'm not the Nevaeh you know. I'm still me, just struggling with a huge life decision I need your opinion on," I say and move my hands to sign the words at the same time, resting my forearms on the back of the chair in front of me.

Papa's eyes have already gone wide from reading the offer, so he isn't surprised when I explain it to the rest of my family. Nova sits upright, surprise written all over her face. Aileen smiles from excitement, but the one who doesn't have to say anything to express her feelings is Mama.

Anger and sadness battle on her face.

"You can't just leave to live in Monaco all by yourself!" she exclaims, capturing Papa's attention. He places a hand on her shoulder, which Mama pushes off as she stands up. "You're not doing it, I forbid you from taking this offer!" she goes on, storming out of the dining room and slamming her bedroom door moments later.

"That was definitely not the reaction I was hoping for," I say, my heart sinking slowly.

"She's only upset because she's not ready for her little girl to move out," Papa replies and signs the words as he takes a step toward me. He excuses himself from Aileen before turning entirely my way to look into my eyes. "Give me the facts," he demands, handing the piece of paper back to me while a hint of a smile plays on his face.

"I have money saved up that could last me half a year in a small apartment in Monaco, I'd earn great money, a little more than I would here, and I would finally get the independence I've dreamed of for a long time," I start, listing only positives to see his reaction. Papa remains quiet, waiting for what is holding me back. "I'm scared," I admit, tears shooting into my eyes. "I've never lived by myself, and I didn't expect that when the opportunity presented itself, it'd be in another country," I explain and groan when my voice cracks.

Papa grabs me by the shoulders and lowers his head just enough to be on the same eye level as me.

"Do you want to take this offer?" he asks, and my eyes shift from one of his to the other. There has been one clear answer to this question since Mrs. Lu handed me the contract, but I've been too afraid to admit it to myself.

"More than I've wanted anything in a very long time." My father lets go of me and steps back, a proud grin covering his face.

"Then don't let fear take it away from you. You're a warrior, Nevaeh, one who never hides from anything. Are you going to back down from your dream life?" A small laugh escapes me while I wipe my tears and feel a weight lift off my shoulders.

I'm sure my anxiety is going to be as happy as a kid in a candy store because of all of the worrying I'm going to be doing on top of all of the change and new situations I'll have to expose myself to. But this feels right. This feels like everything I'm meant to be doing at this point in my life.

"You should probably book a flight and go visit Monaco to check out apartments and familiarize yourself with the country before you move there. It makes it easier," my father says as a tear drops down my cheeks.

He wipes it away and gives me a comforting smile.

Nova, Aileen? What do you think? I sign although I've made up my mind already.

"I think you're going to have the time of your life without me," my sister complains but then hugs me and tells me how proud she is.

Aileen does the same before all of them leave, including Papa. I think about talking to Mama, but usually, it's best to leave her until she's ready, which is mostly after Papa has spoken to her. He has this way of calming her, it's always fascinated me. Whenever I'm angry, nothing and no one can calm me except myself.

After booking a flight and hotel, I stare at my screen. There's only one person I want to call right now, one person I want to share this with. The man who has me all sorts of confused.

The rule stands. I can't date a driver, especially not now when I have to write personal articles about them. It's one of the conditions at the top of the contract Mrs. Lu gave me. But it says nothing about being friends with them, and, right now, I need a friend. One that I know will be happy for me.

The phone rings, and I fix my appearance eight times. For some reason, I video-called him because of an inexplicable desire to see his face. Maybe not inexplicable. After all, he's the most gorgeous guy I've ever seen.

A few rings later, his face appears on my screen, making a happy feeling spread through my chest.

"Hi, beautiful. To what do I owe this honor?" he asks, smirking, and I feel heat rush into my cheeks in response.

"I was wondering if you had time this week to show me around my new home," I say, but Adrian furrows his brows. "Well, I just thought since Monaco is your home country, you could show me the best spots." Adrian's eyes go wide before he looks away from the phone only to smile and look back at his screen.

"Are you kidding me? That's the best news I've heard in a long time!" An excited laugh leaves him. He lowers the phone and yells, "Val! Nevaeh is moving to Monaco!" She appears on my screen as both of them beam at me. I return their smiles, so grateful for the friendship they've given me.

"We're going to have so much fun! Oh, and we will help you move, of course!" Val chimes in, and I feel tears flood my eyes.

This is slowly becoming the best day of my life.

"Actually, Val, I need your help apartment-hunting."

An excited squeal leaves her, and we end up planning everything for my short trip to Monaco. I'm only staying for a few days, but Val is making sure I won't be alone for a second of it.

"By the way, you are not staying at a hotel. Gabriel and I would love to have you stay with us." I try to decline politely because I feel bad about intruding, but she won't have it. "I will pick you up tomorrow," Val simply says before disappearing so I can't argue with her anymore.

Adrian is smiling when I look at his face again.

"What?" I ask, tilting my head to the side while a blush settles on my cheek.

I wish I knew why it keeps coming back when he looks at me. I've never blushed this much in my entire life.

"I was talking to James yesterday, about you more specifically, and I said to him 'Man, I really wish Nevaeh would live here.' Did you hear that, *mon paradis*?" he asks, and I narrow my eyes.

"Did you just call me heaven in French? Is that what you've been calling me every time I didn't understand you?" I ask.

"Isn't that your name?" he challenges, and I shake my head, hating and adoring how it makes me feel when he calls me *mon paradis*.

"Stop calling me that," I say, and Adrian chuckles.

"No. I'll see you tomorrow."

And with that, he hangs up before I can respond.

He spoke to James Landon about me, wishing I'd move to Monaco.

Interesting.

A smile so bright it hurts dances onto my face, and I almost sigh. Every single time I think my love life gets less complicated, Adrian pulls me right back in.

Chapter 30

Adrian

Nevaeh is moving to Monaco, and I'm fucking giddy.

I haven't been able to get her out of my stupid head, especially since I've had her pressed against me. I've fucked my own hand more times than I should have thinking about Nevaeh grinding against me, but I was trying to make my dick tired so that when I see her today, it doesn't jump to attention.

I can't go back to high school where my cock got hard because a pretty girl smiled at me, no matter how beautiful Nevaeh looks when she smiles.

Then again, it's been a long time since I've had sex, and as Nevaeh appears in the pick-up area of the airport, I swear on my life, I've never seen a woman look so sweet and sexy at the same time. Her hair is wavy and all over the place, the summer dress she's wearing hugs her curves in a sinful way, and the look of concentration on her face is breathtaking.

She's breathtaking.

My dick seems to agree because *holy fucking hell*, it's never this easily woken up.

I lean against a nearby pillar, holding the sign I made her over my crotch area, just in case. It reads "*Ms. Nevaeh Fuchs.*" The hood of my sweatshirt rests on the cap on my head to make sure no one around us will recognize me. I've also made sure to be at the very far back, out of everyone's sight.

Everyone but Nevaeh's.

Her eyes catch me faster than I expected her to, almost like my very presence calls to her and she would be able to spot me anywhere. Butterflies—*fucking butterflies, can you believe it?*—appear in my stomach as she starts smiling and running toward me. I straighten out my back, getting ready to catch her. My heart hammers in my chest as she finally flings her arms around my neck. She sighs into my throat, so I hold on tighter, running a comforting hand down her back.

"Shitty flight?" I ask, and she lets out a humorless laugh. Her scent, something sweet and fresh, fills my nose as I place my cheek against her temple. She always smells so good, it's frustrating.

She's irresistible in every single way imaginable.

"Shitty day," she replies while I continue to rub her back. My hands eventually drop to her lower back so I can bring her body flush against mine.

"Did you eat something yet?" I ask, holding on as tightly as I can. She grabs my shirt like she doesn't want to let go either.

"If airplane lunch counts as food, yes." Her voice is full of emotion, and when I step back to cup her face and search for an answer, her eyes fill with tears. They spill down her cheeks, so I wipe them away with care. More follow, but I'm patient and wipe those away, too.

"What happened?" My question makes her shift in my hands, but she doesn't step away. "You don't have to tell me, but I will listen if you would like to share," I offer.

Nevaeh takes a deep breath, her hands moving onto my abdomen. Her gaze glues itself to my chest.

"My mother called me selfish for wanting to move here. She took the entire trip to the airport to tell me what a horrible daughter I am because she isn't ready for me to move out, but I'm leaving her anyway. I know she's guilt-tripping me, but it doesn't make it any easier," she explains, her tears slowing.

When she looks up at me, the pain in her eyes makes a stabbing sensation appear in my chest.

"You're twenty-one. You have every right to do with your life as you please. She doesn't have the right to tell you when you're allowed to move out. You have your own money, dreams, and career. This is *your* life. Not hers. You're allowed to live it any way you want to live it," I say, my grip on her face tightening slightly, only enough to make sure she's really understanding me. Her eyes flutter shut at my touch, and I fight every instinct telling me to lean down and kiss her.

This is definitely not the right moment.

"I still feel horrible," she admits, opening her eyes again.

"I know, but I have a solution for you," I say, grabbing her chin between my thumb and index finger. Her eyes are full of hope. "Spend the day with me. I'm incredible. I'll cheer you up in no time." She bursts into laughter, never breaking eye contact with me, and my heart almost flies out of my chest and straight into hers.

Have you ever had someone laugh and look straight at you? When pure joy filters through their eyes and they direct it all at you? When the whole world disappears and all that's left are you and the person you're with? Because that's exactly what Nevaeh is doing right now, and it's the most wonderful thing I've ever witnessed.

"I can't think of anything better than spending my day with you," she says, so I wrap her up in another hug, pressing my lips to her forehead without thinking.

"I'm going to take you to get some proper food," I say to stop myself from overthinking what I just did. I lean back, tugging a strand of hair behind her ear. "Does that sound good?" I ask, and she beams up at me.

Her happiness matters to me, but I've decided it's just because we're friends. That's all it is.

"You need to stop being so damn close to perfect, Romana," she warns, but the smiles remain on our faces.

My hands drop from her neck to her shoulders, squeezing a little because I really can't help myself. I love touching her. It's like a guilty pleasure I can't get enough of, that I don't want to get enough of.

"I have more than enough flaws, Fuchs," I assure her, watching her grin at the way I pronounce her last name perfectly. "You know, I looked up your last name and found out it means 'fox' in English. I read that foxes are quite playful," I state, and she cocks a brow.

Her hands drop from my body, but I wrap my fingers around her wrists to lift them. I inspect her nails for a moment.

"They can also retract their claws and extend them at will. That sounds like something you do, too," I tease with a smirk. Nevaeh returns it, but as I take a step closer, and bring my mouth toward hers, her breathing hitches. "I'm your prey, aren't I?" I ask, making her let out a shaky laugh.

She clears her throat, looking away from me as she fights another laugh.

"If you were, my claws would have already left marks on your back," she says with a wink, stepping back and breaking the contact between us.

I shake my head, letting it fall backward to look at the ceiling. I question whoever is up there why they brought Nevaeh Fuchs into my life if I'm not allowed to let her mark me as much as she would like.

"You're a tease, *mon ange*, and I told you how I feel about getting teased," I reply, grabbing her luggage and making my way to the parking lot.

If we don't put some distance between us, I might throw all of my rules out of the fucking window.

All this is between us is a flirty exchange, something I used to have with lots of other women, but there is something so special about Nevaeh for me, it doesn't feel the same. It feels like it means more, like I'm flirting with someone I want more than one night with, and that's fucking terrifying.

She just... she brightens up my life.

She makes me feel *so much*, all at once, and I don't ever want to let go of that.

"Why 'angel' out of all the things to call me?" she asks as we sit down in my Velocità Rossa.

I chose the Velocità Rossa 93 Web recently when I was looking for a new car. My grandfather has a whole collection, but I didn't take any of them with me when I moved out and into Gabriel's old apartment.

So, I went and bought myself this one instead. It's a matte black with a single orange stripe running over the hood of it.

Nevaeh's fingers trail over the smooth interior, tracing the door handle while she studies the car with an expression of awe. Over the last few months of us spending a lot of time together, I've come to realize just how expressive her face is. Whether she likes it or not, her features give everything away. If something displeases her, she wrinkles her nose. If something excites her, she grins with her whole face. If something fascinates her, her eyes sparkle with awe and curiosity.

If she's happy, her features start shining brighter than any star in the sky.

"Oof, I'm afraid that's my secret to keep," I reply, smiling at her one last time before putting the car into Drive.

Her head falls back against the headrest as she watches me maneuver out of the parking garage, so I do it a little more smoothly, more effortlessly.

We might be just friends, but I still want to impress her.

"You're boring," she complains when I don't give her an answer that satisfies her.

She's as beautiful as I imagine angels to be, so I call her *"mon ange."*

She feels like heaven to me, so I call her *"mon paradis."*

We drive for a while as she stares out of her window, taking in the road that leads to her new home country. Once we're in Monaco, she sits up a little straighter, studying everything. The buildings I've been around my entire life. The luxurious sight of it is simultaneously antique. Monaco is expensive, without a doubt, and it doesn't just look that way through all the rich people driving Lamborghinis, Velocità Rossas, Maseratis, and every other luxury brand you can think of.

It also *feels* that way.

"Are you okay?" I ask when I notice the corners of her mouth are downturned. Man, why is she still so beautiful when she's frowning?

"Yeah, why wouldn't I be?" She turns her head to look at me.

"I don't know, you just look serious," I say, poking her cheek and making her chuckle.

"I was thinking. You know what that is, right?" she teases.

I tilt my head to look at her for a brief moment before focusing on the road again. She's grinning like she knows exactly what she just did.

"Stop playing on my weakness, Nevaeh," I say, glancing at her once more to show her my smile.

Silence fills the car again, but when she looks out of her window, she's smiling. I made her smile.

See, there's a reason why I keep claiming I'm awesome. I make the people around me smile, and that's arguably one of the best traits a person can have.

"When am I going to see Val?" Nevaeh asks a while later, clearly remembering my sister was the one who was supposed to pick her up. Which Val wanted to do, but I had Gabriel steal all of her car keys so I could go to the airport instead.

"She had some things come up, but I will be joining you for your appointments," I promise.

"Oh no. If you're coming, every apartment is going to seem small. Your ego is going to take up all the space," she says, and I swear, I almost hear my heart screaming: *she's the one!*

And now I kind of want to jump out of a moving train.

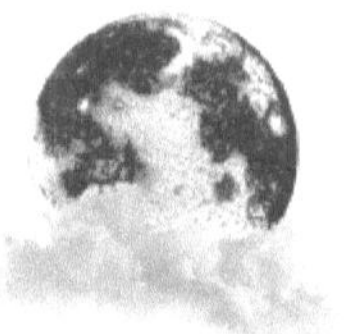

Nevaeh and I have looked at three different apartments, stopped for food, and laughed so much, I'm sure I will be sore tomorrow. None of the places we went to fit her needs, especially because of how expensive they were.

We have one last appointment for an apartment that Nevaeh told me is the cheapest out of all the ones she wanted to look at today. The landlord of the building greets us at the front desk, his eyes going wide when he sees me approaching.

"Mr. Romana, it is an honor to meet you," the short, balding man says in French and extends his hand for me to shake.

"It's a pleasure, but we're here for the lovely woman beside me, so if it's possible for us to speak in English so my friend understands, too, I would greatly appreciate it," I reply in French as I shake his hand, smiling with my usual level of charm.

"Of course, monsieur. Please, follow me." Nevaeh furrows her brows, asking me what that was all about with a single look, but I merely hold out my arm for her to take. She grins at me before lacing hers through mine, letting me lead her toward the apartment.

It's a small, two-room place with a large window at the far back. The bathroom is tiny, with a shower on the left followed by a sink and a toilet on the right. The hardwood floor in the room itself is light, just like the walls.

It's so small, I feel like throwing Nevaeh over my shoulder and carrying her out of the apartment and straight to mine.

But then I notice her spinning around once, smiling like she's never seen a more beautiful place to live. Compared to the rest of the apartments we saw, this one is a lot nicer and cheaper, so I get why Nevaeh looks at it with hearts in her eyes. Even though it's only two tiny rooms, she's in love with it.

"This apartment screams independence to me. It's close to work, in my price range, and I can picture how I would set up the space already," she mumbles, and I'm not quite sure if she's talking to me or herself.

"You could put your bed here," I reply anyway, and she turns to look at where I'm pointing.

"Yes, that's exactly where I'd put it, too," she says.

"Have a closet here and a shelf over there," I go on, pointing all over the apartment. She takes a step toward me, closing the distance between us until I can smell her intoxicating perfume again.

"Put a tall mirror next to the closet," she says, her eyes glued to my lips where I run my tongue over my bottom one.

"I'd place it in front of the bed," I say, smirking at her before clearing my throat to get the landlord's attention. "How much lower can you go on the rent?" I ask in French, and he shakes his head, not impressed by my question.

"I already went as low as I could, Mr. Romana. I cannot lower it more," he replies, but I turn on my charm again and within a minute, we're shaking hands once more.

"Alright, I managed to convince him to lower the rent by two hundred euros, but that's as far as he will go," I tell Nevaeh once the landlord leaves to get her a contract.

"What? Are you serious?" I nod.

Nevaeh covers her mouth with her hand, looking around the room again like she can't quite believe this is all happening. That it's real.

I know that look.

It's how I look at her.

The landlord, Nevaeh, and I go over a few more details before she signs the contract and he tells her she'll get the keys as soon as she makes her first rent payment. He leaves moments later to give us another few minutes to look around while Nevaeh moves toward the window, looking down at the people strolling by. I step toward her, keeping my distance even though wrapping my arms around her from behind is more than a little appealing.

She turns around, running straight into my chest. Okay, maybe I was standing a bit closer than I thought, but she's laughing, the sound light and happy. My arms are finally back around her so I can drag her against my chest again.

"Thank you," she mumbles, and I rub her back. "For coming with me and helping me get this apartment," she adds.

"You're very welcome." I pull her impossibly closer. "To be honest, this was also a very selfish move because now you're here, and I get to see you more often," I admit, making her step out of the embrace to nudge me. "Hey," I complain, my fingers poking her sides to make her giggle.

She attempts to walk away, but I grab her wrist gently, guiding her back against my chest. Our laughter fills the empty apartment, but when she lifts her chin so her mouth is closer to mine, I can't help but lower my lips. My nose brushes over hers, our breaths becoming one as I fight with myself.

"If I kiss you, would you hate me for it?" I find myself voicing the question without even thinking the words.

Nevaeh's breath trembles as it hits my lips, but she doesn't pull away. No. She takes a subtle step into me, lips almost brushing.

"I think it would do something more opposite, Adrian, so you really can't kiss me," she says, and yet, she still doesn't move away.

Not until another breathless moment passes and we both realize nothing can happen, not right now.

"We better hurry. Knowing my sister, she made dinner as a bribe for us to get back as soon as possible."

CHAPTER 31
Nevaeh

Gabriel is sharing a story from his childhood while we eat the food Valentina and he made. She smiles at her fiancé while he goes on to tell me about Jean, his brother, who is studying business. The love I see in Val's eyes and then in Gabriel's when he catches her staring at him turns my stomach upside down. I've never felt a love like theirs. I can't help but wonder how many people are lucky enough to experience it in their lives.

Adrian pulls me out of my thoughts as he guides my hair behind my shoulder, resting his head on his hand and watching me with half a smile.

"What?" I ask, and he looks down at his plate, a faint smirk on his full lips.

"I like having you here," he admits, and my stomach turns for an entirely different reason.

His eyes drift to his sister before he looks away again and clears his throat.

"Anyway, I should probably head home," Adrian says and sits up straight.

The words falling from my lips come out too fast for me to stop them.

"Take me with you."

Surprise laces his features, and when I check to see Val's and Gabriel's reactions, they have the same shock on their faces as Adrian.

I let out a nervous laugh before adding, "I'd love to see where you live."

Nothing is going to save me from this awkwardness. If anything, I'm only digging myself a deeper hole.

"And then I'll drive you back here later?" Adrian asks, obviously unsure what I want. I don't even know what I want. My first instinct was merely to spend more time with him because whenever I'm with him, I don't think about work, Mama, or anything else that makes my blood boil. I only see him, *feel* him.

"Sure. I mean, if you want."

Oh God, this is getting worse by the second.

A chuckle vibrates off his chest, and he grins with his tongue pressed against the inside of his cheek to hide his amusement. He stands up only to lean down and whisper something into my ear.

"If we start talking about what I want, *mon paradis*, then we're going to have a very simple conversation we're not allowed to have," he says and holds out his hand to help me up from my seat.

With a blush settling on my cheeks and my heart racing, I take it but keep my distance from him. Val and Gabriel have luckily moved on by making conversation with each other, which takes some of the embarrassment off my chest.

I attempt to pick up my plate, but Val frowns at me.

"You leave that plate where it is," she warns, and I raise my hands in surrender. "Good. I'll see you later."

Her face lets me know she doesn't think I'll be back, and, if I'm being honest with myself, I don't think so either.

Adrian grabs my hand and leads me back to his car. We don't speak the entire drive, but my heart pounds rapidly anyway. Nothing is going to happen between us, so why doesn't my body understand that? The drive to his apartment in Monte Carlo is short. There are lights all around us, and we pass the famous casino. I've never been a big fan of gambling, but since I'm moving here, I doubt I can get around going at least once. The city is buzzing with life. People are everywhere, enjoying the spring evening weather as it slowly turns to summer.

Adrian drives into the parking garage of his building, and we walk by a row of expensive cars. Grenzenlos, Porsche, Maserati, any luxury brand can be found here. I let out a low whistle when we pass by a baby blue Bugatti.

"No way," I blurt out and study the car more closely. Adrian stops and turns toward me, pointing at my camera bag.

"Do you want to take a picture?" he asks with a teasing grin, and I narrow my eyes before giving him a playful glare.

"No, I've just never seen a beauty like this one in real life before," I reply, and he lets out a hurt huff.

"You've met me," he defends, and I stop myself from face-palming my forehead.

"I stand by what I said," I assure him, and he lets out a groan that makes my heart skip a beat.

"Let's go before you frustrate me even further," Adrian points out while we're walking toward the elevator.

"How am I frustrating you?" I ask as the doors open and we step into the small confinement.

Adrian presses his floor, causing the machine to start up and take us there with a rumbling noise.

"The list is long. Would you like all the reasons or just the top two?" My jaw almost drops, but I manage to catch it before it hits the ground.

"Why are there so many?" I twist my head to study his face, but he's covering it with his hands.

"Okay, bottom of the list? You're stubborn in a way that makes me want to shake some sense into you sometimes. You pretend you're okay when you're unbelievably overwhelmed. You tease me even though I told you it turns me on. You have so much talent but doubt yourself anyway. And you didn't talk to me about how much it bothered you to see me with Melanie at the club," he says, and I struggle to find the breath he knocked out of me.

Adrian leads me out of the elevator and opens his apartment door. We walk inside while I wish I could focus on anything other than his words. He grabs my shoulders before his hands slide onto my neck, causing my eyes to close from his touch.

"Melanie and I slept together once, Nevaeh. She's very nice, but a little touchy, and thinks she might have another chance with me. She doesn't. I don't want her," Adrian explains, rubbing his thumbs along my cheeks.

My eyelids flutter open so I can look at his sincere expression.

"You don't have to justify yourself, Adrian. You're free to sleep with whomever you want. We're just friends," I say, but he cocks a brow, not believing me.

"It bothered you anyway, didn't it?" he asks, and I step out of his embrace. He watches me like a hawk, and my emotions spill out of me before I can stop them.

"Yes, it bothered me. I hated that she touched you. It made me jealous."

There is no anger in the way he looks at me. If anything, there's understanding, and that only frustrates me more.

"It bothers me, Adrian, so much, because I have no right to be jealous. We're friends. That's all we can be. There you go. All my secrets laid bare for you so you can hate me or be upset with me," I say and run my hands over my face.

"I also don't want you to touch anyone who isn't me, let alone have someone else touch you," he admits, his hands lifting to my hips to drag me closer.

His mouth falls back down to mine, his lips almost brushing mine when we're interrupted by the sound of my ringtone filling the room. I take it out of my pocket to turn off the jerk who destroyed what could have been the moment Adrian and I first kissed when my heart sinks into my stomach.

Lincoln's name flashes on my screen, causing Adrian to step away from me.

"Answer it. He'll be worried if you don't," the Monegasque says before leaving the room.

I hit Answer, concern stretching through me. We haven't spoken in a long time, and now he calls me. Something's not right. What if it's Elena? What if something happened to my parents? Anxiety spreads through me, taking me captive until I'm wheezing out a breath.

"Lincoln? What's wrong?" I ask, covering my stomach with my hand.

The silence on the other side makes me nauseous.

"'What's wrong?' I'll goddamn tell you what's wrong, Nevaeh. You're in Monaco looking at apartments because you're moving there and didn't tell me? Are you kidding me? We don't speak and you decide to fucking leave the country to avoid me?"

Relief floods through me.

"First of all, calm down. That's not the reason I'm moving. My boss offered me a job here, and I took it. It has nothing to do with you, and we're not on speaking terms," I say quietly, softly, keeping my anger at bay and also trying to avoid Adrian from hearing how angry Lincoln makes me.

"Why are you speaking so quietly?" Of course, that's what he wants to focus on. I'm about to respond when he draws his own conclusion. "Oh my God, you're with Adrian, aren't you?" he asks, and I let my silence answer his question. "I see how it is. I'm sorry I interrupted date night—" I have to stop him right then and there.

"You're impossible, Linc, absolutely impossible. I'm sick and tired of you pretending to have some fucking claim on me. I'm not yours and never will be," I remind him, but he lets out a harsh laugh. "I didn't want to let go of you for a long time, Lincoln, because you were my best friend for my whole childhood, but this is toxic. You are toxic for me, and I don't want to have you in my life anymore," I reply and hang up before he can yell at me again.

As I raise my head, I notice Adrian walking out of what I assume is his bedroom and leaning against the door frame.

"Are you okay?" he asks, and I let out a deep breath, which sounds more like a sigh.

"Some people in my life want to make things more difficult than they need to be. Lincoln is one of those people," I explain honestly, earning a small smile from the tall blonde.

"But you love him," Adrian points out, and I almost laugh.

"I don't remember my life before him. He was my best friend for a long time, and I love that version of him, but this version, the one who has to fight with me about everything and chose silence as a solution, is not someone I share those feelings for," I say and shift my weight from one foot to the other.

Adrian's gaze is on me as he crosses his arms in front of his chest.

"Lincoln hasn't learned how to properly treat a woman he's interested in yet, and it shows in his behavior toward you," Adrian states, shaking his head in disapproval.

"You deserve someone who knows what he wants but doesn't make you feel like shit when he can't get it," he goes on, and I finally manage a smirk.

"Hmmm, I wonder who you could possibly mean?" I say sarcastically, making him chuckle as he pushes off the wall. "The good thing is, I'm way too busy for a relationship. Plus, drivers are off-limits," I say and step past him and toward his balcony.

"For now," he mumbles from behind me, and I smile.

The view is breathtaking. The sea is straight ahead with countless yachts at the harbor. Lights highlight the buildings on each side of us, but it's quite dark where we're standing. Adrian hung a few lights on the railing, and there is light brown outdoor furniture with a cocoon patio chair on the very left. It's cozy and elegant at the same time.

"I've always wanted one of these," I admit as I move toward the cocoon chair.

It's quite large, enough to fit at least three people. My fingers trail over the woven material as Adrian walks past me and sits down, pulling me with him. I fall onto his chest and let out a wholehearted laugh. We shift around until I'm on my back with my head resting on his thigh so I can look up at him while he stares down at me. His fingers push my hair from my face before his thumb runs over my bottom lip, sending shivers down my back.

"You're very smooth, Mr. Romana, I'll give you that," I say and Adrian's body shakes with a laugh, his other hand moving onto my stomach. I suck in a sharp breath, and he immediately removes it.

"I'm sorry," he says, but I'm already reaching for his hand to place it back on my body.

He smiles down at me, but my eyes close as he traces the shape of an eight along the exposed skin on my hip bone. I feel the ache grow between my legs as his finger continues to work its magic on me. He should stop, and I should tell him to, but that's the last thing I want right now.

The back of his hand runs over my cheek before his index finger follows a path from one of my freckles to the next until he's touched almost all of them. My head lifts in the direction of his hand when he removes it, making him furrow his brows.

"Nevaeh, do you normally kiss your friends?" he asks quietly, his voice strained even as he tries to laugh and lighten the mood.

Everything inside of me is yelling to guide his head down and press my lips against his, everything but my head. My head reminds me of work, my fear of failure, my parents and their expectations, of the life I'm working toward.

"I really like you, Adrian. Kissing you has been on my mind since we first met, but everything's too complicated, and you deserve better than that. You deserve easy," I say, looking away from him.

"*Mon beau paradis* Nevaeh, you should start focusing on what you deserve instead of worrying about me."

A tear falls down my cheek.

"If you don't know, I will gladly tell you. You deserve someone who thinks of you first. You deserve someone who doesn't fight with you every chance they get. You deserve someone who sees beyond your outer beauty and realizes how priceless you are on the inside, too. You deserve someone who knows all of your smiles. Who would wait for you no matter how long. Who'd fight themself to make you happy."

I move off him and toward my bag.

I can't take this, any of it.

"Nevaeh," Adrian pleads, but I'm already by the front door.

"No, Adrian, I can't—" I cut off and cover my face with my hands.

I have no idea what I'm doing, and I'm so scared I'm making the wrong choices, scared I'll lose another dream, turn my parents against me, and ruin my reputation as a reporter.

Adrian's fingers wrap around my wrist to remove my hands and reveal my tear-stained face. Confusion and panic decorate his gorgeous features, and I feel my knees give in a little. Adrian shouldn't be dragged along while I figure my shit out, it's not fair.

"I can't give you what you want," I say, but he merely smiles at me.

"You're so stubborn. Have you ever asked me what I want?" he asks and moves me from side to side to cheer me up, but it doesn't help.

"It doesn't matter. I can't give you anything," I reply.

"I want to be friends, Nevaeh. Do you know when the last time was that I had as much fun as today?" he says, and I bring my gaze to him, waiting for him to tell me. "It was three years ago when I beat James' ass in table tennis while he was drunk. He could barely stand, and I took advantage of it, aiming for his body every time I hit the ball," he explains, and I start laughing. "Like you said, all we can be right now is friends, and I'd much rather be your friend than a stranger you fuck once. Don't make assumptions, and for the love of God, please don't push me away because of them."

He lets out a deep breath, his eyes drifting to the mirror on the wall behind him. Adrian sticks his ass out and frowns.

"You know, since you laughed at me for having a flat butt, Daniel's been helping me build muscle."

For some reason, a roar of laughter escapes me, and I have to sit down on the ground to catch my breath.

"No, you haven't," I blurt out, but my words are barely audible.

"Yes, I have been, but I don't see progress yet," he complains, and I have to concentrate really hard not to pee myself. This man is unbelievable.

Finally, I manage to calm down enough to see he's settled down in front of me.

"Oh my God, Adrian, you have a great ass, please don't be insecure," I say and wipe the tears of laughter away.

"Fine, but only if you watch a movie with me," he replies and stands up, holding out his hands to help me get up, too. I take them, but, this time, he doesn't linger. "Actually, come with me, I'm going to show you something else first."

Adrian grabs my hand to lead me to the room next to his bedroom. I assumed it was for guests, but in it stands a piano. The white, upright instrument rests against the wall, but apart from a bookshelf on the opposite side and a couch to the right, the room is empty.

"When I was younger, I used to take piano lessons, but I stopped for a while. I've been practicing again since I moved into this apartment. This is the only thing I have that no one really knows about," he explains. "People tend to make things about themselves or blow it out of proportion or start expecting things I don't want to give them like writing my own music or some shit. So, I kept this a secret, wanted this to be just mine," he adds while walking toward his piano and carefully pushing me onto the bench in front of it.

"Why are you sharing this with me?" I ask and watch him as he settles down next to me.

"Because in a moment, you will look at me with that smile of awe that makes your eyes glow, and I'd give anything to see it as often as possible," Adrian says, his fingers running over the keys as he hesitates. "I also know that I can trust you, and I haven't trusted a woman apart from Val since my mom left," he goes on, his eyes shifting to my face.

Pain is written all over his features, which makes some shoot through my chest. I run my fingers over his cheek and study the way his eyes close in response.

"Your trust is safe with me. I'll keep it in my heart and fight off anyone that comes close to it," I promise, and he opens his eyes again to look at me, giving me a warm smile.

Adrian feels the keys for another moment before running his fingers over them, creating a soft melody that instantly warms my insides. He's precise about every single note, but I've never heard this song before. I pay close attention, feeling that expression of awe that he was talking about spreading over my entire face until the smile settles deep within my chest. I see one spreading over his face when he looks at me.

A few minutes pass of him playing, but I almost complain when he comes to an end. I could listen to him forever.

"That was beautiful," I say, but he takes a deep breath, looking uncertain and a little like he's in pain.

"Let's go watch a movie." I can sense sharing even one song with me took him stepping out of his comfort zone by a mile, so I nod and stand up, following him out of his private room.

We walk into his bedroom where everything is neat and in its proper place, as if no one lived in here. There isn't a sock anywhere where it shouldn't be.

I place my fists on my hips and tilt my head his way.

"Did you know I was coming and cleaned up?" I ask, but he brushes it off by blowing out a breath like that's the most ridiculous sentence he's ever heard.

"You really think you're *that* special?" He imitates my position by putting his hands on his hips as well. I laugh again.

"We both know I am, and we both know you cleaned up in case we went to your apartment." I cock a challenging brow, and he chuckles at my words.

"I'll have you know, I'm a very clean person in general," he says.

"But you went the extra mile for me." I fill in what he isn't saying, making him grin.

"Fine, yes, I cleaned for you. Happy now?" he asks, and I give him a satisfied nod.

"Yes."

Adrian and I agree on *Captain America: The Winter Soldier* since it's in both of our top ten Marvel movies and he's been meaning to rewatch it for a while now. I lie down on his bed, but he stands on the other side for a moment, his eyes fixated on me.

"What? Did you want me to lie somewhere else?" I ask and sit up, but he shakes his head, a puzzled look on his face.

"No, right there works," he assures me and settles down next to me.

I brush off his strange behavior and focus on the television. Chris Evans jogs onto the screen, and I feel myself inching closer toward Adrian. Noticing, he grabs my hand and brings me to his chest so I can lie my head on it, listening to his quick heartbeat.

I make him nervous. We make each other nervous.

Jesus, I'm bending the rules so far, they could crack any second. If things didn't feel so right with Adrian, I would have stopped this before we got here, but I couldn't. Considering the way his body responds to my proximity, he probably didn't want me to either.

At this point, I'm not even playing with fire anymore, it's something beyond that.

Adrian's fingers run through my hair, messaging my aching head and calming my racing thoughts.

"I've never had a woman sleep in my bed before," Adrian blurts out halfway through the movie.

"Is that your way of telling me to leave?" I ask with a laugh, tilting my head to look up at him. He meets my gaze, his thumb lifting to my lips to trace them. To study them. To memorize them.

"No, I don't want you to leave, Nevaeh, and that terrifies me if I'm being honest," he says, taking a deep breath before he adds, "And while I'm already being honest, you are the most beautiful woman I've ever laid my eyes on, inside and out, and if you stay with me tonight, I doubt I'll ever get over it."

He smiles down at me, pulling my bottom lip down just to release it again and watch it bounce back into place.

"So fucking beautiful, I can't believe you're real," he whispers, biting his bottom lip as he traces my face with his gaze.

"I'd tell you you're the most handsome man I've ever seen, too, but I think your ego is already taking up too much space. Can't let it get any bigger," I tease, and his grin brightens up his entire room, leaving nothing but a ray of sunshine in its wake.

"One day, when I'm allowed, I'm gonna kiss you for every single time you teased me. I'm keeping track, you know. You already owe me ten kisses." The smile stretching my lips wide is out of my control, but even if I could stop it, I wouldn't.

"Is that right? And how long do you plan on waiting for me, Mr. Romana?" I ask, my hand running over his muscular chest. He grabs it, lifts it to his lips, and presses a single kiss to my pulse point.

"As long as it takes."

And with that, he slips down on his bed to position me in the crook of his arm and guide me to his chest. His heart is racing so fast, I can almost feel his fear with every beat. Everything about what we're doing isn't just new for me. It's new for him, too, and it scares him.

And yet, he doesn't push me away. He drags me impossibly closer, his lips brushing my forehead as he cuddles me while we finish our movie.

"I'll wait forever if I have to," is the last thing I hear him say before I fall asleep in the arms of the first person I've ever allowed to hold me this way when I'm at my most vulnerable.

CHAPTER 32
Adrian

I'VE NEVER BEEN so scared in my entire life. The way Nevaeh feels in my arms is... I don't have words, to be honest. I just love it. So much. I love that I get to study the way her breathing turns even as she falls asleep. The way she nuzzles her nose into the crook of my neck to be surrounded by my scent. The way she is smiling a little as she dreams.

It scares and fascinates me so much, I don't sleep the whole night. Nope, not a fucking wink. Instead, I lie there with Nevaeh cuddling me and study her like a creep. As Gabriel told me he sometimes does with Valentina because it overwhelms him how much he cares for her to the point where he can't sleep.

I almost shudder when I realize that's exactly how I feel right now. I like her so much, I don't know what to do with myself. I can't sleep, can't even comprehend she's here with me. Every single barrier I've carefully built and reinforced with more and more cement my entire life is crumbling to the ground like they were all made out of crackers.

At six in the morning, I give up. Daniel's gonna kick my ass for not sleeping after he made me work out for three hours yesterday morning, but there's no point trying to achieve something that's not happening right now.

So, I slip out of bed as carefully as I can and leave a note for Nevaeh, telling her I'll send Val to pick her up later. I need to get rid of all this energy.

And I need to talk to a friend right now.

Using my spare key, I unlock the front door to my grandfather's house half an hour later. I make my way up the stairs as quietly as I can, knocking carefully on Val and Gabriel's bedroom door.

When no one responds and I'm sure they're still asleep, I open the door and say, "*Psssst.*"

Chase jumps out of bed and runs toward me, wagging and going wild at the sight of me. I crouch down to pet him, smiling at how excited he is to see me. God, I love this little guy. Ever since Val found him at the side of the road and brought him home, I adored him, and he seems to love me too, excitement making the Husky-German Shepherd mix jump against my legs when he sees me.

"I swear to God, one of these days, I'm going to kill you for always doing that," Gabriel whisper-screams at me, sitting upright and squinting while looking at me because he's still half asleep.

"Can you kill me while we go have some hot chocolate and play a game of cards?" I ask, trying to stay quiet so as to not wake Valentina.

For almost a year, Gabriel and I have made a habit of coming to each other in the middle of the night to hang out and talk about whatever bothers us. We usually play cards and drink hot chocolates. I've come to speak to get him for one of our talks a lot more often than he's come to me, but I don't feel bad like I would with most people. Gabriel and I might be teammates and rivals, but he's my brother in every way that counts, and I need him right now. If I'm being honest, I also need my sister, but I know exactly what she'll say to me.

Give love a chance.

Relationships can be worth it.

Nevaeh is wonderful, she won't leave like Mom did.

None of that will help me right now, and I need to speak to someone who understands how scared I am. Gabriel was frightened out of his mind when he realized he was in love with Valentina. It made him push her away, and if my sister wasn't so deeply in love with him, I doubt he could have gotten over his fear of letting someone in.

My sister's always been stronger than both of us in that regard. Yes, she was scared too after all of our grief, but she figured her shit out a hell of a lot quicker than Gabriel or I did and have.

"Let's go, Adrian," Gabriel says, sliding out of the bed when Val grabs his arm and sits up a little, looking around to find me in the door frame.

"Adrian? Are you okay?" she asks, worry creasing her forehead.

"Yeah, all good, Val. Just need to talk to Gabriel for a bit," I say, and she releases her fiancé immediately, nodding several times as she clearly processes my words.

"Okay, I'm here if you need me," Val replies, readjusting herself until she's facing me. Her eyes are still closed, but I know she's awake enough for what I'm about to say.

"Can you go to my place and pick up Nevaeh later?" This makes her eyes pop open and even though she's barely awake, she has enough energy to shoot me a disapproving look.

"You left her at your apartment all by herself?" When I don't answer, merely tense up from her words, my sister scoffs. "I knew you were stupid when it comes to relationships, but I didn't think you were that dumb. At least tell me she isn't sleeping in your bed," Val adds, sitting up and wiping a hand down her face.

Chase runs toward her now that she's awake, and she pets his head as she waits for my answer.

"I left her a note," I defend, but my sister looks at me with a combination of disbelief and shock.

"I know you're new to this, but you don't leave a woman you have feelings for, who asked to go to your apartment and you took into your bed in there by herself," Val says as she stands up, stumbling around her room to pick up some clothes.

"How do you know she's in my bed?" I ask, surprise making my heart beat a little faster.

"Because at dinner yesterday, you looked at Nevaeh like you finally get it. Like it all makes sense now, and she gave you the same look in return." My sister grabs a towel before stepping in front of me with a sympathetic smile.

"I don't know how not to be afraid of my feelings," I admit, and my little sister nods like she understands because she does. She understands me better than anyone, except maybe Gabriel.

"Do you want to know why I let her in? Why I chose to make myself vulnerable, Adrian? It isn't just because I think she is one of the most incredible people I've ever met, which she is. But I let her in because the way you look at her like she's the very oxygen in a room is something I didn't want you to lose. I let her in so you'd see she's worth trusting, and she is."

Val pauses to look at Gabriel, who sees something in her face that has him closing the distance between them.

"I know you're not allowed to date her because of her job, but so what? All the best people are worth waiting for," she goes on as Gabriel wraps his arms around her and presses a kiss to her temple.

"I told her last night I'd wait for her, however long it takes," I mumble. Val beams up at me in response and Gabriel snickers to himself. I slap his shoulder to get him to stop, but he only bursts out laughing. "I don't know why you're laughing. You're the fucking reason why I'm like this with all of your 'Oh, I'm so good at expressing my feelings. I'm a fucking ray of sunshine for my fiancée because I remind her how much I love her every second of the day' bullshit." Gabriel cocks an unimpressed yet slightly amused brow while I rant.

"Alright, let's go. We're not playing cards today. We're going for a run to help you get rid of all of your pent-up frustration," Gabriel says, smacking me on the shoulder before kissing Val once and leaving his bedroom to go get ready.

My sister's eyes meet mine.

"I'll go to your apartment to get her here, but please, don't run from Nevaeh, big brother. She could be so good for you if you just let her, even if it'll take some time for the both of you to get there. She won't be forbidden from dating you forever," Val says, pressing a swift kiss to my cheek and disappearing into the bathroom too.

I'm a fucking idiot for being here instead of with Nevaeh right now, aren't I?

"I've never seen you so motivated to work out," Gabriel teases as we make our way down the same trail I've taken a thousand times in my life.

"I'm leading the championship at the moment. I have to be on the top of my game," I reply with a breathless laugh.

"Yeah and that goddamn Lincoln Nash is right behind us in the points, too," Gabriel complains, and anger boils inside of me. Not because the rookie threatens me. I'm going to beat him, but I hate him. I hate him for being such a spoiled little asshole. For upsetting Nevaeh. For upsetting Nevaeh.

Wait, I listed that twice.

Whatever, it should be there twice. Once is not enough to describe how much it pisses me off that he's hurt her feelings, over and over. That he thinks he has some weird claim on her. God, I hate him.

"So, you told her you'd wait for her, huh?" Gabriel says, throwing a smug smile my way.

"Fuck off." I'm even more out of breath now than before and it's definitely not because I'm thinking about Nevaeh.

"I think it's nice. I'm proud of you for taking such a big step," Gabriel goes on as we make our way down the slope leading toward one of Val's favorite cafés.

"Don't be proud of me. It feels like I'm going to spontaneously combust any second." That makes him laugh.

"Whether you realize it or not, you've taken a million steps toward Nevaeh already. You may have taken a thousand backward, too, but I want you to acknowledge the forward ones. You hug her, protect her, seek out her affection, and *let* her give it to you. You took her to your place and she spent the night. You brought her *home* when you've never brought anyone to your grandfather's house. You fight for her, even if you don't see it."

Gabriel stops in front of the café my sister loves, slipping his hand into his pocket to retrieve his wallet.

"Sometimes, it's all about the little things," Gabriel adds before walking inside and ordering my sister's favorite drink, clearly making his point.

Once we bought coffee for all of us and an iced chocolate drink I got for Nevaeh, my future brother-in-law and I make our way back home. The sun is burning my skin, making sweat trickle down my spine. My t-shirt sticks uncomfortably to my body, so I take it off and shove it into my pocket.

When we get back to the house, my sister's voice comes from the pool area.

"Gabriel is..." Val trails off for a moment, and I almost hear the smile in her voice. "He's one of the best Formula One drivers to ever walk this Earth, but he's humble and sweet, too. Don't let his angry game-face intimidate you. He's a big softie on the inside."

"You make me sound too nice, *ma chérie*." We join them by the pool when my breathing catches in my throat at the sight of Nevaeh.

In a bikini.

In. A. Fucking. Bikini.

I might have to sit down or take a cold shower or both.

What I definitely need is to stop staring at her where she's lying on one of the lounge chairs with her arms and legs stretched out to show off her curves. Her body is barely covered by the bikini, and she's so, so gorgeous, I don't even know what to do with myself. All the blood rushes south and my heart hammers as I study the swell of her breasts, her thick thighs, her generous hips, her wavy hair all over the place, and finally, the warm smile tugging at the corners of her mouth.

Her eyes trail over my bare chest in the same way I was ogling her, waking me up. No matter how distracted I am by the fact that I very much want to move between her legs and pull her bikini bottoms to the side to get a taste right now, I owe her an apology for leaving this morning.

"Hi," she says, grinning up at me like seeing me brings her the most joy in the world.

"Hi, *déesse*," I reply, handing her the drink I got her. She thanks me and smiles before remembering what I just said.

"What is it with all the French nicknames? I don't even know what this one means," she complains, forcing a low chuckle out of me.

"Trust me, the nickname I used just now expresses exactly what I thought when I saw you lying over there." Because she is a goddess. At least in my eyes.

The goddess of heaven, perhaps, just like her name claimed her to be.

She sits up and crosses her arms under her chest, pouting playfully at me, but I'm hanging on to the thinnest of threads of my self-control because her breasts are almost spilling out of her little top. I'm not gentleman enough to keep my gaze averted entirely, and she knows it, which is probably why she laughs at me.

"Then again, *démon* would probably be more accurate," I tease, entranced by the way she runs her tongue over her bottom lip. "Alright, that's enough," I say and take her drink away, placing it beside her lounge chair before lifting her into a standing position.

"What are you doing?" she asks with a laugh, but I don't respond, merely guide her toward the pool.

Sensing what I'm about to do, she tries to fight me, but she's laughing so hard, she has no more energy to be stronger than me. I throw her in with ease, watching as the water envelops her within seconds.

Val and Gabriel snicker.

Nevaeh resurfaces, sucking in a sharp breath.

"Adrian, I think I scraped my knee when you threw me in. It burns," Nevaeh says, her face pulled into a pain-filled grimace, making a wave of panic crash through me.

"Fuck, *mon ange*, I'm so sorry," I say, stepping toward the edge of the pool to help her out.

She lets me, but as soon as she's out of the water, she turns us around and pushes me in instead. A laugh bursts out of me underwater, but I push up to reach the surface and get back to Nevaeh.

"You play dirty," I say, wiping my face to get my hair off my forehead.

"You started it," she reminds me as I push out of the pool and stand in front of her. She swallows hard once I'm barely a centimeter away, my chest brushing against hers.

"Yeah, and if it were up to me, you'd be the one finishing," I say low enough to make sure only she hears me. Her gaze attaches to my lips, her chest brushing against mine with every fast breath of hers.

"I think you missed a word there," she replies, so I flash her an innocent smile.

"Well, English isn't my first language," I explain, and she nods several times as if that explains it. "Then again, I grew up bilingual from the age of three."

A nervous laugh bubbles out of her as I reach behind her for the towel she was lying on, wrapping it around her shoulders. Her cheeks are pink, but she's still grinning at me, and it's at this moment that I wonder if buying all of *Griffin Sports* to get rid of the no-dating-driver's rule is a little too extreme.

"I'm sorry I left this morning. It won't happen again," is what I apparently decide on instead of telling her I'm thinking about buying the company she works for so she can date me, which would be highly inappropriate for many reasons.

"Yeah, because I'm never sleeping in your bed again. It's unprofessional," she says, holding the towel closer to her body.

"We'll see," I reply with a wink before making my way inside and allowing myself to take a deep, full breath.

I'm about to go upstairs to shower when my sister's voice fills my ears.

"Nevaeh?" she starts, sounding serious. "It's great to prioritize your career, I did too, but you shouldn't fight your feelings either. Life is about more than work."

My sister is my favorite person for many reasons. This is one of them.

"Plus, secrets can be fun when they don't harm anyone," Val says, the sound of her and Nevaeh's chuckle making me smile.

I'd be Nevaeh's secret any day of the year.

CHAPTER 33
Nevaeh

PAPA HANDS ME SOME tape for the box I'm holding shut at the bottom. I release the flaps to find the beginning of the tape on the roll, groaning when I run my fingers over it five times without any luck. I give it back to Papa, who smiles at my incapability to do such a small task when a moment ago I was basically lifting half of my bed off the floor to look for a missing sock.

He instructs me to close the box again so he can fasten it for me. An unspoken question lingers on his features the entire time.

No, you started without me? Aileen signs, running over to me and wrapping her arms around my neck. I hug her back, smelling the familiar vanilla scent emanating from her. *I can't believe you're leaving me alone with that sister of yours,* she playfully complains, and I let out a short laugh as sadness creeps into my chest while she pulls me into another hug.

Leaving my family is the only bad thing about this move.

You're always welcome to visit me when she gets on your nerves, I offer after stepping out of the hug to look at her. Her brown eyes filled with tears. Guilt consumes me in return. This is the most selfish thing I've ever done, but I hope they will forgive me for it.

How many times can I come to visit? she asks, and I chuckle. She spins around to look at my father, her black, curly hair almost hitting my face. *Rob, you promised I could turn this room into a Nevaeh shrine, and I need you to keep your word,* Aileen signs, and I almost choke on my own breath.

"Oh my God, what?" I ask, but my sister's girlfriend waves my words away with her hand. She's waiting for a response from Papa.

"Of course, I'm keeping my word. I'll even help you build it," he replies, moving his hands to form the words, and I grin.

You're both so weird, is all I say before concentrating on packing my clothes and jewelry into a box.

Aileen neatly folds my things before placing them in my suitcase. I will be flying to Monaco tomorrow morning to drop off my things, then catch another plane to Australia in the evening. Luckily, Adrian and I both have a layover in Frankfurt, which means we will be traveling together from there on.

"Oh no, did I miss the fun part?" Nova asks once we're all done.

She drops onto my bed, grabbing Aileen's hand as she falls. My sister has never been one for physical touch to display affection, but it's different with Aileen, and it makes me smile every time. Nova is so in love with her girlfriend, it's the cutest thing in the world.

"Are you not taking your paintings?" Nova asks. I look at the art that had me in tears a few months ago.

"No, I won't have space on the walls, and I don't want to go through the trouble of sending a painting. It would be too expensive," I explain, a pain shooting through my heart as I do.

Papa puts a hand on my shoulder and squeezes to reassure me everything will be fine. The question from earlier is still on his face, and I finally cave.

"You're going to get more gray hairs holding back what you want to ask me," I say with a smile. "Not that it would be obvious, but—" Papa cuts off my teasing by tickling my sides. I jump out of his reach after letting out a horrendous squeal.

"You should show me more respect," he says and signs with a glare I don't buy.

You're right. After all, you always taught me to respect my elderly, I sign back and run around the bed to get out of his reach. Nova and Aileen are crying from laughter, and I join them while my father smiles.

"It's a good thing you're moving out, Nevaeh. You're too mean," he complains but ends up grinning as he looks down at my boxes in front of him. It fades quickly as a serious expression causes his features to drop. "Your mother isn't really at the nail salon," he starts, and I feel my heart sink. Mama told me she couldn't help me pack because she had an appointment. "She's at Elena's," Papa says, making me sigh.

"Avoiding me," I add, and he nods. "Why are you telling me that?" I ask, unable to come up with a good enough reason why he couldn't just leave me in the unknown. It was painful enough before, I didn't need to know this.

"Because I need you to do something for me, and you're not going to like it." I raise a brow. "You two need to have dinner by yourselves tonight."

He's right, I don't want to do this. Mama is only going to tell me how disappointed she is, and I'll have to convince her what a great choice I'm making.

Since she's even more stubborn than I am, that's an impossible task.

"Fine, but you owe me a big bowl of gummy bears," I reply and lift my hair up to tie it into a ponytail.

Deal, he signs, and I look at Nova and Aileen, who are already staring at me. I widen my eyes and then roll them, making them laugh. I wish they could come to dinner, too, but Papa's right. I have to be the one to talk to Mama without any distractions or influences from other people.

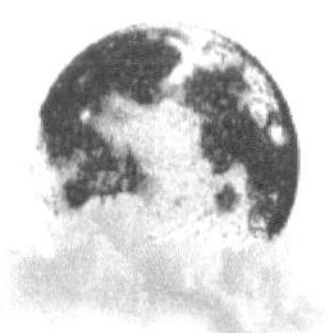

Mama hasn't said a word to me since we sat down at the dinner table. I've tried making conversation multiple times, but she hasn't responded once with anything other than an "mhmm."

"Alright, Mama, I know this is incredibly hard for you, but can you put yourself in my shoes for one minute and see how difficult it is for me? After my injury, I was lost, and now that I'm finally doing well and starting to be happy, my own mother is solely thinking about herself. Why can't you see that this is the right thing for me to do?" I ask while she watches my mouth move with every word.

"I think you're being selfish," she mumbles, picking at her broccoli and avoiding my furious gaze.

"And I think you're being selfish. So, where does that leave us?" Her blue eyes lift back up to my face before she makes my blood boil with her next question.

"It leaves us with this question: are you moving to Monaco because of Adrian Romana?"

I'm going to lose my mind before this dinner is even over. Right now, I'd actually love nothing more than to be with him, but I won't tell her that.

It'll only convince her that she's right.

"Adrian didn't even come to mind when my bosses offered me the job in Monaco. My life doesn't revolve around men, Mama, even if it may include them."

She scoffs at my response.

"Please, you've let them control your actions and decisions for years." This makes me sigh, and not a surface-level sigh either, but a deep one that has been brewing since I first told her about my move.

"How? How have I done that?" My curiosity gets the better of me, and, for now, I let it. I'd like to hear whatever story she has come up with in her head.

"You started pursuing tennis because your father told you you'd make it far. You allowed Lincoln to control your emotions for years and only recently, it made you disrespectful toward guests in this house, young lady. Now, that Adrian guy has you moving to Monaco, doing free-lance type of work when you should be working in a team, and a lot more you probably don't tell me about."

Wow, that's a lot of imaginary facts to take in. I swallow down the angry words lingering on my tongue.

I neatly place the cutlery next to my plate, taking another deep breath.

"I started pursuing tennis because I was in awe of the strength the women showed in their battles for greatness. I didn't let Lincoln control my emotions. It was pain and anger that did. Lastly, I am not, and listen closely here, moving to Monaco for Adrian Romana. He and I are friends, just like I'm friends with Valentina and Gabriel." I push my chair back and stand up, my heart aching from her negativity.

Mama's eyes flood with tears, but she still glares at me.

"You can lie to yourself all you want, but your selfishness will be your biggest mistake. When you realize that, when you want to come home begging for forgiveness because you messed up, don't count on me being there. I've warned you, and you have decided to ignore me. You choose this path, and I'll not wait around for you to come crawling back, which you will. Your father may baby you and hand-feed you as if you were still a child, but I won't," she says.

"What the hell is that supposed to mean?" I ask, but my mother just shakes her head.

I take a deep breath to fight back my anxiety. There's a reason I hate confrontation. That reason is standing right in front of me. My entire life, I've never been allowed to be upset, angry, my own person outside of this family. I've been told to be a good child who does everything she's told because my father had an image to protect. Being in the spotlight of Formula One means he has a reputation he carefully crafted over the years. If one of his daughters were to do something stupid, like discredit herself as a journalist for falling for the most beautiful and seemingly perfect Formula One driver, it would reflect badly on him.

And it isn't just this, it's everything we did as kids. It's throwing a tantrum in a grocery store. It's not wanting to dress up in outfits that made me feel like I was dressed in layers of duct tape. It's not finding a job for months after I've finished university.

My fear of failure isn't something my mind invented as a fun way to mess with me. It was born out of familial expectations, taking away things I wanted and replacing them with things I was supposed to want.

My mother used to yell at me and send me to my room as a child when I didn't know what to do with all of the feelings I had. For a long time, I thought parents were supposed to do that, but after going to therapy, I realized it wasn't. Parents aren't supposed to punish their children for having feelings they don't agree with. They aren't supposed to punish their children for not playing the role that they came up with in their own heads. They aren't supposed to send you away when you're telling them you're upset because they hurt your feelings. But they did. Even with Lincoln, they dismissed my hurt and focused on how I wasn't the perfect daughter who just got along with a family friend.

So, I stopped being honest with my mother. I shut my mouth and fought my hardest for a job I didn't even want because they kept pushing me toward it. They were the ones who told me to apply. I would have been fine finding something else, a job not in my field while I waited for a journalism company to open a spot in my department.

But they didn't want me to waste my time in a retail position. And I didn't want to risk disappointing them.

If my mother wants to blame anyone for the decisions I've made over the course of my life, she can blame herself because all I've ever done, every decision I've made, was in accordance with what they deemed was acceptable for me to do.

"Mama, I don't want to fight anymore. Can we please find a way to figure this out?" I ask, watching her stand up.

"*You're* sick of fighting? Well, how do you think I feel? You're the one who's breaking my heart and all you can talk about is yourself. I gave up everything to raise you. My job, my time, and this is the thanks I get. An ungrateful daughter who just *leaves*," she says and starts crying as she storms off without speaking to me again.

This isn't the first time she's given this speech either. Like I asked her to give up her life to raise me. Like I *forced* her to. I almost laugh at the absurdity of her throwing this at my head when I'm doing everything my parents ever wanted from me. I'm making a name for myself. I'm succeeding, in a way, at my new job. I'm doing what I thought they wanted me to, so I can't fathom how she could be so angry with me.

I love my parents, but, sometimes, I never want to see them again.

CHAPTER 34
Adrian

NEVAEH IS SITTING IN one of the seats at our terminal, her eyes fixated on the article in her hand. She told me her boss gave her a bunch of suggestions on what to do differently for the next one, and Nevaeh's studying them like they hold the world's biggest secrets. She looks stressed, her hands shaking like she's anxious.

"Come on, Nevaeh, get up. You're not torturing yourself any further," I say after approaching her, grabbing the article in her hand, and placing it on the empty seat next to her.

"What are you doing here? I thought you were only landing in an hour," she asks when she realizes it's me.

A little smile appears on her lips.

I'm fucking dying to kiss her.

"My flight landed early. Now, I need you to focus," I start, and she lets out a shaky breath, her anxiety obviously still weighing heavy on her chest. "Your article was great, and you need a distraction while we wait. Lucky for you, I am incredibly creative," I go on, hoping my distraction will help. "Do you have a piece of paper and a pen?"

Nevaeh fishes around in her bag for a moment before handing me both. I scribble a bunch of things onto it, grinning to myself.

"I have something for you, a present, but I'll only give it to you if you manage to get all of the items on the list before I do. The first one back here wins. What do you say?" I ask, handing her the paper so she can see what she'll have to check off the list.

XL Toblerone bar.

A perfume bottle for no more than five euros.

A hat without a logo on it.

A game you love to play.

An 'I love Germany' shirt.

"Whoever gets back first wins whatever you have?" she says to clarify, but I watch the way she picks up her backpack to get ready to run.

"Yeah, whoever—" Nevaeh doesn't let me finish my sentence before she sprints away and toward the first little shop. A little laugh bursts free because she's so fucking sweet, I could watch her forever and not get bored.

I have no intention of winning, which is why all of the things I wrote down for Nevaeh to get are already in my backpack. Instead of running around, I make my way toward the nearest food place in the airport and get us both something to eat, a little more for Nevaeh because I have a feeling the woman forgot to eat again with work taking up all of her thoughts.

Before I saw her so stressed and anxious, I'd already planned all of this, but I'm happy it'll be able to distract her now.

She looked so excited to get started...

It's always made me happy to make the people around me happy. That's the way my heart works.

But it feels a little different with Nevaeh. It feels like making her happy doesn't just do the same for me in return. Seeing her smile is like a year's worth of happiness flooding through me in an instant.

The man at the food place gives me a strange look, but I merely smile at him. I'm well aware of how strange I look with my baseball cap on and my hood over it. It's necessary for trips when I don't want anyone to recognize me. The sunglasses might be overkill, but I'm only wearing them while walking around. Plus, there are hardly any people at the airport today, which makes hiding a lot easier.

I love my fans to death, I do. They mean so much to me, but even I need a break sometimes. It's taken me a while to come to terms with the fact that I'm *allowed* to want privacy, too.

By the time the food is done and I make my way back to where Nevaeh was sitting before, she's already back and waiting for me. A smile lingers on her lips, spreading even wider when she notices me strolling toward her.

"Well, oh well, look who is finally done," she teases, her eyes sparkling with pure joy.

"I brought the winner something to eat," I reply, holding out the food for her to take.

An excited expression takes over her whole face as she takes one of the iced teas and sandwiches.

"Hold this please," I add and hand her my food too to dig around in my backpack.

I press my tongue against the inside of my cheek and put the ugliest concentration face on, making Nevaeh laugh as she watches me.

I fucking love that sound.

"Ah, here it is," I announce and tuck my backpack under the seat to turn to her and place a box in her lap.

I grab my food out of her hand so she can open my gift.

"Open it." A nervous feeling sets in, my heart reminding me how unsure I am that this was the right gift to give her.

"I'm so scared," she blurts out, a nervous laugh leaving her full lips.

"Just open it. I promise I kept the kinky stuff to myself," I say, watching a wonderful blush cover her round cheeks.

"What if I don't want you to keep it to yourself?" she asks, placing her food to the side to turn to me. "What if I want everything you have to offer?" Nevaeh says, sliding her hand onto my thigh and upward until my breath catches in my throat and my dick takes attention to how close her hand is to it.

Fucking traitor.

I'm also a fucking idiot for wearing sweatpants around Nevaeh.

Do you know how well sweatpants hide a raging hard-on?

That's right, not at all.

So, as her hand trails even higher, my cock grows harder and harder, becoming more visible by the second.

"What if I want to play another game? One where we're both naked and play with each other?" she asks, sliding her hand toward my knee now and grinning at the outline of my needy cock.

Alright, if my little tease wants to play, I'll fucking play.

My thumb and index finger lift to her chin, holding it between them as I tilt her face toward me.

"And what if I want to bend you over one of these uncomfortable chairs, slide down those sexy as fuck yoga pants you're wearing, push your panties to the side, and fuck you with my mouth until you scream my name? What if I want to slip my cock inside of you while you're still high on the first orgasm? What if I want to fuck you slow and gentle one second, then go fast and hard the next until you're writhing in pleasure underneath me? What if, Nevaeh?" My voice is low and husky, and my lips somehow move closer to hers with every word.

Nevaeh's breathing hitches, her bottom lip slipping between her teeth, but I pull down her chin to watch it bounce free again. There's so much I want to do with her pretty mouth, so much I'm not allowed to.

"What if I want that, too?" My hand immediately drops from her face and down to her neck, my fingers wrapping around her throat gently and carefully, just firm enough to feel her heart racing underneath my fingertips.

"Nevaeh, all you have to do is say the word," I say, but she gives me a sad smile like she wishes things were that simple when they're the opposite.

When complicated doesn't begin to cover the situation we're in.

"Open your gift. I want you to put it on," I say instead, releasing her completely.

Mon paradis stares down at the box, undoing the ribbon at the top by pulling both ends apart. Nevaeh lifts the lid, her whole body slumping at the sight of the bracelet I got her. Her fingers wrap around the piece of jewelry to raise it out of the box and study the charms dangling from it.

"There's a nine for Val, an eight for me, a Formula One car to tie it together, and a camera for, well, obvious reasons," I say with a small laugh.

She traces each charm, the numbers, then the car, and the camera. She stops at the last charm, running her thumb over it.

"The blue heart is for anxiety. I read that blue can be calming for the mind." Her gaze slips to me, a storm of emotions in them.

A little bit of panic grabs hold of me.

If she doesn't like it, I'll take it back, no big deal. I'll find her something else. But I want her to like it because I love it. And I was really hoping she would, too.

"This is the most beautiful bracelet I've ever owned," she says and places it in my hand. "Will you help me put it on?"

"Of course," I say and watch as she extends her arm, holding out her wrist for me.

I place it on her with care, closing the clasp again and letting my fingers linger on her skin for a moment longer. Goosebumps appear in the wake of my touch, and I almost smile at the thought of having such a visible effect on her.

"We can keep adding charms, too," I say after Nevaeh retracts her hand to admire the way the bracelet looks on her.

"I'd like that," she replies before lifting her hand to my wrist and rubbing her thumb over my pulse point. "Thank you."

"You're welcome," I manage to croak out, my voice raspy and filled with something I'm not sure I want to identify.

I'm still terrified of my feelings. Terrified, but also slowly starting to feel like it'll be okay because this beautiful woman in front of me makes it seem that way. I'll be okay.

But what if you get attached and then she leaves? my subconscious, the dickhead, chimes in.

Fuck off, I reply.

"What game did you get?" she asks, forcing me back into reality.

"An Italian card game I want you to try out," I say and show her the cards Gabriel and I always use to play Scopa. I picked this game up years ago, playing with Chiara and Leonard. "What did you get?" I ask with a smile, and Nevaeh grins at me.

"Plain playing cards so I can show you a German game called *Schwimmen*. My grandfather taught me, and now I'll teach you," she says, no longer visibly worried about work or anything else.

Nevaeh looks at peace and next to my heaven, how could I feel any differently?

CHAPTER 35
Nevaeh

THE NEXT TWO DAYS, Valentina, Gabriel, Adrian, and I spend almost every single moment together. Gabriel is excited to be my next victim for the interview, and Val keeps teasing him, telling him to behave or she'll punish him afterward. He gave her a wicked look that let me know he'd very much like getting a punishment from her, and I burst into laughter when Adrian let out a hurling noise beside me.

Today is Qualifying. I'm just pulling on a pair of jeans and a new top I bought yesterday when someone knocks on my door. I adjust the top, realizing it's way too tight around my chest for my anxiety to be okay with it.

The person behind my door knocks again, this time harder and a little more impatiently. I abandon my hope of changing and go to speak to whoever is bothering me this early in the morning.

"Mr. Fender, what can I do for you?" I ask with surprise.

We may not be best friends, but he holds a higher position at the company than I do, and I will show him respect.

He gives me a small smile.

"Listen, I'm very sorry about everything that went down between us. I hope you know it was never my intention to overwork you to the point where you fainted," he says.

I honestly consider telling him about my anxiety, that a combination of it and my lack of sleep and dehydration made me faint, but I don't want to make him feel better. He was a horrible boss to me, and now I don't work for him anymore. I work directly for Mrs. Lu and Ms. Martin, and they've been nothing but kind to me.

"I appreciate your apology," I say, shaking his hand when he holds it out for me.

"Great, now, come on, we have to go. I got us a car and Fallon and Liz are already waiting downstairs. You don't want to be late for your day with Mr. Biancheri," he reminds me, and I hesitate for a moment.

I really need to change, but he's staring at me in a way that tells me it's best not to make him wait any longer. Instead, I grab my purse and follow him downstairs while he watches me with a forced smile and his eyes speak volumes. He doesn't like me and is probably just being nice to me because our bosses told him to be.

This man is really starting to piss me off.

At the track, I get my badge for the weekend from a security guard, who seems to be incapable of taking his eyes off my tits in my tight top. It's disgustingly obvious, but he doesn't seem to mind that fact at all.

"Do you stare at all the women's tits when they walk through here or am I the only one you're trying to make uncomfortable?" I ask and lift my purse to cover my breasts. The shirt I'm wearing is *revealing*, yes, I'm aware, but for god's sake, dude, have some self-control.

"In a shirt like that, you're asking to be stared at, lady," he replies, laughing with one of his colleagues. Still waiting for my badge, I lift my phone to my ear, pretending to have dialed someone's number. I may hate confrontation, but I despise disgusting men more. "The hell are you doing?" he asks, holding onto my badge.

"Me? Oh, I'm trying to get a hold of my father, Robert Fuchs, the team principal at Grenzenlos. If he doesn't answer, I think I'm going to call my friend, Valentina Romana, or maybe her fiancé, Gabriel Biancheri. I could of course also call her brother, Adrian Romana. I don't know if you know this, but he almost had someone very influential in this sport fired because they disrespected me. What do you think he'll do to someone like you?" I ask, still holding my phone to my ear.

The security guard's face has drained of all color.

He hands me my badge and mumbles an apology, his eyes trained on the floor now. I wish him a wonderful day before making my way toward the Velocità Rossa garage where Gabriel told me to meet him.

I find Adrian instead, leaning against a wall and listening to one of his team members talk. My heart stops for the briefest moment, then stumbles all over itself to restart. All because Adrian looks incredible in his red Velocità Rossa shirt and plain blue jeans. His blonde hair sits in perfect curls on his head, and his blue-green-brown eyes shine in the sun. I studied their color enough times to have memorized every aspect of them, like the tiny freckle he has in the corner of his left iris. How the colors seem to change depending on what color shirt he's wearing. How they're more enchanting every single time I look at them.

When they drift to me, he stands up straight and a smile covers his lips. We've spent so much time together these past few days, but he still looks at me like he hasn't seen me in weeks and couldn't be happier that I'm here, making my way toward him. His attention briefly moves to the man he is talking to while he seems to apologize for walking away.

As soon as I'm close enough, he says, "Come with me." I follow him into the building behind him, and the next thing I know, he's turning around and hugging me to his chest. I fling my arms around his neck, giggling a little.

"Hi," I say eventually, making him squeeze me even tighter.

"*Bonjour, déesse,*" he replies and steps back to plant two kisses on my cheeks.

My face burns long after his lips are gone. His hands hold onto my hips for a moment longer before he steps back and lets out a low whistle.

"That top on you should be illegal," he tells me with a slight laugh. I wipe my hands down the front of it and frown at him.

"It should be, especially because I haven't been able to breathe properly since I put it on," I admit, causing all of the amusement to leave his beautiful face. "My ex-boss hurried me out of my hotel before I had a chance to change," I explain, but Adrian's eyes and lips reveal how upset he is to hear that.

"Let me get you a different shirt. I should have another like the one I'm wearing in my bag." He tries to walk away, but I grab his hand to stop him.

"Don't worry, it'll be fine," I assure him, but he doesn't look convinced. "I can't be seen walking around in your shirt, Adrian." It's his turn to frown.

"You look beautiful, but I need you to promise me that you'll come to me to get a new shirt if it gets too uncomfortable. I'll get you a plain one without any teams on it," he says, using one of his hands to tuck my hair behind my shoulder and then ear. Seeming to realize what he's doing, he quickly retracts his hand.

"I promise," I reply.

"I have to go, Nevaeh, but come to me if you need anything."

He should be focused on his race weekend, not me, but that's not the type of man he is. No, he's the type of guy to look over his shoulder to smile at me again, even though he's now getting yelled at by Daniel to hurry up.

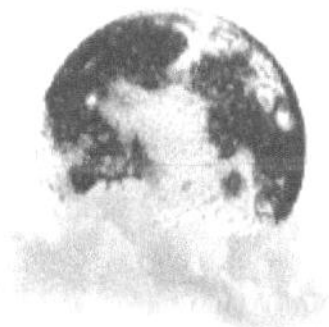

Gabriel and I have a fun time working together.

He shares his routines and rituals with me and even draws me a Formula One car during his break. I take a few photos of him and the team, just like I did last time, and eventually, I sit to write down all of my thoughts. Hector, his performance coach, takes the seat in front of me and hands me a cup of non-caffeinated tea. This is the third time today that someone from Gabriel's team has randomly given me something to eat or drink, which must have everything to do with Adrian.

"Your father is Robert Fuchs, isn't he?" Hector asks. I force a smile before taking a sip of the beverage he brought me.

"Yes. Have you met him?" I don't know how he found out about my relation to the great Robert Fuchs of Formula One since I make sure to introduce myself with my first name and never mention my father in conversations. I want to make a name for myself in this sport and not because of Papa. If we already have to share it, I want to be known as a great journalist, not someone's daughter.

Or someone's girlfriend.

Hector tells me all about meeting my father, one of the kindest people in the world according to him, and I muster a smile while I listen. I love my father, but there is a limit to how many times I can hear Hector say how great he is. That man has enough flaws they will never know about, like forgetting about his children's existence when he's gone to work. I wouldn't dream of telling Hector about that, but it lingers in my head while the performance coach speaks.

Luckily, he gets up to check on Gabriel a few minutes later. I stand up as well, moving around to stretch my legs. It also allows me to breathe better in this ridiculous top.

All of a sudden, a group of people hurry past me and into the room, filling it until we're all squished together. They are staring at the monitors, but I'm too far in the back now to see what's going on. I attempt to make my way out of the crowd, but I'm being shoved against people, unable to escape.

The air becomes thick, and my heart starts to race. Anxiety and this ridiculous shirt cut off my air even more until the atmosphere around me becomes unbearable. I try to breathe and slow my heart rate, trying to ignore the claustrophobic feeling that wraps around my throat, but then someone pushes past my right shoulder, causing a horrible pain to shoot through my arm that soon spreads through my whole body.

I can't breathe.

Pain makes my eyes sting with tears.

Oh my God, I can't breathe.

I can't scream for help.

I can't do anything.

My hand moves onto my chest while I choke for air.

I start to hyperventilate, my vision blurring.

I manage to push past a few people, the exit out of this maze somehow too complex for my anxiety-ridden brain to figure out.

Fingers wrap around my wrist and pull me out of the crowd. They bring me all the way into a separate room where I'm still not able to catch my breath. It feels like the top is restricting my chest. I reach for the zipper in the back when Adrian appears in front of me.

My entire body is trembling from my anxiety, tears streaming down my face. I sink to the ground, my legs shaking too hard for me to keep standing

"Nevaeh, tell me what to do," he says and drops to his knees in front of me, so I point to my shirt.

"I can't breathe," I manage to croak out while my hands tug on the neckline. "Take it off," I beg, his hands moving onto the back a second later.

He fumbles with the zipper for a moment before he groans and then rips the shirt apart. I let out a gasp and remove it from my chest, sucking in several deep breaths.

Adrian pulls me into a hug, and I sigh into his chest as his familiar cologne fills my nose. He falls backward onto his ass with me still in his arms, making me straddle his lap while my head tries to catch up with the present.

"It's okay, I've got you," he murmurs into my ear, stroking a hand down my back.

I take my time, deep breaths in, holding them, and then letting them out.

Over and over.

My breathing slows and my anxiety subsides a little, giving me the chance to acknowledge that I'm almost half-naked with my chest pressed against his.

"Out," I hear Adrian bark at someone after a while of us staying on the floor.

His hands are still caressing my back while mine rest between us and against his chest. My face is nuzzled into the crook of his neck.

"I told you to come to me before this happened," he scolds, and I let out a short laugh.

"The crowd of people made me feel claustrophobic and I think the shirt heightened that feeling. Then, somebody hit my shoulder, and the pain just made everything worse. My anxiety didn't like that," I explain as I lean back to look into his eyes.

A cold breeze hits my body, suddenly making me very aware of the fact that my hard nipples are only covered by a bralette. I wrap my arms around my body to hide my breasts, but his gaze is trained on my face.

Sensing my discomfort, Adrian reaches behind him and into a bag to take out a plain, black shirt. He lifts it over my head, but I hesitate when it's time to put my right arm through the hole.

"You got this, *mon paradis*," he encourages. I suck in a breath through my teeth while I lift and then push my arm through the opening, wincing at the discomfort rippling through me.

As soon as the shirt is on, Adrian slides the short sleeve to the side and studies my scar. His hand is so gentle, I can tell he's scared to hurt me if he presses harder. He brings his mouth closer, watching me as his lips brush over my scar.

Tingles replace the pain I was feeling until my breathing hitches. Desire spreads through me at the way he looks at me, settling between my legs until my clit gives a needy throb.

"Are you feeling better now?" Adrian asks, his hands slipping over my hips before he kisses my shoulder again.

My hips rock forward and against his groin, my clit searching for any sort of friction. Adrian hisses, his fingers digging into my hips.

"Much," I admit, my voice cracking and revealing how breathless his small kisses have me.

He kisses my scar once more, and my hips roll again in response, my body on fire from lust.

"We shouldn't do this, Adrian. It's not allowed," I say, but he's kissing up my neck now, and I'm grinding against his growing bulge, whimpering when the tiniest wave of pleasure rolls through me.

I want more, *need* more.

"We should definitely stop," he says and cups my left cheek to tilt my head to the side. He takes advantage of the new position to scrape his teeth along my neck. "Do you want me to stop?"

"Not really," I admit, breathless and desperately rolling my hips back and forth. "I want you to kiss me, Adrian." And I don't want to pretend that I don't, not anymore.

My eyes flutter open to look at the bracelet he gave me, but he grabs my attention by trailing kisses along my jaw and toward my lips.

"You'll regret it later," he says, and while I might regret it later because of my job, I won't regret kissing the man I have feelings for.

"No one has to know," I whisper, his mouth now hovering over mine. He's breathing heavily as if he's trying to restrain himself. "Please, kiss me. I want you to," I say, but he leans away from me to study my face.

Right when I think he's about to tell me this is a mistake, he says, "Fuck it," and presses his lips to mine.

Chapter 36
Adrian

No one pinch me.

If this is a dream, I don't want to wake up.

Nevaeh's lips are on mine, kissing me like I'm her oxygen, and I kiss her back just as fiercely because, fuck, *she* is *my* oxygen. I breathe her in, dragging her closer against me while she keeps rolling her hips in search of friction. We're both wearing jeans, so the easiest way to get her what she wants is to unbutton her pants and slip my hand inside her panties, but her kiss is clouding my brain to the point where I can't even think of the words to ask her if she wants me to do that.

Nevaeh consumes me.

With every move of her lips on mine, every teasing lick of her tongue inside my mouth, I feel her weaving herself into every fiber of my being. Tethering us together. Our breaths intertwine. My groans fade into her moans. My heart beats in rhythm to hers. All of me becomes all of her in this one single kiss, this moment of passion that's been building for the past three months.

Part of me expected her to taste like heaven, another part hoped she wouldn't. But as I slip my tongue inside her mouth, as I move my hands on her hips to draw her closer, I realize she tastes like every single one of my fantasies combined. She tastes like what I imagine the sky would taste like, and she makes me feel like I'm falling through the softest of clouds in the process.

I've never been kissed the way Nevaeh kisses me.

I've never kissed anyone like this either.

I can't get enough.

So, I kiss her again and again, exploring her mouth like my life depends on it, and, to be honest, it might. I think I might die if I stop kissing her now, but luckily, Nevaeh isn't in a rush to pull away either.

"This is so wrong," she breathes out when I move to kiss her neck again, still rolling her hips to find friction.

"But it feels so right, Nevaeh, I don't wanna stop," I say, my hands slipping onto her ass to roll her hips for her.

My cock is unbearably hard, straining against my jeans to get out of its confinement. Nevaeh's moan when I suck on a sensitive spot on her neck only makes me more desperate to get the layers of clothing out of the way.

"Adrian, I need—" She cuts off and lets out a low moan when I move my hand under her shirt and over her pebbled nipple.

"What do you need, Nevaeh? Tell me, and I'll give it to you. I'll give you anything," I say and drop my hand lower to feel the soft skin on her stomach underneath my fingertips. If I go just a little lower, I can unbutton her pants and give her what she wants, but she has to tell me. I need her words.

"Hey, Adrian, we gotta—" Gabriel's all-too-familiar voice fills our small room, and Nevaeh jumps off my lap in an instant. With the weight of her on top of me gone, I feel empty and cold all at the same time.

I haven't killed Gabriel yet for all of the dumb things he's done since I met him, but I might just kill him now for interrupting my moment with Nevaeh.

The scowl on my face must speak volumes because he retreats and calls out, "Yeah, I got it. I'll just go throw myself off the roof so you don't have my death on your conscience." I almost laugh, I probably would if Nevaeh didn't look like she already regrets our kiss.

"Come here," I say, holding out my hands to get her to join me on the floor again.

"No, I have to go and check in with Gabriel, see if he has any more information for me to write into my article," she says, wiping a hand down her face before reaching up to fix her hair.

"Nevaeh, come here," I repeat, getting up and closing the distance between us. She takes a step toward me too, looking up at me as I grab her chin between my fingers. "No pressure, okay? It was a kiss, but I don't want you to think I have any sort of expectation now. If you want me to kiss you, I'll kiss you until you're sick of it. If you want to do more than kiss, I'll fuck you so right, we'll never want to do anything else ever again. If one kiss is all you want right now, that's fine. We'll do whatever you want, always. Okay?"

Who the hell have I become?

Nevaeh studies my lips for a moment after I'm finished talking. She steps on her tiptoes and presses another, swift kiss to my lips before stepping back and frowning.

"You don't do relationships, Adrian, and I can't be with you without risking my job. Tell me what those two things add up to," she says, and I know where she's going with this, exactly where I was afraid she would.

"Think about what you want, Nevaeh, not what you think I want or what your job tells you to want. No one has to know, just us. Figure it out. When you know, I'll still be here, and nothing will change in the meantime," I promise her, placing my hand on her cheek one last time before exiting the room and making my way toward my private room.

Once I'm there, I flop into the chair in the corner, dropping my face into my hands and cursing several times under my breath.

I don't do relationships, but I want one with Nevaeh.

And I'm not going to deny it any longer.

I like her, and I'll be damned if we can't be together because of me.

CHAPTER 37
Nevaeh

It's race day.

The starting line-up of the grid is Gabriel in first, Lincoln in second, then Adrian, Kyle, James, Grant Irwin, Cameron, Val, Leonard, and the rest of the drivers. I do my best to stay out of Gabriel's way while taking notes simultaneously. He raises seven fingers in the air—his number—when I point my camera at him, causing a smile to grow on my face. I get what Val sees in him. He's cute and funny but can also be serious and determined to get what he wants. I'm convinced that's exactly what won her over.

That and his ability to draw anything he sees.

I study the Formula One car Gabriel drew me, contemplating how incredible it is that simple lines can be put together to create a perfect replica of the actual model.

My head moves against the wall behind me, and I fold my legs under my butt on my chair, studying the people running around in a hurry. I've gathered all of the materials I need for my article for now, and Hector promised to bring me to get a better view of the cars later.

The screen across from me replays yesterday's post-Qualifying procedures, the moment when Adrian took off his helmet and ran a hand through his sweaty hair. I'm thrown straight back to our kiss, the way it felt to finally have his mouth on me. If lips could be a person's weakness, his would be mine.

I wasn't supposed to kiss him, I know I wasn't, but I've come to realize that I'd defy the rules for him any day of the week.

We've both been so reserved. Him because he doesn't believe in love. Me because of my job. But something has shifted. I can't quite pinpoint what it is, if I'm sick of acting like I don't want to be with him or if it's him telling me he'd give me everything I want.

Either way, things aren't going back to how they were before. I don't want them to. I want us to be more.

A hand appears on my shoulder, ripping me out of my thoughts. I look up at the person who is trying to get my attention and melt a little when I see it's the gorgeous blonde from my thoughts. He's in his red racing suit, an easy smirk on his full lips.

"What are you doing here? You're supposed to be focusing on the race," I blurt out and stand up.

"I came here to steal a kiss for good luck," he says, making excitement and hesitation battle for dominance in my head. "Have you seen Gabriel?" Adrian asks.

I burst into laughter. There may be a hint of disappointment in my amusement, but the consequences of kissing him in front of everyone to see push that feeling to the back of my mind.

"He was just here," I reply before pulling half of my bottom lip between my teeth and shaking my head.

"He must have left. Oh well, I guess I will have to find someone else." His eyes move around the room, and mine do the same. Once I'm sure no one's paying attention, I place my hands on his neck and then my lips on his cheek.

"What could be luckier than a kiss from someone you call 'angel?'" I ask, and his attention drifts to my lips as I let go of him and attempt to wipe my kiss off his face. His fingers snake around my wrist to stop me.

"No take-backs, Nevaeh. That kiss needs to stay there for the duration of the race." I swallow the lump in my throat. His scent fills my nose, drawing me closer to him. "I should go. Thank you for the luck," he says and winks at me before leaving again.

Adrian treats me like a goddess. Like he'd happily fall to his knees and worship me without hesitation. How am I supposed to dismiss it? Ignore it? Pretend like he doesn't and I don't love it when he does?

My mother's voice appears in my head, screaming that that's exactly what I'm supposed to do. To focus on my career and never, ever let a man make me feel any sort of way that could risk it. And I agree. My career comes first, but trying to ignore one's feelings for another person is like trying to control the tide when you're not the one in charge of it.

The moon is.

Adrian is my moon.

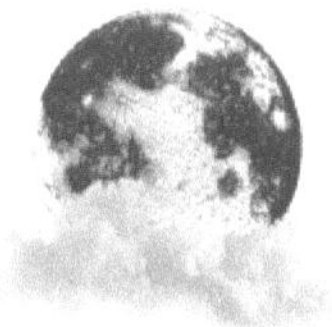

The drivers take their formation lap before standing in their assigned places on the grid, waiting for the lights to go out. My heart thumps in rhythm with every red dot that appears and skips a beat when they all vanish. Gabriel gets a phenomenal start, but so does Adrian. He races right past Lincoln and into second place. An excited gasp escapes me as I clap my hands together and cheer internally for him. His overtake maneuver was beautiful. It was easy and smooth, just on the inside of the Grenzenlos.

Adrian stays there for the next ten laps, but Lincoln is right behind him the entire time. Val is making her way up to sixth place, and James is still in fourth. The rest of the drivers are switching positions, some moving up while others fall behind. Cameron struggles with his tires and makes an early pitstop that costs him eight places.

"Come with me," Hector says and leads me outside to an area by the fence where no one is standing.

I put my better lens on my camera, the one that catches movement best, and place my eye over the eyepiece while closing the other. Gabriel, Adrian, and Lincoln shoot past me like bullets, and I'm barely able to get a few pictures when a deafening sound fills my ears.

Metal hitting metal.

I swing my head around to see Lincoln and Adrian spinning off the track and into the barriers.

Out of shock, I drop my camera, forgetting I didn't place the strap around my neck. My hands cover my mouth as my body goes into shock.

Hector yells for me to come inside with him, but I only start walking when his hand wraps around my wrist to pull me with him.

"Hector, I need to see if they're okay," I say when he doesn't stop once. He hands me my camera and leaves me in the garage to check on something else.

My eyes shift to the screens before relief consumes me. Adrian and Lincoln get out of their cars before the Monegasque turns to the English man and touches his fingers to his head to say "Are you fucking crazy?"

Lincoln simply storms off toward the marshals and medical team.

The replay of the incident reveals that he was the one who drove carelessly into the back of Adrian's car. Anger takes over, along with anxiety and relief until I'm shaking.

Minutes later, while I do my best not to spiral into what-ifs, Adrian walks through Gabriel's garage and toward me.

He removes his helmet before wrapping his arms around me.

"I'm okay, I promise," he says, and, suddenly, I feel tears shooting into my eyes. Adrian tightens his grip, and I slide my hands onto his sweaty back.

I've never been so terrified in my life, and the more the shock washes off, the clearer the fear is. My hands are shaking while I push my lips together to hold back a sob.

"Everything's okay," he repeats, stroking my hair with his left hand.

"I'm pretty sure I'm the one who should comfort you," I reply and step back, my fingers moving to my mouth and his to my shoulders. Adrian gives me a small smile, which I can tell he doesn't mean in the slightest.

"It happened right where you were, Nevaeh. I can't imagine how scary that must have been. I'm sorry." I shake my head slightly, confusion probably evident on my features.

"Are you seriously apologizing to me right now? Are you crazy?" I ask, and he smiles.

"If by crazy you mean that I saw you taking photos, got hit by Lincoln, and my first concern after was to make sure you were alright, then yes, I am crazy. Plus, I'm fine, I barely felt pain," he explains while I lift my hand to wrap them around one of his wrists.

His eyes drop to my camera.

"What happened?"

He takes it between his hands to inspect the damage.

"I dropped it when the crash happened."

The lens is broken and so is the screen. If my body wasn't still shaking from the incident, I'd probably care more about the camera, but that sadness will come later.

"I'll get you a new one," he says, but I frown at him.

"No, you won't," I scold.

A moment of silence passes between us before I cross my arms in front of my chest, hiding how my hands are still shaking. I'm going to have to grow a stronger spine if I'm watching all of the races in person.

Crashes happen. All the time.

I'm just not entirely sure how one is supposed to get used to this.

"I guess my kiss wasn't good luck, after all," I mumble, and he lets out a laugh.

Sweat drips from his forehead, and I realize he has to talk to his team and take care of his needs.

"Next time you should try giving me one on the lips. It will be more effective and last longer," he replies, nudging my chin with his fingers to get a smile out of me. It works like a charm.

"Okay, go get yourself checked out. I think you hit your head," I say, making him give me my camera and step back.

The smile stays on his lips as he walks away.

CHAPTER 38
Nevaeh

GABRIEL ENDED UP WINNING the race with James coming in second, Kyle in third, and Val in fourth. I was so happy for her, I gave her the biggest hug afterward. We didn't go out to celebrate that weekend. Instead, I stayed in my hotel room, completely immersing myself in my article for Gabriel.

On Monday evening, I submitted it along with the photos I took, but I got no response from Mrs. Lu or Ms. Martin. It's Tuesday afternoon now, and I haven't slept much in the past forty-eight hours. It's one of the reasons why I hate flying, I can never sleep on the plane.

My heavy eyelids barely stay open while I look at my broken camera, trying to see how bad the damage is. The screen is shattered and beyond salvageable. The lens I was using is broken, too.

I scroll through the cameras Papa and Nova sent me as replacement suggestions.

Since I need one for work now, I won't get around buying a new one as soon as possible, but it has to be in my price range, which makes choosing a new one infinitely more difficult.

Ms. Martin's name appears on my screen, and I suck in a sharp breath through my teeth. My boss calling me unscheduled is definitely not a good sign.

Maybe she hated my article.

Maybe she's going to fire me, after all.

Maybe I'm not good enough.

Overthinking in situations like these is my specialty. Any situation really.

"Hello?" I answer the phone, holding my breath while I wait for her to talk.

"Nevaeh, how are you?" she asks, and we small-talk for a moment about my trip back to Monaco and how she's been. "Listen, there is something I need to discuss with you," Ms. Martin starts, making my hands shake uncontrollably.

"Am I in trouble?" I can't help but ask. Not knowing what she's going to say is killing me.

Uncertainty is poison for a person with anxiety.

Ironic because the antidote isn't always certainty either.

"That depends, and I'm sorry to have to ask, but are you involved with Mr. Romana? It has been brought to my attention that the two of you have been growing closer."

My heart drops into my stomach.

"What has prompted this line of questioning?" I ask, my heart racing and a cold sweat breaking out across my back. Fuck, fuck, fuck.

"Mr. Fender has mentioned seeing you and Mr. Romana sharing a hug on Sunday after his crash."

Of course, *he* mentioned it.

"Mr. Romana and I have been growing closer, as friends and only friends. I have also been growing closer to Ms. Romana, Mr. Biancheri, as well as Ms. Romana's race engineer, and many other people I'm working with. Formula One is a community with caring and kind people. It's difficult not to befriend them," I reply, hoping it will convince her that I've been doing everything right.

I hate lying, but it's also not fun that my job is controlling my life.

"I understand. Just remember the rule," she reminds me, even though it's not necessary. I've memorized this rule.

"I will," I promise and wipe my face.

My Omi used to say, "Promises, promises. They're as thin as paper, but, sometimes, they can tie you to a decision for a lifetime."

I didn't understand what she meant at the time, that a piece of paper could hold so much power. As I got older, learned about contracts and marriage certificates, the meaning became a lot clearer.

I don't want to be tied to this promise when I have no intention of keeping it.

"Now, for the good part of this call, I wanted to tell you how wonderful your article was. It will be published tomorrow. I'm just waiting for Mr. Biancheri's team to approve it," she says, and I smile brightly.

"Gabriel loved it, so I hope they do as well," I reply and stand up to stretch my legs.

My apartment looks so empty, it irritates me. Luckily, Val is picking me up to go bed and mattress shopping soon. I can't sleep on the floor tonight, after all. It's my first night by myself in the apartment, and, as excited as I am to have independence and freedom, I'm also a little scared.

"You sent it to him before giving it to me?" Ms. Martin asks, pulling me back to the conversations.

"Yes, of course. I believe the driver should have a say first, considering this is a very intimate article and interview that we do," I explain, my finger trailing over my window sill.

"That's very thoughtful, Nevaeh. I'm proud of you." A smile grows on my face at her praise.

We hang up soon after, and I make my way downstairs to meet Val at three o'clock, just like she told me to. A pick-up truck stands in front of my building, and I cock a brow at it before looking for my friend's car instead.

"Get in," his familiar voice fills my ears.

Sunglasses cover his light eyes, and the way he sits in the truck, one hand on the wheel while the other lies on the middle console, has my knees a little weak. He's annoyingly attractive.

"I'm taking you mattress shopping," he says, and I shake my head.

"No, thank you. I'm waiting for Val," I reply and pull out my phone to call her.

If she let him come instead of her and didn't tell me, then I have a bone to pick with her. We had a girl's day planned.

The phone rings for a moment before her ringtone appears from inside of Adrian's car. He places the device to his ear and smiles.

"Hello?" I hear his voice through the phone and in front of me. "I took her phone and keys so she couldn't stop me from going with you. Now, please, beautiful, get in the car," he pleads, and I let out another laugh.

This man is impossible.

I climb into the truck, and Adrian holds out a to-go cup for me.

"Your favorite, a hazelnut hot chocolate."

"How did you find that out? I didn't tell you," I reply and he gives me a satisfied smirk.

"I asked your sister," he says nonchalantly, still grinning at me.

"Nova needs to stop telling you about my favorite things," I say, making him nod in agreement.

"Damn straight. You should be the one telling me so I can spoil you more efficiently."

"You shouldn't spoil me at all. I'm not your girlfriend." Especially not after that phone call with Ms. Martin.

"Technicalities," he mumbles, waving his hand like he's dismissing my comment.

I laugh a little before thanking him for my drink.

My eyes study the simple, black interior design of the truck. The familiar "new car smell" fills my nose, and I notice there isn't a single speck of dirt anywhere.

"Did you buy this truck?" I ask him, but he shakes his head while turning the key in the ignition.

"I rented it for today. Now, before we go, are we okay?" he says, causing me to shift my head in his direction. "Since we kissed, we haven't really spent time together, so I just wanted to make sure you don't hate me now," he says, lifting his sunglasses to show me he means every word.

"Of course we're okay."

Adrian has done nothing wrong. My feelings are complicated. They are causing all the trouble in my life when the only thing that matters is how happy Adrian and my relationship makes me. Friends or friends who like each other more than friends, it doesn't matter. I like how I feel when I'm with him.

"Good, because I have something else for you, and I didn't want you to think I'm bribing you into agreeing we're okay if that's not how you feel," he admits while reaching back to grab something.

He brings a camera to the front and places it on my lap. My jaw drops as my heart forgets its rhythm.

"Adrian—" I start, but he interrupts me before I can complain.

"None of that. Thank me or don't say anything," he instructs, rolling his lips to keep from laughing and stay serious.

"Thank you," I say and lean over to press a kiss to his cheek.

The corners of his mouth curl into a smile while heat settles on my cheeks, most likely painting them a deep shade of red.

He turns on the radio to break the tension, and I stop breathing when Dylan Scott's voice fills the car.

"You like country music?" I ask when I see him mouthing the lyrics of 'Can't Take Her Anywhere.' He grins, but his eyes stay on the road, making me feel safe and giddy at the same time.

"Yeah, but we can change it if you want," he offers. I reach out to turn up the volume.

"Dylan Scott is one of my favorite artists," I explain.

Seconds later, we're singing our hearts out to the music. No one has ever enjoyed country music with me, not my sister, Aileen, Papa, Mama, or even Lincoln when we were still friends. None of them, except Adrian now.

My chest fills with a sweet warmth as the biggest smile covers my lips. 'New Truck' starts blasting through the speakers, and we both scream along, not caring how horrible we probably sound. I'm laughing so hard, my stomach starts to cramp in the best way.

"Not there, Nevaeh, how many times do I have to tell you it goes on the other side?" Adrian asks, and we both burst into laughter. He points to the instructions, making me almost fall over.

"It's in fucking French, are you kidding me?"

Tears of amusement push out of my eyes while I place my hand over my now cramping stomach. I can't remember the last time I laughed this hard. We've been trying to build my bed for the past two hours, but neither of us is good at these kinds of things.

"I have to teach you. You have to learn French if you're going to live in Monaco," he points out and studies the paper again.

This is hopeless. We're obviously incapable of accomplishing this tonight.

"Okay, I'm calling time of death. I'm too tired to keep going," I say and stretch my arms into the air before yawning. Adrian yawns too, making us both chuckle.

"Val and James will be able to help tomorrow," Adrian assures me, standing up and walking over to my mattress.

He rips the plastic off while I watch, admiring the way his arm muscles are flexing with the motion.

"Well, I was supposed to do this with her, not you," I remind him with a smile.

Adrian frowns for a split second before dropping my mattress onto the floor and walking over to the sheets we bought.

"She wouldn't have made you laugh as much as I did." He unfolds the sheets to spread them over what will have to do as my bed for now.

"Yes, because she would have been able to read the instructions properly," I tease, and he throws the bedding down.

"You know what? I'm done helping," he says.

"Sure, call it 'helping,'" I reply, and he grabs his jacket before walking toward the door. "Adrian! I'm joking. Please, stay," I laugh, and he spins back around, crossing the room and falling on top of me with a heavy *thud*. "Oh my God," I choke out and try to push him off me, but Adrian has become limp and heavy as a rock. "I can't breathe," I say, but he doesn't release me. I try to heave him off again and fail since my back is flat on the ground and I've always been horrible at bench pressing.

"Have you learned your lesson?" he asks, and I giggle uncontrollably underneath him.

"Yes, I've learned my lesson. Please, get off," I beg, and, finally, he rolls over.

My laughter still fills the almost empty room, and he joins with a chuckle that makes my heart warm. We're both on the floor now, me on my back and Adrian on his stomach. He studies my face with the same intensity that I do his.

Silence surrounds us, allowing me to listen to my racing heart.

His fingers move to my cheek, cupping my face as his thumb runs over my bottom lip.

"I have a really hard time not touching you," he says softly. My eyes close as his thumb continues to trace my lips. "You're *mon paradis*, Nevaeh." I tilt my head to get closer to his touch.

Adrian's lips are barely a few centimeters away from mine now. Our breaths are one, but I lean away again to clear my mind.

"I think you have the wrong person, Adrian. You might be attracted to me, but you're not *that* attracted to me that I'd tilt your whole word on its axis and make you want things you never have before," I say, trying to convince myself as much as him of this. Maybe the reminder will help me keep a healthy distance between us.

Adrian stands up and holds out his hand to lift me off the ground, too. I slide mine into his, the air *whooshing* out of me as he helps me up, pulling me close. My hands slip onto his hips, enjoying the hardness of his body against mine.

"You really are stubborn once you've set your mind on something," he points out, and I'd laugh if my body wasn't pressed up against his if the ache between my legs didn't make me dizzy. "If you're questioning how attracted I am to you, then you've not been paying attention to me, *mon ange*."

Adrian grabs my hand and places it over his chest, allowing me to feel his accelerated heartbeat.

"Feel that? Now, if I wasn't so incredibly attracted to you, didn't want you as much as I do, having you pressed up against me wouldn't excite me this much, would it? It wouldn't make my heart race," he says, and I lower my arms until my fingers rest on his stomach.

"I guess not," I mumble with a shy smile that heats up my face.

"You guess not? *Mon Dieu*, Nevaeh, you are so frustrating," he replies and lets go of me to make my bed.

I join him, but neither one of us says another word until we're finished.

Adrian is fluffing out my pillow when I realize, like I do every time we spend the day together, that I'm not ready for him to leave yet.

"You know, I fell asleep before the movie ended last time. Do you want to watch it again?" I ask, and he pulls his sweatshirt over his head before removing his socks without a second of hesitation. He drops onto my bed, and I laugh as I grab my laptop and join him.

Adrian opens his arms for me when I've hit play on the movie, and I bury myself in them, nuzzling into his side.

"If you fall asleep, try not to snore so much this time, yeah?" he asks after a while, and I push off him to show him the scowl on my face.

Adrian places his arms under his head while smirking, looking like sex on a platter. Not good... not good at all. I lie on his chest again and smack his stomach.

"I won't snore if you contain your farts," I reply, and he tickles my sides to make me giggle.

He releases me quickly, sliding his arm back around my shoulders. The sound of his heart racing fills me in a different way now, one I've never felt before. It's racing *for me*, for the feelings it harbors inside of it *for me*.

Adrian's lips press against my head, lingering for a moment.

"Will you tell me about your anxiety? I would like to understand it better if you're comfortable sharing." I run a hand over his stomach, leaning my head back to study his mouth.

"I get anxiety attacks sometimes, mostly when I'm overwhelmed, stressed, tired, or when I get close to having my period. I get anxiety-induced insomnia at times, too, which is a pain because I get so frustrated that I can't sleep, it gives me more anxiety. I hate the feeling of claustrophobia, it triggers an anxiety attack. Going out of my comfort zone and trying new things? Even worse, but I do it. I push myself because life doesn't go easy on anyone, especially on those with mental illnesses.

"Some days feel like fighting a battle when your limbs are glued to the ground and you can't get up. Other days are much better. There's no single explanation for my anxiety but a hundred different ones that could apply to how I feel, how lost I get. My anxiety comes in different shapes too. It can be an uneasy feeling in my chest, barely there but reminding me it exists. It can also be a heavy weight on my body."

I take a break to breathe, watching Adrian's thumb lift to my lips and tracing my bottom one. He's concentrated on my mouth, on the words falling from it.

"I have symptoms too, handshaking, heavy and shallow breathing, hyperventilating, and so on, but I usually have enough time to call my sister and ask her to help with my 'Code Blue.' That's what we call it." Adrian's fingers drop to the bracelet he got me, trailing over the blue heart charm.

"What does she say to help you?" he asks, sliding his hand over my hip and toward the small of my back to drag me against his chest.

"She helps me breathe. Counts with me, you know? Inhale, hold, exhale," I explain, and he nods, rubbing an infinity symbol onto my back. Or maybe it's an eight. I'm not entirely sure. I don't care either way because both are sweet.

One is his number.

The other is a promise of forever.

"So best if I'm nowhere near you when you have an anxiety attack, considering I take your breath away, right?" A laugh bursts out of me, and I nudge him. Adrian chuckles with me, holding on tight. "I've got you, you know? Whenever you need me. If you can't get a hold of your sister, call me. Come to me. I'll breathe with you," he promises, so I tilt my head up and kiss his jaw.

"Thank you."

Silence engulfs us for a moment, the movie already over when he trails a hand down my spine.

"I love spending the night with you, which is a weird thing for me. The only two reasons why I sleep next to a woman are either when Val doesn't want to sleep alone or when I pass out next to a random girl I fucked." I frown at his words, but Adrian tickles me a little to make me giggle.

"Why do you?" I ask, and he raises both his brows.

"Why did I have sex with strangers?" I nod as he pulls me closer. Our noses brush before he focuses on answering my question. "I think it has to do with my mother abandoning Val and me at a young age. I loved her more than anything, I remember it clear as day, but, all of a sudden, she was just gone. The thought of falling in love with someone and risking the destruction a heartbreak can bring wasn't appealing. At least not until—" He cuts off abruptly, but Adrian doesn't have to finish the sentence. We both know he means me and suddenly, my heart is racing.

"Until the girl from the club, I know," I tease, making him roll onto his stomach to groan into my mattress. He swears in French for a few moments, and I wait patiently for him to lift his head again. A chuckle escapes me when he shakes his head.

"You're the woman who teases me, makes me laugh from deep within, and has me on my knees without trying to. You're the one I can't fucking get over, and I haven't even been under you. It's ridiculous," he complains.

Maybe Adrian didn't say this, and I'm simply so sleepy that I'm making everything up in my head, but when he brings his mouth closer to mine to make our noses touch again, I know he really said it.

"You like me," I whisper, but he doesn't give me a response. All he does is move his head from side to side to make our noses brush one another. "You can't like me,"

I say, our words causing tears to shoot into my eyes. "I'm so confused and selfish with my career," I add.

"You're not selfish. If anything, I'm the one who keeps confusing you more," he says, and I lift my gaze to meet his. "If all I could ever have with you was this, I want you to know, it'd be enough for me." He presses a kiss on my forehead. "Any version of us is enough for me."

"I feel the same."

My words tumble out of me, making a strange realization settle inside of me. I'd risk a lot for this man, but I'm the one who would be risking everything while his job would not be affected.

But I have a feeling that risking my job means little compared to the risk he's placing on his heart.

"But I want more. And you deserve more," is the last thing I hear myself saying as my eyelids grow heavier.

Although I try not to, I fall asleep with his familiar cologne filling my nose and strong arms bringing nothing but comfort.

CHAPTER 39
Adrian

I SLEPT.

And I slept well, probably better than I have in years.

My eyes are closed, but I've noticed her breathing getting more shallow. I peek through one half-opened eye to find her staring at my lips. Her hand trails a bit lower on my chest, and my already aching cock gives a needy throb in my boxers. I don't know if this woman likes making me hard when we can't do anything about it or if she has no fucking clue what she does to me. Either way, I lower my lips a little, my fingers moving to her chin to grasp it between my thumb and index finger.

"Do it," I say, and she looks up at me, so beautiful even in the morning.

"Do what?" she asks, so I lean down to press my nose against hers. I can almost hear the thumping of her heart, *thud, thud, thudding* faster and faster with every centimeter I close between us. It matches mine perfectly. I brush my nose from side to side once, then say what I've wanted to say since our first kiss.

"Kiss me, *mon paradis*. Kiss me until you stop regretting it," I say, but Nevaeh pushes me away a little, bringing distance between us.

"I got a call from Ms. Martin yesterday, telling me that Gillian Fender saw us hugging and assumed we were getting closer. She gave me a warning, and I don't think I'm going to get another one of those."

All the color drains from my face. I can't see it, but I can feel the way my cheeks grow cold and the blood rushes out of them.

The thought of Nevaeh losing her job because of me ties my stomach into knots.

"I'm so sorry," I blurt out, leaning away from her to give me space to think.

"Don't be. I'm incapable of not touching you, Adrian, just like you seem to feel about me."

Nevaeh smiles at me, then sits up in bed and stretches her arms above her head. A yawn slips past her perfect lips before she gets up and walks toward her wardrobe.

"I love your ass," I say in French without thinking, making her spin around and place her hands on her hips with a cock of her brow.

Uh oh. I'm in trouble.

And I'm smiling like a lottery winner.

"You wanna say that again to my face?" she asks, and I roll over until my face is buried in pillows.

"Your French is better than I thought," I admit with a laugh, my words muffled because my face is trapped between the pillows. "Your ass is unreal, *mon ange*," I say as I lift my head to look at her again.

"It's real, Adrian. Would you like to touch it and see for yourself?" she asks, closing the distance between us.

"Fuck yeah, I do, baby," I reply, sitting up in bed and moving toward her, too.

"Maybe if you're a good boy, I'll let you one day," she adds, leaving me where I am without another word.

I roll onto my back and stare at the ceiling for a moment, smiling to myself because, despite not being able to be together right now, I'm happy. Truly happy.

Spending time with Nevaeh is slowly becoming one of my favorite things in the world.

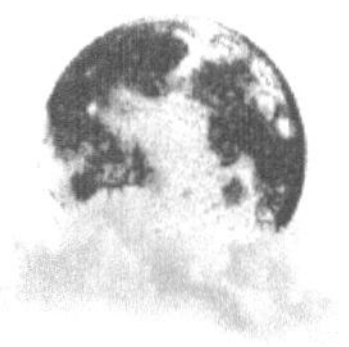

Val and James manage to assemble the bed within half an hour while Nevaeh and I hand them the tools they need. They're fucking show-offs, if you ask me, but I enjoy watching Nevaeh and James get to know each other.

My best friend talks about his son and how he lives with Gabriel's aunts since Annabel, the child's mother, ran away.

I've never been able to comprehend how a parent could do such a vile, cruel, and disgusting thing. My mother did it, she left without ever looking back, and my father was never the same. Luckily, James isn't like that with Damian. He made a hard decision to let Gabriel's aunts adopt his son so he could be in a loving home with parents who don't travel the whole year for work.

"So, when is it my turn to be interviewed?" James asks, and Nevaeh pulls out her phone to check.

"Next week will be Nolan Matts from Carousel," she replies, and I watch my best friend smile at her. Even though I know he means it in a polite way, I kick him.

He's too single to be smiling at my angel that way.

"Your turn is four races from now," Nevaeh adds and turns to Val to remind her she'll come before then.

"Ha," my sister says to James.

They start pretend-fighting, so I take the instructions Nevaeh was holding and hit James over the head with them. Then, I throw them back in Nevaeh's lap so that when James turns around again, she looks like the culprit. She bursts into laughter, unable to explain it wasn't her but me.

"There is an event at the *Casino de Monte-Carlo* for the Formula One drivers tomorrow. Will you go with me?" I ask after a while of silence, Val and James watching me with surprise as I turn to look at Nevaeh.

"I'd love to, but I'm not sure that would help make us look like friends," Nevaeh replies, sliding her hand toward mine where it rests on the ground. I stare at her fingers inching closer, trying to figure out a way I can take her without her boss making a big fuss.

"Nevaeh will be my plus one. Since I'm already engaged, it won't be suspicious," Val says with a wink, and I watch Nevaeh's face light up as she looks at my sister. "Although, it does depend on what you wear because if I can't take my eyes off you, the suspicion will return," she adds, but I shoot my sister a warning look. Happily engaged or not, Nevaeh is mine, and if my sister turns her charm on, I'm not sure I have a competing chance.

"I appreciate the invitation, Val, but I have nothing to wear. My clothes are only arriving on Saturday," Nevaeh explains, but my sister is on her feet a moment later. She's all giddy as she pulls Nevaeh onto her feet too.

"I know just the place to get you a dress or suit, whichever you prefer," Val says, grabbing Nevaeh's camera bag because she knows, just like I know, that she never goes anywhere without it. "I'm sorry to do this to you, Nevaeh, but I've never had someone to go shopping with, and you're going to be my victim today," Val informs my angel with a serious expression, making Nevaeh laugh as my sister pulls her toward the door. "The bed better be put in its proper place with the mattress on it by the time we get back," she calls out before letting the door slam shut so James and I can't protest.

"How's Damian?" I ask when I catch James grinning at me in a way he never has before.

"He's fine. Sleeps a lot, poops a lot, screams a lot. You know, like a baby does," he replies, still grinning.

"What's the fucking face for?" is my next question. James shrugs before picking up the screwdriver and going back to cleaning up.

"The fact you don't know what the face is for when you look at Nevaeh like she's the Driver's Championship title and all of your other dreams combined into one person is baffling," he says matter-of-factly.

"I do not look at her like that," I say and scoff, but a smile covers my lips anyway. "Fuck, I do look at her like that, don't I?" James throws an unopened bag of screws in my direction and lets out an annoyed huff.

"What do you think?" he replies, smiling down at the screwdriver in his hand while I grin at him.

CHAPTER 40
Nevaeh

"I FEEL BAD. THEY shouldn't have to do this all by themselves," I say, but Val doesn't stop. She leads me all the way to her baby blue Mustang, a classic car I've only ever seen in photos. "Holy fuck. Do you mind if I…" I trail off and lift my camera, aiming it at her car.

"Go for it, love," she replies, and I take a few photos before we both get into her car.

My phone rings a moment later, Ms. Martin's name flashing on my screen. Twice in twenty-four hours. That can't be a good sign.

"Hello, Nevaeh. I'm sorry to disturb you, but I've just received a very exciting email. I have a job for you if you're feeling up for it," she says, and relief and excitement course through me.

"Yes, of course. What's the job?" I ask, holding my phone away from my mouth to apologize to Val, but she waves my apology away and smiles.

"There is a charity event happening in Monte Carlo tomorrow. The press officer of Formula One reached out and asked us to do an exclusive. More specifically, they asked for you," she says, and my chest almost bursts from pride.

All the years I spent studying, writing, and interning, are all paying off now as I'm making a name for myself in the world of Formula One. I never thought this sport would be how the world would get to know me, but I can't lie.

It's exciting.

"You'd go around the room, ask the drivers some questions, and enjoy yourself. How does that sound?" Ms. Martin asks, and I start grinning from ear to ear.

"Sounds great. What exactly do you want me to ask them and put into the article?" I ask, trying to contain my excitement.

Val parks the car as my boss tells me more details for tomorrow, and we hang up a couple of minutes later. My friend smiles at me as I share what just happened, leading me down a row of little antique shops at the same time.

We arrive at one called *Rush*.

It looks newer than the rest of the buildings we walked past and yet strangely old, too. It's absolutely charming.

"She remodeled it recently, expanded from one floor to two," Val explains, and I raise both my brows. "Evangelin is the owner and a dear friend of mine. Her husband, Carlos Klein, bought it for her after he won his first championship," she says and opens the door while I pick up my jaw off the floor.

Carlos Klein is a legend in Formula One. Papa has spoken about him many times. Never in my entire life did I expect to meet someone as close to him as his wife.

I manage to move my feet to follow Val inside. A tiny woman with long, white hair comes up to us, greeting Val with a hug and me with a warm smile.

"It's a pleasure to meet you," I croak out in the best French I can muster. Evangelin holds out her hand, and I give it a gentle shake.

"We can speak in English, dear, don't worry," she says, and I barely hold back a sigh. "Feel free to call me when you need something," she adds as I study her shop.

Casual clothes sit on the racks that are neatly distributed downstairs, so Val leads me upstairs with her instead.

"What are we looking for?" she asks while I move to one of the racks on the far right.

A sleeveless silk dark-orange dress with a slightly low v-neck, a slit up the thigh, and lace around the breast area catches my attention. I run my hands over the fabric, falling in love with the soft feel of it.

"Try it on," Val says and pulls me out of my thoughts.

"I could never. My shoulders are too broad. It won't look good," I reply and walk past it, my heart staying with it as I browse through more options that will hide my scar and shoulders.

"Can I ask you something?" Val's voice reveals how unsure she is about whatever she wants to know. I nod, my eyes and attention on her. "Do you not notice the way people fall at your feet no matter what you wear?"

A nervous chuckle escapes me, but she shakes her head, giving me a serious frown.

"I mean it. You put on that dress, and I promise you, you'll knock the breath out of everyone, especially my brother."

This makes a blush and a smile settle on my face.

The thought of Adrian drooling over my body does give the dress an advantage I can't deny.

"Where are the dressing rooms?"

CHAPTER 41
Adrian

"Stop fussing with the tie. I just fixed it," Gabriel says and slaps my hand away from where I was about to place it on my tie for the third time in three minutes.

"It's gotta look perfect," I mumble, taking a deep breath and acknowledging the nervous feeling in my chest with a small groan.

"Why?" Gabriel teases, smirking at me because he clearly already knows the answer.

"Because Nevaeh is going to look perfect, and her date-not-date should match that," I reply anyway, running a hand over my pocket square, the one Val gave me because it's made of the same material and color as Nevaeh's dress.

"You really, truly like her, don't you?" Gabriel asks, a serious expression replacing the amused look he was wearing a moment before.

"So much," I admit.

My heart confirms my words a second later when my eyes catch Nevaeh as she gets out of my sister's Velocità Rossa SUV. Every single word in the English, Italian, and French vocabulary is knocked out of my head at the sight of her.

Good fucking God.

I don't know what I did to deserve laying my eyes on her, but I'd do it over and over again if it meant I'd get to look at her every single day of my life. Preferably in that dress.

Who am I kidding?

Any piece of clothing on Nevaeh makes me a weak man.

Weak for her.

The dress she's wearing is my favorite shade of orange. It's made of silk and flows around her legs perfectly, the slit on the side exposing one of her beautiful, thick thighs as she walks. Her heels look painfully high, but Nevaeh steps one foot in front of the other with elegance. The neckline is low and her breasts fill that dress up in a way that makes my mouth water. The fabric clings to her ass too, and I find myself jealous of another piece of fucking clothing.

Her hair is perfectly wavy, just like always. She's smiling at my sister, accepting her invitation to hook their arms together.

"Breathe," Gabriel whispers to me, and I suck in a sharp breath, hoping it's not obvious.

"Is that a thing I'm supposed to do?" I ask sarcastically, and Gabriel nudges my side.

"Only if you want to live long enough to kiss her again," he says with a mean smile and a simple shrug of his shoulders.

Nevaeh's attention shifts to me, and the rest of the world vanishes. There's only her and me now.

The smile spreading across her face has me breathless all over again. She rimmed her eyes with brown eyeliner. Her lips are painted a dark orange to match the dress, making the smile on my face spread without my permission.

Valentina flings her arms around Gabriel's neck while Nevaeh steps in front of me, her hands clasped together.

I shove mine into my pockets to resist the urge to touch her.

"Neveah," I say, the usual softness in my tone as I address her.

"Mr. Romana," she replies with a shy smile. Her eyes trail over my black-on-black suit before her features soften at the sight of my pocket square.

"Come on, Nevs, let's go," Val says and grabs my angel's hand, leading her away from me.

Biting back a groan of disapproval, I follow Gabriel, Valentina, and Nevaeh inside.

The inside of the casino is fucking bright in comparison to the night sky outside. I blink several times before studying the interior. It reminds me a little of the inside of one of the million cathedrals Val has made me visit over the years.

The walls are made up of paintings and gold flecks while expensive chandeliers dangle from the high ceilings. There are people in fancy clothing everywhere, more older people than young, and I spot some of the other drivers at one of the tables. Nolan Matts and his teammate Jason Young stand at one of them, raising their glasses in our direction. I give them a small nod before walking to another game table with Nevaeh, Val, and Gabriel.

It's quite crowded with the four of us joining now, and I notice Nevaeh shooting Val an unsure look. I move halfway behind Nevaeh, caging her in my arms a little to make sure I can give her enough space on each side of her body to keep her comfortable. Her shoulders sag in relief while I move her hair out of the way to make sure she can hear my next words clearly.

"I see you've chosen to wear something to drive me wild tonight." My voice is low and quiet so no one else, not even Val who is next to us, can hear me. She tilts her head back a little more to make sure I alone hear her answer.

"How wild?" she asks, making a chuckle roll from my chest.

"Move your ass a little backward and you'll feel what you and that dress do to me," I tease, never in a million years expecting she'd actually move her ass toward my half-erected cock to actually get a feel.

A quiet gasp leaves her lips while I fight to hold a moan in. I grab her hips and move her away from me, self-control a concept I hardly know anymore.

"Don't do that, *mon ange*, not if you'd like to keep that dress on," I warn, dropping my hands from her body and placing them on the gaming table on either side of her again. I know people can see us, but it's also really crowded, so I'm hoping we don't stand out.

"So, tell me, what is this event for?" she asks to change the topic.

"It's for charity. We gamble some of our money and all the proceeds go to a charity of our choice. Not all the drivers wanted to bet their money, but most are here.

Look," I point at James, Cameron, Leonard, and Kyle, who are enjoying themselves at another table.

"Yes!" Val exclaims as she wins a round of blackjack. "Sorry," she apologizes after with a small laugh.

"Here, you play for me. You're my lucky charm," I say, pulling Nevaeh's attention back to me. She turns her head, not realizing how close our mouths would be, and it takes all of my willpower not to kiss her again.

"But I wasn't very lucky last race weekend," she says, her gaze switching between looking at my eyes and lips.

"I didn't even have a scratch after the crash. If you don't think I had your kiss to thank for that, then you clearly don't see things the way I do," I reply, making her bite her bottom lip to hide a smile.

"You're such a flirt," she says, and a deep laugh bursts out of me.

"That wasn't flirting, Nevaeh. You pressing your ass against my cock was," I remind her, watching the most beautiful of blushes take hold of her cheeks. My sister flashes Nevaeh a curious look, but my angel doesn't say a word.

"You pushed me away so quickly, you can hardly say it was more than a brush," she defends, so I place my hands back on her hips and drag her backward until my cock presses against her round ass. It's so subtle, I doubt anyone could possibly realize what I'm doing unless they stood right behind me. "You told me not to do it again, but you get to? That doesn't seem fair," she complains as my sister wins another round.

She's having the time of her life, jumping up and down out of excitement and pressing sloppy kisses to Gabriel's lips every time she wins.

"If only you'd come home with me tonight, so I could show you how frustrating the barrier of our clothes really is," I say, watching her bet some money and join the game.

"Maybe I will, or maybe I'll take you back to my place. I don't care either way as long as you're the one taking this dress off me," is the last thing she says before winning a big chunk of money and stepping away to start doing the interviews she told me she'd be doing.

I watch after her for a long moment, trying to process what she just said.

Fuck.

She wants me.

I'm gonna take her dress off tonight and make her come so many times, she'll be as addicted to me as I am to her.

CHAPTER 42
Nevaeh

I know I'm being all of those things, telling Adrian I'd like him to take me home later, but I'm done.

I'm done pretending he's not the one I want when seeing him in that tux, wearing an expression of pure, unfiltered joy and lust made me feel wanted in a way I never have before.

I'm done pretending because there is no one like Adrian Romana, no person who'll ever treat me like I'm so much more than just good enough. Like I'm the very reason he breathes.

I've been with men and women, but none of them could ever compare to him.

There are a million things we have to figure out, whether or not he really wants a relationship, and if yes, can we keep this a secret until my job no longer prohibits us from being together? It won't be easy, but I don't care anymore. No good thing is ever easily accomplished, but they're so much sweeter when you have them.

Adrian is my moon, in complete control of the feelings I have for him, and there's no fighting his gravitational pull anymore.

"Nevaeh! You look beautiful," Cameron Kion says as I approach, and I grin at him.

"You all look very handsome tonight," I compliment him, James, and Leonard, who thank me before smiling at the same time. The synchronization makes me smile. Well, all of them but Leonard. He gives me a polite nod, as unhappy to be here as I would imagine a loving man to be when his wife and daughter are thousands of kilometers away from him.

We fall into a casual conversation, and I ask them some questions for my article, which they happily answer. I leave them shortly after and notice an area being cleared for dancing. Music fills the room as a hand grabs mine and guides me against Lincoln's chest.

"Lincoln, what the hell are you doing?" I ask, a little uncomfortable that he's touching me. We haven't spoken in person in a long, *long* time. Now that I live in Monaco, I was hoping I'd see him even less.

He sways me to the music for a moment, not a single word coming from him.

"I'm getting very uncomfortable, Linc," I say, attempting to step out of his hold, but his grip tightens.

"Please, stay for a moment. I want to apologize," he says, but I push against him again. He doesn't let me go.

"I don't want to hear your apology. You were right when you said I didn't want to hear it all those months ago. I didn't. I still don't. You've hurt me too many times in the past, have staked a claim on me when I have not and never will be yours, and then we stopped speaking. It should stay that way." He frowns at me, and his hands hold on even tighter, his fingers digging into my hips.

"So, you admit to being stubborn, and yet it's still my fault? Do you see the problem, Nevaeh? It's you. It was never me, and that isn't fair." Anger makes my cheeks heat and my heart race.

"We're only here because you made a mistake four years ago that you can't accept, the one that broke something between us I'll never be able to fix." Lincoln shakes his head with an angry look.

"You don't even want to try!" he says, and I tug on the grip he has on me once more.

"You're right, I don't. Lincoln, you used to be everything to me. You were my best friend, the guy I fell in love with when I was a teenager. We were inseparable, but after we fell apart, I fell out of love. We drifted away from each other because you broke my trust when you stomped on the pieces of my broken heart. I'd just lost my dream and then I lost my best friend and first love in the same breath. That can't be fixed. I don't want it to be fixed. I want to move on with my life and leave us in the past, where we belong," I explain, stopping my movements, but he still doesn't release me.

"How could you be so selfish?" I'm so sick and tired of people throwing this at me whenever I make choices that will heal me, that can make me happy.

"Lincoln, let go of me. I'm done with this conversation," I say, but he doesn't. He holds tighter. Trying not to make a scene, I resist the urge to knee him somewhere very private.

"You heard her. Get your hands off before I remove them, and you don't want to find out all of the career-ending ways I'm imagining doing so right now," Adrian says as he walks up to us, placing a hand on my shoulder.

Once Lincoln releases me, the Monegasque pulls me behind him, shielding me.

"Touch her again, and I'll destroy your career. I'll go to Robert Fuchs and tell him how you treat his daughter to get you kicked off the team. I'll go to the media and tell them when a woman asks you to let go, you hold on tighter. I'll tell them all the truths until you're nothing. Until you're done in the world of Formula One. Do you understand me?" Adrian asks, anger tensing his shoulders.

"You think you're so high and fucking mighty when you have no idea what you're talking about. Get out of my way. Nevaeh and I aren't done talking."

This whole conversation is making me nauseous. The prospect of a fight breaking out makes me feel physically ill, and that's all Lincoln has been doing. Picking fights with me, making me miserable. He's toxic, and I don't want him in my life anymore.

"Are you done talking to him, *mon ange*?" Adrian asks as he turns to me.

"I've been done since he dragged me onto the dance floor," I reply, wrapping my arms around myself and taking a step back.

"There's your fucking answer, rookie. I suggest you don't come near her again." A hand slips into mine, and I look over my shoulder to see Valentina by my side,

Gabriel beside her. Leonard, Cameron, and James have joined them as well, making sure this situation doesn't get out of hand.

Lincoln takes a step forward, closing the distance between himself and Adrian. I spot Leonard walking toward them now, scowling and looking ready to murder someone.

"Take another step, and you won't be dealing with Adrian, you'll be dealing with me," the World Champion says, moving to stand between Adrian and Lincoln. "And trust me, I'm a far worse option than the sunshine boy behind me."

Lincoln lets out a huff, anger turning his face red. Without another word, he storms off, away from the dance floor.

Cameron spins Valentina into a dance right after, and I find myself in Adrian's arms, swaying to the music. My heart is still racing, and he seems to take notice because he traces his usual infinity figure on my back to soothe me.

"I have to go finish my interviews," I say, but I don't step out of Adrian's arms yet, and he doesn't push me away either. If anything, sensing I need a bit of comfort, he guides me closer as we slow-dance to the music.

"I know," he replies, keeping a respectful distance between our lips when I want nothing more than to kiss him. To thank him for helping me avoid this fight I didn't want to have. "I just want to hold you for one more minute, make sure you're okay. Then, I'll let go, okay?" he asks, and I nod several times.

Neither one of us speaks as we continue swaying, listening to the music as he presses his cheek to my forehead and I close my eyes.

"I meant what I said. I want to go to your apartment with you. I want to spend the night together," I blurt out quietly, but by the way his body tenses a little, I know he heard me.

"There's nothing I want more." My heart flutters from his words.

"My boss won't like it, so we can't tell anyone," I say, stepping out of his arms to bring some distance between us. A few people to our left were giving us strange looks, so space it is.

"I don't need to parade us around, Nevaeh. If you want me the way I want you, I'm all in. In any way this will work," he replies, shoving his hands into his pockets. I want to do the same because not being able to touch him while he tells me he wants a relationship, probably for the first time in his life, is torture.

"I want that, too," I whisper, and the brightest of grins spreads across his face.

"Then we'll sneak out of here. Gabriel will show you the back exit, and I'll meet you there with my car in half an hour," he says, taking a step toward me to add, "I want you to do something for me when we're in the car."

His voice is low and full of a delicious promise, making more goosebumps spread over my skin.

"Anything," I reply before my brain even processes the word.

"Spread your legs for me so I can slip my hand into your panties and make you feel good, okay?" the Monegasque says, and I nod slowly, words vanish from my brain.

He steps around me and toward where they're taking donations without another word.

CHAPTER 43

Adrian

AFTER WASHING MY HANDS, I rush outside to grab my car from the valet. My body is fucking vibrating from desire. My mind is playing through all of my fantasies, every little thing I want to do with her, and my cock stirs at the possibility of finally kissing her again, undressing her, sinking deep inside of her.

I've never, ever wanted a woman so desperately, and knowing she wants me too? Nobody. Fucking. Pinch. Me.

The valet gives me a strange look when I politely—okay, rudely—tell him to get my car as quickly as humanly possible. I make up for it by giving him the biggest tip of my life and racing to get to Nevaeh's and my meeting point. She's already standing outside with my teammate and my sister, smiling at something they're telling her.

She'll never stop mesmerizing me. Merely seeing her smile is enough to make my heart palpitate.

"Get in, *mon paradis*," I say as I step out of the car to open her door, watching her face light up with lust at the sight of me. I may have undone most of the buttons of my shirt on the way over to get this reaction.

"Bye," Nevaeh says to Val and Gabriel, slipping into the passenger seat while running a hand across my chest.

My cock hardens uncomfortably from this simple, little touch, embarrassingly quickly, too.

As soon as I'm in the car, I tell Nevaeh to get her head down as we speed past a dozen reporters. It's nothing new that people see me with a mystery woman. The women I've slept with in the past loved the attention of the press and being seen with me, and I gave it to them without blinking twice. I didn't mind the world knowing I never settled down, but, right now, I mind it a whole fucking lot because I don't want Nevaeh to be grouped together with the people in my past.

She's my present and future.

So, I tell her to duck, both to avoid anyone seeing us together for her job and to prevent them from assuming she doesn't mean anything to me. That she's a fling.

She's not.

She's so, so much more to me.

Once we're out of sight, I watch Nevaeh spread her legs for me, tilting her head in my direction to smile.

"Good girl," I praise, slipping my hand onto her bare thigh where her dress has a slit. A blush creeps up her cleavage and neck before settling on her cheeks.

"Adrian," Nevaeh says on an exhale, but I take my time trailing my fingers up her leg before letting them disappear underneath her dress.

"Did you get all your answers from the drivers?" I ask, dropping my hand between her thighs but far away from her pussy.

Nevaeh's legs clench together, trapping my fingers between them.

"Yes," she says, pulling at her dress to give us more room without the fabric constricting us.

"Fuck, Nevaeh, you're such a dream," I say, slipping my hand higher until my index finger can run over her soaking wet panties. "Is this for me?" I ask, rubbing the fabric and making her squirm in the seat.

"No, I just really like your car," she lies with a naughty smile. I stop rubbing her, and she whimpers. "Fine, yes, it's for you. It's always for you. You turn me on, Adrian, and I need you. Please," she says, and I reward her by sliding her panties to the side and playing with her clit.

"Atta girl, I like hearing you say that," I say and keep rubbing my fingers in circles before slipping them over her wet center. Fuck, I want to slide right in—

"Oh my God, Adrian," Nevaeh moans, her walls clenching around my index finger. She's so tight, I go slow, barely past the first knuckle.

"Are you okay?" I ask, and she nods several times, her hand grabbing the door handle.

"Yes, it feels so good. Keep moving, please," she begs, so I slip my finger out of her, playing with her clit for another moment and then thrusting back inside her pussy.

"You have no idea how hot that is, baby. I could feel your dripping wet pussy all day," I say, feeling her clench around me again.

My eyes are on the road up until the moment we make it into my parking garage. Once we're parked, I turn to her, adding a second finger as I thrust into her.

"Fuck," she moans loudly, covering her mouth as her eyes flutter shut.

"Don't muffle your moans. I want to hear you."

She smiles and screams for me when I thrust back inside and find the little spot that makes her entire body buck.

"I need you to focus on me, Nevaeh. Eyes on me, just for a moment," I say, although watching her lose herself in the pleasure I'm giving her is by far one of the best sights I've ever laid my eyes on. When she doesn't look at me, I stop my movements. "Before we go upstairs, I need you to tell me what you like in the bedroom. The quicker you do, the sooner I keep going and make you come on my fingers," I promise, watching her gaze drift to me with uncertainty writing itself all over her face.

"What do you mean?" she says like no one has ever taken the time to ask her this question.

"What turns you on? What do you like done to you? Do you like coming on cocks or faces better? Hands? What do you need? I'll give you anything," I say and mean the promise with every fiber of my being.

Her mouth forms the most beautiful O-shape, and I lean forward to trace her lips, picturing slipping my cock between them and into the heat and wetness of her.

"Tell me, *mon ange*, what do you like?" I ask when all she does is roll her hips to get the friction back. She manages to grind down on the heel of my hand, eliciting a moan out of herself. I smile, rubbing my hand against her clit until her back arches off the seat. "Nevaeh," I remind her, using her name as softly as I always do.

"I like how bossy you are and when you praised me just now," she admits, so I reward her by thrusting my fingers back inside of her and curling them to play with her G-spot.

She cries out, making my cock throb uncomfortably in my pants. It wants to be touched, to be deep inside Nevaeh.

My angel tilts her head away from me as she says, "I get really turned on by making someone moan." Embarrassment heats up her cheeks, so she covers her face to hide.

"We have that in common," I assure her, my thumb tracing her clit.

"Oh God," she moans, grabbing my arm for stability as I bring her closer to her climax.

"You have nothing to be ashamed of. I'll make every single one of your fantasies come true, Nevaeh, and then we'll come up with some on our own," I promise.

Nevaeh grinds against my hand, frantically trying to reach her release as I play with pussy until she drenches my hand.

"I've always wanted to have sex somewhere that's a little public. Where nobody is, but anyone could walk in. Like right now, but a little more dangerous," she explains, and I lean over the middle console of my car to grab her face.

"I'll make it happen," I say before leaning forward and kissing her right as my fingers thrust inside of her again, feeling her orgasm tremble through her.

I taste it as she slips her tongue into my mouth, her hands sliding into my hair as she brings me closer and grinds against my hand. She's moaning and whimpering through her pleasure, and I almost reach for my cock and give it a rough jerk just so it doesn't hurt so much from the build-up anymore.

I wasn't lying when I told her hearing women moan for me turns me on. It turns me on even more because Nevaeh is the one falling apart for me.

"Fuck, you're too beautiful when you come. How am I ever going to stop?" I ask as I lean back to take in the satisfied smile on her face.

"I want to make you come," she says and brings her hand to my lips.

"Let's go upstairs, baby, then you'll get your wish while I get mine again."

We sprint up the stairs, too impatient to wait for the elevator. I'm right behind Nevaeh, grabbing her ass on the way up and making her squeal uncontrollably. She turns around and flings her arms across my neck, pulling my head down to kiss me again.

We're in the middle of the staircase, but I push her up against the wall and explore her mouth anyway, not giving a fuck who can see us. Her hands slip onto my ass, bringing my cock right against her lower stomach. Nevaeh rubs herself against me until I'm groaning into her mouth.

"Hmmm, there he is," she says, breaking the kiss to smile at me and reach for my cock.

"Touch my cock, and I'll fuck you right here, Nevaeh, up against this wall," I warn because I don't have enough self-control to wait anymore unless she tells me to.

Knowing which floor and what apartment to go to, Nevaeh runs off without waiting for me, holding up her dress. Her shoes dangle from my fingers as I follow behind her with a chuckle and my cock so hard, even walking is uncomfortable.

My girl's waiting for me in front of my apartment door, leaning against the wall and grinning like I'm the best thing in the world. And I know I have the same look on my face because how the hell could I not?

She's *everything*.

I unlock my door and wrap an arm around her, pulling her against me as we stumble inside, my mouth back on hers. My teeth graze her bottom lip, getting a sigh of happiness from her.

My hand slips to her throat, pressing down on each side to feel her heart racing. She moans from the pressure, fumbling with my pants until she has the button undone and the zipper down.

"Can I touch your cock?" she asks as I kiss along her jaw.

"You can touch every single part of me. I'm yours."

Nevaeh slips her hand into my pants, palming me through my boxers until I groan, my kiss growing hungrier.

"Bedroom," I say, pleasure rolling through me until I have to grit my teeth and breathe through the wave that has my orgasm embarrassingly close. Nevaeh keeps rubbing me, ignoring my instructions, and making me hold on for dear life.

Too impatient, I distract her by kissing her again and leading her into my bedroom, throwing her onto the bed the first chance I get. She giggles, stretching her arms into the air until her body is on display for me. She's so fucking sexy, I can't breathe.

"Undress," she instructs, but I shake my head.

"You don't get to tell me what to do tonight, *mon paradis.* I'm in charge and you're going to let me take off your dress so I can finally get a look at that perfect body of yours," I say, and Nevaeh rolls her neck for a second, pressing her legs together at my command.

I pull her upright again, spinning her around until her back faces me. My fingers glide over her arms, slowly, teasingly making their way toward the back of her dress. They slip across her collarbone, over her shoulders, before dropping to her zipper and carefully pulling it down. My lips move to her neck, kissing her lovingly and gently for a moment while I work on removing her dress. I want her to be comfortable, to know how much she means to me while I take away this barrier and we step into a more intimate and vulnerable zone.

I kiss her neck again, but as soon as the dress hits the floor, she spins around to kiss my mouth, giggling from happiness as I guide her back toward the bed. Nevaeh drops down on it, still smiling as she shows off her curves, which are only covered by a set of black lingerie. A simple bra and panty combination I've seen on hundreds of women, but none of them have ever made me feel quite so out of control.

I shrug off my tux jacket and undo the last couple of buttons on my shirt, letting both fall to the ground. My pants follow while she watches me, her eyes glued to my body. Once I'm only in my boxers, Nevaeh reaches behind her to undo the clasp of her bra, letting it fall down to the floor.

Her breasts bounce free of the containment, her nipples pebbled and demanding my attention. I want to give them my mouth, my hands, anything, but I'm so mesmerized, all I can do is stare at Nevaeh.

I don't think I've ever seen anyone so perfect.

"Fucking hell," I mumble, sucking in a sharp breath.

"Everything you dreamed they would be?" she teases, always playing on my weakness. I nestle myself between her legs, grabbing her chin and forcing her to look straight into my eyes as I answer.

"None of my dreams compare to your body, to you," I say, lowering my head to kiss down her collarbone, all the way to her left breast. I suck her hard nipple into my mouth, tugging until she's moaning.

"Adrian."

My name has never sounded so sweet.

My lips trail kisses in a horizontal line across her chest until they wrap around her right nipple to show it the same level of attention. My fingers curl around her panties, but I look up at her for permission before dragging them down.

"Please," she begs, anticipation making her breathing shallow and heavy. "I need you inside of me." I slide down her panties, kissing her as I do because I can't help myself. I've never kissed anyone this much, and I never want to stop either.

Kissing Nevaeh is like taking your first breath after being underwater for too long. Fucking ironic considering I can't breathe when I'm around her because I'm so scared of allowing myself to feel, of her breaking my heart and leaving me, that I forget I need oxygen to survive.

Before I spiral into my panic, Nevaeh places a hand on my cheek, caressing the skin there.

"I'm here. I'm not going anywhere," she promises, almost as if she can sense my fear, so I kiss her even harder to let her reassure me with more than just words.

Her hand reaches for my cock again, stroking me over my boxers. My knees buckle from pleasure, and I thrust my hips forward, my dick toward her hand, for more contact. Her tongue plays with mine, and, although I said I'd be the one in charge, she's the one holding all of the control.

Stepping back to catch my breath, I let my eyes trail down her naked body, stopping at the V between her legs. Her pussy is dripping wet and pink, her clit swollen again and needy for attention. I lick my lips, desperate for a taste, but Nevaeh's words echo in my head, and my cock gives an agreeing throb.

"Such a pretty pussy," I mumble, leaning down to kiss her neck and slip my boxers off at the same time. "Lie back," I instruct a second later, but her eyes linger on my cock, panic written all over her face. "Don't worry, *mon ange*, we'll go slow. It'll fit," I assure her, and she lets out a nervous laugh.

"How do you hide that thing when you're in your racing suit?" she blurts out with another nervous laugh, and I chuckle in response, watching her cheeks heat yet again.

"When I'm not around you, it's a lot easier," I explain and grab a condom, spreading her legs wider so I can move between them.

Nevaeh reaches out to stroke me, smirking as she watches me tremble from the pleasure. I wait for her to finish exploring me, wanting to give her the same time I took before putting on the condom and slipping inside her beautiful pussy.

She releases me and watches with fascination as I roll the condom down my hard length, concentrating on making sure it's on right. I suck in a sharp breath once it's all the way down my cock, and Nevaeh trails her hands up the sides of my thighs, then over my ass where she squeezes to bring me closer. I tumble forward with a laugh, taking her with me and claiming her mouth again as we fall backward. She giggles against my lips, but when I rub my dick over her pussy, over her clit, letting her coat me in her desire, the sound quickly turns into a moan.

"You're perfect, Nevaeh," I say, slowly pushing inside of her. "Every inch of you."

She sucks in a breath, tensing around me.

"Do you want me to stop?" I ask and attempt to slide back out, but her hands move to my ass cheeks to stop me.

"No, don't stop, please. I'm in my head," she says, running a hand down my face. "I wanna feel good for you," Nevaeh admits in a whisper, averting her gaze. I grab her chin between my fingers, tilting her head my way again.

"Feel me, baby," I say, grabbing my cock and gliding it over her pussy. "Feel how hard you make me, how my cock aches to be inside of you. Your touch, your body, *you* feel like heaven to me, Nevaeh," I add and drop my hand from her chin to her breasts to rub my thumb over her nipple. "I'll make you feel so good, I'll slip right in." My promise is followed by a shudder and a small moan when I pinch her nipple between my fingers.

I touch her all over, kneading her breasts, rubbing her clit in slow, tight circles until she's whimpering. I glide the head of my cock over her again before pressing into her.

"More," she says, so I slide in another few centimeters. Nevaeh moans, reaching for my neck to pull my mouth to hers.

"You're such a good girl, stretching to fit my cock deep inside of you," I praise. My angel moans as I thrust all the way in, her thighs squeezing me. "You feel so good, squeezing my cock," I say and kiss her, giving us both a moment to adjust to this new sensation before I slip out of her and thrust back inside. "Shit, shit, shit," I breathe, my mouth dropping to her nipple again. "You're doing so well for me."

The way she melts into me every single time I praise her has me on the verge of coming so quickly, I slow my thrusts to prolong this moment.

Nevaeh whimpers in complaint, but I angle her hips up and fuck her in shallow thrusts right against the spot that makes her cry my name over and over.

"Just like that, Adrian," she begs as I press down on her lower abdomen, moaning so loudly, all of my neighbors are going to know how well I fuck my girl. I lower her hips again to lean down, sucking her nipple back into my mouth to play with it.

Hearing my pleasure makes her clench around me again, so firmly that my arms and legs shake while I fight off my orgasm. My balls tighten and my cock aches with the need to release, so I fuck her harder and faster, slowly increasing my speed to see her reaction.

"God, yes!" she screams, so I go deeper, harder, faster. Then shallower, softer, slower.

My groans escape without my permission, but I don't try to hold them back either. Instead, I kiss her, my hand moving between our bodies to stroke her clit and drive her straight over the edge with me.

One more thrust and I'm coming so hard, I'm seeing stars. Nevaeh trembles beneath me, moaning through her orgasm as I spill into the condom, still pumping in and out to let us ride out our pleasure for as long as possible.

Pressing a kiss to each of her breasts, I take my time catching my breath. I lower myself on top of her, not ready to slide out of her and break our connection just yet.

"That was so fast," she says, placing her hands in my hair. She's smiling, her lips perfectly swollen from our kissing.

"It has been long overdue. All those months were like the longest foreplay in history. After all that build-up, the release comes quick," I say, moving up her body and pressing my lips to hers. "But don't worry. We have the whole night to go again." Kiss. "Again." Nibble on her bottom lip. "And again."

My tongue briefly slips into her mouth before my lips move to her jaw, kissing her until my cock hardens again.

"I want you to ride me, Nevaeh, let me see those breasts bounce."

And fuck, they do as she rides me like I've never been before.

CHAPTER 44
Adrian

I ALWAYS FEEL LIKE a fucking creep, staring at Nevaeh while she's fast asleep in my arms, but I also can't bring myself to stop.

A satisfied little smile lingers on her full lips, making one slip onto mine. I put it there. Her happy, "I just got fucked until I passed out" expression is there because of me, and my heart is racing at the thought.

Sex has always been about pleasure for me. Feelings were never present, and I had no clue how differently it would feel with someone I feel this way about. I had no idea that the connection I share with Nevaeh would end in the best orgasms I've ever had.

Her tight walls wrapped around me while she repeated my name over and over gave me something I've never experienced, never thought I would in a billion years either.

It gave me a safe space.

Nevaeh is my safe space.

My fingertips run over her soft cheek, memorizing every single birthmark, freckle, mole, little vein, anything I can see in my dark bedroom. I try to make sense of my feelings, but I'm so lost, so new to all of this, I have no idea what any of them mean.

Nevaeh giggles when I kiss her? My knees go weak.

She leans into me and inhales my scent like her life depends on it? My heart explodes into a million colors of joy.

She sighs out of happiness? I'm a goner.

I'm so desperately wrapped around her finger, my chest hurts when I'm not near her.

What does that mean?

And more importantly, what the hell happened to me?

That question resurfaces less frequently now than it did a few months ago, but I still have no answer for it. Just last year, I was set on growing old by myself. Well, myself and James since he has been too in love with Val to notice other women.

I thought that'd be it.

We'd sit on our veranda, looking back at the exciting life we had as race car drivers. Now he has a son, and I found a woman I don't ever want to let go of again.

Her eyelids flutter, a little moan leaving her. I want to lean down and kiss her because of it, but I also don't want to wake her. It's been a long, emotionally and physically exhausting day for her, and she needs to rest.

My thumb glides over her bottom lip, which is slightly thinner than her top one, tracing the shape until I'm hoping it'll never leave my memory. Who am I kidding? Nothing about this woman will ever leave my mind.

Every moment with her turns into a core memory.

Just like right now.

Doing something as simple as studying the way her steady breathing pushes her chest against mine every few seconds is perfect. I drop my fingers to her stomach, finding a new area to memorize. My thumb brushes over her stretch marks down to the ones near her belly button. I suck in a sharp breath before trailing over the lines of indents near her hips.

Stretch marks.

Such simple things, insecurities for most women because of society's stupid expectations, but they're the most beautiful thing I've ever seen on Nevaeh. Just like the scar on her right shoulder, which is the next area I trace. Her biggest insecurity is my second favorite place on her body. It's a physical representation of her strength and determination.

I'll never get tired of looking at it.

How could I?

Another little moan leaves her, and I smile. She's so happy and I'm the cause. I'm right for her, and I have never been right for anyone in my life. My sister is the only exception, but I was raised to be everything she could ever need. With James, Leonard, Cameron, and Gabriel it's different, too. They keep me around because I'm funny and like them enough to do anything for them. Fine, *love* them enough to give my life for them if it comes down to it.

But with Nevaeh?

Nothing makes sense. I don't constantly have to work to be everything she wants. I don't have to offer her the world. I *want* to do all of those things. It comes naturally to me because she makes life easier. She's made breathing easier since I met her all those months ago. The sexy, proud smirk on her face as she studied her photos. Her gorgeous body was covered in so many layers, that I chuckled at the time. Her face was so bright and glowing, I didn't even have time to fixate on anything else.

"Adrian," she mumbles in her sleep, and I inch closer to her. Fuck, my name falling from her lips sounds so different than when anyone else uses it. It sounds so much better.

"I'm here," I whisper, and the tension that briefly entered her shoulders washes away.

"Cold," she says, but I doubt she'll remember any of this tomorrow because she's mostly asleep.

I reach behind me for the shirt I was wearing before I went to the event, and somehow, and I have no idea how, manage to place it on her naked chest without waking her.

She snuggles against me at the same moment my phone starts to vibrate on my nightstand. I snatch it off the wood before it wakes... my girlfriend.

Damn, I like that way too much.

"What?" I hiss into the phone without looking at the caller ID. A deep voice rumbles through the speaker.

"Open the front door, arsehole. I have questions," Leonard's familiar voice drowns into the speaker, but I have to hold the phone away to make sure I'm not imagining this.

"Are you having a laugh?" I say, imitating his English accent while I use a phrase he loves to say to me. "It's two in the morning. I'm not opening the door for you," I blurt out, but I'm also already slipping out of bed.

He won't go away until I let him in and give him answers.

"Do you have a beer cold?" he asks, and I walk over to my fridge, pulling out one of the ones I bought for Nevaeh, in case she ever decided to stay over again. Nova told me Nevaeh likes a good German beer, and I will always have what she needs.

"You're one persistent and annoying person, mate," I say as I open the door and shove the beer into his hand. He takes a sip before even entering my apartment, making his way toward my balcony and placing his finger over his lips.

"Come on, we don't want to wake the poor thing you've somehow managed to deceive," he replies in a whisper, and I nudge him in the ribs so hard, he lets out a strained breath. "I was just teasing. Bloody hell. No need for violence." He takes another swig, his throat working as the liquid shoots down.

"Well, it wasn't fucking funny," I retort, walking over to the table and sitting down. My eyes shift to the cocoon chair, the memory of Nevaeh with her head in my lap replaying before I can stop it.

A bright smile slips onto my face.

"Sorry, I've just been where you are now, except I didn't give up the life of a fuckboy for the woman I love," he says, and the smile vanishes, irritation replacing it on my face.

"I'm not *giving up* anything. I'm *getting* everything by being with Nevaeh." His jaw drops a little at my angry tone. I've never, ever raised my voice at Leonard. I respect him more than anyone else because of his experiences. He's lived longer than me, seen more things than I have, and is an irreplaceable friend. "How do you even know Nevaeh and I are... something?" I can't tell him we're going to date in secret if he knows nothing yet.

"Because it's clear as fucking day, Adrian. I saw you two at the event, I know you left together." He cocks a brow, and I hide a frown by running my hand over my face. That's not good. "Don't worry, Val told me about Nevaeh's job. I will take this to my grave," he promises, and I know he's good for it.

Leonard doesn't tell anyone about people's personal lives, including his own.

"I'm surprised you didn't tell me your feelings were so strong. You usually ask me for advice," he says and fakes a pout. I roll my eyes at him, but he merely returns to his scowling expression as he sips his beer. Grumpy old man.

"All you need to know is we're going to date in secret, but I've never been happier." Leonard's brown eyes stare into mine from the other side of the table.

"You've changed," he says, pressing his lips together to fight back a smile.

"I don't know why you're so surprised. You changed completely after you started dating Chiara." The mention of her name makes his eyes twinkle.

"Yes, she warmed up my life and made me smile, but I wasn't the one who swore off relationships until I reached my grave," he says, and the reminder of that conversation sends a shiver down my spine.

"That was before Nevaeh," I mumble.

"Maybe, but it doesn't change that if you're not one hundred percent sure, you're going to break that girl's heart by pretending you are," Leonard says, and I look up at him.

"Her heart is not the one that's in danger of being ripped to shreds," I reply, staring out at the ocean and sucking in a sharp breath to gather courage for what I haven't admitted out loud to anyone yet. "Mine is."

CHAPTER 45
Nevaeh

WE'RE ON THE TENTH race of the season. Mrs. Lu threw my schedule around so that my interview with Valentina has been rescheduled to the weekend of the Monaco Grand Prix. My friend wasn't happy about it, but when I reminded her how special it'd be for the article to be written about her at her home race, she beamed up at me.

We're in Austin, Texas this weekend, and I have yet to take some time to go explore the city I grew up in for three years of my life. I meant to go when we first got here a few days ago, but then Adrian showed up at my hotel room with a pint of ice cream. We shared half of it before he buried his face between my legs until they were shaking and I was screaming his name. He did that over and over until I lost count of how many times I came and he finally sunk inside of me.

Adrian and I have been secretly dating for the past seven weeks, and something that's become very clear is that he loves to watch me orgasm. All the time. Every chance he gets.

We've been good about keeping our distance and sneaking around undetected. We've also somehow managed to hug a lot less or touch each other in general, which I hate but has been good for Gillian to get off my case. Ms. Martin hasn't asked me about Adrian anymore, and I've been handing in articles that have gotten a lot of attention from fans.

I'm making a name for myself and I'm loving every second.

Adrian has been kicking ass too, having won five out of the past ten races. Gabriel is currently second in the Drivers' Championship standings, Lincoln only a point behind him, and ten points behind Adrian. They're close, but there is still over half a season left. Nothing's written in stone yet, or on a trophy, I guess.

Today is Qualifying, and James has been preoccupied with his responsibilities without paying too much attention to me. He's the driver I'm interviewing this weekend and he warned me about his quiet behavior a few days ago, but I don't mind it one bit.

We've been getting along well these past few days, and I'm already working on the article. It fascinates me how different the rituals are for every driver. James focuses on reflex training while Gabriel focuses mostly on stretching and warming up his muscles.

"Can we talk?" James asks me, surprise settling in my chest.

"Of course," I reply, and he motions for me to sit down with him at the table in the empty conference room I was planning to work in until Qualifying was over. There is a small screen in here, showing live footage of the session. "What's up?" I ask, slightly worried about the answer. James and I hardly know each other, and, even though I like him, we've never been alone, not even at any point during this weekend.

"I'm sorry to bother you like this, but I need you to promise me something," he starts, and I watch him carefully as he wrestles to phrase his request. His blue eyes drift to mine, his gaze holding mine. "For the article, please don't mention Damian. I know we've talked about him, but I'd like to keep him as far away from the spotlight as possible," he explains.

I offer him a small smile.

"You have my word, I won't say anything about him nor will I send it off to my boss without letting you read the article first. That's how it works with me," I assure him, earning myself a dashing smile I'm convinced could make anyone fall in love, given that they aren't already with someone else.

"Thank you. I appreciate it, Nevaeh." I smile at him, but there is more he wants to say. I can tell by the way he scans my face as if answers were written in my features. "At the end of last season, a man wrote an article about Damian without any knowledge of my actual relationship with him or that he was adopted by Gabriel's aunts, Dominique and Nicolette. He called me a terrible father," James admits, breaking eye contact and looking away. I slide my hand onto his shoulder and squeeze it, bringing a comforting expression to my face.

"I would never write lies like that, especially considering how great of a father you are. You made a difficult decision that got Damian two amazing moms and you. If I wrote about you as a father, and I won't, that's what I'd say," I reply, squeezing his shoulder again before dropping my hand.

He studies me for another moment before smiling to himself and nodding.

"Your heart," James says, and I furrow my brows.

"What about my heart?" I ask with curiosity and confusion laced in my tone.

"It stole my best friend's, and I had no idea why until a moment ago. Now, I know," he adds, standing up and grinning down at me. "I'm glad you're in his life."

Then, the Englishman walks away, leaving me with the sweetest feeling spreading through my chest.

I attempt to go back to my article, but the empty room fills with the sound of my favorite voice a moment later.

"God, you're so beautiful," Adrian says, and I close my notepad to look up at him. A smile dances over my face, mimicking his: one of pure happiness. His green-blue-brown eyes scan my body as I stand up to be in front of him.

Adrian's fingers instantly move to my nape, pulling my mouth to his.

"What are you doing here? Qualifying is about to start," I remind him, but he merely cocks a brow before closing the door behind him to make sure no one sees us in here.

"I have come to establish a new tradition." He bends down to press his lips to mine, letting out a sigh when he breaks the kiss again.

"For good luck?" I ask, his nod serving as a response while he lingers in front of me with his eyes closed and a satisfied look on his face.

"I can feel it coursing through me already," he says or jokes, I'm not sure, but I burst into laughter either way.

"My God, get out of here before I question why I like you," I tease, and he smiles at me.

"Always with the teasing, Nevaeh. I'm already on my knees for you, what more do you want?" he asks before giving me a wink that weakens *my* knees. "I'll see you later," he adds with a serious look, and I step on my tiptoes to place a swift kiss on his lips.

"Be careful," I remind him, making him hesitate in front of me for a moment, panic in his eyes. "What? What did I say?" I ask, and he shakes his head.

"Nothing, I just realized that if something were to happen to me, I'd never get the chance to—" Adrian cuts off and stares deeply into my eyes, a little smile now on his lips. "Well, I'd never get the chance to do a lot of things with you. Kind of scared me there for a moment," he admits, and I take a step toward him to place my hands on his hips.

"Go kick some ass, and if you get pole, I'll give you the chance to fuck me in your private room," I suggest to take some of the tension off him.

It works like a charm.

Desire replaces his panic, and he bites down on his bottom lip.

"Is that a deal?" he asks, and I move backward to hold out my hand for him to shake. He does so with a ridiculous amount of enthusiasm before walking away, more determined than ever.

An excited laugh escapes me as I imagine having sex in a somewhat public space. Grenzenlos has been predominantly first during practice, so I don't think Adrian will get pole, but the thought still sends a thrill through me.

Qualifying starts a few minutes after I regain the ability to think about anything other than Adrian inside of me.

Q1 goes smoothly, all of my friends making it to Q2 with ease. The problems start in the second round. Valentina struggles with her car and doesn't make it to Q3 and neither do Leonard and Cameron. Disappointment washes over me for my friend, but I remind myself of something she said to me recently.

"You have to approach every race and Qualifying with a winning mindset, but you can't let that destroy you when you lose. That's the difference between a sore loser and an aspiring champion."

I know she will be sad about this result, but she will do her best tomorrow, learn and grow from today. I have no doubt in my mind.

Q3 has me on the edge of my seat. Adrian is fast and so is Gabriel, but neither of them seems able to keep up with the two Grenzenlos drivers. By the time they all take their last lap, I have lost the ability to breathe properly.

Lincoln crosses the finish line for the last time this session, his lap putting him on the provisional pole—the pole a driver gets when the rest have not finished their last lap of the session. Kyle comes in second, Gabriel in third, and James in fourth while the others place anywhere below that. I feel my heart skipping a beat when Adrian crosses the line, his lap a tenth of a second faster than Lincoln's.

"Yes!" I scream and jump out of my seat to clap.

My earlier excitement returns when I realize what this means. I let out a nervous laugh as I walk out of the conference room and over to James' performance coach to inform her that I've gathered all of the information I need for today and that I'll see her tomorrow. She gives me a warm smile before I head toward Adrian's box to find Daniel.

"Nevaeh! It's nice to see you. What can I do for you?" he asks, and I put on a serious face.

"Did Adrian tell you about—" I cut off and gesture around the room as if that would fill in the blanks. Daniel grins at me in response.

"No, but I'm not oblivious. I know that man very well," he says, making my cheeks heat.

"Okay, could you let him know I'm in his room when he's done with his interviews? There is something important I have to talk to him about," I say and he gives me a knowing smirk.

"Of course. Take the room. I will make sure no one interrupts so you can have some *privacy*," he replies with a wink, and I laugh in response.

Daniel opens the door of the room for me, leaving me alone a moment later. I suck in a sharp breath as my fingers reach for the buttons of my blouse. The material feels light as it drops to the floor, followed by my heavy shorts. I sit down on the single chair in the corner, crossing my legs and praying Daniel makes sure nobody intrudes.

It takes a while until the door opens again, but, luckily, Adrian steps into the room, taking the tension off my shoulders. His eyes look me up and down appreciatively as he closes the door and locks it.

"Fuck," he swears under his breath, and I dip my tongue out to run it over my bottom lip. Adrian watches me closely, his shoulders rising and falling rapidly. "*Mon paradis*," he says while approaching me with a smirk that would make my knees weak if I was standing. "I've been fantasizing about this since I was told I got pole. Please, get on the table for me, baby. I'm starving," he begs before holding his hand out to help me up. I let him pull me against his chest and lift me onto the massage table where he spreads my legs to move between them.

"Take off your suit," I say, but he grabs my legs and throws them over his shoulders, pulling me to the very edge of the table.

A gasp jumps out of me, followed by a muffled moan when he drags his nose over my panties where my clit is already swollen and begging for attention.

"In a minute," Adrian replies before bringing his lips to the inside of my left thigh, trailing kisses toward my pussy. His nose brushes over my panties again as he inhales and smiles. "*Mon petit paradis*, I've missed you," he mumbles before slipping down my underwear, his eyes on mine.

"I should be the one rewarding you for getting pole," I point out, pushing myself up on the table to get closer to him. Adrian's eyes drop to my pussy before his cool thumb runs over my clit, making me flinch.

"I'm sorry it's cold, I just washed my hands," he explains before lifting his fingers to warm them with his breath. "And to get back to your comment, this—" He cuts off to run his thumb over my swollen clit again. I cover my mouth to moan loudly.

"This is my fucking reward." His head moves between my thighs once more before his tongue swiftly flicks over my clit.

"Oh fuck!" I moan but immediately cover my mouth so no one can hear.

"You need to stay quiet, Nevaeh, otherwise I can't continue," he reminds me, and I nod to assure him I won't make another sound.

I sit up a little so I can watch him as he flicks his tongue over my clit for the second time, his fingers dipping inside of me and curling at the perfect spot. I scream into my hand, muffling the sound enough to make sure no one hears me.

Adrian looks up at me as he repeats the same two movements, watching my reaction closely. I try to keep eye contact, but pleasure consumes me. My eyes flutter closed without permission. My hand is still on my mouth, biting on it, while more inevitable moans leave me.

"Adrian, please, oh God." I'm a mess.

I don't even know what I'm begging for, but everything inside of me lights on fire as he speeds up, his lips wrapping around my clit to suck gently on it. The familiar build-up appears in my stomach, and I almost sigh in relief.

"Fuck," I breathe, and he moans against my clit, his fingers hitting my G-spot again.

My body starts to shake before an orgasm washes over me, taking me to my own personal *paradis*. I can barely feel his fingers and mouth leave me as I come down from my high, but when my eyes open, I find him smiling at me.

"I love how your body responds to me, how quickly I can make you come on my face," he says, his smug smile almost challenging me. My mind refocuses on the present as I sit up, my fingers moving to the zipper of his racing suit to pull it down.

"I bet I can make you fall apart quicker," I say, looking up at him with a naughty grin.

"I made you fall apart in two minutes. I can last longer than that," he defends, but happiness sparkles in his eyes. He's enjoying this playfulness just as much as I am.

"Are you sure?" I tease, my hands sliding under his suit so I can push it down his arms and chest. Adrian is patient as I undress him before panic settles on his face. "What?" I ask and stop my movements.

"I didn't bring a condom," he says, and I let out a shocked gasp.

"You, Adrian Romana, went somewhere without a pack of condoms ready? Damn. Are you okay?" I ask, but he merely chuckles. "It's a good thing your girlfriend is just as horny as you then," I explain and nod toward my shorts, which he picks up to stick his hand into the back pocket. Adrian pulls out a row of condoms and chuckles.

"How much sex did you plan on having with me?" he says, and I shrug.

"Don't judge. It's been days, and see, I'm the prepared one now. *I* made this possible," I remind him, making him laugh.

"You, Nevaeh Fuchs, truly are my perfect match." His sweet words surprise both of us, but he simply smiles at me after he realizes what he said. "What have you done to me?" he asks and steps toward me, his gaze warm as it fixates on my face.

"I don't know, but I hope you don't mind," I reply and start removing his clothes again.

"Not one bit," he whispers while I slide his suit down further along with his boxers. His hard cock excites my entire body as I get on my knees for him.

Adrian grabs my chin to force me to look up at him right as I reach for his cock.

"I have one rule about oral. I don't want head if I didn't shower before, okay?" My confused expression makes him smile. "I don't like the thought of tasting bad for you," he explains, and my eyes go wide.

"Oh okay," I say, watching him grab my chin and leaning down to press a swift, gentle kiss to my lips.

I take the condoms from his hand and carefully slide one down his cock before standing up again and pushing him backward, guiding him to sit in the chair I was in earlier.

"Bra," he commands, and my fingers slip onto my back to undo the clasp, letting the material drop from my breast and exposing my hard nipples. "Fucking perfection," he says and leans back in the chair, staring at me like he truly believes those words. "Come use me, Nevaeh," he says and pats his thigh, sending a thrill through me.

I admire his body, the way his fireproofs are barely lifted enough to expose his lower stomach. The way his racing suit still hugs his legs, but his cock is out and ready for me to play with.

Fuck, he's so hot.

"I have to warn you. I will do anything to win that bet," I mumble as I get on my knees and crawl toward him.

Desire spreads all over his face, making him shift in his seat as he watches me closely. He strokes his cock, probably desperate for a release, and I watch his movements with fascination. Adrian's groan fills the room and my ears until my body aches with the need to replace his hand with mine. To stroke it along his cock and guide it toward my clit to play with it.

When I'm in front of him, I place my hands on the armrests, keeping eye contact while I move on top of him, my pussy hovering over his cock. Adrian's smirk is easy and sexy as he waits for me to do or say whatever I want.

"As soon as I'm inside of you, start the timer. You won't win," he teases, but he just shot himself in the foot with that wording.

"If I can, I get a photo shoot where you have to do and wear as I say," I offer, and he chuckles.

"Okay, fine. If I can last longer, you have to wear a remote-controlled vibrator on a race weekend of my choosing," he counters, making my lips part in surprise. At the same time, excitement accompanies the surprise.

Why do I like the idea of that?

"Deal," I say and hold out my hand for him to shake.

Adrian does but then guides my hand under his shirt and onto his abs. I lean forward, my lips barely brushing his before they move to his neck, finding his soft spot and sucking on it. A deep moan leaves him, making me smile as my kiss moves to his earlobe where I nibble on the skin.

"Neveah, fuck, you can't do that. Don't cheat," he complains, but I keep trailing kisses from his ear to his neck and then slide down to lift his shirt and lick down his stomach. "Shit," he moans when I wrap my hand around his cock, rubbing the head with my thumb.

"You said the time starts when you're inside of me. You said nothing about me touching you before," I explain, but I doubt he hears me over his low groan.

More moans leave him as I slip my hand between my legs, dipping my fingers inside of me to coat them with my arousal. I start sliding my hand all the way down and then back up his cock, his eyes glued to where I'm stroking him.

"Please, I need to be inside of you," he begs, his palms moving to each side of my face before his thumb slides over my bottom lip. "And I need your mouth on mine." He guides me up until I'm standing only to pull me in by my hips, bringing me back on top of him. My legs straddle his, his cock close to my entrance again. "No more teasing," he says, but I'm not done yet. My hand reaches for his cock again so I can slide it over my clit, making me gasp from pleasure. "Fuck, I'm not gonna last if you do that," he says, so I keep going, feeling him tense under me.

"Are you already struggling?" I ask with a teasing tone, and he grabs my hips once more to stop my movements.

"I started struggling the moment I set my eyes on you," he replies, aligning my entrance with the head of his penis. "Now, please, I'm begging, I need your walls wrapped around me," he pleads, and I instantly sink down on his cock, desperate to feel him too.

We gasp when he's completely inside of me, but he guides my head down to kiss me, swallowing my moan. It momentarily distracts me from moving, which is probably why he's doing it.

I lean back to start bouncing up and down on him.

"Fucking hell, baby," he says, and I cover his mouth so he stays quiet. He chuckles against my hand, his fingers lifting to play with my tits

I sink down hard and lift fast before rolling my hips back and forth to rub my clit against his pelvis, switching back to bouncing a moment later. His moans vibrate against my hand, encouraging me to keep going. Pleasure consumes me, takes over until my brain barely remembers the deal. I want to make this last forever. But I'm also competitive and like to win.

When he's completely inside of me again, I tighten my walls around his dick, making him grab my hips and dig his fingers into the soft skin there.

I bring my lips to his earlobe and let out an "hmmmm" that makes him tense even more. "I'm yours, Adrian, and so is this pussy. All yours. Come for me."

He shakes his head, so I start switching between bouncing and tightening around him, my mouth close to his ear so he can hear my moans loud and clear.

"God, you feel so good, Adrian. You make me feel incredible," I say because I can tell from the way he grips the armchair, my words are getting him closer to his orgasm. I guide his hands to my breasts, which he squeezes again with a groan.

"Fuck," Adrian breathes, and I moan into his ear. I can feel my own build-up return as his cock continues to hit that perfect spot inside of me.

"Please, Adrian, I'm so close. Your cock feels so good, I need you to come inside of me," I beg, causing his legs to shake and a loud moan to leave him. I'm barely able to keep my hand over his mouth again to shut him up.

His eyes close as his orgasm blindsides him. His hands hold onto my breasts, pinching my nipples as I grind my clit against his pelvis again and follow him straight over the edge. My body trembles, stars exploding behind my eyelids as pleasure sweeps through me.

I stay on top of him, running a hand over his naked chest and smiling victoriously. It couldn't have taken more than a minute and a half, tops.

When he opens his eyes, he frowns at my happy grin.

"That's not fair, *mon ange*, you can't say those things and moan into my ear while your pussy does its magic and then place my hand on those breasts of yours. No one could last long with that combination," he complains, but I simply give him a kiss and attempt to move off him.

He holds me close for a moment, his fingers running up my thigh and slipping between my legs to feel the place where his cock is buried deep inside of me. Shivers run down my body from his fingertips' exploration, and he smiles at them like he's never seen a more beautiful sight.

"We have a few more condoms. Let's use them," he says, rolling his thumb over my nipple until I'm grinding against him again.

A knock on the door breaks the tension his touch brought back. "Hey, Adrian, we need you to come and look at something," Daniel says, making Adrian sigh.

"I'll be right there," he replies and looks up at me. "Moment ruined, isn't it?" he asks, and I give him a small smile.

"There is no such thing with you, but you need to go see what they need." I attempt to get up again, but he holds me down once more. I giggle involuntarily as his hands brush my sides. He takes my chin between his thumb and index finger, a serious expression on his face.

"*Mon paradis,*" Adrian says, and I lean forward to press a kiss to his lips.

"*Mein Mond.*" He cocks a confused brow, but I simply give him one last peck before getting off and putting my clothes back on without explaining what it means.

Mein Mond.

My moon.

I've always been fascinated by the moon. By the phases. By its beauty. By how bright it shines in the dark night sky.

Adrian is like that.

He's the brightest light in the darkest world.

CHAPTER 46
Adrian

Last day of the weekend before I get to take my angel out tonight. I have something very special planned, something Nevaeh will never see coming. She's been meaning to go out in the city to explore it because this is the first time she's returned to Austin since she left as a kid, but work—and my insatiable need to make love to her every chance I get—has kept her so busy, she hasn't had a chance to.

I'm going to change that tonight.

"Breathe, race, and win, as long as it doesn't cost you a limb," my sister, Gabriel, and I say at the same time. We move toward our respective cars where they are on the grid, the U.S. anthem already sung and the race about to start.

I kiss my sister on the crown of her head and give Gabriel a half-hug with our hands clasped together.

They exchange 'I love you's as I walk away, trying to ignore the stabbing sensation in my chest to make my way toward James' garage and kiss Nevaeh again. I stole a kiss this morning in her hotel room when I surprised her there, but I want to kiss her here, for everyone to see. As much as I'm enjoying keeping us secret from the world—except for my nosy family of course because they kept that secret from each other for all of three seconds, those jerks—I'd enjoy it a hell of a lot more if I got to touch her without her having to risk her job.

"Head out of your arse and helmet on," Daniel says, and I burst into a surprised laugh, taking my balaclava from him.

He grins at me, but I can tell he's a bit nervous.

After what happened with Lincoln last time, I'm also nervous. He's a chaotic, dangerous racer. He's aggressive and doesn't seem to mind risking his own race to fuck with someone else's. I only hope Robert Fuchs put him in his place after last time, reminding him that you can't do whatever the fuck you want to in Formula One. There are rules firmly set in place to avoid someone getting *killed*.

We've lost a few drivers to reckless driving already since the sport was established almost eighty years ago. The number doesn't have to rise because Lincoln fucking Nash drives with his dick doing the thinking instead of his head.

He's in love with Nevaeh. I get that. How could you not be? But it doesn't give him the right to mess with me on the track. Formula One isn't a high school game, and Nevaeh isn't a trophy he can win.

Before I can stop myself, I'm moving toward where Lincoln is standing with his performance coach. I force a smile even though I'd rather punch this guy's teeth out than be polite to him.

"Good race?" I say and extend my hand in a peace offering.

He eyes it like I've slattered the thing in poison, which I should have considering how big of an asshole he is. I wait another second before retracting it and shaking my head at his immaturity.

"Try not to take me out this time, yeah? Let's both make it over the finish line without amateur mistakes ending our race, rookie," I say and watch his eyes grow dark with anger.

"Get the fuck out of my face, Romana," he practically growls, so I give him several nods, my expression as unimpressed as I feel.

"I know this is your first year driving among the big teams, so I'll let you in on a little secret. If you want to stay on top, you have to earn it. Earn your seat. If you don't, they'll take it away as quickly as they gave it," I say and step back when he moves toward me.

"Why are you still talking? You're leading the championship, you got the girl. You don't have to rub it in," he says, pointing a finger at my chest as anger consumes him.

"The championship is far from decided," I grind out, hating that I have to say this. "And Nevaeh isn't mine, nor is she something to 'get,'" I add. "Drive with your head, not your heart, and we'll be good."

It's a bad idea to let your emotions control your actions when you're racing. It's also hard not to because when you've got so much adrenaline pumping through your veins, your emotions spill all over the place without a filter. Some drivers are better at keeping them locked down, like me. Others, Lincoln, haven't quite figured out how to glue their mouths shut or keep their limbs from moving before thinking.

Don't get me wrong, passion and emotion are important in F1 too, but there are moments for that and none of them occur when you're racing down the track, driving three hundred kilometers per hour.

I walk away from Lincoln and to my car, hoping he'll get a fucking grip on himself so we can start and end the race without an incident like last time.

The scent of hot asphalt fills my nose as I slide the balaclava over my head. Daniel is giving me an unsure look, but I give him a cocky smirk to ease his nerves. Lincoln won't do anything stupid now. He won't give me the satisfaction of being exactly who I've called him out to be: a rookie.

"Remember, the track is bumpy," Daniel reminds me as I slip my helmet on.

"I know. My ass is still fucking sore from the last few days," I joke when in reality, my entire body is sore. It feels like I have bruises all over.

"I know," Daniel says with a comforting smile.

After making sure I'm in the car with my earpieces working and my gloves on, he leaves me to let my crew work on the car for the last two minutes before the formation lap.

My heart starts racing just like it always does. Burning rubber fills my nostrils, the scent dulled by my helmet, but I still smell it. I let it pump more adrenaline through me. I let it consume me.

When I was younger and found my love for racing, I never thought I'd become so addicted to this feeling. To how alive I'd feel. They have a name for people like me, like everyone on the grid. They call us adrenaline junkies. When your life is at risk every single time you step into the car but you crave the thrill, the excitement, and the weightlessness as you race, it's hard to argue with that title.

Maybe that's why being with Nevaeh is so addictive, too. Being with her feels like I'm risking my life in the same way I am when I'm racing. Tying myself to her feels strangely like tying myself to the car, becoming one with it for the goal of reaching a dream that seems impossible.

Winning a championship.

Growing old with someone who loves me and wants to start a family with me.

They've started feeling a lot more possible when I changed teams and met Nevaeh.

Velocità Rossa will get me that title.

Nevaeh... will she get me my other dream?

The way I feel about her, I fucking hope so.

"Focus," Chloe says into my ear when I've slowed down during the formation lap a little and Lincoln almost drove into my ass because he wasn't paying attention.

"It was on purpose, there's a huge fucking bump there," I reply, telling the truth. I may have gotten lost in my thoughts, but I know this track inside out. I've studied it, before and during the free practice.

"Mhmm," my grumpy race engineer mumbles into the earpiece, and I almost chuckle.

"Have a good race to you, too," I say, lining up on the grid and feeling my heart pump nervous energy through me, mixing uncomfortably with the adrenaline.

The first light turns on, then the second, the third, the fourth, and lastly the fifth. I hold my breath, anticipation wrapping around my lungs. I stare up, my fingers hovering over the buttons on my steering wheel, my engine roaring with the need to drive.

I feel the same.

I let out the breath the moment the lights turn off, slamming onto the throttle and shifting into gear to push ahead. Lincoln's start doesn't compare to mine. My reaction time is better than his by miles, but he brakes later into the first corner, his front wheel lining up with my rear one. I take my corner well, leaving him behind as I shoot forward.

A glance in my mirror shows Gabriel attempting to overtake Lincoln, my teammate already halfway ahead when Lincoln's front tire touches Gabriel's side, causing him to spin off track in circular motions. He slams into the barrier as I keep racing, my heart dropping a little at the sight.

"Fuck, is he okay?" I ask Chloe, but she tells me to focus and that she'll give me an update when she gets one.

Goddamn Lincoln.

Yellow flags are waved as soon as I enter the second sector. I slow down my speed to the required percentage.

"Gabriel's out of the car. He said he's okay, but there'll be a safety car," Chloe informs me, but I already knew this would happen before she told me.

Gabriel crashed in a dangerous section of the track, and if they don't get the car out of there, it could pose a safety hazard.

"Safety car, not a red flag?" I ask.

"No red flag," Chloe confirms. It wouldn't be ideal two laps into the race, but safety comes first.

A red flag means the race would be paused and all of the drivers would return to the pitlane, lining up in their respective places to restart the race once all of the debris is moved and the car is no longer standing in a dangerous zone.

"Who else is out?" I ask, watching the safety car appear in front of me. This vehicle, a Grenzenlos for this race weekend, comes out to control our speed until the track is safe to race again.

"A Klein and a Carousel. Everyone else is still in," she says, and I can't help my next question.

"Where's she?"

"Worked her way up to P6. Had a hell of a start," Chloe says proudly, and I smile at the thought of my sister overtaking everyone in the back to get into sixth place.

"Put her in a competitive enough car, no one else will stand a chance."

My grandfather's words echo in my head. I remember the day he said this to me when Valentina won her Karting Championship after Christian fucking Crovetto, her biggest childhood rival, tried to cheat and push her off the track to win. He didn't succeed. My sister came out on top, just like I know she will as soon as her car is fast enough to keep up with the rest of the teams. Talent and skill will only get you so far without a competitive enough car.

If everyone had the same car on the grid, my sister would win every single time. But we don't. We have cars with different top speeds and advantages, and that prevents her from winning at the moment. But if she keeps this up, assholes like Lincoln won't get to keep their seats for much longer. She'll be the one the top teams consider for a seat.

I'm waiting for that day.

"Safety car ending in two laps," Chloe says as sweat drips down my back.

"About fucking time," I mumble to myself because the longer we're doing this slow tempo, the more my adrenaline will wear off.

"One lap."

I grit my teeth.

"You can restart," Chloe says once the safety car is gone.

I take a deep breath, slowing a little to confuse Lincoln behind me. Restarting a race after the safety car is tricky. You have to somehow manage to deceive the driver behind you that you won't restart the race or restart it at moments you're not. Then, you have to shoot away at the moment they least expect it, catching them off guard. Because Lincoln is an idiot, it should be easy enough to trick him.

And it is. It's embarrassingly easy.

I slip ahead, and my race continues smoothly from there.

Until my first pitstop.

My pit crew can't get the screw off one of my tires until ten seconds have passed. I'm cursing, counting the time in my head, and asking Chloe what the hell is going on at the same time. I see more of the crew running around, my car on three new wheels now, the left, front one still stuck with the old tire.

"They can't get the tire off!" Chloe says, and I let out more curse words, not giving a fuck if the race control, the people in charge, can hear me. I'm fucking furious.

This just ruined my race because, by the time I get back onto the track, I'm last.

From first to last.

"Lincoln's P1," Chloe informs me, which is the worst part of it all.

The little rookie is in first place.

As soon as I'm out of the car, I'm throwing myself off a fucking cliff.

CHAPTER 47
Nevaeh

ADRIAN WAS FURIOUS AFTER he ended the race in sixth place because his team fucked up his tires. He hardly spoke to anyone, but I didn't push him either. I texted him, telling him we could reschedule our plan to go out. He texted back right away, telling me the only thing that can cheer him up is me.

I know he isn't just upset about the race. He's angry because Lincoln is leading the Drivers' Championship now. Kyle may have won the race because Lincoln got a five-second penalty for causing a collision with Gabriel, but he still got enough points to replace Adrian as first in the standings.

I'm furious for my boyfriend.

Now, Valentina and I stare at the huge package on my hotel bed for a minute, shocked at its size. It was on my bed when we got to my room to get ready for tonight.

I'm the first to reach out and lift the lid, curiosity taking over. A pair of, probably very expensive, dark orange cowboy boots sit inside along with a matching cowboy hat.

My friends in Austin and I used to dress up in cowboy boots and hats when we hung out, learning every type of line dance there was. The memories of dancing the night away to my favorite artists replay in my head.

I can't believe Adrian is taking me somewhere I'll be able to show these things off.

I quickly disappear into the bathroom to put on a pair of jeans and a crop top that fits tightly enough so it won't expose anything but loosely so I can move and breathe freely. Every curve that should be highlighted is, and I step into my boots with an excited giggle. They have a bit of a heel, but nothing too high.

When I walk into the room again, Valentina's mouth opens. Gabriel is sitting in the corner, drawing something, but even he looks up to give me an approving nod. Then his eyes drift to Val before he smiles at her shocked expression.

"Holy shit. You can't wear that," Val says, and I let out a confused laugh.

"What? Why?" I ask, lifting the hat and finding a note underneath.

It reads,

Don't worry, none of it is made from real animal leather.

He knows me too well.

Val's reply grabs my attention again.

"You'll give someone a heart attack, Nevaeh," she swoons, and Gabriel looks at her with an amused smile.

"You know, I'm starting to think you'd leave me for Nevaeh if you could," he says, and Val bursts into laughter as she walks over to him.

"I love you, *mon soleil*, I'd never leave you," she assures him and continues to step toward him.

"No, don't come closer, I'm not done yet," Gabriel warns but shuts his notebook so she can go to him anyway.

Val presses a kiss to his lips before settling down between his legs and facing me. She winks at me before Gabriel wraps his arms around her stomach, holding her against his chest and nuzzling his nose into her hair.

"Now, what do you want to do with your makeup?" Valentina asks, but when I look at myself in the mirror, I smile.

"Nothing, actually. The mascara is enough," I reply and straighten out my back as I reach for the cowboy hat.

It's been years since I've worn one, but it feels right as I place it on top of my head. Nostalgia combined with happiness floods my body.

Soon after, while Val and Gabriel make conversation about the weekend with me, a knock on the door interrupts us. I open it to see Adrian dressed in a pair of jeans combined with a flannel shirt that makes me laugh.

He's not wearing cowboy boots but a hat rests on his head.

"And? How do I look?" he asks with a sweet smile, and I shake my head at him as his eyes trail down my body. Adrian has clearly lost his train of thought as he tugs his bottom lip between his teeth while an appreciative smirk settles on his face. "Gabriel, Val, get out of the room. Nevaeh and I are going to need a few minutes," Adrian says, and my knees go a little weak at the lust in his gaze.

"Well, we were just leaving to go change anyway," Valentina says and grabs Gabriel's hand to guide him out of the room. "See you at the bar," she adds, and I watch them kiss all the way down the hallway. Adrian grabs my attention by slipping inside my hotel room with me, kissing me until I forget about the rest of the world.

"I'm sorry about your race," I say as he wraps his arms around me and just hugs me for a while.

"Next one will be better," is all he replies, leaning back to grab my chin between his thumb and index finger. "How do you feel about going tonight?" His other hand lifts to my bracelet, rubbing the blue heart to let me understand what he means.

"Surprisingly okay." He smiles down at me, gliding his nose over mine for a moment. "Thank you for the boots and hat," I say.

"My pleasure. You look like the *déssee* you are," he replies, forcing a blush to settle on my cheeks. No matter how desperately I try to control it, my body responds however it wants to to Adrian, and I can't stop it. "Let's go?" he asks and holds out his hand for me.

"Yes, but no touching tonight," I remind him, and he groans with displeasure.

"Hardest task of my life." I snort at his dramatics.

James, Leonard, Cameron, and Cameron's boyfriend, Elijah, are all waiting for us outside of the bar already. Adrian keeps his distance and I keep my cowboy hat low on my head when I hear a very familiar voice appear behind me.

"Nevaeh!" I turn around to see Scarlette approaching with a very attractive man walking beside her.

He has dark golden skin, wavy brown hair, two differently-colored eyes, a muscular build, and a scowl resting on his face. A birthmark is painted across his cheek, and I realize this is her husband. She showed me a picture of her MotoGP championship-winning man a few weeks ago.

"Nevaeh, this is Julián. Julián, this is Nevaeh." I shake the stoic man's hand and he gives me a curt nod.

"Pleasure to meet you," he says before wrapping an arm around Scarlette's waist and bringing her against his chest.

"Good to see you, mate," Adrian says and shakes Julián's hand, too. "Everyone ready?" he adds and spins around to look at his other friends.

They all give an agreeing hum, so we step through the old, wooden doors and into a crowded space filled with laughing and cheerful people. There's a neon sign right above the bar that reads "Bourbon House." The ground is sticky, the music blares through the speakers, and laughter flows through the room in waves. It's crowded in here, everyone enjoying their Sunday night.

"I beg of you, if you don't want me to break anyone's face tonight, stay close to me, yeah?" Adrian says while we make our way past men who can't stop staring at my chest. I step in front of him before flashing him a promising smile and leading him toward the bar to get drinks. He's right next to me, scanning the crowd of people around us with a frightening intensity.

"Relax, would you?" I ask right as the bartender turns to ask me what I want.

I decide on something non-alcoholic because Adrian doesn't drink and I'm not the biggest alcohol drinker either. The occasional beer is more than enough for me. Adrian asks for water, and both our drinks are pushed toward us a minute later. Leonard and Cameron carry drinks for the rest of our group, and we follow them to a high table.

"Now, what do you want to do?" I ask. I take a sip of my iced tea while Adrian takes one of his water.

"Let's enjoy our drinks and then dance our asses off," he suggests, and I let out a chuckle before watching Leonard scoff in horror and Julián look at Scarlette with a begging expression. It says, "Don't make me do this" and I'm laughing so hard, it catches his attention.

"I'm not dancing," Leonard says, and Julián gives an agreeing nod.

"Oh, you're dancing," Cameron chimes in, and I notice he's put on cowboy boots and a hat too. He looks incredible.

"You're not my wife, so I don't have to do as you say," Julián replies, and Leonard snorts in response.

"My sentiments exactly." They're both so grumpy, complete contrasts to the shining bright light standing beside me. Adrian is close but keeps his respectful distance, as always.

We spend a while at a high table near the dance floor, laughing and talking about the most random things. The weight of my anxiety slowly lifts off my shoulders as I start to get swept into the moment.

My anxiety is always more difficult before an event but during it? I get lost in the now, in the carefreeness.

Valentina and Gabriel join us half an hour later, Val dressed in a short, red dress and Gabriel in a matching red polo shirt.

My head is enjoying the calm and familiarity these amazing people bring with their funny stories and friendship that feels like a warm hug.

'Can't Take Her Anywhere' by Dylan Scott blasts through the speakers, and I look up at Adrian with the brightest of smiles. Since we found out that we both adore country music, we've listened to this specific song a hundred times, at least.

We burst into song, laughing as we confuse everyone else at the table. He spins me around where we're standing, pulling me close once I'm in front of him. Adrian releases me when he realizes how close we've gotten, even though everyone here already knows we're dating.

They're keeping it from the rest of the world for me, for which I'll be forever grateful.

"Come on," I say as the song changes to a faster rhythm, and hold out my hand for Val to take. She intertwines our fingers to follow me onto the dance floor.

People all around us get into one line, preparing themselves for when the beat drops and the line dancing begins. My friends and I danced to this specific song so many times, I know it by heart and can join the other people with ease. Adrian, Valentina, Gabriel, Scarlette, Julián, Cameron, Elijah, and Leonard, on the other hand, watch me like a hawk, trying to get the steps right for the first minute of the song. They're doing all sorts of movements, just not the right ones, and I can't hold back my laughter when Adrian runs into me.

"The other way!" I complain over the loud music, and he lifts his hands to apologize. My moon tries again, a serious expression taking over his face, but it's no use. The song is over long before he even gets a single foot placement right. I bend over at the waist, the amusement causing my stomach to cramp up.

"How do you do this shit?" he complains as he leans down so I can hear him. I straighten out my back, wiping away the effect of my laughter from under my eyes.

"Practice," I reply, and he shakes his head.

"I looked like an idiot, didn't I?" I cover my mouth to keep from answering his question, although I don't need words to do so. My eyes probably tell him exactly how hilarious his stumbling over his own feet was to me. "Let me try again, this time, teach me first," he says, but I place a hand over his stomach and watch our friends mess up for a second.

They're stumbling all over themselves too, Leonard stiff and Gabriel more confused than anything. Cameron and Elijah are doing whatever they want, and Julián is dancing with Scarlette in his arms now.

"I'll teach you," I finally reply, and Val steps in front of me.

"I need some help too, and so does my husband," she says as Gabriel wraps his arms around her, lifting her off the ground and tickling her.

They pick up what I show them quickly, and by the time the next song comes on, we're back on the dance floor and things go a lot more smoothly for us, but eventually, Adrian just stands there and watches me with pure fascination.

"I want to kiss you so badly," he says, and without thinking, I step on my tiptoes and close the distance between our mouths. I cover my face with my cowboy hat, even though I don't give a damn who saw when Adrian smiles like I've just given him the best thing in the world.

"Move those feet," I call over the music, and he goes back to dancing clumsily, almost as if my kiss has put him in a trance and he isn't entirely in the moment anymore but still stuck on our lips pressing together.

Who would have ever thought a single kiss could unravel the heartbreaker of Formula One?

Chapter 48

Nevaeh

THE SOUND OF THE piano fills Adrian's little apartment while I build up the backdrop for the photoshoot Adrian owes me. I'm hoping what I have planned will cheer him up since he's been feeling a bit down with Lincoln leading the championship and the last race not going well.

I place together the metal pieces before hanging the white backdrop from it. Then, I stand up the lights and my tripod before walking into the bedroom and putting on a pair of jeans and a shirt without anything underneath. I grab a pair of Adrian's matching ones—yes, he bought us matching jeans a week ago for reasons he wouldn't disclose—before walking into the room where he is.

A soft melody fills my ears as I make my way toward him. A small smile dances onto his lips when he notices me. His fingers keep running over the keys and his eyes drift to my face.

"*Mon paradis,* Nevaeh," he says as I settle down next to him, making my heart skip several beats.

"Hi," I whisper, and Adrian keeps playing the same melody.

"I wrote this for you," he admits, his fingers flying over the keys. "Do you like it? It reminds me of what you sound like to me." The soft melody is incomparably beautiful. It's calm, peaceful yet a little mischievous and naughty, too.

"It's wonderful, Adrian," I reply, emotion heavy in my throat. No one's ever written a song for me before.

"For the past two days, every single time I have sat down at this piano, I have heard nothing but this in my head." I swallow hard, and Adrian finally stops running his fingers over the keys. "It won't leave me, constantly reminding me of what you mean to me," he says, and I lift my hands to his cheeks.

He pulls me onto his lap instead.

"I'm sorry it's stuck in your head," I mumble, but Adrian gives me a small chuckle.

"I'm not." He grabs my chin and tilts my head down to kiss me. "You came in here with a mission. Tell me what it is," he says, and I can't help the way my face lights up.

"Okay, so, you still owe me a photoshoot, and I need you to put these on for me. Take off your shirt and socks and meet me in the living room." I press one more kiss to his lips before skipping out the door and toward my camera. I turn it on and change it to the right setting just in time for him to walk up to me.

"Is it going to be just me?" Adrian asks, his smile brighter than I've seen it in days. It warms my heart to see him happy and know that I'm the reason why.

"For now, yes, but later I will take some with you," I explain, and he gives me a small nod. My eyes trail over his naked torso, appreciating every hard ridge, every carved-to-perfection part of him.

"I've done photoshoots before, but I've never been this nervous. The thought of an unflattering photo when you're the one looking through them later is terrifying," he says, and I bite my lip to keep from bursting into laughter.

"I promise I won't tell you if there's one," I say and tell him to stand in front of the white backdrop. He does, lifting his arms to his hair. My mouth starts to drool as his muscles flex with every move he makes, and my heart starts beating faster, more unevenly.

"If you keep looking at me like that, I will have to reschedule this photo shoot," Adrian warns, so I shake my head to refocus.

I lift my camera to take some photos, telling him exactly where to stand, what to do with his arms and legs, and basically how to make the ache between my legs more irritating. Every photo is perfect to me, every smile priceless. His body is incredible and it controls mine with ease, but his face makes me weak. His full lips, defined jaw, and light eyes have me wrapped around his finger.

With other people, the poses I make him do wouldn't look this good, but everything I ask of him has him looking like an angel sent from heaven.

"Okay, okay, you have enough of me for now. Get in here," he complains when I simply keep taking more photos. There must be two hundred of him on my SD card now.

"Fine," I reply with a smile as I place my camera on the tripod. Adrian watches me closely while digging his hands into his pockets. I go into the settings to turn the timer on before removing my shirt, leaving me in nothing but jeans, and turning to my boyfriend.

An easy smirk slips onto his face.

"Now this is my kind of photoshoot," he says with lust gleaming in his eyes.

"Alright, so, I was thinking—" I start and cut off because I'm not sure how to explain myself.

"That I use my hands as your bra?" Adrian asks, making me grin and heat settle in my cheeks at the same time. Being naked in front of him doesn't make me blush, but admitting that I've wanted a photo like that since I first laid my eyes on him does.

"Yeah, I think it will be hot," I reply, and he takes three steps toward me, his bottom lip tucked between his teeth.

"It will be beyond hot, Nevaeh. So fucking hot, I hope you know this photoshoot will end with you bent over my couch," he says as his hands move to the sides of my face, lowering his mouth onto mine. The kiss is demanding, rough yet gentle. His tongue slips into my mouth, and my knees instantly go weak.

Adrian drops his fingers to my hard nipples before squeezing gently.

"Oh God," I moan and step back. "No, no, no, no, no," I add and shake my head. "This may have been a bad idea." My moon chuckles as he wipes his thumb over his bottom lip.

"The second you took your shirt off, this became a great idea," he says with a cock of his brow, challenging me to deny the truth behind his words.

"You're right, but you'll be able to control yourself for a few minutes, won't you?" I ask, crossing my arms in front of my chest, challenging *him* to prove *me* wrong. Adrian's eyes drop to my pressed-together tits, and he inhales deeply as his self-control grabs onto the thinnest rope.

"Just be careful not to rub your ass against my cock right now, okay? I don't think I can handle it," he admits and turns away from me, walking back to where he stood before.

I smile to myself the entire time I set up the timer and then rush to him so he can wrap his hands around my breasts. He does so without hesitation, his long fingers snaking around me and his palms covering my nipples.

We take a few photos in that same position, then some from the side with my chest pressing against his.

We're laughing and grinning at each other the entire time.

The tips of his fingers wrap around my bracelet for one of them as he stares deeply into my eyes, reminding me just how much I mean to him.

"I want to take one with your hand down my pants," I say while putting the timer on for the twentieth time. I really need to get myself a remote.

"Really?" he asks, surprise all over his beautiful face.

"Yeah, why? Is it too weird?"

"No, not at all. I just didn't think you'd want a photo like that, you know, with my hand on *mon petit paradis*," he says, and I let out a combination of a gasp and a laugh.

"I was thinking on my ass, Adrian," I explain, and, for the first time since I've met him, he blushes.

"Oh, fuck, sorry," he laughs and nods. "Okay, yeah, we can do that."

"How about we do both?" I ask, stepping on my tiptoes to press a swift kiss to his jaw. I make my way into his bedroom and walk back out with a Polaroid camera.

"You can keep it in your wallet," I suggest with a smile, and his jaw drops ever so slightly.

"Where did you come from?" he jokes, and I chuckle in response.

"I came from your personal heaven." Adrian attacks my lips for the second time before nibbling on the sensitive skin on my neck until I'm giggling uncontrollably.

We manage to separate long enough for him to walk toward the backdrop again while I put the timer on for the last time today. My fingers drop to the buttons of my pants undoing them so he can easily place his hand on my ass. I face the camera with my back while his fingers dip into my jeans.

Since I'm wearing a thong, his hand slips over my bare ass cheek. My breathing hitches as my chest pushes against his torso and his lips capture mine. The flash goes off, but all of my attention is on Adrian's lips. On the way they envelop mine so easily, so perfectly, it makes me wonder if they were made for me.

"Okay, take the Polaroid one so I can get you out of those jeans," he says after gently kneading my ass cheek, and I rush to set it up only to move back to him. "I can't believe we're doing this," Adrian whispers into my ear. He uses his left arm to cover my breasts and his right hand slips on top of my panties. "So wet for me," he mumbles and bites down on my earlobe, making me moan at the same time it takes the photo. "Perfect," Adrian adds, his finger running over my swollen clit.

"Fuck, Adrian," I curse as I fall into the pleasure of his touch.

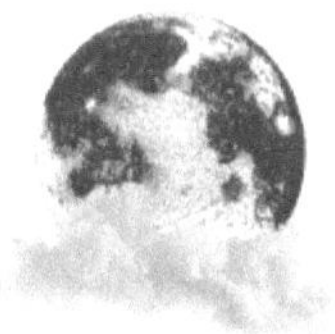

We end up on his couch an hour later, sweaty and trying desperately to catch our breaths. His naked skin against mine, while he draws an infinity symbol over my back, causes a feeling of immense peace to spread through me.

Ever since Adrian and I started dating, no, ever since we started spending time together months ago, I've found myself more at ease than I ever have before. He doesn't just make me happy. He calms me, and for a person with anxiety, the source of a calming feeling is rare and priceless.

Adrian silences my racing mind.

He settles the storm inside of me.

He gives me a safe place, a sanctuary where nothing can hurt me.

"Thank you," Adrian says after a while of me listening to the beat of his heart, his even breath. I tilt my head to look up at him, his fingers reaching out so his thumb can trace my bottom lip.

"For what?"

"For cheering me up. For taking my mind off my grief and replacing the feeling with happiness," he explains, his thumb moving to my chin to grab it between his fingers. "Tomorrow is the anniversary of my father's passing, which means it's the anniversary of my mother abandoning our family, too." I move up his body to get closer to him, his thigh between my legs as they straddle it.

"It happened on the same day?" Adrian takes advantage of my proximity and brushes his nose against mine.

"Same day, years apart," he says, leaning his forehead against mine. "He always got drunk out of his mind on the anniversary of her leaving us. It was his way of coping with his pain. To this day, I don't know if he just gave up on life when he got into the car, hoping it would end his suffering, or if it really was an accident. It's one of the few things I wish I could ask him." I trail a hand up his chest to his neck where I rub my thumb along the side of his throat.

"Do you think the answer would bring you peace?" Adrian considers my question for a moment.

"I hope so, but, at the same time, I doubt anything out of that man's mouth could have brought or would bring me peace."

He leans his head back against the armrest of the couch, his hand on my hip going back to trailing the infinity symbol.

After taking a deep breath, he tilts his head toward me again and says, "But you bring me peace, Nevaeh." My heart flutters at his words, at the reciprocation of my feelings.

"And you me."

Adrian smiles, then kisses me, the rest of the world fading away until all that's left is the feeling of his lips on mine.

CHAPTER 49
Nevaeh

MY FINGERS RUN OVER the keyboard of the computer at the office while I make a plan for my interview with Leonard Tick. Genevieve, my supervisor here in Monaco, brings me a cup of tea at lunch and sits down in front of me, a smile on her young face. She's only five years older than me, but she's in charge of everyone. I put aside my work to be polite and also take advantage of the break.

"Thank you," I say and point at the tea.

We've barely spoken since I started coming to the office a little over a week ago, but she's been kind to me ever since.

"How are you?" she asks while taking a sip of her drink. Her brown hair is in a tight bun, as always, and her matching brown eyes are highlighted through her purple eyeliner. Her bronze skin almost glows today, and I wonder what has her in such a good mood.

"I'm fine, just getting everything ready for the race weekend," I reply, hating the small talk, even though it's one of the most human things in the world.

"You're flying in a few days, right?" I give her a small nod.

"How are you?"

"I found out I'm pregnant this morning, so I'm pretty happy right now," she says, and I can't stop my jaw from dropping.

"Oh my-—Congratulations," I manage to blurt out, a bit confused why she'd want to share this with me. Genevieve grins, and I finally realize why she's glowing. It's happiness. She's, without a shadow of a doubt, happy.

"Thank you." She adjusts her collar before clearing her throat. "You're probably wondering why I'm telling you, but I promise there is a good reason. I have to leave for a doctor's appointment, but Mrs. Lu and Ms. Martin are coming by for a debriefing. Would you mind doing that for me? I have all of the information here," Genevieve says and hands me a folder full of papers.

I hesitate because I had no idea that Mrs. Lu and Ms. Martin were coming. I've been leaving Ms. Martin messages since yesterday, asking her if my newest article was okay or if she wanted me to change anything. She hasn't gotten back to me yet.

"Sure, no problem," I reply, sensing there will be an opportunity for me to speak to my boss.

Genevieve stays at my desk a little longer, sharing her story of her partner and her trying to get pregnant for the last year, but not having any luck until now. I congratulate her a few more times before she leaves, and I go back to my planning.

Leonard is polite, but he's also quiet and keeps to himself, especially during race weekends, according to Val. So, I will have to find a way to make the four days entertaining for him as well as for me. It will be difficult considering that, even after all my research and the few evenings I went out with him and our friends, I've barely found out anything about this man.

Giving up, I text Val to ask her if there is any connection I can build on. He's her mentor and teammate, not to mention a friend. She must know something.

Valentina: He likes photography.

I almost jump out of my chair from excitement.

"Good news?" Ms. Martin's voice interrupts my victorious moment, and I clear my throat before answering.

"Not news, but what I found is very good, yes," I reply and share what has me feeling giddy at the moment.

An approving smile spreads over her face as she settles in the seat in front of me, the same one Genevieve occupied only an hour ago. There's something familiar now about her smile, something oddly comforting. Like I've seen her smile and eyes a hundred times by now even though I've only met her in person a few times before. The feeling unsettles me a little, especially because when I smile at Mrs. Lu to greet her, I don't feel the same connection.

Maybe it's because I've been working closer together with Ms. Martin.

"I'm very impressed with your performance at this company, Nevaeh. You take every criticism under consideration, every tip I give you, and you continue to surprise me with your implementation of said advice. I have to admit, I did not expect this when I hired you," Ms. Martin says, and I let out an uncomfortable laugh. Praise and honesty like that from her are two things I'm not sure how to handle.

"Thank you for your guidance and the opportunities you've given me," I simply say to both of the women in front of me, but a strange expression briefly covers Mrs. Lu's face. It's gone so quickly, I don't have time to ask her about it.

"Genevieve tells me that you received the honor of debriefing us on what has been going on," Mrs. Lu states while settling against her chair, crossing her legs in the process. I pull the folder out from under my notebook, showing them everything Genevieve told me to. Mrs. Lu and Ms. Martin listen closely, taking the papers I hand them with every explanation of what is on them.

"What about the new client list?" Ms. Martin asks, and I skim through the documents to look for them.

The first list I find has around ten names and reads *New Tennis Clients.* Under the reason for some of their joining it says: *Articles of Formula One drivers written by Nevaeh Fuchs.* My heart sinks from shock when I read Sabrina Barlow's name along with Catalina Sanchez's and Santiago Castillo's, all of the famous players I've been watching for years.

The dates of their signing reveal that this happened almost two weeks ago.

"Did you know about this?" I ask Mrs. Lu, pointing at the paper. She scans the page quickly, her eyes widened ever so slightly before she looks at me. Her lips are pulled into a thin line as she contemplates her next words.

"I didn't, but I will look into it and get back to you, I promise. I know how desperately you wanted to get a job in the tennis department," Mrs. Lu assures me, but for some reason, I don't think she will spend a minute on this to help me.

These famous tennis players signed as clients, which means that they agreed that exclusive content and information will be given to *Griffin Sports*, and it's all thanks to me.

"Now, is there anything else?" Ms. Martin asks, pulling me back into the moment.

"No, that's it." I try not to read into this, to believe my boss when she says she didn't know, but it feels strange for the head of a company not to be aware of ten big, brand-new clients signing. Clients that bring in a lot of money.

No, I don't believe her when she says she didn't know. But what I don't understand is why she didn't tell me.

What could she possibly gain by keeping this from me?

Mama, Papa, Nova, and Aileen are all standing in my apartment, inspecting it with various degrees of disapproval or excitement. Mama looks personally offended by how small it is, Papa is murmuring something about how practical the space is, Nova is horrified by the size of my bathroom—big enough for one person but tiny in comparison to the one she has—and Aileen is signing how wonderfully charming she finds everything.

We had a very awkward dinner where my mother and I didn't speak and Nova couldn't stop talking to fill the awkward tension with conversation. I love my sister, I do, but it didn't help. The looks I got from Mama were enough to tell me she still hasn't forgiven me for this decision, for choosing to live my life the way I want to, not the way she thinks I should.

"I will personally pay you monthly so you can move into a place with a bigger bathroom," Nova calls out before a dramatic gasp escapes her. I translate what Nova said to Aileen, and she giggles at her girlfriend's words. "You only have one drawer for your bathroom things?"

"Leave my bathroom alone," I say as Papa walks up to me and wraps an arm around my shoulder. I lean my head on his torso, listening to the steady beat of his heart.

"I can't believe you live here," Mama says, scrunching her nose up in disgust. "You had a house, a home with so much space, and you gave it all up for... *this*?" Aileen frowns at my mother, so I place a hand on her shoulder to assure her it's okay.

"Yes," I say, not hesitating. *And I'm happy*, I add, signing the words because if I said them out loud, I have a feeling it would hurt her more.

My mother has been many things for me in my life. A friend, someone to lean on when times got tough, a patient listener when my anxiety first started. She's been overbearing and controlling too, but she's never been cold. That's not who she used to be to me, but she's grown so fucking cold, I don't know what to do anymore.

"There's something you wanted to discuss with me," Papa chimes in, hugging me a little before stepping away to stand in front of me and block my view of Mama.

"It's work-related," I say, hoping he hears in my voice that I want to discuss what happened in private. I give Papa a look when he furrows his brows at me, and understanding washes over his features.

"Then, let's go get some ice cream and discuss. I'll see you all back at the hotel," he announces to Mama, Nova, and Aileen, signing the words with his hands at the same time.

We all make our way outside of my building, Nova and Aileen hugging me goodbye and telling me they're excited to spend the day together tomorrow. Mama simply disappears into the taxi, not looking back once.

My heart hurts a little now.

"Will she ever forgive me?" I ask Papa, and he holds out his arm for me to take.

"She doesn't see how successful you are yet, so she thinks you made the biggest mistake of your life. But, everywhere I go during the race weekend, I hear people praising you. 'The young journalist who has exceeded everyone's expectations,'" he says, and half a smile tugs on my lips. "She wants you to move back home, but I can see now how well you've been handling everything. I'm so proud of you," Papa goes on, and I squeeze his arm.

A tear slips down his cheek, but he wipes it away quickly.

"It's just hard for both of us that you're not around, which doesn't mean that you should move back. It's just, you grew up so fast, and we miss you."

My own tears stream down now. I want to respond, but it takes me a second to get rid of the lump in my throat.

"I miss you both a lot. There is still so much I need you both for, things that have me tossing and turning all night that I can't seem to answer for myself. I will always need you, no matter what," I point out, and he nods, his eyes fixed on the street in front of us.

"Then tell me, what has you tossing and turning?" Papa asks as we make our way toward the gelateria.

"My boss has been hiding that new tennis players have signed with *Griffin Sports* to have articles written like the ones I write for the Formula One drivers. She told me she didn't know, but I have a feeling she's lying to me," I explain.

"Why do you think that?" He looks down at me, his face void of any emotion.

"Because these are famous tennis players, top tennis players. They're probably paying a lot of money to get these exclusives. How would she not know about this for two weeks?" I ask, and he nods, clearly agreeing with my train of thought. "I wanted a job in the tennis department, but they didn't have a spot for me. Now they do. I've proven to be a good journalist. There's no reason for her to keep this from me," I say, frustrated all over again.

"Maybe there is one that she didn't want to share with you," he guesses, shrugging a little. "Give her some time. Now she knows that you know. She won't be able to hide it from you anymore," Papa adds, and I already feel a lot better now, having spoken to him.

"Yeah, you're right. Thank you," I say as we stop in front of the gelateria.

"Your mom will come around too." I appreciate his reassurance, but, right now, it feels like I'm the villain in her story, and I'm not even sure I want her to forgive me.

There shouldn't be anything to forgive.

Maybe if I say it a few more times, I'll stop feeling so guilty.

Chapter 50

Adrian

Leonard, James, Cameron, Gabriel, and Damian are staring at me. I notice it too late after I've already grinned at my fucking phone because Nevaeh told me she can't wait for our date tomorrow. We haven't seen each other in days because her family is visiting, and I miss her already.

Yes, she also said a few other things, but her "Can't wait for tomorrow, baby" had me beaming at the screen. The happy look faded as soon as I saw my family's confused, yet slightly amused expressions.

"Hay fever?" Cameron asks, his Australian accent thick as he addresses everyone but me.

"Maybe. There's definitely something wrong with his head so it has to be fever-related," Leonard chimes in, and I think about flipping both of them off for a moment.

"No, there is only one logical explanation," James says, bouncing his son on his knee. "This isn't Adrian. The real Adrian was kidnapped, and we have some kind of shapeshifter in front of us."

Oh my fucking God, they can't be serious. I smiled at my goddamn phone, it's not a big deal. Even if it is. Even if I'm a completely different man when it comes to love and romance now.

"Careful, boys, this shapeshifter can do more than put on the face of the most handsome man on planet Earth," I say, and they all let out a laugh that sends a wave of happiness through me.

"At least he's still as arrogant as before, maybe more so now after convincing one of the most beautiful and fascinating people in the world that dating him was a good idea," Cameron adds, and I roll my eyes at all of them.

I don't understand why it's so surprising that Nevaeh would choose me... am I *that* wrong for her? I don't think so. I hope not. I've done everything in my power to give her the world so far, but maybe it's my way of lying to myself. Maybe I'm just wrong in every way, and I've managed to convince everyone I'm not. Oh God, my brain hurts from overthinking the most ridiculous things.

Nevaeh is happy with me. I'm good for her as long as I keep her this way. Right? Fuck. Relationships are so stressful.

"Oh no, now he's thinking. Don't hurt yourself, mate," Cameron says, and I stand up, walking into my kitchen while they chuckle at my expense.

Why the hell did I invite them over again? Oh yeah, I missed them. Silly me.

"Come on now, Adrian, don't pout. We're glad you managed to rip yourself out of Nevaeh's arms long enough to spend some time with us," Leonard explains, and, although I want to tell him how ridiculous that is, he's right.

I haven't given them much of my time. They've asked me to, but I had no interest in leaving my girlfriend's side. I still don't, but she put the phone into my hand a few days ago, dialed James' number, and told me to have a night with my friends. I tried to argue that she's also my friend and should stay, but then she told me about her family visiting and Val inviting them all over for dinner.

If anyone is ever going to be a threat to my relationship with Nevaeh, it's my sister. I'd laugh at the thought if it weren't an actual concern at this point.

"Yeah, I'm hooked. I like her so much, it fucking hurts to be away from her. The last time I checked, every single one of you feels the same, except James of course," I add the last part with an apologetic smile, but he shrugs off my comment, looking into his son's eyes with a warmth like no other. He's also holding his ears closed because I'm swearing, and he doesn't want his son to adopt that "filthy" habit, as he put it.

"We do feel the same," Gabriel says, grinning now. "Which is why we're teasing you. It's too much fun when we know how accurate our jokes are." I roll my eyes again.

"Can we get to the part of this evening I invited you all for?" I ask, settling back down in my chair. Five sets of eyes are on me again, and I let out a long, hard sigh. "Fine, you freaking butt faces, ask your god darn questions," I say, and James gives me an appreciative smile.

The rest of the group has curiosity spilling onto their faces like blush would on Nevaeh's cheeks. Cameron is the first to speak.

"Are you actually making plans for your future with her? I remember you telling me that's the last thing you'd ever want with someone." Fuck no, I'm going to have to tell them corny shit, don't I? No, I don't. I'll answer, but my cheesiness is only meant for Nevaeh.

"Yes, I am." Three words, enough to answer his question, but he pries because he knows he can.

"One kid? Two kids? Five? None? Settle down here in Monaco or somewhere else? Big wedding or small ceremony? Big house or small apartment? Any pets?" Man, he's annoying.

So why the hell do I answer all of this?

"However many kids Nevaeh wants. Wherever Nevaeh wants to grow old. The biggest or smallest ceremony she could ever dream of. A mansion or a shoebox, anywhere with her. Lots of pets because she loves animals. Happy?" None of them expected me to give them this much, to be so vulnerable without hesitation.

"Son of a bench, you're in love," Leonard says, and panic creeps into my chest.

"No, I'm not," I argue, even though I have no idea how to describe what I feel. It's more than like, but I've never been in love before, so how the hell would I know what it feels like? "Am I?" I find myself asking. All four men across from me look at each other before bringing their gazes back to me.

"Only you can answer that question," Gabriel says, but Leonard snorts.

"Of course, you're in love, you idiot. It's so obvious." I let out a pretend shocked gasp.

"No need to get so rude," I say and place a hand on my chest in mock offense. Leonard scowls at me, but the familiar half-smile he's given me for years tugs at the right side of his mouth.

"Alright now, let's give Adrian what he wants. We came here for game night, not to tease him about his sappy behavior," Gabriel says, but Cameron snorts.

"Speak for yourself. I'll do both, you'll see."

And he stays true to his word the entire night.

CHAPTER 51
Nevaeh

MY LAPTOP SHUTS DOWN on me in the middle of a photo edit, and I curse under my breath. This is the third time in two days it has done that. Luckily, the edits were just for myself and not for the article I sent to Ms. Martin this morning. She wanted me to write one for the upcoming weekend, try out something new. She already sent back feedback, telling me she really enjoyed it and will publish it sometime this week. Meanwhile, I slam my laptop shut and sit back in the cocoon chair, my favorite place in the apartment besides the bedroom or anywhere in Adrian's arms. He said he has something planned for us to do today but that he needed another hour, so I've been working instead.

"Come with me," Adrian's voice fills my ears, and I look up at him with a smile slowly creeping onto my face.

"You're so bossy, do you know that?" I ask, but he's already lifting me out of the chair and pulling me toward the door.

"I'll stop when you stop loving it so much," he replies and turns to me to briefly flash me a sexy smirk that heats up my cheeks. I do love it when Adrian's bossy because I know I still have a choice. He would never make me do anything I didn't want to do.

"Before we go anywhere, is my outfit appropriate? This is Monaco, after all, and I know you told me to wear sweatpants, but *I'm wearing sweatpants*, in Monaco," I state, and he spins around, looking me up and down with an appreciative smile.

"No one on planet Earth pulls off sweatpants like you. Fuck," he says before his bottom lip slips between his teeth. A low sigh escapes him, and he shakes his head to refocus. My body catches fire from his gaze, and I suck in a sharp breath when I remember to breathe. "Let's go before I forget how important today is." I cock a brow but follow him without asking questions. He pulls a cap over my head and an oversized sweater on my body, making sure I'm unrecognizable, just like I always am when we go out.

We drive for a bit, the noon sun shining brightly onto us in the car, the benefit of having a convertible. Adrian is silent and the radio is quiet. I watch my boyfriend almost the entire way, getting lost in the way his blonde hair flattens out and then gets poofy depending on how the wind moves it. His smile, however, stays consistent the entire way.

"You're so beautiful," I can't help but say, his grin growing wider from my words.

"I've never been called beautiful before," he replies and takes my hand in his to press a small kiss to the back of it. "Never thought I'd like it this much," Adrian adds, and I lift my fingers to his cheek to run them over his defined cheekbone.

"Well, you are. You're the most beautiful man I've ever seen in my entire life, *mein Mond*," I inform him, and he lets out a sound that I can only describe as a combination of a groan and laugh.

"You keep giving me new weaknesses." I shake my head at my man before my gaze shifts to *Stade Louis II*, the football stadium here in Monaco. "We're going to play a bit of soccer," Adrian says, driving all the way to the underground parking area where a security guard waits for us.

She hands Adrian a ticket, and he takes it with a "thank you" and a kind smile. He's so polite to every single person, always making sure to spread kindness. And I like him all the more for it.

The parking garage is completely empty, not a car in sight as Adrian parks. I open my own door very slightly, but he reaches across me and pulls it shut again, making me burst into laughter.

"You don't open your own doors when I'm around, Nevaeh," he scolds, and I watch him with a laugh as he runs around his car to open my door for me.

"You rented out a whole stadium just for us to play soccer?" I ask to change the subject, and he nods. "That must have cost a fortune!" I say, but Adrian shrugs nonchalantly.

"It barely cost me anything. The manager owed me a favor because I got him seasonal F1 tickets, and I cashed it in. Please, never worry about something like my money, okay?" Since it is none of my business anyway, I give him a nod, which he replies to with a satisfied smirk.

We walk into the grand stadium, past the players' lockers, and then out onto the field. An impressed gasp leaves me as I spin around, taking in the size of it all.

"You made the same sound the first time you looked at my cock. If that isn't an ego boost, I don't know what is," he says, and I press my lips together.

"Like you need it," I mumble with a smile before walking onto the artificial grass and letting out a short laugh. Adrian moves over to the benches where he grabs a ball and then kicks it over to where I am.

"No one is here, I made sure of it in case you—" He cuts off, and I tilt my head. "In case you wanted your fantasy to come true," he says, and I slowly make my way over to him, every step fuelling the excitement inside of me.

"We're all alone? No people? No cameras?" I ask, and he flings his arms around me, dragging me against his chest.

"Yes." I wrap my arms around his neck and touch my lips to the lobe of his ear.

"Care to play a game?" I whisper, making him tense. He always tenses when I turn him on, which is why I nibble on his lobe, making his hands slip onto my ass. "One where we'll end up naked?"

"Are you suggesting strip soccer?" he asks as I step away from him, breaking all skin contact.

"I score a goal, you remove a piece of clothing. You score a goal, I do," I say, licking my lips when his eyes attach to them.

Adrian holds out his hand for me to shake, so I slide mine into his briefly before running toward the soccer ball and kicking it toward the goal closest to us.

"Cheater!" Adrian calls after me with a laugh, but I don't stop until I kick the ball right into the empty goal.

"Oh yeah!" I scream and turn to him.

He's a few meters behind me, pushing his tongue to the roof of his mouth and placing his hands on his hips.

"Let's start with something small. Your shirt, please, baby," I say and smile as he reaches for the hem of it.

"Usually, people start with a shoe or a sock," he reminds me, but he doesn't have to. I'm well aware of how these things are supposed to go, but I want his torso naked and exposed to me, even if it may distract me.

He does as I instructed, his trained body only covered by a pair of shorts now. My eyes dip to the dusting of hair leading from his belly button all the way into his boxers, and I run my fingers down its path as he steps in front of me. His chest is rising and falling against mine, adrenaline shooting through us from anticipation and excitement.

"Alright then, let's play this your way," he says before taking the ball from me and moving backward.

Since the whole field would be too big for two people, we stay close to the goal we're nearest to. He's so quick now, I can barely keep up with him before he scores, and I lean my head back to groan.

"Shit," I mumble and reach for my shoes to take them off, knowing full well he will complain.

"I don't think so, Nevaeh. Shirt, please," he says softly, but I simply stay where I am, lifting my hands to signal for him to remove it.

"If you want it off, take it off yourself." A sinfully dirty smile spreads across his face.

"You make me take it off, and I don't think I could stop myself from removing more. The choice is yours," he says, and I chuckle, lifting the shirt over my head.

His eyes fixate on my breasts instantly, giving me time to snatch the ball from him and step away from the goal just enough to aim properly. Adrian takes the ball from me, sending us into a battle that lasts God knows how long.

By the time I'm completely out of breath, we're both only wearing our underwear. Adrian and I stand in front of each other now, the ball under my barefoot while I try to calm my heart rate. Sweat drips down his body. His defined hands catch my attention more than they should. His long fingers run over the sides of his boxers for a moment, and, suddenly, my eyes fixate on his bulge, which tightens the fabric around his hard cock.

Everything inside of me is drawn to him, to get either on top or under him, rub against him before he pushes inside of me.

"Focus, *mon ange*, unless you want to lose," he reminds me, and I clear my throat to push away my horny thoughts but winning doesn't seem to matter anymore.

Fucking him does.

I run toward him with the intention of "slipping" right in front of him, which works perfectly, bringing both of us onto the grass, him on top of me.

"I really hope they clean this grass between matches," I say when I realize how much the players sweat and spit on the grass.

It's a strange thought to cross my mind with him enveloping my body like this, but I can't help myself.

Adrian chuckles, the vibrations coming off his chest and going through me.

"They just put in completely new grass to prepare for the restart of the season. I made sure of it. We're the first people to be on here," he says, his lips moving closer to mine. His eyes lift toward the goal before he smiles down at me. "The ball is over the line," he adds, his voice barely more than a whisper. I reach for the waistband of his boxers.

"Then you should probably take off your underwear," I say, bringing my hands to his arms on either side of me. He's not close enough for my liking.

"Are you sure?" he asks, kissing me once before leaning back.

"Don't you want to?"

"Of course I do," he replies, so I reach for his cock and start palming him through his boxers. "Oh fuck," he moans so loudly, a wave of excitement courses through me in an instant. "Nevaeh—shit." Adrian's voice is riddled with pleasure, encouraging me to keep going, to keep hearing him. "Nevaeh, stop, please," he says, and I let go of him.

"I'm sorry, I thought—" He cuts me off by placing his lips on mine and taking my hands to pin them over my head.

"You thought right, but I won't last long if you play first," he says, grinding his cock against my covered clit.

My back arches off the uncomfortable, prickly ground as a moan leaves my lips. He restrains my hands by pressing my wrists into the ground, but it excites me. I'm under his control, and, fuck, it feels good.

Adrian rubs against me again, sending shivers down my spine and arms and anywhere else they can reach.

"Fuck, Nevaeh," he moans, and my eyes open to see his lips parted to form a small O-shape. His eyes are on my face, burning my cheeks in the best way. I lift my head off the ground to bring my mouth to his.

"I need your cock inside of me," I say against his lips before meeting his grinding movements by wrapping my legs around his hips.

"Baby, I'll bury my cock so deep inside of you, you'll feel me with every step for days to come," he replies with a smile before getting off me to reach for a condom out of his shorts' pocket.

A warm breeze glides over me now that his body no longer covers mine, and I stretch my arms and legs along the ground. The thrill of what we're doing keeps my heart pumping rapidly against my ribcage.

Adrian settles back down between my legs, his fingers hooking around the waistband of my panties. He waits for me to give him an approving nod before sliding them down and smiling at his *petit paradis*. Out of all the things he could have called my pussy, he chose something so sweet and beautiful...

"You're always so wet for me, for my cock," he says, and I sit up to close the unbearable distance between us.

"You spent the last half hour turning me on, making me wet for you. Don't make me wait any longer," I beg, and he gives me a brief chuckle, sliding his boxers down and revealing his cock. He slips the condom down his length as I watch every little move of his.

"How dare I make you wait?" he asks and pulls me closer by my legs, wrapping them around him again so that my knees touch his hips. His hand grabs my face, forcing my eyes to stay on his as he slowly slides himself inside of me. "Keep your eyes on me like the good girl you are, Nevaeh, and I'll make you come however many times you want," he promises.

My eyes are on his as he stretches me to fit his thick length, filling me in one slow and gentle thrust. His hand roams over my hip and up to my breast, pulling down the fabric of my bralette to watch it bounce free. A groan vibrates off him and right through me as he lowers his mouth to my nipple and sucks until stars cloud my vision.

"Adrian," I breathe out through the pleasure. He trails kisses up my neck and jaw, making his way to my lips, but he doesn't kiss me yet.

"You like getting fucked here, like this, where anyone could walk in and see us?" he asks, his lips brushing over mine with every word and every slow thrust. My core tenses at his filthy words, at the smirk stretching his lips. "Does my perfect angel get off on having my cock buried deep inside of her right here?"

A low, guttural moan escapes me, and he finally closes the distance between us, kissing me to feel the sound deep inside of him.

"Tell me. Let me hear you say it," he says, slipping out of me and fucking into me so hard, the stars behind my eyes multiply by a million.

"I get off on it," I croak out, and he rewards me by picking up his tempo and thrusting harder now. I grab onto his arms, holding on as hard as I can so he can ground me while simultaneously getting me high on pleasure.

"Atta girl," he praises, a hand slipping over my neck as he kisses me again, swallowing my moans. "I fucking love how you take my cock. Just watch how perfect we are together," Adrian says, grabbing my chin and tilting my head down until I'm looking at where he disappears inside of me.

I can barely hold myself up on my elbows as he slams inside of me, his fingers drifting between our chests and over my clit, rubbing it the way I like it. His gaze is full of desire as he switches between shallow and deep strokes, making my head spin until my eyes close.

"Keep those eyes open, Nevaeh, watch how good you make me feel."

"Oh, fuck, Adrian," I moan, my nails digging into his arms. Pleasure dances through me until it settles in my stomach, bringing back the tension I long for. "Yes, right there, please!" I whimper when he uses his thumb to trace circles around my needy clit.

"You like it just there, baby?" I nod, studying the look of pleasure creasing his forehead and making him bite down on his bottom lip.

Adrian keeps moving, too eager to push me over the edge to stop. He slips in and out with ease, bringing an indescribable feeling of completeness to my body. He buries his face in the crook of my neck as he moans my name repeatedly, which only brings me closer to my orgasm.

"*Je t'appartiens*," he says before slamming so hard inside of me that I fall over the edge and right into paradise. The orgasm pulses through me like a wave of adrenaline, shaking my body against his.

I tremble from the intense orgasm. His thumb keeps rubbing in circles as his movements continue, his finger applying just enough pressure. Adrian moans loudly into my neck before his movements slow and his body sinks down onto mine. He keeps sliding in and out, even after he orgasmed, his finger still on my clit, rubbing and circling until I fall apart under him again.

"Shit," I repeat more times than I can keep count, and Adrian lifts himself off me just enough to capture my lips and slip his tongue inside my mouth. My hands move onto his hard stomach, feeling him flex under my touch.

"This is not exactly where I saw us ending up today," he admits, and we both laugh, my head still in the clouds. "Tell me something, Nevaeh," he says, so I open my eyes to watch him lift my panties. "You've been wearing a lot of orange lately. Is it for me?" he asks, leaning back to help me slip my orange panties back on.

"It's your favorite color, so, yes," I reply shamelessly, loving the way he smiles happily.

"It used to be," he says and hovers over me again to kiss me.

"What is it now?"

He rubs his nose along my neck for a moment, then says, "I have multiple now."

"What are they?" Adrian pushes himself up again, pulling me with him until we're both sitting upright.

"The color of your lips, the color of your eyes, the color of your hair, and the color of your blush." He stares down at where my hand is before wrapping his fingers around mine. "Those are my new favorites," Adrian says, a shy smile covering his lips. "I hope that's alright with you."

"As long as it's okay with you if I keep wearing orange because it reminds me of you," I say, doing my best to swallow past the emotion building in my throat.

"I wouldn't want it any other way."

CHAPTER 52
Nevaeh

LEONARD AND I HAVE been getting along really well. He enjoys it whenever I let him take the pictures and answers any question happily. At one point on Friday, he even shared a story about his first F1 race with me. He wasn't as talkative today, but I don't blame him.

Qualifying was brutal. The sun was burning hot in Barcelona today, and all the drivers were battling with the heat throughout the preparations and Qualifying itself. Adrian took pole with Lincoln in second, Gabriel in third, Val in fucking fourth, which I already hugged her for, James in fifth, Kyle in seventh, and Leonard in eighth, followed by the rest of the drivers.

I'm sitting on the bed in my hotel room as a text lights up my screen. Adrian's with his team and told me he'd see me tomorrow so I'm not surprised to see Val's name appear instead.

Val: I have a little surprise for you. Meet me at the track in half an hour.

I smile to myself before assuring her I will be there. My feet bring me into the bathroom where I look at myself in the mirror. My fingers wrap around the bracelet Adrian gave me, my chest tight with anxiety. Today is a very difficult day, especially because there's no trigger, no attack. It's just *there*, in my chest, making me feel heavy and unmotivated. I feel like crying and sleeping, but I'm too on edge to do either of these things.

Maybe being around Val and seeing the surprise she has for me will cheer me up.

I'm about to leave when my phone rings.

"Hello?" I ask as I answer my boss' call.

"Hi, Nevaeh, I know it's late, but I have some great news. After this season, I would like to offer you the opportunity to work with the tennis department, if you're still interested," Ms. Martin says, surprise spreading through me.

"Yes! I'm very interested," I say.

"Great, because I looked over the client list you gave us, and you were right. Some of them came to *Griffin Sports* because of you. They want you to interview the players and write similar articles like the ones you write for the drivers," she explains, but I can't believe what she's saying.

This was my dream job.

She's handing me my dream job.

"Thank you for calling me," I say, hearing her chuckle through the phone.

"My pleasure. Finish out the season, keep doing the good job you are, and I promise you'll be in the tennis department by next year," she replies, and my knees go a little weak. I hold onto the sink in my hotel bathroom, doing my best not to burst into tears.

She hangs up without another word, leaving me to cover my mouth and happiness to spread through my chest. I try to linger on it, to remind myself this is the job of my dreams, that I did it.

But something in my chest revolts against the thought of switching departments.

Something that's grown attached to everyone I've been working with. To the sport I never thought I'd fall in love with.

My heart.

My heart is begging me not to take this job, to stay in the world of Formula One because I didn't just find the man I care for here. I found a family. I found people who care for me unconditionally. I found friends who don't use me but listen to me and allow me to comfort them in return. I've found a love for racing, for the excitement of the sport.

Then I think of Adrian and how we'll never be able to be together as long as I'm working in Formula One.

My head hurts. My heart is all over the place. My anxiety returns tenfold.

What the hell am I supposed to do now?

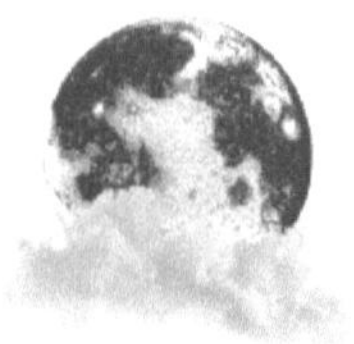

Half an hour later, I arrive at the track and make my way to the Velocità Rossa garage where Valentina is leaning against a stunning red Velocità Rossa. An easy smile lingers on her lips as she speaks to James and Gabriel. Out of habit, I scan my surroundings to look for Adrian, but he isn't here, and a little disappointment shoots through me at that realization.

Val beams at me when I reach her before flinging her arms around my neck.

"Thank you for coming, Nevs!" she says, opening the door and reaching inside the car to grab a helmet. It's one of hers, except nothing is covering the face.

"What's this for?" I ask as I take it from her. Happiness spreads all over her features, and even Gabriel and James are smiling at me.

"You told us once how jealous you are that we get to drive such awesome cars around the track, but you don't have to be anymore. You get to drive this one," Val informs me, making a shocked, swift laugh escape me.

"Are you serious?" She nods with a grin and takes my hand to lead me to the driver's side. "But you're going to sit with me, right?" I ask, excited and scared at the same time.

This is a once-in-a-lifetime opportunity, but I won't accept it if she tells me to go through with this by myself. My anxiety has already spiked, but the comforting smile she offers me settles the feeling a little.

It'll be okay.

Deep breaths.

"Of course, love, I'd never let you do this by yourself," she assures me while opening the door and gesturing for me to get in. "This is going to be so much fun," she adds, shutting it once more and skipping over to the other side to kiss Gabriel once before joining me in the car.

My fingers run over the leather interior and then trace the Velocità Rossa logo on the horn of the wheel. Val gives me a brief instruction and everything I have to know. Then, she tells me to start the engine and drive out of the pitlane and onto the track.

"Go slow, see what speed you're ready for, what you can handle," Val adds, so I start driving slowly instead of speeding down the track.

"My father's taken me to race in cars like these since I was a kid. Sometimes he even let me drive them, but never like this," I say, giggling a little as we make our way into the sixth corner of the track if I've been counting right.

I press down on the gas pedal, steadily increasing the speed but chickening out as soon as I see a corner. It's dark outside, but the track is lit up all around, allowing me to see everything in front of us.

There's just something so beautiful about a Formula One track at night, the way there's nothing around us but the sound of the roaring engine, the lights giving it an orangey hue, and the air just smells different. It's an entirely different feeling in itself, and I think that's why I've always enjoyed the night races more whenever Papa took me with him as a kid.

Sometimes, I forget how big of a role Formula One has played in my life since I was a child. My father has been a big part of that, of course, but I also remember Nova cheering at the top of her lungs for her favorite driver, Adrian's dad.

As I got older, Mama started taking me to tennis games, and once I started playing it too, I no longer cared about anything else. Even after I lost my dream, I thought any connection to tennis, to the sport I fell in love with, would make the pain of losing my dream less consuming. Until now. Until I fell in love all over again.

I'm twenty-one years old. I always thought I knew exactly what I wanted, what I was working toward. I was miserable in this job when I was working with Gillian, but I felt so free when I started working with the drivers. They showed me the beautiful sides of Formula One. The speed, the thrill, the fans that cheer for you no matter what. The family they created here. It almost feels like I'm part of that now, and I don't want to leave.

"You can do it," Val encourages, and I take a deep breath. "There is a straight line coming up, okay? Fucking floor it," she says, and I laugh before doing exactly as I'm told.

"Woohooooooo!" I scream but slow down soon after as the straight comes to an end.

"Good job," she praises and claps her hands together to cheer me on.

Adrenaline pumps through my veins, and I finally get it. I understand why the drivers crave this, the thrill and excitement. The danger and power. The lightness of my body, the speed as we race down the track, it all feels like nothing can touch me. Like I'm invincible.

It's an addictive feeling.

When I tell Val what I'm thinking, she beams up at me.

"It is. It's everything. I've loved it for so long, I did everything to make it my life," she says and smiles at the track ahead of us.

"Can we switch seats? I would love to watch you race for a little," I admit, and Valentina tilts her head my way, giving me a wicked grin.

"Absolutely we can, but I won't go slow or easy on you," she warns, but I'm already bringing the car to the start line so we can switch places.

Once Valentina is behind the wheel, her eyes light up and her body relaxes into the seat. She waits for me to put my seatbelt on before flooring it and racing down the track. If I could, I'd fly out of my seat. A laugh bursts free, one that turns into a squeal as she hits the corner and drifts. She lets out a *whoop* before stepping on the gas again and letting out an evil laugh.

"Hold on tight, Nevaeh," she instructs before going even faster.

I screw my eyes shut, holding back another laugh before looking at my friend. Whenever I see her in this environment, I realize over and over that Val was born to do this. She was born to be a racer, to break down barriers men have built around her for as long as she's been trying to make it into this sport.

But nothing could stop her. Nothing and no one, and I admire her for that. I admire her strength and determination. I admire the way she never gave up. I admire that she knew what she wanted and went for it.

"You were made for this," I say as she races down the main straight once more, drifting into the first corner. My fingers hold onto the door and the middle console as she laughs again, slowing down to, probably, keep my heart from stopping altogether.

"It didn't always feel like that, you know? I felt so lost and worthless more times than not. That's how they made me feel. Like I wasn't worthy of a spot in this world. Sometimes I still feel that way, like if I don't work every single second of the day to earn it, I'm not good enough for it," she admits, turning the wheel to take a corner.

"For what it's worth, I don't think there's a driver on the grid who deserves a seat in Formula One more than you do. You've outperformed Leonard in almost every race. You have pushed Alfa Adrenalina higher on the Constructors' Championship standings than they have been in a long time. On top of all of that, you and Leonard are still working to open your driver academy soon. You're remarkable in every way, Val."

She brings the car to a stop in front of James and Gabriel, turning to me to show the tears that have shot into her eyes.

"I've never had a friend like you, Nevaeh, but I want you to know that I care about you so much. That isn't easy for me to say, but I mean it," she says, so I fling my arms around her and hold on tight.

"I care about you, too," I reply, leaning back and letting a tear fall down my cheek right as two stream down hers.

I wipe mine away and she wipes hers before we get out of the car to greet the two men waiting for us. Gabriel frowns a little when he sees Valentina's teary eyes, but she merely wraps her arms around him for comfort. James looks away at the same moment I do, and our gazes meet, allowing me to see the pain in his eyes. He gives me a smile I know he doesn't mean before walking away.

The helmet is so tight on my head that when the pressure leaves, I almost sigh in relief. Gabriel hands me my camera, and I flash him a smile.

My feet bring me to the front of the car so I can take a few photos. I squat down to find the best angles, like I always do, and then inspect the pictures on the small screen of my camera to make sure they turned out well. Then again, I don't have to check to make sure anymore. The camera Adrian got me takes the best pictures. Even when the photos turn out blurry, there is a special kind of beauty to them.

"So handsome," I mumble to myself, not realizing I'm no longer alone.

"Thank you," my secret boyfriend's familiar voice says, causing me to freeze in place. My head doesn't know whether it wants to focus on the nostalgia of this moment from the day we first met or the fact that he's here with me and everything's perfect now. "But if you wanted a picture of me, you didn't have to hide behind the car to take it," he adds, and I grin at him.

Nostalgia briefly takes over but his presence ends up winning the battle, and I take a step toward him with my heart racing in the way it always does when he's near me.

"Those are the first words you ever said to me," I point out as he closes the distance between us, too.

"Best pickup line of my life," he teases, so I playfully smack his stomach. He wraps me into a hug in response, kissing the top of my head.

"You shouldn't be touching me like that here," I say but don't push away either.

"There's no one here that doesn't know, I promise," he assures me. I melt into him, the emotional rollercoaster of today catching up with me now that I'm in his arms. "Talk to me." I place my chin on his chest and crane my neck to look up at him. God, why is he so tall?

"What do you mean?"

"Something's wrong, *mon ange*, I can feel it. Talk to me, and I'll make it all better," he says, his hands moving to my cheeks to cup them.

"I've been offered a job in the tennis department starting next season," I explain, fighting back my tears.

I don't understand why this choice makes me so sad.

"That's incredible. It's everything you wanted at the beginning of this year. Why are you sad?" His genuine pride makes me even more emotional.

"I've grown attached to the people, to the sport. To you," I add the last two words, making him smile a little.

"I've grown attached to you, too, baby, but we'd find a way to make it work. People do it all the time, and I'm very motivated to make us work because I—" He cuts off and sucks in a sharp breath.

"I know," I assure him, but he shakes his head.

"No, you don't know because I haven't said it. I've been so scared, Nevaeh. Ever since I've met you, I've been confused and terrified, but I couldn't stay away. I couldn't fight the hold you have on me, and I don't want to," he says and leans down to press his nose to mine.

"Adrian—" I start but cut off, unsure what to say.

"I never thought I'd find you," he says, his head dropping to my chest so he can kiss the spot above my heart. "Never thought I'd believe in the possibility of love again."

I lift my thumb and index finger to his chin, grabbing it in the same way he always does with me when he wants my undivided attention.

He didn't tell me he's in love with me, but it's here, in this moment, when he's given me the world, that I realize *I'm* in love with *him*. I'm so in love with him, my heart aches because of how full it is with him. I'm so in love with him, I don't want to hide us from the world. I'm so in love with him, there's no going back for me anymore.

"If you give me your heart, I promise, I'll keep it safe," I say, and his eyes fill with tears, but he blinks them away and kisses me instead.

"*Je t'appartiens, mon paradis,*" he repeats. "I belong to you, and that includes my heart. It's yours."

His lips wrap around mine again, and I lose myself in his taste, in his words, in his feelings.

"You make me feel safe, you tease me, you see me in ways no one else does. You bring me to my fucking knees, and I love it. I love that we were friends first. I love that we have so much in common but also some things we don't because you're always happy to let me introduce you to new parts of my world. I love sleeping in a bed with you and waking up to your face. I love it all. It's sacred to me now, a gift from fate." He takes a deep breath as he drags me even closer.

"But how could you feel safe if I scared you?"

"You scared me like racing scared me when I first started. You scared me because I'd never felt this way before, but I'm not that scared anymore." He kisses me, leaving his lips on mine as he says, "It feels like I've been reserving my heart for you, Nevaeh, like it was only ever yours to take so I never let anyone close enough to it."

He takes a breath for courage.

"*Je suis amoureux de toi.*"

There's no translation needed. Nothing at all as the tears finally stream down my face. Adrian Romana, the man who doesn't fall in love, just told me he loves me for the first time.

"Ich liebe dich," he goes on, butchering the German language perfectly.

He kisses me once more, making me smile against his mouth, but I have to break the kiss to cover my mouth to hold the sob at bay.

"I love you, Nevaeh."

"I love you endlessly, *mein Mond,*" I reply, flinging my arms around his neck and deepening our kiss.

He holds me close for a moment, nothing but the sound of his and my racing heart between us.

"Whatever it is you want to do, I'll stick by your side. If you want to stay in F1 as a reporter, we'll stay a secret. If you choose tennis, we'll make our schedules work. Either way, we'll figure it out. Together. I promise."

And I believe him.

It just doesn't make my choice any clearer.

CHAPTER 53

Adrian

TODAY IS THE LAST race before the summer break.

I'm in a good fucking mood.

Before you ask, yes, it's because I told Nevaeh I love her last night and she said it back to me. Obviously, that's the reason for my good mood. How could it not be? I've never been in love before, but it feels incredible like nothing can touch me as long as Nevaeh is by my side. It's a heady feeling, dangerous, but that's what Formula One is all about, too, and I crave that feeling. I just never thought I'd feel it in my relationship.

"Adrian Romana." Well, that voice certainly has the ability to kill my happy mood.

"What do you want, rookie?" I ask, straightening out my back to tower over him. Daniel gives me a disapproving look, but I'm not the one who wants to fight.

Lincoln is.

"I've thought about what you said last time, and you're right. The championship is far from decided, but I'm going to win. I'm going to take this from you the way you took Nevaeh from me."

He takes a step toward me, puffing out his chest.

I'm as unimpressed by his announcement as he knew I'd be, which is why he adds, "You're not good enough for the trophy. Your grandfather and father were champions in their time, I used to watch them when I grew up, and you're nothing like them. You don't have what it takes to win. It's why Gabriel won last season. It's why I'll win this season. They'd be so disappointed to know you don't have what it takes."

Lincoln steps away again, smiling viciously at me before delivering the killing blow.

"Luckily, they're too dead to watch you fuck up your second chance," he says, making my hands curl into fists at my sides.

All of my grief bubbles up to the top, all of my self-doubts ripping my confidence to shreds. Maybe if I hadn't felt this way before, his words wouldn't rattle me, but they do. They fuck with my carefully crafted mindset until I'm so off-balance, I can't even breathe anymore.

I'm not good enough.

My family would be disappointed in me.

They're all too dead to watch me fail or succeed, too dead to be there for me either way.

I've been so good at distracting myself from my grief, to redirect my thoughts whenever they went to a dark place. I've managed to push it all into a corner and ignore it. Never deal with it. Be the light in everyone's lives. Do my best to never get dragged down by how much I miss my family. How deeply their losses hurt me. Just how hard it broke my heart when my grandmother died, my father accidentally killed himself, and my grandfather passed away from lung cancer.

When my mother *left*.

I breathe through gritted teeth, unwilling to let Lincoln see how big of an effect his words have on me.

"Are you done? I have better things to do than watch children throw tantrums," I say, sounding calm and collected despite the tsunami of pain hitting my system in waves.

"Yeah, I'm done here. I've caused all the damage I needed to unravel your cool-guy demeanor because I've seen right through you from the moment we met. You pretend nothing can get to you, but you have weaknesses. You're confident, but deep inside, you're a broken man, who loves people too fiercely. Let me give you one last tip, don't waste that love on Nevaeh. You make one mistake, and she'll leave you, just like she left me," he says, and I bite through another wave of pain, my molars grinding together.

"You made more than one mistake with Nevaeh. You treated her like a piece of fucking property, and I swear to God, if you go near her again without her permission, I will hurt you. Maybe not physically, maybe not visibly, but I will find the one spot that brings you the most pain, and I'll press until you beg for mercy." I move toward him, leaning down so he's sure to hear my next words clearly. "Now get the fuck out of my face before I punch you in yours," I warn, panic snaking around my lungs and squeezing until inhaling hurts.

He looks a little scared of me now, but I don't care anymore. I need him to leave so I can find Nevaeh.

Lincoln disappears a second later, and I let out a wheezing breath, collapsing against the fence Daniel and I were standing next to. I just got out of my car after driving it to the first place position on the grid and we were about to run through our last-minute pre-race preparations when Lincoln showed up. I don't have a lot of time to break down right now, but it doesn't matter.

This is not a choice I'm making.

"Adrian," Daniel blurts out, catching my arm as my breaths come out faster and more shallow.

"I need Nevaeh."

My hands are shaking. Pain has consumed every part of me, making it impossible to breathe. It feels like the entire planet is sitting on my lungs, preventing them from taking in any oxygen. I've never experienced this kind of suffering, this deep, unconscious pain that has resurfaced after years of suppressing it. It's almost like it increased over time, and now it's eating away at everything good and positive inside of me. All my happy memories, all the joy I've ever felt, everything is getting pushed into a corner of my mind as hurt stacks its tables and chairs against it, keeping it from escaping.

I have to make it stop.

Somehow, and I have no idea how I have to find a way to get rid of this inability to breathe.

Grief is an old friend, I've carried him with me my entire life. I've known him since I was a child. Lived in a certain kind of harmony with him.

Lincoln's words have shattered that harmony.

Tears stream down my face, but I wipe them away, angry at myself for falling apart where everyone can see me. I stumble away from Daniel, toward Leonard's garage where I'm hoping Nevaeh will be.

My brain is spinning from the lack of oxygen, my hands are still quivering from the earthquake within me, and my lungs are burning. They burn and ache, but I can't ease their pain. I can't ease any of it, anywhere in me.

"Come on," I say to myself, trying to inhale as deeply as I can. It doesn't work.

More hyperventilation follows.

How the fuck do I make this stop?

I think about what Grandma would tell me to do. She'd say, "Think about why this is causing you so much pain. Try to understand why it hurts, and then address it. You will be able to move on." It's complete and utter bullshit. I know why this hurts so goddamn much. I know where everything is coming from, the root of all of my problems. It doesn't make them go away, doesn't help me fucking breathe.

Why the hell is it so hard to breathe, for fuck's sake!

Grandpa would tell me to find balance. "You're completely out of balance. You're letting your emotions affect your body and mind. It's why you can't breathe." Blah, blah, blah. None of this is going to help me.

"Drown your sorrows, son. Forget about the rest of the world and grab a bottle. It always helped me. It can do the same for you." My father's voice swims in my ears.

Alcohol. His addiction got even worse after he got kicked off his team. He always told us he'd decided to retire, but I knew better. I knew he was kicked off the team because of all the bullshit he pulled. It's why Grandfather was always disappointed in him. It's why Grandma couldn't bear to look at him anymore, not that she had to for a long time since she died shortly after he became a self-destructive mess.

Fuck.

More pain shoots through me when I realize for the millionth time they're all dead. They're all gone, forever.

As soon as I'm in front of the garage, Nevaeh rushes outside to meet me, catching me a second before I hit the ground.

"What happened? What's wrong?" she asks, searching my face while helping me step away from all the people who could potentially record my breakdown.

"Can't... fucking... breathe..." I manage to croak out, dropping down a wall as soon as Nevaeh closes the door to where she brought me. "Feels... like... I'm dying."

"Okay, it's alright, baby. You're having a panic attack. You're not dying, and I've got you. Let's breathe together," she says before telling someone, I hope it's Daniel, to get her some ice. "Ready, *mein Mond*?" she asks, touching my cheek and making me realize just how hard I'm pressing my eyes shut. The way she addresses me, *my moon*, brings me back into the moment with her, allowing my eyes to flutter open.

There's a comforting smile on her face as I look at her.

"I've got you and I'm not going anywhere. We'll breathe together, and you'll find your way back into your body, regain control. Okay?"

The way she's so calm, so well-versed in what the fuck is happening to me, settles me enough to nod. She takes my shaking hand in hers and presses it to her chest, letting me feel her steady heartbeat. Nevaeh places her hand on my chest, grounding me.

"I'm here. You're going to be okay. Take one big inhale for me, hold it, then exhale."

"I can't," I say, more tears streaming down. I can't stop crying either. Everything hurts. Everything burns inside of me.

"Yes, you can."

Daniel reappears with an ice pack in his hand, and Nevaeh lifts my fireproofs enough to press it against my chest without any warning. The cold sends a shock to my system until I'm hissing out another breath.

"Fuck's sake, baby," I groan, my head falling backward against the wall.

"Breathe in," she says, taking a deep breath with me. "Hold." I hold my breath. "Exhale." Through gritted teeth, I expel it, but she doesn't stop there. She makes me repeat the same three steps until my panic subsides enough to stop my body from shaking. Nevaeh eventually removes the ice pack, handing it to a very concerned Daniel. "Can you give us a minute?" my girlfriend asks sweetly, softly, her voice soothing me all over again.

"Of course," my performance coach and friend says, stepping out of what I just now realize is a break room.

"Talk to me. What triggered it?" she says, rubbing a gentle hand over my chest.

The events leading up to my panic attack spill from my lips without hesitation. Nevaeh's eyes grow dark at my explanation.

"I'm gonna kill him. I'm going to ask him to meet me somewhere private, trick him into a box, nail the lid shut, and throw it into the ocean." I can't help but chuckle at her plan. My fingers wrap around the hand she's still holding against my chest, lifting it to press a kiss to her knuckles.

"What if he's right? What if I'm not good enough? What if everything my father and grandfather were as racers was all given to Val and none of it to me?" I ask, so she moves forward until she's straddling my lap and able to cup my face in her hands.

"I hear you. Your feelings are valid," she says, and I furrow my brows at her, a little smile covering my face.

"But?" I reply, running my hands from her hips to her ass.

"But I would like to smack some sense into you, Adrian. You are a phenomenal driver. When I watch you race, I can't look away. You mesmerize me. You're aggressive but fair. Respectful but determined. Talented but also skilled. You *deserve* the championship. You are good enough. Don't let Lincoln project his insecurities onto you. He's not good enough. He hardly had to work for his seat. Yes, he's a good driver, but he's also a cheater. He's already got enough penalty points to last a season. He's a dick," she says, making me snort a little but mostly smile at her because her reassurance of my ability as a racer means way more to me than Lincoln's degradation of it.

"I love you, mon paradis," I blurt out, telling her I love her for the second time in twenty-four hours. It's a strange realization, knowing I've never done that with anyone but my sister and once James. I could fall in love with her time after time, life after life. Over and over because once isn't nearly enough.

"I love you endlessly, *mein Mond*." Then, she kisses me, and all my grief, all the pain in my chest, goes back to its proper place in my head. "I need you to promise me something," she says against my lips, leaning back enough so her brown eyes are on mine. I trace the freckles painted over the bridge of her nose and cheeks.

"Anything."

"Don't ignore your grief. I tried to ignore mine after my injury. It doesn't work forever. It will come out in moments like these, through panic attacks and anxiety, maybe even depression." I nod because she's right. I can't hide from it forever. I can't ignore it either. "I'll help you. I'll catch you when you fall because you're allowed to take the time to fall apart."

More tears jump into my eyes.

"I am?" She strokes my jaw, then runs her thumb over my bottom lip.

"You are. One more race until the summer break, until you can take a breather," Nevaeh assures me.

"What if I don't win today?" It feels like if I don't snatch the win, if I can't win this race, I'll lose the championship altogether. It's a stupid thought, but after the hit my confidence took today, I'm not sure I can dismiss it either.

"You're Adrian Romana. You get back up after getting knocked down, brush the dust off your magnificent ass, and try again," she says, standing up and holding out her hand.

"You like my ass? All my hard work has finally paid off!" I celebrate, watching her laugh at my comment before letting her help me up.

My arms wrap around her once I'm upright, hugging her to my chest.

"Thank you," I say, inhaling her sweet scent. My tensed-up muscles relax a little as she runs her hands down my back.

"Anytime," she replies. "Breathe, race, and win, as long as it doesn't cost you a limb."

I give her one last kiss, falling more in love with Nevaeh Fuchs every second I spend in her presence.

CHAPTER 54
Nevaeh

Adrian needs to win today.

If he doesn't, I have a feeling he's going to struggle the rest of the season because of what Lincoln said. The urge to go to my ex-best friend and hit him over the head with my laptop becomes more appealing the longer I smack my fingers across my keyboard to write Leonard's article. I'm so angry, I don't know what to do with myself anymore.

All this pent-up energy eventually leads to me standing up and pacing around the room. The drivers are about to take their formation lap, and my anxiety skyrockets as I watch Adrian lead the rest of the pack around the track, warming up his tires and charging his battery. I find myself walking out of the private room I was in and toward where Quinn, Leonard's performance coach, is standing. She hands me a pair of headphones, and I slip them on, my eyes finding the same screen she's watching like a hawk.

"This never gets easier for me either," she says and squeezes my arm. I doubt this isn't nerve-racking for any fan of the sport. Add one of the drivers being my boyfriend to the mix and my anxiety, and I'm standing there with shaky legs and shallow breathing.

I rub the blue heart charm on my bracelet, taking several deep breaths right as Adrian moves back into the first place position behind the starting line.

The lights turn on one by one.

I hold my breath.

Engines roar.

Leonard's garage goes silent.

Everyone and everything seems to stop moving.

Anticipation tenses my muscles.

As soon as the lights go out, all the cars start rolling. Adrian gets away well, but Lincoln has a better start and overtakes him in the first corner. My heart sinks at the sight and shoots back into my chest when Adrian slips beside him in the next corner, overtaking Lincoln to get back into first place. Their tires almost touch. Lincoln's front wing grazes Adrian's.

My hand covers my mouth as I watch Adrian push ahead, reclaiming first place. His team radio blasts through my headphones a second later.

"Fuck! Do I have damage?" Adrian asks, breathless and frustrated.

I hold my breath as I wait for an answer.

It seems like the whole world does, too.

"No damage. Keep going, you're good," Chloe says, causing the breath to release out of me in a silent *whoosh*. "Lincoln's got damage though," she adds the same moment Lincoln slows down, Gabriel shooting past him, Val right behind her fiancé.

Chaos follows moments later.

The Carousel drivers crash into each other, almost taking out Cameron in the process, so the safety car comes out for the fourth time this season. Lincoln changes his front wing, ending up in twelfth, which is only thanks to the other drivers having to decrease their speed.

Adrian stays in first, Gabriel and Val behind him. James is in fourth now, with Leonard and Cameron following. Both drivers involved in the crash make it out and seem okay, but it takes the marshals a long time to clean up the debris. So long, the FIA decides to call for a red flag and pause the race.

All eighteen remaining cars return to the pitlane. I watch Adrian get out of his car, anger tensing his shoulders. He might be wearing a helmet, but I've studied this man enough to know when he's standing relaxed and when he's close to bursting from anger. Right now, I think he wants to rip Lincoln's head off for the second time this season.

Adrian attempts to step toward where Lincoln is getting out of his car, but Val cuts him off, grabbing her brother's shoulder and stopping his approach. Gabriel's behind Valentina then too, taking off his helmet and balaclava, probably to hear their conversation better. Adrian attempts to step past Val to get back to approaching Lincoln, but Gabriel slips in front of his teammate, shaking his head.

James, on the other hand, is determined to defend his best friend and approaches Lincoln. He points at Adrian, gestures wildly with his hands, then pokes Lincoln's chest in warning.

I wish I knew what they're saying.

"Uh oh," Quinn says right as Leonard approaches Lincoln and James, stepping between them to break up their fighting.

He took his balaclava and helmet off too, and all I see as I look at his face is disappointment. And exhaustion. He looks like a parent who's sick and tired of the children's fighting. The scowl on his face is directed at Lincoln, who is yelling something at Leonard. The Englishman's unimpressed expression speaks volumes about what Lincoln is saying. Leonard only answers one word to Lincoln's minute-long rant. I don't have to be a lip reader to see him say "no" because he's shaking his head, too. James walks away and toward Val, Gabriel, and Adrian while Leonard makes his way inside his garage to meet Quinn.

"Fucking children. 'He hit my best friend.' 'No, he hit *me*.'" Leonard shakes his head again. "I'm going to retire after this season. I'm too old for this shit," he says to Quinn, but he's close enough for me to hear. "James is a good kid, but he still needs to learn that racers like Lincoln don't have a rational side when emotions are running high," he goes on, and I almost thank him for clearing up what happened.

"Lincoln could have cost Adrian his race... again," Quinn replies, and I press my lips shut at the thought.

"I know, and I'm fucking furious, too, but approaching Lincoln won't help. You've got to take shit like that to the FIA." Leonard catches me staring at him and nods his head at my concerned expression. "Adrian's got this. Don't worry." His reassurance, his cool determination, feels like a warm hug.

I let it envelope me while we wait for the race to restart.

Once the marshals have cleared all the debris and the cars have been taken off the track, the FIA announces the race will restart in five minutes behind the safety car. Adrian stops in front of Leonard's garage for a second, winking at me before continuing to walk toward his car, leaving me to go back to worrying.

I don't know how the rest of the drivers' partners do this. I text Elijah, Cameron's boyfriend, asking him how he's doing. We only recently exchanged phone numbers after we met at the honky tonk bar in Austin, but we've chatted a couple of times to discuss how stressful the life of a Formula One partner during the race is. He also loves sending me videos of Adrian and Cameron, which I love.

Me: How are you doing?

Elijah: Peed my pants. Did you see how close Cameron was to the Carousel?

Me: I did.

Elijah: How is the state of your pants? I'm guessing it's similar to mine considering what Lincoln pulled.

Me: I peed before the race started, so I'm good.

Elijah: Writing that down for next time.

I can't help the laugh bubbling out of me.

At least I'm not the only one feeling on edge.

The race restarts with Adrian following behind the safety car. I watch as it enters the pits two laps later, allowing Adrian to restart the race. Gabriel is right behind him, and Val is creeping closer to her fiancé while James is waiting to overtake her.

Adrian shoots ahead, but Gabriel's reaction time is flawless. He's right there with his teammate, pushing him far but not so far that Adrian's car slips into the gravel. My hand flies back to my mouth to suppress a gasp when James' car slips past Valentina's by a hair-width. My friend doesn't give up though. She might have the slower car, but she fights until she's back in third place. Unfortunately, a lap later, James is ahead of her again, his car too quick and hers too slow to keep up with him. Adrian and Gabriel have drifted apart a little, my boyfriend now over a second ahead of his teammate.

By the time the first pitstop rolls around, I'm holding my breath again. After what happened in Austin, I don't trust the pit crew anymore. Quinn laughs at me when I look away from the screen, but there is no way I'm watching what might be another horrible stop.

Luckily, everything goes smoothly and Adrian ends up in fifth place, as expected. Unfortunately, Lincoln has worked his way up to sixth place, and with warmer tires, he overtakes Adrian as they race down the straight. A string of German curse words flows out of me, even though I know Lincoln still has to pit and Adrian will get back ahead.

At least, that was the plan before James' engine catches fire and he has to pull off to the side of the track to jump out of his car and let the marshals put out the fire. The safety car comes back onto the track, giving everyone who hasn't pitted the advantage of losing less time. Gabriel pits, Val pits, Leonard pits, and lastly, Lincoln does, too. I'm watching the screens closely, Adrian now in third place, right behind Val and Gabriel.

If he hadn't pitted before them, if he'd waited, he wouldn't have lost the lead of this race for good, but luck was not on his side today. More curse words fall from my lips as the race restarts for the second time, Adrian fighting with Val for second place. She fends him off for a lap before he races past her by braking later as they go into the corner. He zooms ahead, chasing down Gabriel.

My heart is racing.

"It's like last year all over again," Quinn says to me, and I study her amused expression for a second. "Those two are so evenly matched, it's hard to figure out who'll win, you know?" she adds, and when I bring my attention back to the screen, I see Adrian's DRS flap open to gain a speed advantage over Gabriel. The breath catches in my throat. Adrian attempts a dangerous overtake, a single centimeter further to the left and he'd touch Gabriel, but he makes it past his teammate without an incident.

Ten laps later, he wins the race.

And I barely keep from screaming in joy when Valentina snatches third place, too.

Adrian is back to leading the championship, and there's nothing that could ruin the high we're entering the summer break with.

At least, I hope so.

CHAPTER 55
Adrian

I'M STILL HIGH ON my win when Nevaeh and I stumble through the door of her hotel room, my tongue slipping through her parted teeth and her hands gliding into my hair. She tugs on my curls as I grab her ass and drag her further against my chest, pushing my groin against her stomach. She smiles against my lips, clearly happy to feel how fucking hard I am for her already.

I told Nevaeh I wanted to celebrate my win with her alone, away from everyone else, and she didn't hesitate. We rushed to her hotel and as soon as we were alone in the elevator, my woman attacked me, flinging her arms around my neck and kissing me senseless.

It was the best feeling ever.

"You're so hard," she says, another moan slipping past her lips when I cup her breasts over the thick fabric of her shirt.

"And you're perfect," I reply in French, not even realizing I switched to my mother tongue until Nevaeh giggles. I'm so wrapped up in her, I'm surprised I still know words in any language.

I kiss her again, tasting her until she steps away to rip her shirt off and tug on mine. I chuckle at her impatience, pulling my shirt over my head and dropping to my knees to slide down her skirt and panties. She steps out of it, her hands slipping on top of my hair as she slowly guides my mouth toward her beautiful pussy.

"Use your words, baby. Tell me what to do. I'm on my knees and would do anything for you. Just say the word," I say, watching a wonderful blush settle on her cheeks.

"I want your tongue on my pussy," she says with a shy smile, her head falling backward as I run my hands up and down her legs. Goosebumps appear all over her skin, so I take my time, kissing her inner thigh and making my way toward where she wants me most.

I look up at her right as I lower my mouth to her clit, flicking my tongue over it. Nevaeh shakes from pleasure, her fingers grabbing my curls and pulling on them with every lick, with every suck.

"Shit, Adrian, that feels so good," she says, her legs quivering as I continue eating her out. I could taste Nevaeh all day, every day. She tastes like my forever, and I'll never get enough.

My cock gives a needy throb, so I lower my hand, undoing the button of my jeans and sliding the zipper down. I slip my fingers over Nevaeh's pussy, letting them enter her for a moment before using the same hand to start stroking my cock.

"Adrian, I'm gonna come," she says right as I use the tip of my tongue to flick it over her clit faster until I have to band an arm around her legs to hold her up. I give my cock another rough stroke while Nevaeh screams through her orgasm, covering her mouth to muffle the noise.

As soon as she stops shaking from her orgasm, I guide her toward the bed, kissing her while she moans happily into my mouth. She can taste herself on my lips and seems to enjoy it because she slips her tongue into my mouth and groans in response.

"Get on the bed and spread your legs for me, baby. I want to slip into my paradise," I say, watching Nevaeh follow instructions without a moment of hesitation.

She parts her legs and arches her back, her perfect breasts bouncing a little with the movement. I could watch her forever, too. Just study every little move of hers, study the way her body responds to me, how her eyes light up with mischief as she guides her hand to her pussy and slips a finger inside. She plays with herself until her toes curl, and I watch it all as I slide my boxers down and take my dick in my hand again.

"Replace my finger with your cock, Adrian. I need you deep inside of me." *Fuck, yes.*

"You're so fucking hot when you boss me around, Nevaeh," I say, grabbing a condom out of my bag and slipping it down my sensitive length.

A groan escapes me while I move onto the bed, grabbing her hand from between her legs and lifting it to my mouth. I suck her finger into my mouth as I align myself with her entrance, loving the way she whimpers in pleasure. I sink inside of her in one, swift move because she was so wet and ready for me. At the same moment, I'm seated all the way inside her, a knock on her hotel door startles both of us.

"Nevaeh, it's Gillian," her former boss says, and I watch panic cross Nevaeh's features.

"Fuck," she whispers, but she makes no attempt to push me away. If anything, she rolls her hips a little to get friction, a smile dancing onto her lips that she tries to hide. My perfect, dirty girl wants me to fuck her while her former boss is outside her door because it's forbidden. And she loves the danger of it.

I lean down, pressing my lips against her ear before whispering, "Be quiet."

Nevaeh gives me several eager nods. I watch her chest rise and fall more abruptly, adrenaline and anticipation exciting her. Her walls clench around me too as she puts her weight on her elbows and watches me slip out of her. I place a finger over my lips and wink at her before driving into her so hard, she slams a hand over her mouth to keep quiet.

"I want to talk to you," Gillian goes on while I fuck my woman with long, savoring strokes that have her eyes rolling into the back of her head.

A rush rolls through my body.

This is forbidden. We shouldn't be here. And yet, it feels so fucking good, I can't stop. I never understood the appeal of doing something for the thrill of it being forbidden. I never understood it until I started dating Nevaeh.

"Come on, Nevaeh, I thought we moved past this pettiness." *Why the fuck is he still talking?*

"Do you want me to make you come with him right outside this door? Hmm? Is that what you want?" I whisper, quiet enough to make sure she's the only one that hears me. Nevaeh nods, her hand slipping between us so she can rub her clit in tight, fast circles.

Gillian knocks again while I thrust into her, this time harder and quicker until Nevaeh's biting down on her hand to keep from screaming. I can't help but smile at her, at the way she whimpers and moans so quietly, desperately trying to keep Gillian from hearing.

"Stay quiet, Nevaeh. We don't want him to hear," I say right as her former boss knocks again.

"Okay, fine, I'll speak to you tomorrow," Gillian adds so I slow my movements just enough to listen to his footsteps depart.

"Finally," I say and fuck into her so hard, she moans louder than ever before.

"Again," she begs, so I repeat the same movement. Over and over. "Adrian," she says softly while I play with her nipples, rolling them between my fingers.

"Scream it," I say, so she does, my merciless thrusts becoming quicker with each one.

"Adrian," she pants, pulling my head down to feel my lips press against hers. "Faster," she begs against my mouth, and I pick up speed, turning her into a loud, moaning mess. My groans fill the room, and she revels in them, the sound exciting her. I can see it in the way she smiles. "Oh, yes," she moans, reassuring me for the thousandth time.

"Fly for me, *mon ange*," I whisper into her ear, burying my face into the crook of her neck.

Everything inside of me tightens. Pleasure sweeps through me. And then, I'm the one who's flying, my head in the clouds as I thrust into her, letting her ride out her orgasm while enjoying wave over wave of pleasure myself.

My movements slow, my body still shaking from the orgasm as I groan her name several times and sink onto her chest. I roll my hips for a little longer, trying to savor every moment.

"I can't believe we just did that," she says, pushing my hair off my sweaty forehead. She's just as sweaty and breathless as I am, completely unraveled by something as simple as a goddamn orgasm.

"I think this weekend has just made the top ten of my favorite race weekends," I say, slipping out of her and discarding the condom. Nevaeh laughs a little while watching my ass as I walk away, and I smile to myself.

Once we're both cleaned up, we fall back into bed. Nevaeh wraps herself around me, and I drag her even closer, inhaling her sweet scent. I kiss her forehead once before tracing that all too familiar infinity symbol on her back.

Because I want to keep her in my life forever.

I never want to let go, and I hope nothing will ever take her from me.

"I love you so much, *mon paradis*," I blurt out, so fucking incapable of keeping these words to myself even though I used to be the best at it.

Nevaeh tilts her head and grabs my face in her hands before she says, "I love you endlessly, *mein Mond*." Then she seals those words with a kiss, one so full of emotion, I feel it deep inside my soul.

CHAPTER 56
Nevaeh

It's Tuesday morning, and I'm a little late for work. I sent in the article yesterday after getting Leonard's approval, but Ms. Martin hasn't emailed me back any improvement suggestions, which made me smile. She must think I'm improving if she has nothing to comment on.

My feet bring me to my desk, but no one seems to be missing me yet. Relief briefly washes over me before I concentrate on everything that I have to do today. I haven't finished editing the photos from the weekend yet, the ones Mrs. Lu sometimes uses for different articles written by Gillian.

I'm about to start on the first one when Genevieve appears in front of me, tapping the papers on my desk to get my attention.

"Come with me," she says, and I swallow hard. Disappointment lingers on her face, a frown playing on her lips.

"I'm sorry I was late," I blurt out as I follow her to the main office, thinking that must be the reason why she is upset with me.

"It was only three minutes, Nevaeh. That's not why I have asked you here," she explains, sending a wave of fear through me. My eyes shift to her desk where Mrs. Lu and Ms. Martin sit.

Anger has taken over my bosses' features and I'm convinced panic mine. I stop at the door, not moving another centimeter. I couldn't, even if I wanted to.

"You lied to me," is the first thing that comes out of Ms. Martin's mouth. Disappointment also covers Mrs. Lu's face, but she doesn't say a word.

Genevieve gently grabs my arm to pull me inside, closing the door behind me to keep this conversation private. I'm about to ask my bosses what it is I've lied about when Ms. Martin finds her voice again.

"How many times did I ask you if something was going on between you and Mr. Romana?" she asks but doesn't give me a chance to respond. "Many times, Nevaeh, and you lied to me every single time. Before you attempt to do so again, I suggest you come to take a look at what a good friend of yours sent me," she states and holds out her phone, a video of Adrian and me dancing and kissing at 'Bourbon House' playing on the screen.

My face is barely visible, and if someone hadn't told her it was me under that cowboy hat, I doubt she would have recognized me. It was too dark, too crowded.

I cover my mouth both because I've been caught and because I feel extremely violated. A friend of mine sent that video? Who the fuck would do that to me? Certainly, no one I went there with, right?

"I'm sorry," I manage to croak out, but my throat is dry. It's the only thing I can say, not that Ms. Martin would have given me a chance to speak more anyway.

"What are you sorry about? Hmm? That you got caught?" I shake my head, too stunned and overwhelmed to reply. "That's the problem with sleeping with two men, Nevaeh, one of them will always get hurt and look for payback."

My breathing hitches as realization dawns on me. Lincoln took the video. He must have gone to that bar, too, recorded us, and sent it to my bosses.

Nausea consumes me, and I try to keep the room from spinning. The pain of his betrayal rips my heart in half. We aren't on speaking terms, but I never thought he'd ruin my career to get revenge.

"Listen, I can explain. Lincoln and I have never had a physical relationship, and Adrian and I—" I start, but Ms. Martin stands up and slams her palms onto the desk, making Genevieve, Mrs. Lu, and I jump.

Ms. Martin's pink dress sways from side to side at the movement, anger covering her features. A few strands of her blonde-gray hair fall over her face, but she doesn't seem to care as she yells at me.

"No, you listen, child. You have given us a lot of headache for someone we only hired because her father paid us to!" she yells, making my body freeze.

Time stops as all the blood rushes out of my face.

"He what?" I ask, making Mrs. Lu's eyes go wide.

Clearly, Ms. Martin wasn't supposed to tell me that, but her anger let it slip. Tears shoot into my eyes as I sink onto one of the chairs, my legs no longer capable of holding me upright.

"Did you really think things just came that easy, Nevaeh? That a journalist who just started at a company would climb up the ladder so quickly?" she asks, shaking her head in disbelief. "Wake up, child. The world doesn't work that way, especially not the world of Formula One."

"Tell me what he did, please," is all I manage to say, tears collecting in my eyes at the betrayal.

"He paid us to give you a chance. For the first two months, your salary was paid by him as well," Mrs. Lu explains, but my head is spinning and her words sound distorted. "We didn't have a position open, so he paid us to open one. He asked for you to be in the Formula One department too, but he wouldn't tell us why."

Ms. Martin's voice is a lot harsher as she continues explaining what my father did.

"When he found out what happened with Gillian and the deal you made with Adrian, he started contacting all of the Formula One teams, convincing them to let you write those articles for every other driver. The ones who didn't want that, he paid to convince them otherwise. He was behind everything, your success, the reason you got to write those articles. It was all him, none of it you."

Tears spill down my cheeks as my heart shatters into a million pieces.

"You can't seriously have thought things would be so... so easy. Do you think other journalists whose fathers aren't the team principal of one of the biggest Formula One teams would have made it as far as you without much of an effort?" Ms. Martin asks, but it's a rhetorical question and one she answers as quickly as she phrased it. "No, Nevaeh, they wouldn't have."

I can't take this anymore. The lies, the betrayal, all of it makes my heart ache worse than I've ever experienced before, worse than when the doctor told me I'd never be able to play tennis competitively again.

"We can't keep you on any longer. If a video like this were to get out, the credibility of our company would be questioned. Not even your father can pay us enough money to keep you on, Nevaeh. I'm so sorry." Mrs. Lu is a lot gentler and more understanding about this situation, but it doesn't make it any easier either.

"I can't, I can't breathe," I say as I stand up once more and make my way toward the door.

They already fired me so there really isn't a reason to stick around and have an anxiety attack right there in the office where I don't feel safe.

My fingers barely hold onto my phone as I struggle to make my way down the stairs and into the hot summer day. I cover my mouth once more when I'm outside, this time to muffle a sob combined with a scream of pain.

None of it was my doing.

None of it was my achievement.

It was Papa's money, the one thing I've been trying to get away from since I started working at *Griffin Sports*. I was so proud of myself for getting the job, but it was all because of him, not because of who I am, my achievements, nothing.

My arms wrap around my chest while I look around the place I call home. Ms. Lu and Ms. Martin sent me here for what? Why did they turn my life upside down if they only hired me because of my father? Or was it Papa's idea, too? Is that why he was so adamant about me moving, to chase my independence? Because it was his idea all along?

I feel sick to my stomach.

I guess it makes sense that my father is capable of something like this. He helped Lincoln get a seat at Grenzenlos because of his best friend. He meddles, interferes, and buys people the chances they wouldn't be given otherwise.

"Are you okay?" a woman asks in French, and I nod, not realizing how much of a scene I'm making until that very moment.

Everything is so messy and complicated now, I don't know what to do with myself. I've risked everything for a job that wasn't even mine to begin with, and I hate my father for what he's done. All I've tried to do is establish my own life. Why didn't he let me? Why did he have to interfere?

Everything was a lie.

Tears stream down my cheeks, but I wipe them away when determination takes over.

I have made a life for myself. Monaco is where I feel at home, which is not something I have ever been able to say about any other place I lived in. None of the other places felt like this, but they also didn't have the family I found in Val, Gabriel, and Adrian.

I'm running now.

My apartment is only a ten-minute walk from here, and I make it there in seven. I'm texting Adrian to meet me there, more tears streaming down my face. I've just lost everything. I lost my job, my relationship with my father is even more damaged than the one with my mother, I'm going to lose my apartment and will probably have to move somewhere cheaper, find a job somewhere else. But I've got him, and he'll catch me now.

I know he will.

He's at my apartment ten minutes later, not bothering about knocking but simply bursting inside to wrap me up in his arms and let me sob into his chest.

It's not even anxiety that has me breaking down. In a way, I wish it was. It hurts a lot less than the heartbreak that's making me cry.

The last five months have been a lie. Everything I was working toward wasn't mine, and I can't help but fall apart a little at the thought of only having made a name for myself because my father paid people to get me a job, paid them to further my career. He told me people were praising me, but it was all because of him.

When I manage to say this out loud, Adrian holds me even tighter.

"He may have been the one to get you the job, but you earned it, Nevaeh. You were such a brilliant journalist, the press officer of Formula One hired you through *Griffin Sports* to write that article for the charity event. If your first article hadn't impressed at least some of them, they wouldn't have agreed. I know my team was mind-blown by your work, and that has nothing to do with him. That's your achievement, Nevaeh, not his."

I try to acknowledge his words, but I'm hurting too deeply right now to accept them. To let them sink in.

"How could he do this to me?" I ask, leaning back to look into his eyes.

"I don't know. Maybe he thought this would be good for you, that you'd never find out. It was his way of meddling, like parents do, without realizing the repercussions of his actions," he explains, and I nod along to his words before more tears and sobs leave me.

"I feel so lost now," I admit, wiping my face with my hands.

"I know, but, I promise, I'll stay by your side while you find yourself again. I'll remind you of who you are until you don't feel so lost anymore."

He seals that promise with a kiss, one I desperately melt into and cling onto because I love him. I love him so much, a part of me is glad we don't have to hide our relationship from the world anymore.

I just wish that part was big enough to make my father's betrayal sting less.

CHAPTER 57
Adrian

Nevaeh's sobs have slowed.

She's lying in my arms on her bed while we watch *Captain America: Civil War*. I stroke her hair gently, calming her until she melts further into me.

All of her pain sits like a building on my chest, heavy and immovable.

I hate her father for what he did, for making her think she could never achieve anything unless it was with his help.

I hate Lincoln even more for recording us and sending that video to Nevaeh's bosses. The next time I see him, I'm going to kill him. Val, Gabriel, Cameron, Leonard, Chiara, and James will help me, too, so I'm pretty sure we could get away with it. After all the shit he's pulled, he deserves to get hurt in return.

Nevaeh's growling stomach tears me out of my murderous thoughts and back into the moment. I rub an infinity symbol onto her back, leaning down to press my lips to her forehead and linger there for a moment.

"Hungry?" I ask, and she nods, the movement sleepy and slow. "I'll go get us some food," I assure her, kissing the crown of her head before slipping out of bed.

Nevaeh sits up, too, scanning her little apartment before worry creases the area between her brows.

"Fuck," she mumbles, so I move in front of her, taking her chin between my fingers.

"What's wrong?"

"I left my wallet at the office," she says, attempting to move out of bed, too, but I grab her shoulders and push her backward.

"I'll go get it. You stay here. I'll be right back." She opens her mouth to protest, but I kiss her so thoroughly, by the time I lean back, she's smiling a little.

"Okay," is all she replies.

"I love you endlessly, *mon paradis*," I say, her chin still between my fingers.

"I love you endlessly, *mein Mond*."

I slip out of her apartment after another long kiss, walking toward her office. Part of me wants to tell all of them to burn in hell, that they lost one of the best fucking journalists on the planet, but I know Nevaeh wouldn't want me to do that, so I keep my mouth shut.

A woman named Genevieve shows me to Nevaeh's desk where I grab her wallet, scowling at everyone who passes me.

This must be what it feels like to be Leonard, Chiara, Chloe, and Julián.

Right now, I get their inclination to frown at everyone because that's exactly how I feel.

"Adrian?"

That voice.

The softness of how she addresses me.

The way she pronounces my name like no one else in my life.

"Adrian," she repeats, but this time, it isn't a question.

It's a plea.

I turn around to find her standing behind me, uncertainty painted all over her aged features. She's wearing a pink dress, her favorite color from what I remember. Her once blonde hair is now starting to gray, and her eyes, they're exactly like Val's and mine.

"Mom?"

To be continued...

Sneak Peak

Untiled Second Book of Adrian and Nevaeh's Story

Prologue

Adrian
15 years ago

"I don't want you to go," I say, grabbing my mother's hand as she packs a suitcase for some trip she only told me about ten minutes ago.

"I'll be back before you know it," she assures me, ruffling my hair once before disappearing into her closet again to grab more clothes.

"Does Dad know you're leaving?" I ask because I know something isn't right. I can feel it deep in my gut. My mother is acting weird, and I need to find out why. Maybe then I can stop her from leaving.

"Of course he does, Adrian. I wouldn't just go without telling him," she promises, but her left eye twitches a little, something it always does when she lies.

"Mom, please, stay. At least until Dad gets back," I beg and pull on her shirt again. She yanks her arm away and grabs both of my shoulders.

"Go ask Tini if she wants to play with the new Carrera track and remote-controlled cars your father got you," she says, leading me out of her bedroom and toward my sister's. I knock on Valentina's door as I look over my shoulder at my mother one last time.

My little sister, the most important person in my life, opens her door to show me she's wearing one of Dad's Velocità Rossa baseball caps and a bright smile on her face. She's holding the remote in her hand, already playing with the gift our father got us.

When I ask if I can join her, she grabs my hand and pulls me into her room, leading me to where the track is set up.

Valentina hands me the other remote and settles down on the ground again, patting the spot next to her to get me to sit with her. Tears fill my eyes as I take a seat, watching my sister's mop of dirty-blonde curls dance as she wiggles from side to side in excitement. I try to swallow them back down, but they fall when I wrap an arm around her, knowing that I won't be able to protect her from what's about to happen.

I won't be able to protect her from all of the pain our mother will inflict because I can't even spare myself.

I let the tears fall down my cheeks as I press a kiss to the crown of her head, hating that my little sister will know heartbreak before she even knows what that word means.

Acknowledgements

The first person I'd like to thank in my acknowledgements is Adrian Romana. Over the past few years, Adrian has become my favorite character, and I doubt anyone else will take his place any time soon. This book was so easy to write because out of all my characters, I feel most connected to him. So, I'd like to thank him for being exactly who he is (and my deepest apologies for that end, Adrian!)

Secondly, I'd like to thank Nevaeh because her strength and determination will forever inspire me to keep going.

Next, I'd like to thank the person that never gives up on me, that does everything for me. My sister. I could have never asked for a better sibling or business partner.

Over my years on Bookstagram and Booktok I've also made a lot of friends that help me keep going, that push me to become a better writer. So, I'd like to thank Drew for always being there for me. I'd like to thank Chloe for inspiring me to be a better author. I'd like to thank Sophie and Emma for being my longest readers and now very close friends who always stand by me. I'd also like to thank Ams, Esha, and Teigan for cheering for me all the way. Lastly, more people that have support me that I'd like to thank are Apoorva, Amber, Solène, Ana, Lauren, Tanisha, Hali, Renee, Jessie, Beth, and many more! Your support will forever mean the world to me.

I'd also like to thank Natalia. I would not be here without you.

Lastly, I'd like to thank the rest of my family, my mom, my aunts, and my grandparents, for always pushing me, for encouraging me to never give up.

All of you make it possible for me to keep writing, and I promise I'll keep going.

About the Author

BRIDGET L. ROSE IS a half-German, half-Italian author, who was born and raised in Germany until the age of thirteen. She fell in love with books from a young age, and soon discovered her passion for writing as well. She likes to spend her free time with her family, reading a book, or writing one herself. She also adores the sport Formula One, which led her to write her Pitstop Series.

Books by Bridget L. Rose

The Pitstop Series

Jump-Start

The Inside of a Rainbow

Rush: Part One & Two

Chase: Part One & Two

From Angels to Devils Series

From Devils to Angels

www.ingramcontent.com/pod-product-compliance
Lightning Source LLC
Chambersburg PA
CBHW051432190726
48289CB00001B/154